After a successful c
Wingfield turned
created the charac
featured in six n
adapted for televisi
A Touch of Frost starring David Jason.
R. D. Wingfield died in 2007.

DON'T MISS THE OTHER TITLES IN THE DI JACK FROST SERIES

A TOUCH OF FROST

A wealthy businessman's daughter is missing, the son of an MP is suspected of a hit-and-run and a multiple rapist is on the loose . . .

'What impresses most is the extraordinarily vivid interplay between the police characters. Frost himself is splendidly drawn' *The Times*

'A funny, frantic, utterly refreshing brew'
Sunday Telegraph

FROST AT CHRISTMAS

Ten days before Christmas a child goes missing. Then Dead Man's Hollow yields up a skeleton . . .

'Affecting, frightening and, especially in Frost's dialogue, extremely amusing' *Listener*

'A crisp, confident, ripely-characterized novel; exciting, ingenious, roundly satisfying'
Literary Review

NIGHT FROST

A serial killer is terrorising senior citizens and a seemingly perfect couple is the target of an arson attack just as the police are hit by a flu epidemic . . .

'Multiple cases, multiple bodies and lashings of police in-fighting. Fast, furious and funny'
Daily Telegraph

'Meaty police procedural; bawdy, funny . . . enough material here for cult hero status' *Literary Review*

HARD FROST

One boy is found dead, another is missing and a psychopath is on the rampage. Then a supermarket MD is sent a ransom demand . . .

'Crime pick of the year. Darker, funnier and more violent than the television adaptation, but just as high quality' *Daily Telegraph*

'Inspector Jack Frost (is) deplorable yet funny, a comic monster on the side of the angels' *Guardian*

WINTER FROST

A serial killer is murdering local prostitutes, a man uncovers a skeleton in his garden and armed robbers hit the local minimart . . .

'Frost is a splendid creation, a cross between Rumpole and Colombo' *The Times*

'If you enjoy crime fiction at all, read this. If you've never read a crime novel in your life, start with this one' *Morning Star*

A Killing Frost

R. D. WINGFIELD

CORGI BOOKS

TRANSWORLD PUBLISHERS
61–63 Uxbridge Road, London W5 5SA
A Random House Group Company
www.rbooks.co.uk

A KILLING FROST
A CORGI BOOK: 9780552156899

First published in Great Britain
in 2008 by Bantam Press
a division of Transworld Publishers
Corgi edition published 2008

A CIP catalogue record for this book
is available from the British Library.

Addresses for Random House Group Ltd companies outside the UK can be found at: www.randomhouse.co.uk
The Random House Group Ltd Reg. No. 954009

The Random House Group Limited supports The Forest Stewardship Council (FSC), the leading international forest certification organisation. All our titles that are printed on Greenpeace approved FSC certified paper carry the FSC logo. Our paper procurement policy can be found at
www.rbooks.co.uk/environment

Typeset in 11/12.75pt Caslon 540 by
Falcon Oast Graphic Art Ltd.
Printed in the UK by CPI Cox & Wyman, Reading, RG1 8EX.

6 8 10 9 7 5

To Boofy. With all my love.

A Killing Frost

Prologue

A blinding flash of lightning etched the trees in sharp relief against the night sky, followed almost instantly by a rumble of thunder overhead which seemed to make the ground shake. Heavy, stinging rain drummed down.

The man sheltering under the oak tree, his raincoat soaked through, cursed his luck for venturing out on such a lousy night just to take the flaming dog for a walk. As soon as the rain eased off he would make his way home, but where was the dog? Probably cowering under a bush somewhere, terrified by the noise.

'Rex! Come here, you bloody animal.'

An answering bark resounded in the darkness, but he couldn't locate it. 'Rex, here! Now!'

There was a whimpering yap, then the dog bounded over to join him, its fur flattened and rain-blackened. It had something in its mouth.

'What you got there?' The lousy dog was always picking up and eating pieces of ancient carrion, usually making itself violently sick on the mat once they got home. But this didn't smell ancient. It stank to high heaven.

He tried to pull it from the dog, which growled menacingly and clenched its teeth even firmer, reluctant to yield its prize. The man pulled his hand back. Whatever the dog had found felt like bloated, squishy flesh.

'I said drop it!'

Another menacing growl. He grabbed the dog by the collar and shook its head until it released its grip and whatever it was holding fell to the ground.

He dragged the torch from his raincoat pocket and clicked it on. The horror of what he saw jerked him back.

'Bloody hell . . . Bloody bleeding hell!'

The dog made a leap to retrieve its find, but just in time he snatched its collar again and clicked on the lead, holding it awkwardly as he unbuttoned his mac to get to his mobile.

'Operator,' he shouted over the thudding rain. 'Get me the police . . . Denton police.'

Detective Inspector Jack Frost, slouched at the desk in his office, glanced up as lightning flashed and the overhead lights flickered off and on. He went to the window and looked out on the darkened car park, where stair-rods of driving rain broke the reflections in the puddles.

'Look at that bleeding rain,' he muttered to himself, glad he wasn't out in it. One good thing about heavy rain: it kept most villains indoors.

He returned to his desk and his car expenses. Picking up his ballpoint he carefully altered a '6' to an '8'.

There was a perfunctory tap at the door and Bill Wells, the station sergeant, entered. 'Jack . . .'

Frost didn't look up. 'I can't come out to play now, Bill. I've got my sums to do.'

Wells grinned. 'You're going to get caught fiddling those expenses one of these days, Jack.'

'Not a chance,' murmured Frost. 'The devil looks after his own.' He put his pen down. 'Any chance of a cup of tea?'

'No time for that, Jack. Just had a bloke on the phone. He's in Denton Woods – his dog has found a chopped-off human foot.'

'Tell him to phone again when he's found the rest,' said Frost. Thunder rumbled and the lights flickered again. 'I pity the poor sod you're sending out to answer the call.'

'There's only you, Jack. Jordan and Simms are still at the hospital with that girl who was attacked in the car park.'

Frost chucked down his pen and took another look out of the window, hoping the rain was showing some signs of easing up. 'Shit!' he muttered. It was bucketing down worse than ever.

Bill Wells yawned, knuckled his eyes and checked the time. Two o'clock. Not a word from Frost yet. Time was creeping. The cells were empty. The usual quota of yelling, singing and vomiting drunks had been kept indoors by the weather. He didn't have much to do. He yelled for PC Collier to make some tea and picked up a copy of the *Denton Echo*. As he turned the page, the main doors crashed open and a gust of wind blew across the lobby. A rain-soaked, fed-up-to-the-bloody-teeth Detective Inspector Frost squelched over to the inquiry desk and dumped a dripping transparent plastic bag in front of Wells. Inside the bag was a bloodless, bloated, dirt-encrusted human foot, the pale skin flecked with green and black mould. It had apparently been sawn off at the base of the fibula; the toes bore puncture marks from the teeth of the dog.

'If anyone reports a foot missing, we've found it,' said Frost, shrugging off his mac and shaking it over the lobby floor.

'Flaming heck, Jack,' said Wells. 'You should have left it on site. This could be a murder inquiry.'

'What – just leave it there and have some poor sod standing over it, guarding it? Besides, we don't know where the dog got it from and I wasn't going to go crashing about in Denton Woods in the dark trying to find the rest.' He prodded it through the bag. 'It's from a hospital, I reckon . . . some prat of a medical student's idea of a joke.'

'What am I supposed to do with it?' asked Wells.

'Fifteen minutes at gas mark five,' said Frost. 'Or stick it in the bloody fridge and if no one eats it send it over to Forensic in the morning.'

Wells wrinkled his nose. 'It's a bit flaming whiffy, Jack.'

'I thought that was you,' said Frost. He looked at the foot again. 'And first thing tomorrow, Bill, get a couple of spare bods to go through the motions of searching for any more bits. But don't let them waste too much time on it.'

'Something else, Jack. That fifteen-year-old girl who was attacked. Sally Marsden. PC Jordan has phoned through – she was raped. Looks like the same pattern as the other two girls.'

'Damn,' sighed Frost. 'It never rains, but it flaming pees down.' He gave his mac another shake. 'Right, I'm on my way.'

Wells shook his head. 'No need, Jack. The hospital say she's in no state to be questioned until the morning.'

Frost yawned. It was too late to go home. 'Got an empty cell I can kip in?'

'Take your pick,' said Wells.

Frost yawned again. 'Send the maid to wake me at around seven with a cup of tea in one hand and her knickers in the other. If that kid's been raped I want to get down to the hospital first thing. We've got too much to bleeding do, now that Hornrim Harry's sucking up to the Chief Constable by lending half our manpower to Hockley Division for a drugs bust. "You can have as many men as you like, sir. Frost has got sod all to do. He can manage." '

He collected his cigarettes from his office. Rain was crawling down the window. It was a sod of a night.

1

Frost hated hospitals, especially the dawn chorus of patients coughing and groaning, weak voices calling out for nurses who never came, the clinical smells. Sheeted, rubber-wheeled trolleys pushed by grim-faced porters swished past him as he trudged the long curving corridor, looking for Ward F3. Most of all, he hated the 'NO SMOKING' signs. What was it about 'NO SMOKING' signs that made him lust for a cigarette? He passed the staircase that led up to the room he had visited every day when his wife was dying. He shuddered. What a bloody awful time that had been.

Outside Ward F3, Harding, head of Forensic, was talking to a junior doctor who looked even more tired than Frost felt. Harding hurried across to meet him. 'Bit of luck for a change, Inspector. We've got a semen sample.'

Frost frowned. 'A semen sample? I can't see it being the same bloke who raped those other girls. He's always used a condom.'

'Everything points to it being the same man, Inspector,' insisted Harding. 'He probably saw his opportunity, didn't have a condom on him and raped her anyway.'

'I like these bastards to be consistent,' said Frost, still not convinced. 'How's the girl?'

'Tired and emotional – he must have knocked the poor kid about – but the doctors say she can go home. Her mother's on her way with her clothes. We've taken those she was wearing for forensic testing.' He jerked his thumb at the ward door. 'End bed with the screens.' He scuttled off down the long corridor.

Frost pushed open the door and walked past the rows of beds to a curtained-off area at the end, near the windows. 'I'm Inspector Frost,' he called. 'Are you decent? If you are, I'll come back later.'

A young policewoman he didn't recognise opened the curtains. 'Come in, Inspector.'

Sally Marsden – pretty, with fair hair, blue eyes and a scrubbed, tear-stained face – was in an armchair by the side of the bed, a blanket draped over her pale-yellow hospital nightdress with DENTON GENERAL HOSPITAL stitched in blue across the chest. She looked a lot younger than her fifteen years.

Frost sat on the bed and pulled out his cigarettes. A warning cough from the WPC made him put them away again. 'Stylish nightdress,' he said.

The girl gave a weak grin. 'I keep shaking.' She held out her quivering arms so he could see.

Frost nodded sympathetically. 'Shake away, love. You've had a hell of an experience. We've got to catch this bastard. If you feel up to it, I want to know everything that happened. Every bloody thing, no matter how unimportant you think it might be.'

Sally pulled the blanket tighter around her shoulders. 'I'd been with a friend from school, listening to music round her house. I hadn't realised the time and my mum doesn't like me staying out late. It was nearly quarter past ten and I'm supposed to be home by ten.'

'Where does this friend live?'

'Twenty-nine Kestrel Terrace. I've given the police lady the details.'

The young WPC nodded her confirmation. Frost waved a hand for the girl to continue.

'To save time I cut through the multi-storey car park in the town centre – it saves walking all the way round the block.'

'Bleeding dangerous at that time of night,' muttered Frost. 'If it's the same bloke, he got one other girl there.' The car park was always dark and cold, and after the shops had closed, very echoing and empty.

'I couldn't face my mum's nagging if I got in late. She's very strict.'

'Not always a bad thing,' said Frost, his hand caressing the cigarette packet in his pocket. God, he was dying for a fag. 'Then what?'

She screwed up her face and shuddered at the memory. 'I was hurrying. At first I couldn't hear anything, just water dripping somewhere and the echo of my own footsteps. Then – and I had to stop to make sure – I could hear footsteps behind me. Quiet footsteps as if whoever was making them didn't want to be heard. I walked faster. The footsteps quickened. Then, suddenly, he was right behind me. He clamped a hand round my mouth. I tried to bite his hand but he punched me – hard.' She was shaking violently and had to pause to compose herself.

'Take your time, love,' soothed Frost. 'When you're ready . . .'

'He said, "Scream, you bitch, and I'll kill you." ' She shook her head. 'I don't think I could have screamed, even if I'd tried. I was paralysed with fear.' She paused again.

Frost waited a moment for her to calm down. 'When he spoke, how did he sound? Old, young, any sort of an accent?'

Sally shook her head again. 'Youngish I think. Twenty – thirty perhaps . . . I don't know. He was trying to sound Irish, but you could tell he was putting it on.'

Frost nodded. It was the same bloke. The other victims had reported the same.

'He pulled a cloth thing over my head so I couldn't see, then grabbed my hair and kicked my legs so I fell to the ground. Then he pulled up my clothes . . . He . . .' She faltered, then, shoulders shaking, broke down in tears.

'There, there,' soothed Frost. 'Take your time. I know it's bleeding upsetting, but we've got to know everything.'

She wiped away the tears. 'He had sex. He

was rough. He hurt me. Then he said, "Stay there, you little cow. Don't move. Don't make a sound or I'll cut your effing throat. We're going for a car ride."'

Frost's head jerked up. This was new. 'He said that? He said you were going for a car ride?'

She dabbed at the tears with a sodden handkerchief and blew her nose. 'I still had this cloth over my face. I heard him hurry off, then I heard voices. Other people coming. So I screamed and screamed. I could hear his footsteps running off, then other footsteps . . . the two young guys who found me. They called an ambulance and the hospital called the police.'

They were interrupted by the clatter of hurrying footsteps. The cubicle curtains were jerked open and a sharp-faced woman in her late thirties toting a white plastic carrier bag barged in. Jerking a thumb at Frost she demanded, 'Who the hell is he?'

'He's a detective, Mum,' said the girl.

'Well, he don't flaming look like one,' she snapped, dumping the carrier bag on the bed. 'Here's your clothes. I'm taking you home.' She spun round to Frost. 'Fifteen years old. Never had a boyfriend. I've told her – not until you're sixteen. You see too many of these kids dressed like tarts – barely eleven years old, some of them. She's a good girl – never out late. I make certain she don't get into any trouble and this bastard . . .' Words failed her.

'I know, love,' agreed Frost. 'But we'll catch

him, don't you worry.' He hoped he sounded more certain than he felt.

'I'm against abortions,' continued the mother, 'but if that bastard's made her pregnant . . .' She shook her head. 'Other kids are at it like bloody rabbits, she keeps herself pure and this happens.'

'There's no bloody justice,' sympathised Frost. He stood up. 'I'll be in touch, and I'll keep you informed.' He almost raced down the long corridor, ready to light up the minute he was outside. He nearly made it.

'Inspector Frost.'

He stopped and turned to see Sophie Grey, the young social worker.

'Could I have a word, Inspector? It's very important.'

Frost groaned inwardly. Everything was bloody important these days.

The train rattled round the bend before shuddering to a halt with a squeal of brakes as it reached the station. The carriage window was dirt-grimed, but Detective Chief Inspector Skinner could see enough to confirm what he had let himself in for. He dragged his case down from the rack and opened the carriage door.

'Denton . . . Denton . . .' bellowed the Tannoy. 'Alight here for Denton.'

Skinner, the only passenger to alight, nodded ruefully. He didn't need to be told. The whole drab, miserable look of the place screamed 'Denton' to him. He gazed wistfully at the train as it moved on, taking its passengers to happier destinations.

Outside the station, thick black, low-lying clouds added to the gloom, and a cold wind slashed his face. He looked up and down the empty road. No sign of the police car that was supposed to meet him. Just bloody typical of Denton! He dragged the mobile phone from his pocket and rang the station. The idiot at the other end did nothing to improve his temper.

'What did you say your name was?' asked a bored-sounding Sergeant Wells.

'Skinner. Detective Chief Inspector Skinner,' he snapped, jumping back just too late to avoid being doused with dirty water as a passing lorry drove through a puddle. He couldn't read the mud-splattered numberplate, but he noted the firm's name on the side. He'd get Traffic to nail the bastard. 'A car is supposed to be picking me up.'

'That's right, sir,' agreed Wells cheerfully. 'Isn't it there?'

'Would I be bloody phoning you if it was here?' hissed Skinner. 'Of course the bleeding thing isn't here.'

'If you'd just hold the line, sir, I'll check,' said Wells, putting him on hold. A tinny synthesiser played the first few bars of the 'William Tell Overture' over and over again. After what seemed ages, Wells returned, sounding puzzled. 'Are you sure it isn't there, sir?'

Skinner took a deep breath. 'Of course I'm bloody sure, Sergeant. Do you think I don't know what a flaming police car looks like?'

At that moment an area car crawled round the corner.

'All right, it's here now – and it's taking its bloody time.' He clicked off the phone and shoved it back in his pocket.

As the car drew up alongside him, he opened the door, chucked his case inside and slid into the passenger seat.

'Are you DCI Skinner?' asked the driver, PC Jordan.

'Who the hell do you think I am?' snarled Skinner.

A big, fat, pig-headed bastard, thought Jordan, but he kept the idea to himself. 'You could be someone who thought this was a taxi and just climbed in, sir. It has happened before, so I always like to check who my passenger is.'

'Well now you bloody know,' snapped Skinner. This officer was too cocky for his own good. He'd better watch his step or he'd be following Frost out of Denton.

Jordan exchanged raised eyebrows and pulled-down mouth with his observer, PC Simms, then spun the car round to head back to the station. They drove in silence.

The radio crackled. 'Control to Charlie Simms. Are you anywhere near Milk Street?'

'Just passed it,' answered Simms. 'Why?'

'A Sadie Rawlings, 13 Milk Street, has reported an abduction – her two-year-old baby son. Inspector Frost is on his way. He wants you to meet him there.'

'We're taking Detective Chief Inspector Skinner to the station. We'll drop him off first. Shouldn't take more than a couple of minutes.'

A stubby finger jabbed him in the arm. 'Take the shout now,' ordered Skinner. 'I'll handle it.' He rubbed his hands with glee. A child abduction on his first day. This should earn him some Brownie points.

'It's Inspector Frost's case,' Jordan told him.

'Well it isn't any more. And when I want something done, Constable, you do it. You don't query it – *comprende*?'

'The Chief Inspector says he'll handle it,' reported Simms. 'We're on our way.'

Jordan spun the car into a U-turn.

Milk Street – a cul-de-sac blocked off at one end by the brick wall of a monumental mason's yard – had more than its fair share of boarded-up windows and rusting abandoned cars waiting for the council to get round to towing them away. Black plastic dustbin sacks, put out days too early for the weekly collection, had been ripped open by dogs and their contents spewed over the pavement.

Skinner stepped gingerly over a slurry of discarded Indian takeaway containers and rapped on the door of Number Thirteen with the flat of his hand.

It took several raps before Sadie Rawlings, an over-bleached blonde in her late twenties, opened the door and squinted at the warrant card. 'Took your bleeding time,' she said. 'I'm at me wit's end. I phoned bleeding ages ago.'

'Five minutes ago, actually, madam,' said Skinner as they followed her into the house.

'Broke in through the window,' she said. 'Smashed half my crockery and took the kid. There's blood all over the place.'

'Blood?' Skinner's head snapped up. It was the first time this had been mentioned.

The woman was walking unsteadily and reeked of cheap gin. A cigarette with a tube of ash quivered from her lips. Her make-up had been trowelled on. 'I woke up this morning and he was gone – bloody gone!'

The house had a stuffy smell, the lingering aroma of past meals intermingled with stale cigarette smoke and cat's pee.

'Right, madam,' said Skinner. 'From the beginning. What time did you put the baby to bed?'

'Six o'clock. He went straight off to sleep.'

'And what time did you go to bed?'

'Questions, bleeding questions. Just bloody well find him. They'll blame me. They'll say I neglected him. I'm a bloody good mother.'

'I don't dispute that, madam,' said Skinner, trying to stay patient, 'but I need some answers first. What time did you go to bed?'

'I don't know. I don't study the bleeding clock. Just after ten – something like that.'

'You heard nothing during the night?'

'Not a sodding thing and I'm a light sleeper. The kid's only got to cough and I'm in there like a shot. I'm a bloody good mother.'

'So you said, madam. And what time did you go into the baby's room this morning?'

She tried to focus bleary eyes on her wristwatch. 'About half an hour ago. When I phoned you. As soon as I saw he was gone, I phoned.'

'So he must have been taken some time between six o'clock yesterday evening and nine this morning?'

'Bleeding marvellous. I could have bloody worked that out for myself.'

Skinner took a deep breath. She was beginning to get on his nerves. 'Could I see the baby's room now, please?'

She led them down the passage and flung open the door to a small room, barely furnished with a chair and a white painted cot. A sour smell came from a heap of discarded Pampers nappies on the floor. She kicked them under the cot. 'I was going to tidy up but with all this bleeding upset . . .' She pulled back the curtain and daylight tried to claw its way through a dirt-engrained window. The bedclothes on the cot, which looked as if they hadn't been washed for weeks, were pulled back. The pillow, which showed the indentation of the baby's head, was splattered with blood.

Skinner nodded grimly. This was looking nasty. 'Don't touch anything.' He went to the door and bellowed down the passage to Jordan, 'Get SOCO down here now!' Returning to the woman, he said, 'Show me where they broke in.'

He followed her back down the passage to a tiny kitchen. Below a shattered sash window, the battered draining board was smothered with pieces of broken glass. Glass and broken crockery scrunched underfoot. Skinner's nose wrinkled. There was no way he would eat any food prepared here. The walls were dirty and greasy; unwashed saucepans and food-encrusted plates were piled in the sink, which was awash with cold, grey, greasy water. There were more dirty nappies in the corner, next to a heap of unwashed clothes.

Treading carefully to avoid the mess on the floor, Skinner moved to the broken window and peered at it closely. Rivulets of blood had run down the jagged edge of the pane. He gave a sigh of relief. It looked as if the intruder had cut himself when he smashed the glass, so the splashes on the pillow probably didn't come from the baby. He kicked aside a piece of cup. 'You had crockery stacked up by the window?'

'I was going to wash them up,' Sadie sniffed. 'You never get any free time with a kid.' She flicked ash from her cigarette into the dirty water in the sink.

'He would have knocked them over as he clambered through the window. Don't try and clean up the blood. Our scene-of-crime team are on their way. They'll take samples for analysis.' Fat chance of her cleaning anything up, he thought. He looked through the broken window to the yard. 'How do we get out there?'

A back door at the end of the passage opened on to a tiny yard, which contained an overflowing dustbin surrounded by a carpet of sodden disposable nappies. The door was bolted so the abductor obviously hadn't taken the baby out that way. He would have had to use the front door. Odds were he'd have had a car waiting outside – he wouldn't carry a baby through the streets. Skinner slid back the bolt and opened the door.

'Hardly Kew Gardens,' muttered Simms.

Skinner stepped carefully over the mess and studied the gardens on each side and those running back to back. 'He would have to climb over quite a few garden fences to get here from the street.' He turned to Jordan. 'Check with the neighbours. See if they saw anyone climbing over their fences during the night.'

'If they had they'd have been straight on to us,' said Jordan.

He received a paint-blistering glare from Skinner. 'That wasn't a subject for debate, Constable, that was a bloody order. Just do it. *Comprende?*'

'*Comprende*,' muttered Jordan. He wasn't taking to this new chief inspector.

Skinner turned his attention to the adjacent gardens. 'All those fences to climb,' he muttered. 'Whoever did this was determined to get the kiddy.' He clicked his fingers for Simms's attention. 'Let's cover the worst-case scenario – a paedophile. Radio the station. I want everyone on the sex offenders register checked, then visited. I want to know if any of them are wearing bandages or plasters to cover cuts from broken glass. And I want their premises searched

– plasters or not. If anyone refuses, we get a search warrant.'

Simms radioed the station.

'And where are we supposed to get the flaming manpower to do this?' demanded Wells. 'What prat authorised this?'

Skinner snatched the radio from Simms. 'Chief Inspector Skinner here, Sergeant. I authorised it and I expect my orders to be carried out without question. Just do it!' He clicked off and thrust the radio back at Simms. 'There are going to be some changes here. Denton seems to be staffed by idiots.'

'You don't think it's a kidnapping then, sir?' asked Simms.

'Use your flaming common sense, Constable. How much money do you think the mother could raise? I'd say a tenner, top whack.'

'Perhaps the kid's father wanted custody?' suggested Simms. 'He wouldn't have been happy leaving his kid with her.'

'My thoughts exactly,' said Skinner, although until then it hadn't crossed his mind. His money was still on paedophiles. 'Let's ask her.'

Back in the living room, Sadie was draining the dregs from a near-empty gin bottle which she hastily put down.

'Has the child's father ever tried to get custody of the baby?'

'He only need bleeding ask,' slurred Sadie. 'He could have it gift-wrapped.'

'We'd better check him out anyway. What's his name? Where can we find him?'

'I don't know his flaming name. Charlie something. I only met him the once and he hardly said a flaming word once his trousers were off.' A rat-tat at the front door made her look round. 'Who the hell is that?'

Skinner jerked a thumb at Simms. 'Get it. It might be SOCO.'

Detective Inspector Jack Frost, maroon scarf dangling from his neck, pushed past Simms and made his way up the passage. 'Strong smell of cat's pee. Sadie must be in.'

Sadie scowled at his arrival. 'Oh, it's you,' she sniffed.

'Only the best for you, Sadie,' breezed Frost. He kicked at some of the broken crockery on the floor. 'Had a Greek wedding?'

Sadie scowled. 'My baby's been kidnapped and he's making bleeding jokes.'

Skinner pushed forward. 'That remark is out of order.'

Frost stared at him. 'Who the hell are you?'

'Skinner. Detective Chief Inspector Skinner.' He emphasised the 'Chief'. This scruff was obviously Frost, the man Mullett wanted him to get rid of, the man whose days in Denton were numbered.

'Pleased to meet you,' grunted Frost without conviction. 'Thanks for keeping my seat warm. I'll take over now.'

'You are not taking over, Inspector,' declared Skinner. 'This is my case.' But Frost had his back to him and was talking to the mother.

'What's this story about a kidnapping, Sadie?'

'I've already told the fat bloke.'

Skinner pushed his way between them. 'I've got all the details, Frost, thank you. The abductor got in through that window some time during the night. He cut himself on the broken glass and knocked all this stuff on the floor as he clambered through. He then went to the child's room. This way –' He moved to the door of the baby's room, but Frost seemed to have something else on his mind and was showing no inclination to follow. 'This way,' repeated Skinner. Was the fool deaf?

'Oh – all right,' said Frost vaguely.

In the baby's room, Skinner indicated the cot. 'Blood on the pillow, but I don't think it came from the kiddy. I'm getting SOCO down to check.' He turned and realised he was talking to himself. Where was the idiot? 'Frost!' he bellowed.

'In here,' answered Frost from the next room.

Skinner rolled his eyes to the ceiling in exasperation. The silly sod was in the mother's bedroom. As Skinner moved to drag him out, Frost stuck his head round the door and yelled down the passage, 'Fanny! I want you!'

'Don't call me Fanny!' she snapped.

'Sorry,' said Frost. 'Association of ideas, I suppose.' He nodded at the bed, which had clothes sprawled all over it. 'This your bedroom?'

'Well, it ain't the bleeding scullery, is it?'

'All those tatty clothes. It looks like an Oxfam shop's remnants sale.'

Fed up with the scruff's time wasting, Skinner again tried to take control. 'If you can tear yourself away, I want you in the other room, Inspector.' But Frost, completely ignoring him, poked a finger at the woman. 'I've just realised what's been bugging me, Sadie. Why are you all tarted up?'

'What do you mean?'

'Half past nine in the morning and you've got your glad rags on.'

'I can wear what I bloody like!'

Frost ambled over to the dishevelled bed and picked up a pair of jeans and a grubby T-shirt. 'These are what you usually wear in the morning, Sadie.'

'I never said they bloody weren't.'

'Then what are they doing on top of the bed? A bed you were supposed to have been sleeping soundly in all night? A nice tidy girl like you wouldn't have left them on the bed before going to sleep – she'd have chucked them on the floor.'

Sadie spun round to Skinner. 'Do you know what the sod's on about?'

Skinner hadn't the faintest idea, but before he could ask, Frost was off on another tack. 'Did the bastard steal your hearing aid, Sadie?'

'Hearing aid?' she shrilled. 'What hearing aid? What would I want a hearing aid for?'

'Well, you must be bloody deaf if you slept through all that crockery crashing down on the floor.'

'I'm a heavy sleeper. I get so worn out looking

after the baby, I sleep like a log the minute my head hits the pillow.'

'Ah,' nodded Frost. 'I thought there'd be a logical explanation. And what time did your head hit the pillow last night, Sadie?'

'I already have that information,' intervened Skinner, who saw himself getting elbowed out of the investigation. But he was puzzled. He wanted to ask his own questions. The woman was now telling Frost she was a heavy sleeper, yet she had told him that the slightest noise woke her. He checked his notes. 'Just after ten.'

Frost ignored him, his eyes riveted on the woman. 'Come off it, Sadie. At ten o'clock you were still in the bloody pub being bought gin and limes by some short-sighted git who thought he was on to a good thing.'

Her eyes blazed. 'How bleeding dare you!'

'I bleeding dare because I *know*, Sadie. I'm not flaming guessing, I *know*!'

Her eyes spat hatred. 'All right. So I might have popped out for a quick drink. Where's the harm in that? I slave for that kid. I'm entitled to a bit of relaxation. A quick drink, then I came straight back. I was in bed by half ten.'

'But whose bed, Sadie?' demanded Frost.

Furiously, she turned to Skinner. 'Do I have to put up with flaming insults like this?'

Frost answered for him. 'Yes, you do, Sadie. You left that poor sod of a baby all alone in the house from around eight o'clock last night until you staggered back home, half pissed, still in your glad rags, just before you phoned to report him missing.'

She clawed her hands, looking ready to scratch his eyes out with her long, red-painted fingernails. 'All bleeding lies. I'll have you up for defamation of character. What sort of a bleeding mother do you think I am?'

Frost smiled sweetly. 'I'm a policeman, Sadie, and we're not allowed to use that sort of language, even to a slag like you.' His expression changed. 'Now stop sodding us about. I've got better bloody things to do. I've got a rapist to catch and bits of leg to find. I *know*. I know everything. I even know where your baby is at this precise moment in time.'

Sadie stared at him. 'You know? I'm flaming worried sick and you know!'

'Worried sick? You've been out all night. You didn't give a sod about the kid. The poor little mite was screaming at four o'clock this morning. It woke up your next-door neighbour. He got out of bed, banged on your front door, then when he got no reply he climbed in through the kitchen window.'

'The interfering bastard,' she shrilled. 'He can pay for that smashed crockery.'

'He banged and shouted at your bedroom door, just in case you were spending the night in with the kiddy for a change. He looked inside. The bed was empty. The kid was screaming and throwing up, so he and his girlfriend took it to Denton General Hospital, from where I've just come. Your baby is there now.'

Sadie dropped down into a chair. 'The bastards. They break into my house and take my kid. They don't give a sod that I'd be worried sick.'

'I doubt if they thought that was even an outside possibility. Anyway, they said they stuck a note through your letter box, telling you where the baby was.'

She gave a scornful sniff. 'What bloody note?' She frowned as a thought struck her. 'Oh – *that* bloody note!' She flapped a dismissive hand. 'They know I never read their flaming notes. They're always complaining about something with their lousy notes. They've always got something to moan about – the noise . . . the smell . . . I didn't read it. I tore it up.' She rummaged in the ashtray, found a dog-end and lit up, coughing as she exhaled smoke. 'So all's bleeding well that ends well. Thanks for your trouble. I'll collect my kid now. You going to give me a lift?'

'A lift to the nick for wasting police time, Sadie. Now tell us exactly what happened last night, and keep the lies down to a minimum.'

She dragged smoke down to her lungs, coughed and spluttered, then wiped her mouth with the back of her hand. 'All right. Forget what I said before. I was so upset with that tosser next door nicking my baby, I wasn't thinking straight.' She managed one last drag before the filter tip started burning. 'Any chance of a fag?'

'No,' said Frost. 'They're bad for you. It says so on the packet.'

She flopped down on the bed. 'Bastard! OK. Last night. I put the kid to bed around seven. He went straight off. He wasn't bloody crying like those bastards said otherwise I wouldn't have left him, would I? I thought I'd nip out for a quick drink. One drink – there and back, ten minutes, top whack! I didn't intend to stay.'

'But you tarted yourself up in your glad rags, just in case?'

'I'm not like you, Mr Jack bloody Frost. I don't go out dressed like a tramp. Do you want to hear what happened, or are you going to keep chipping in with your stupid remarks?'

'Both,' said Frost, waving a hand for her to continue.

'Right. Like I said, one drink, straight back – that's what I intended. Anyway, I was chatting to this bloke and the sod must have put something in my drink because when I woke up I was in his bed, it was eight o'clock in the morning and the bastard had gone to work. I didn't have enough money for a cab so I had to wait ages for a bleeding bus.'

'Is that what you charge these days, Sadie?' asked Frost. 'Your bus fare?'

Sadie spun round on him. 'Shut your shitty mouth, you ignorant bastard.'

'Kindly address those sort of remarks to my superior officer,' said Frost, nodding towards Skinner.

Skinner glowered. Was the fool trying to be funny? He thought he heard PC Jordan sniggering in the background, but wasn't sure. *All right,*

Frost, he thought grimly, *you'll be laughing on the other side of your face, Sunny Jim, when you know what I've got in store for you.*

'Anyway,' Frost continued, winding the maroon scarf more tightly round his neck, 'I've got bits of leg to find, so I'll leave you in the capable hands of Detective Chief Inspector Skinner. It's his case, not mine.'

As Frost breezed out there was a knock at the door. 'I'll get it,' he called. 'Probably that bloke from last night, Sadie, asking for his change.'

They heard the door open, then Frost asking, 'SOCO? What silly prat asked you to come here? No, forget it!'

Skinner fumed. He could see the two PCs were having difficulty stifling their laughter.

The bedside phone rang. Sadie answered it. 'Just a minute, you want the fat bloke.' She handed the phone to Skinner. 'It's the hospital.'

Skinner hesitated. He wanted to chuck this case back to Frost. It was now too trivial and time-wasting for a detective chief inspector to handle. But Frost had gone.

He took the phone, which reeked of cheap scent. 'Yes?' he grunted. His expression changed. 'Say that again . . . OK, I'm with her now. Leave it to me.' He put the phone down and turned to Sadie. 'Right, get your coat on.'

She pulled a red coat with an acrylic fur collar from the wardrobe and slipped it on. 'We going to get my kid?'

'You're not going to see your baby for a while, I'm afraid. Social Services have got him.'

Her eyes widened in indignation. 'Social flaming Services? What are those interfering sods sticking their noses in for?'

'The hospital reckon your baby's been poisoned.'

Her jaw dropped. She stared at him. 'Poisoned?'

'His milk had been doctored.'

'Doctored? What do you mean, doctored?'

'You had another child, didn't you? And it suddenly died.'

'A cot death. A bleeding cot death. I found her dead. I couldn't wake her. There was an inquest. They said it was a cot death.'

'One dead baby I'll accept as accidental,' said Skinner. 'But when the other one is poisoned it gets me suspicious. I'm taking you down to the station for questioning.'

'What sort of a flaming country is this?' shrieked Sadie, shaking off the hand Skinner had placed on her arm. 'People break into your house, steal your kid, smash your best china, and instead of getting sympathy you're accused of flaming murder. You wouldn't have treated me like this if I was an illegal immigrant.'

Ignoring her, Skinner signalled to Jordan. 'There's a baby's bottle with milk in it by the side of the cot. Get it. Forensic can have a look at it. And check her cupboards. You're looking for baby milk and salt.'

'Salt?' said Sadie.

'There was enough salt in that child's milk to kill a dozen babies.' He smiled inwardly. This was more like it. Thank goodness he didn't hand the case back to Frost. Attempted infanticide – and on his very first day at Denton. He beckoned to Simms. 'Come on. Let's get her down to the station.'

Police Superintendent Mullett took a sip of coffee and beamed across his mahogany desk at his newly arrived detective chief inspector. 'So glad to have someone of your reputation with us in Denton, John.'

Skinner faked a beam back. 'I'm looking forward to a long stay, sir.' A lie, of course. *Once I get my promotion you won't see my arse for dust.* He let his eyes flit round Mullett's office with its polished oak panelling. The old log cabin, as Frost called it. The rest of the station was a tip, but Mullett had done all right for himself. Skinner would make certain his own office was done up to the same standard during the short time he had to spend in this lousy division. He drained the coffee from the poncey little cup Mullett had given him and replaced it in the tiny saucer. 'As you know, sir, I'll be travelling backwards and forwards to my old patch over the next few weeks. I've got cases to clear up, court appearances and so on.'

Mullett nodded. 'I fully understand that, but we are extremely short-staffed at the moment, what with people on courses and the uniforms we've had to loan to County for that drug-smuggling operation. The sooner we can have you full-time, the better.'

'Shouldn't take more than a couple of weeks to tie up most loose ends, but I want to get shot of Frost as soon as I can. I met up with him today and I agree with you, sir. The man is useless.'

With a look of alarm, Mullett raised a warning finger to his lips, then hurried across to his office door, opened it and peered cautiously up and down the corridor to ensure no one was in earshot. Back at his desk, he clicked the switch which lit up the red 'ENGAGED – DO NOT ENTER' sign. 'This must be kept absolutely confidential, John. If it got out prematurely . . .'

'Don't worry, sir,' Skinner assured him. 'It will get out when I want it to get out, and not before.'

Mullett gave an approving nod. He could hardly believe that what he had been wishing for for so long was actually going to happen. 'But what if he doesn't agree to a transfer out of Denton?'

Skinner gave a smug smile. 'He'll have no choice but to agree. I've done this many times before, so I know what I'm doing.'

Mullett sighed with relief. 'It's good to have you aboard the Denton flagship, John. I can see we're going to get on very well together.'

Skinner smiled back. Mullett looked the sort of man he could twist round his little finger. If he played his cards right, he could end up sitting in that very chair behind that mahogany desk. He stood up. 'I'd better get back to my suspect now – the woman who tried to kill her baby.'

'I'm impressed by the way you've got stuck in on your very first day,' said Mullett. 'Very impressed.' As Skinner left, he switched off the red warning sign. It would be good to have someone like Skinner in the division to do all the dirty jobs Mullett didn't have the guts to do himself. Yes, this was going to work out very well.

Frost squeezed his car into the only available space, narrowly avoiding scraping the paint off Mullett's brand-new, metallic-blue Porsche. He mooched across the car park to the rear entrance of the station. He was not feeling very happy. The semen sample from the rape victim didn't match any known offenders – but perhaps that would have been too easy. And Forensic, while admitting that the severed foot could have come from a hospital dissecting room, refused to rule out the possibility of foul play, which meant he would have to treat it as a possible murder inquiry. And his team was already stretched to the limit now that Hornrim Harry had sent half the force out to catch some other division's drug barons, and the other half were on courses to improve efficiency. The way to improve sodding efficiency was to be on the spot, solving the flaming crimes, not writing poncey essays about understanding the criminal mind. If Forensic had to provide the manpower, they'd flaming soon classify the foot as a medical student's joke, he thought glumly.

Ahead of him, Jordan and Simms were escorting a weaselly-looking man they had arrested for shoplifting, who was bewailing his luck. 'I had to do it, officer,' he told Simms. 'I haven't eaten for three days.'

'So what were you going to do with the bra you nicked?' asked Jordan. 'Boil it or fry it with the knickers?'

'It's easy to be funny when you've got a full stomach,' whined the man.

Frost followed them down the passage and through the swing doors leading to the lobby, where a frazzled Sergeant Wells was with a frosty-faced elderly woman who was clutching a shopping basket. When the woman caught sight of the shoplifter, she dropped the shopping basket and raised a shaking finger, her eyes wide. 'That's him. That's the man. He did it!'

'Did bloody what?' blinked the man. 'What's the silly cow on about?' He moved towards her, but Frost pushed him away.

'Get him to the Charge Room now,' he ordered the two constables. 'I'll sort this out.' He turned to the woman, who was now trembling and panting with fright. 'What's this all about, love?'

She waited until the Charge Room door had closed before answering. 'I'd just drawn my pension. I went down that little alley at the side of the post office and he jumped out, snatched my handbag and legged it. How am I going to get through the week with no money?'

Frost sighed. There'd been a spate of these handbag-snatchings over the past few weeks, usually from elderly women. 'Are you sure that he was the man who robbed you?'

'Positive. I'd stake my life on it. I'd know him anywhere.'

'And when did you say this took place?'

'About half an hour ago. I'd just drawn my pension . . . You ask them in the post office.'

Frost held up a hand to stop her. 'It couldn't have been him, love. Half an hour ago he was in Marks and Sparks nicking bras.'

'If he says that then he's lying to protect himself,' she snapped. 'I'm not senile. It was definitely him. Have you searched his house?'

'From top to bottom,' lied Frost. 'All we found were nipple-less bras and crotchless knickers.' He waited in the lobby while Wells found a WPC to make the woman a cup of tea and see her home safely.

'Bloody woman!' moaned Wells. 'She's positively identified every face in the flaming mug-shot book. We haven't the faintest idea what the bloke looks like. She's identified men of every colour, any age, hairy, bald, giants, flaming midgets. As long as they wear trousers, she'll identify them!'

'Show her a picture of Mullett,' said Frost. 'If she identifies him, I'll arrest him for you. I suppose no one's come hobbling in saying they've lost their foot?'

'No,' grinned Wells. 'Did you know the new DCI has arrested Sadie Rawlings on suspicion of attempted infanticide?'

Frost stopped in his tracks. 'Sadie? He's bloody mad.'

'He reckoned there was enough salt in her baby's bottle to kill an elephant.'

'I can imagine her killing an elephant, but not

a baby. She's a long way from being a bloody saint, but she'd never try to kill her kid. The man's a bloody fool.' He sniffed. The siren call of sausage and bacon was wafting from the canteen. 'I'm off for some breakfast.'

The phone rang. Wells answered it. 'Hold on, Jack! It's the manager from Supersaves. They've had a letter from some nutter claiming he's poisoned some of the food on their shelves.'

'Supersaves? Half their stuff tastes as if it's been poisoned anyway. Send DC Morgan.'

'He's out collecting the CCTV tapes from the multi-storey car park.'

Frost frowned. 'The car park?' Then he remembered. 'Oh – the rape. Send an area car – it's probably a hoax.'

'Jordan and Simms have just gone out to see the parents of a girl who went missing last night.'

'I'm flaming starving. There must be someone else you can send?'

Wells shook his head. 'Only you, Jack.'

Frost took a farewell sniff of the heady fry-up aroma which was trying to Pied Piper him upstairs. 'Sod it! Tell him I'm on my way.'

2

The letter, handwritten in block capitals on cheap A4 paper, read:

> I HAVE POISONED A BOTTLE OF SUPERSAVES OWN BRAND EXTRA STRONG MOUTHWASH, A BOTTLE OF SUPERSAVES 'VINTNERS CHOICE' WINE AND AN ECONOMY SIZE TIN OF SUPERSAVES HAPPYBABE MILK POWDER. TO IDENTIFY THEM, I HAVE MARKED THEM WITH A BLUE CROSS. YOU WILL NOT FIND THEM IN THE PROPER AISLE. I HAVE HIDDEN THEM AROUND THE STORE. GET TO THEM BEFORE YOUR CUSTOMERS DO OR YOU'LL HAVE DEATHS ON YOUR HANDS. INSTRUCTIONS TO PREVENT A RECURRENCE WILL BE SENT TO THAT SHIT BEAZLEY.

Henry Martin, the store manager, a man in his late forties, looked underpaid and overworked. His desk overflowed with papers and his in-tray spilled over. It reminded Frost of his own office. Skilled at reading typescripts upside-down, he squinted at a charming, red-inked, underlined memo to the manager from the store owner, Mr Beazley, which was headed 'ARSE-KICKING TIME' and began: 'If that stupid useless prat who thinks himself a greengrocery manager . . .' Frost nodded to himself. Typical Beazley. A bullying bastard. He had met him before and knew what an arsehole the man was.

Martin was pacing up and down the office in agitation, sucking nervously at a cigarette.

'What do we do?' he pleaded. 'What the hell do we do? There's no way we can shut the store down. The boss would do his nut.'

Frost gave a non-committal grunt and returned his attention to the blackmail letter. Beazley, the owner of the store, would do a lot more than his nut. 'Do you have the envelope?'

Martin shook his head. 'Why should we keep them? When the post is opened, envelopes are shredded.'

'Great,' said Frost. 'Saves us the bother of finding out where it was posted.'

'Of course it might be a hoax, but we can't take the chance,' said Martin, plonking down in his chair.

'Then shut the store down until you find the marked items,' said Frost.

'If I shut it and it's a hoax, I'll be queuing up at the Job Centre before lunch.'

'If it's not a hoax,' said Frost, 'I'll invite you and Mr Beazley to the post-mortems.' He took a sip of coffee and shuddered. It tasted foul. Probably Supersaves own economy brand. He pushed the cup away and read the letter again.

'... GET TO THEM BEFORE YOUR CUSTOMERS DO OR YOU'LL HAVE DEATHS ON YOUR HANDS.' 'My feeling is that this isn't a hoax. But if you're prepared to take a chance ...'

'I've got the staff out now, checking the aisles,' said Martin, 'and the check-out girls are keeping their eyes open just in case a customer has put one in their trolley.'

'You should close the store down until you find the lot,' Frost told him.

Martin looked horrified. 'Mr Beazley would never allow that. We're trying to contact him, but he hasn't reached his office yet. If we shut down without his consent, he'll be furious.'

'It won't make him happy if customers come in with dead babies as proof of purchase, asking for their money back,' said Frost. 'Kick everyone out and shut the flaming place down.'

'But if it turns out to be a hoax ...'

'Flaming heck,' said Frost. 'Is that your theme tune?' He moved to the window and looked down at the store, its aisles thronged with customers, mingled with hordes of red-overalled Supersaves employees searching the shelves.

There was a tap at the door and a thin, bespectacled man sporting a lapel badge reading ASSISTANT MANAGER came in, followed by a young, red-overalled assistant clutching two bottles to her chest. 'We've found these so far, Mr Martin. One wine, one mouthwash.' He took the items from the girl and handed them to the manager.

Frost groaned. 'Why don't you pass them

round the store so everyone can have a turn mauling them about? I'd hate the blackmailer's fingerprints to be nice and clear so we can find out who he is.'

'Sorry,' flushed the assistant manager. 'I didn't think.'

Slipping a polythene bag over his hand to avoid adding any more fingerprints, Frost carefully took the items from Martin and placed them on the desk. 'Where were they?'

'We found the wine in the Grocery Warehouse, on a shelf by the door. The mouthwash was in the Household aisle.'

Frost unscrewed the cap of the mouthwash and sniffed. The smell was unmistakable. 'Bleach,' he said. 'Well, one thing's for sure – we can stop deluding ourselves it's a hoax. This bastard means business.' He turned to the assistant manager. 'What about the baby milk powder?'

'We're still looking.'

'Find it,' ordered Frost, 'and quick.' He turned to Martin. 'Shut the bleeding place down.'

'Yes,' agreed Martin. He turned to the assistant manager. 'Close the store. Say there's an electrical fault or something – we can tell Mr Beazley it was on police orders.'

Frost waited until the assistant manager and the girl had left. 'They found the wine in the warehouse area. Who's allowed in there?'

'The warehouse staff and staff from the shop floor who help to unload and stack.'

'Members of the public?'

'Oh no. Staff only.'

'Then it's odds on it being an inside job. Can you think of any member of staff who would have a grudge against Supersaves?'

'Every bleeding one of them,' said Martin bitterly. 'Me included. Mr Beazley is not the nicest person to work for.'

'I've met him,' sympathised Frost. 'I wouldn't work here for a thousand quid a day. Let me have a list of all employees – include those who have been sacked or left within the last month or so. We'll run them through the computer.' He read the letter through again. 'It's not dated. It came today, did it?'

'I think so,' said Martin.

Frost stared at him. 'You *think* so? Don't you flaming well know?'

'It could have come on Saturday. We have limited clerical staff on duty at weekends. Head Office correspondence gets priority; other stuff is left unopened until Monday.'

'Bloody brilliant,' muttered Frost. 'He says instructions to stop his actions will follow. I take it you would have told me if you had received a blackmail demand.'

'We haven't received it, and of course I'll let you know when we do.' Martin looked through the office window down to a store now devoid of customers. 'I wish they'd hurry up and find that missing jar. Mr Beazley will be furious. He's not renowned for his tolerance.'

Frost's stomach rumbled to remind him he

hadn't eaten yet. 'Do you serve breakfasts here?'

Before Martin could answer there was a tap at the door. His eyes brightened as the assistant manager came in.

'You've found it?'

The man shook his head. 'We've exhausted all possibilities, but we're going over everything again.'

'It could have been sold to a customer,' said Frost. 'We'll have to get the media on to it to warn the public.' He reached for the phone.

'Hold it!' said the assistant manager. 'It might not be necessary.' He pulled a computer printout from his overall pocket. 'That baby powder is a brand-new line. We didn't put it on the shelves until all stock of the old line had gone. It went on display late on Sunday, just before closing time. A box of twenty-four. I've checked and there are twenty-three left – only one has been sold, and that must be the adulterated one.'

'So how does that help us?' asked Frost.

Martin took over. He could see what the assistant manager was getting at. 'We can check the printed receipts. When it goes through the check-out, the product is registered. If the customer paid by credit card we can easily get their name and address from the credit-card company.'

'That could take flaming ages,' said Frost. ' "If you have lost your credit card, press 8; if you want to trace a customer with contaminated baby milk, press 9." Get on to it right away.'

'We're checking late-night-Sunday till

receipts now,' the assistant manager told him. 'If our luck's in we'll get to the customer before the tin is opened.'

'And if your luck's out, they could have paid with cash. Make it quick. If you haven't turned anything up in a quarter of an hour, I'm going to local radio and the rest of the media.' His stomach rumbled again. 'Do you do breakfasts at the restaurant here?' he asked the manager again.

'We do an excellent full English – it's on special this week.'

'How do I pay for it?' asked Frost.

'Oh – we take credit cards.'

Shit, thought Frost, who was hoping the stingy sod would let him have it on the house. 'Right, I'll nip over and get something to eat. Tell your assistant where I am.'

As he crossed the shop floor he could see the staff were doing a thorough job with the search. Everything was being taken off the shelves, examined and put back again.

In the restaurant, he was just dipping his fried bread in his egg when Taffy Morgan burst in and came running towards him.

'Ah – there you are, Guv.'

'Yes,' said Frost. 'I know where I am.' He took a swig of tea.

'I tried to get you on your mobile, Guv.'

'I keep it switched off,' said Frost, 'in case some Welsh git tries to ring me. Sit down and watch me eat.' He forked a piece of bacon and surveyed it gloomily. 'This pig was solid fat.'

Morgan dragged out a chair and sat opposite him. 'That rape case, Guv, I've run through the CCTV tapes from the multi-storey car park. Got a shot of a car roaring off at about the time the girl said. A Ford Focus. It's got to be our rapist.'

Frost pushed his unfinished breakfast away and lit up a cigarette. 'Well done, Taff. About time our flaming luck changed. You got the registration and checked it out?'

Morgan nodded. 'Graham Fielding, 29 Castle Road, Denton.'

'Any previous? Has his dick got him into trouble before?'

'No, Guv. Shall I pick him up?'

Frost dribbled smoke from his nose as he chewed this over, then shook his head. 'No. Don't let's jump the gun. We've got nothing on him other than the fact that his car was in the vicinity at the time of the rape. Call on him, Taff, use your Welsh charm, and if that doesn't put him off, ask if he will give us a DNA sample – Forensic will tell you what to get. Take a paper bag in case they want poo. If it matches, we've got the bastard; if not, we can forget him.'

'Supposing he won't give a DNA sample, Guv?'

'Then reason with him – punch him in the stomach. If that doesn't work, bring him in. If he's innocent there's no reason why he should refuse.'

As Morgan left, Frost noticed Henry Martin hovering. He didn't look at all happy. 'What's up?' asked Frost. 'Have you eaten one of these breakfasts?'

The manager forced a smile and slid into the chair vacated by Morgan. 'Mr Beazley doesn't like people smoking in here.'

'It does less harm than eating the food,' said Frost, making no attempt to put the cigarette out. 'So what's the news?'

'We've been over the shelves thoroughly three times. No sign of the missing jar. We've been through the till receipts – it hasn't been checked out. I don't know what we can do. We can't open the store until we find it. I dread to think what Mr Beazley will say.'

'If no one's bought it and it's not still in the store, then it's gone out without being paid for. So either a member of your staff has helped himself or . . .' His eyes widened and the hand holding his cigarette paused in mid air. A light dawned and he grinned. '. . . or it could have been nicked by a shoplifter.'

'Speculation,' moaned Martin. 'We could never prove it.'

'This might be your lucky day,' said Frost. He pulled his mobile phone from his pocket and dialled a number. 'Jordan? Inspector Frost here. That milk powder you picked up from Sadie's house – did it have a blue cross on the bottom? . . . Well check it out now.' He drummed his fingers on the table as he waited. 'Yes . . . What? Brilliant. No, don't send it to Forensic yet. Hang on to it until I get there.' He dropped the phone back in his pocket. 'We've traced it,' he told

Martin. 'You can open up again. But let me know the minute you get another letter demanding money – and make certain as few people as possible smear their fingerprints on it.'

'I can go, can I?' shrilled Sadie. 'Oh, bleeding nice! Locked up, falsely imprisoned, insulted and then kicked out. What about compensation?'

'Your compensation is that we're not nicking you for shoplifting,' said Frost. 'Now push off before I change my mind.'

'What about my kiddy?'

'Sort that out with Social Services, Sadie, and next time you nick something, make sure it isn't contaminated.'

'You wouldn't treat me like this if I was an asylum-seeker.'

'Then go and seek bleeding asylum and come back and see, but for now, push off.' He held the door wide open for her to leave. 'Another dissatisfied customer,' he told Bill Wells and mooched back to his office.

Frost looked up from the crime-statistics report where a column of figures was dancing before his eyes. A tap at the office door heralded the arrival of Simms and Jordan.

'Whatever it is, the answer's no,' he told them. 'I've got my sums to do.'

Jordan grinned. 'We've just been out on a call, Inspector. Teenage girl missing from home.'

'She's not here,' said Frost, 'and I wouldn't tell

you if she was.' He put his pen down and sighed. 'All right. Tell me about it.'

'She's Debbie Clark. Told her parents she was going to a sleepover with her schoolfriend Audrey Glisson – she's done this many times before. Went off on her bike about half seven yesterday evening. When she didn't come home this morning, the parents phoned Audrey's house. Debbie hadn't been there and hadn't arranged to go there.'

'So she's been missing overnight? Probably having a sleepover under her boyfriend. I bet she's now at his place having a fag,' said Frost dismissively, picking up his pen again. 'Fill in a missing-persons report.'

'The parents claim she isn't that sort of a girl,' said Jordan.

Frost snorted. 'As I've told you a million times, lads, every time a teenage girl goes missing from home, the parents swear blind she's a pure, sweet, home-loving girl training to be a nun, and nine times out of ten they turn out to be little scrubbers, on the game, pumping themselves full of coke, who've run away for the umpteenth time.'

'She's only just thirteen, Inspector. Today is her birthday . . . they were throwing her a party tonight.'

'If I had the choice between jelly and ice cream or a bit of the other, jelly wouldn't stand a chance,' said Frost.

'We've a feeling about this one, Inspector,' said Simms. 'I really think you should see the parents.'

Frost dribbled smoke through his nose. He, too, often had feelings that weren't borne out by the evidence, feelings that sometimes proved correct. 'All right, lads. Book her in as a missing person and when I get the chance I'll see them, but I'm tied up right now.' He reached out for his internal phone as it rang.

'Frost!' It was Bill Wells. 'Superintendent Mullett says he wants the crime-statistics report right now, Jack.'

Frost looked down at the untidy mess of scribbled figures and crossings-out in front of him. He got up and snatched his scarf from the hook on the wall. 'Tell him I'm out interviewing the parents of a missing thirteen-year-old girl.'

The Clarks lived in a large four-bedroomed house situated on the outskirts of Denton, overlooking Denton Woods. As the area car scrunched down a long driveway flanked by miniature conifers, Frost admired the extensive lawn. Studded with flower beds, it encircled a large fish pond with a statue of a naked woman pouring water from a jug.

'Very tasteful,' he nodded. 'I'm glad she's not doing a pee like that boy in Brussels.'

A gleaming black E-class Mercedes-Benz estate was parked outside a double garage. 'They're not short of a few bob, are they?' muttered Frost, climbing out of the car.

They had hardly reached the front door when it was flung open by the missing girl's father, Harold Clark, an angry man in his mid-forties, with slicked-down dark hair and a neatly clipped moustache like Mullett's, which turned Frost off him right away.

'About bloody time,' snapped Clark, jerking a thumb towards the hall. 'In here.'

They followed him into a large, thickly carpeted lounge. One wall was dominated by a huge fire, with gas flames licking at artificial logs, the other by an enormous plasma television screen. Clark's wife, some ten years younger than him, sat huddled by the fire in one of the cream leather armchairs. Behind her, wall-to-wall patio doors gave a panoramic view of Denton Woods, which at this time of year, with black clouds hovering, seemed to have a sinister aura. Mrs Clark would have been pretty if her hair had been combed and she had put make-up on. She didn't look well, staring blankly into space and twisting a damp handkerchief in her hands.

'The police,' announced her husband curtly.

She looked up through tear-swollen eyes at the men. 'Have you found her? She's dead, isn't she? I know she is.' She dissolved into tears. Her husband put an arm round her. She abruptly twitched her shoulder to shake him off, then shrank back into the armchair.

Clark gave a 'you can see she's upset' shrug and moved away.

'We haven't found her yet,' said Jordan. He indicated the inspector. 'This is Detective Inspector Frost.'

Clark scowled at the shabby figure of Frost, who tended to look even shabbier against luxurious backgrounds. He was clearly not impressed. 'Have you got a search party out yet?'

Frost shook his head. 'Not yet, Mr Clark.'

Clark's face darkened. 'What do you mean, "Not yet"? My daughter's gone missing.'

'It's early days,' explained Frost. 'Young girls go missing all the time. They run away from home, they come back.'

Clark was spluttering with rage. 'Run away from home?' he shrieked. 'You stupid, bloody fool. I told these two officers earlier, there is no way my daughter would run away from home. It's her thirteenth birthday today.' He flapped a hand towards the mantelpiece where a stack of unopened birthday cards were piled. 'She's having a party. She was looking forward to it. There is no bloody way she would run away.'

'Do you know how many teenagers run away from home every year, Mr Clark, and how many of them come running back in a couple of days with their tails between their legs?'

Clark jabbed a finger at Frost. 'My daughter is not a bloody statistic. I want search parties out now, do you hear? Now!'

Frost unwound his scarf. It was sweltering in the lounge with the gas fire going at full blast. 'Let me have a few facts first, sir, please. She went out yesterday evening on her bike, I understand. What time would that be?'

'How many more bloody times? She had her evening meal and left about half past seven. Said she was going to see her friend Audrey and might stay the night. She's done it before, so we didn't worry.'

'She often went there for sleepovers?'

'Yes.'

'Audrey used to come here for sleepovers,' said the mother flatly, staring into space, 'but not any more.'

'Oh?' asked Frost. 'Why not?'

Clark shot a warning glance at his wife, then answered for her. 'We've no idea. You know what kids are.'

'I see,' nodded Frost, who didn't see at all. He'd have a word with Audrey himself. 'And you've checked with this girl?'

'Of course we've bloody checked. Do you think we're stupid? Debbie hadn't been there. She hadn't even arranged to go there.'

'Has Debbie got a boyfriend?'

'She's only thirteen! Of course she hasn't got a boyfriend. There was some lout sniffing around some months ago, but I soon got shot of him.'

'He was a nice boy,' said his wife tonelessly. 'I liked him.'

'Oh yes?' snarled Clark. 'A nice boy! So what was he doing in her bloody bedroom with his hand down her blouse? I slung him out of the house and said if I ever caught him with my daughter again . . .' He let the threat hang.

'Have you contacted the boy to see if Debbie is with him?'

'I phoned his house, but got no reply. She'd better not be there – I'll break the dirty bastard's neck.'

'His name and address, please.' He waited as the mother scribbled it down. 'Has Debbie got a mobile phone?'

'Yes. I've been ringing, but it's switched off.'

'Did she take any clothes – money – her bank book?'

The Clarks looked questioningly at each other. 'I'll check,' said the wife, rising unsteadily from her chair, again shrugging off her husband's helping hand.

There was a silent, uneasy wait as she went upstairs and Clark exuded his dislike of the shabbily dressed inspector. Frost was dying for a smoke but couldn't see any ashtrays.

Mrs Clark returned, shaking her head. 'All her clothes seem to be there – and her bank book.'

Frost stood up. 'Could I take a look round her room?'

She led him back up the stairs to a room decorated with pop posters. A single bed with a light-blue coverlet stood against one wall, a cream-coloured wardrobe against the other. Everything was neat and tidy. By the window a wire-mesh waste-paper bin nestled under a desk housing a flat-screen computer and an inkjet printer.

'Is she on the internet?' asked Frost.

Mrs Clark nodded. 'Always messaging her friends, even though she sees them every day at school.'

Frost jabbed a finger at the keyboard, pulling it away quickly as the computer bleeped. He nodded knowingly as if the noise meant something to him, but he was completely computer illiterate. One of the technicians would need to have a look at the machine to see what secrets it held if it turned out that Debbie really was missing and not just having it away with the boy whose hand had been discovered exploring the contents of her blouse. He took a look at the waste-paper bin. This was more his sort of thing. He bent and pulled out some crumpled gift-wrap. A stuck-on label read '*Happy birthday, darling, from Mum.*' He frowned. 'I thought her birthday was today?'

Mrs Clark took the wrapping paper from him and stared at it in puzzlement. 'She's opened it. Before her birthday . . . she's opened it!'

Her husband came in the room. 'What's the matter?' he barked.

'It seems that Debbie opened one of her presents from your wife before her birthday and took it with her,' Frost told him.

Clark turned to his wife. 'What present?'

She paused before replying. 'That bikini she wanted.'

Her husband exploded. 'You bought her that bloody bikini? A twelve-year-old school kid? Didn't I specifically tell you—'

'All her friends had one,' cut in his wife.

'Most of her friends are sluts – jailbait. My daughter isn't!'

'Perhaps you could discuss this some other time,' said Frost wearily. 'She was obviously going somewhere on her bike last night. Could it have been the swimming baths, to show the new costume off to her friends?'

'It's possible,' said her mother. 'She often went swimming there.'

'Right, we'll check it out,' said Frost, winding the scarf back round his neck, ready to leave. 'Oh – do you have a recent photograph?'

Mrs Clark stared at her husband, who paused before mumbling, 'Nothing recent, I'm afraid.'

'Oh?' said Frost. 'A school photograph, perhaps?'

'No,' said Clark, not looking Frost in the eye. 'There are no school photographs.'

'Oh?' repeated Frost, waiting for an explanation, but none came. 'I see,' he said eventually. But he didn't see.

'I take it you are going straight back to the station to organise a full-scale search for my daughter?' demanded Clark.

'As I said, it's a bit too early for that at this stage,' Frost told him.

'Too early?' echoed Clark angrily. 'Too bloody early? She's been missing since last night. How much longer are we expected to wait while you sit on your bloody arse, shuffling papers, while my daughter is out there, probably in the hands of some sexual pervert.'

'I appreciate your concern—' began Frost.

'Then bloody well do something about it.'

'I've been involved in over a hundred missing-teenager cases, Mr Clark. All the parents were worried sick, quite rightly, and in nearly every case the parents refused to accept the possibility that their child might have left home of their own accord. But in over 95 per cent of cases that is exactly what happened and their kids were only too glad to creep back home after a couple of days.'

'You can quote your lousy statistics at me until you are blue in the face, but I want a full-scale search carried out now – this very minute . . .'

'I'm sorry—' began Frost, but before he could continue, Clark moved towards him, his face contorted with rage.

'You're sorry? I'm the one who's bloody sorry. I've been sent a useless, do-nothing idiot. Get out of my house. I'm having you taken off this case. I've got friends in very high places, as you will soon find out.'

With a nod to the weeping mother, Frost jerked his head for Jordan and Simms to follow him. They left the house.

Back in the car, Frost lit up a much-needed cigarette. 'Friends in high places,' he mused. 'I bet they live on the top floor of a tower block.'

'What do you reckon, Inspector?' Jordan asked.

Frost exhaled smoke. 'I don't know. I still think she's having it away with the boyfriend, but I've got a nagging suspicion that something nasty has happened to her. If we had more manpower down here instead of on loan to flaming County, courtesy of Superintendent bloody Mullett, I'd start searching – but we haven't. Right, after you drop me off, go to the boyfriend's house, check his hands for bra marks and check that Debbie isn't there. Then go and see this girl Audrey, see if she knows more than she is telling – and find out why she stopped coming for sleepovers. Oh – and check the swimming baths. See if anyone remembers Debbie there last night. I still reckon she'll be back in time for her birthday party, but we might as well pretend we're thorough for a change.'

Superintendent Mullett, the Denton divisional commander, held the phone away from his ear. The shouting from the other end was overpowering.

'. . . And I want a proper detective on the case, not that scruffy, rude, ignorant individual you saw fit to send to me this morning.'

'Inspector Frost is a very capable officer,' said Mullett, trying to sound as if he believed it.

'Inspector Frost is an incompetent, ignorant oaf. A disgrace to the force. Are you going to organise a search party to look for my daughter, or do I have to go direct to my friend, the Chief Constable.'

Mullett straightened up in his chair at the mention of the Chief Constable.

'He's Debbie's godfather – did you know that?'

Her godfather! Mullett's heart skipped a beat. 'Leave it to me, Mr Clark. I'll get a search party organised right away.'

'Is that a promise?'

'You have my word,' floundered Mullett, nodding furiously to emphasise the fact.

'Good, because I have recorded this conversation.'

A click and the dialling tone.

Mullett carefully replaced the receiver, mopped his brow and picked up the internal phone to summon Frost.

Frost's radio gave an attention-snatching cough as he coasted into his place in the station car park. It was PC Jordan reporting.

'Inspector, we checked the swimming baths. Yesterday was senior citizens' night. A twelve-year-old girl in a bikini would have stuck out like a sore thumb.'

'Lots of other things would have stuck out as well,' said Frost.

'Next, we went round to the boyfriend's house. No reply. I checked with the neighbours. His parents are away for a couple of days and he is looking after himself. They saw him cycle off around seven yesterday evening, but didn't see him come back and didn't see any lights come on. There's milk on the doorstep, the paper's in the letter box, and no answer to our knocks.'

'Have you spoken to that girl, Audrey?'

'We're on our way there now.'

'Right. Let me know what she says.' He clicked off and drummed his fingers on the steering wheel. Boy missing, girl missing, both on bikes. It was looking more and more obvious that they had done a bunk together. But a nagging doubt kept chewing away.

As he opened the door to his office, the insistent ringing of his phone greeted him. Before he could pick it up, Sergeant Wells burst in.

'Just had Beazley – the boss of the supermarket – on the blower, Jack. They've heard from the blackmailer – he wants fifty thousand pounds.'

Frost re-buttoned his coat. 'Tell him I'm on my way.' As he left the office, he jerked a thumb at his phone. 'Answer that, would you?'

'It came this morning,' grunted Beazley, a short, piggy-eyed man in his late fifties. 'The bastard wants fifty thousand quid.' He passed a sheet of paper with an envelope clipped to it over to Frost.

Frost held it carefully by the edges and skimmed through it. Like the previous note, it was handwritten in block capitals:

> THAT WAS ONLY A TASTER. I'VE PLENTY MORE POISONS LEFT. PEOPLE WILL DIE. TO STOP ME PAY £50,000 INTO ACCOUNT NUMBER FDZ32432, FORTRESS BUILDING SOCIETY. DO IT TODAY OR THERE'S MORE POISON TOMORROW.

As Frost was reading, Beazley stripped the wrapping off an enormous cigar and lit up. 'I phoned the building society to get the bastard's name. They wouldn't give it to me. Said they had to respect their client's confidentiality. The sod's trying to screw me for 50K and they want to respect his bleeding confidentiality.'

This is a copycat crime, thought Frost. There had been a similar extortion case in London some years before, where the blackmail money was paid into a building society account which the villain had opened with a false name and address. But today building societies insisted on proof of identity, so this bloke, obviously an amateur, must be a real prat giving away a traceable account number.

'Are you going to pay it?' he asked as a cloud of cigar smoke drifted across his face.

'You tell me,' grunted Beazley. 'I'm not risking a single penny unless you can guarantee you can catch him. The sod could take the money and do it again.'

'Pay it,' said Frost. 'He's got to contact the building society to withdraw it. We'll catch him.'

Beazley shook ash from his cigar and stared at Frost in disbelief. 'Pay him? You're saying I should cough up 50K on the off chance you might catch the sod as he withdraws it? Supposing you are up to your usual standard of efficiency and he draws the lot out while you're arresting some poor sod for a parking offence? No way.'

'Your choice,' said Frost, standing and buttoning up his mac. 'Let us know when he puts rat poison in your baby food and cuts holes in your condoms.'

'Hold it!' barked Beazley, flapping Frost back into the chair with his hand. He tugged at his lower lip in thought, drumming the desk with a gold fountain pen. Then he chucked the fountain pen down on the desk and jabbed a key on his phone. 'Archer, get your arse in here now.'

Barely had he released the key than there was

a timid tap at his door and a little man with thinning, sandy hair blinked nervously at him.

'You wanted me, Mr Beazley?'

'Yes,' snapped Beazley. 'I want a cheque made out right away for fifty thousand pounds.'

'Who shall I make it out to?' asked Archer.

Beazley stared at him in mock surprise, as if he was being asked a stupid question. 'How the bloody hell do I know?' He turned to Frost. 'Who does he make it out to?'

Frost read from the blackmail letter. 'Fortress Building Society account number FDZ32432.'

Archer had barely left the room before he was back, breathlessly clutching a large chequebook which he placed on the desk in front of Beazley. He stood back deferentially. With barely a glance at it, Beazley uncapped his fountain pen and slashed his signature as if signing for petty cash, then ripped out the cheque, more or less along the perforation, and handed it to Frost, who stuffed it unceremoniously into his mac pocket.

'Right, Mr Beazley, leave the rest to us.'

Beazley flailed a podgy hand of dismissal and returned to his study of the store's trading figures with a series of grunts and groans. As Frost left, Beazley was already on the phone to his hapless grocery manager. 'Hoskins, what the bleeding hell is up with your weekend sales figures . . . ?'

Once outside Beazley's office, Frost dragged his cigarettes from his pocket and lit up. As he walked away, someone called out that he had dropped something. He looked down. Bloody hell! It was the flaming fifty-thousand-pound cheque. He scooped it up and put it in the comparative safety of his inside jacket pocket. 'Your money's safe with me, Mr Beazley,' he told himself.

The note on Frost's desk, pinned down by his ashtray, screamed in red block capitals: 'MR MULLETT WANTS TO SEE YOU URGENTLY'. His internal and outside phones both rang together. Mullett would be on the internal, so he answered the other one first. It was PC Jordan.

'Inspector, we're over at that girl Audrey's house. I think you'd better get over here right away and hear what her mother has got to say about Debbie's father.'

Audrey, a serious-looking twelve-year-old wearing glasses, looked troubled.

Her mother – dark-haired, plumpish, in her late thirties – nodded grimly to Frost in greeting.

'What have you got to tell me, Mrs Glisson?' he asked.

She took one of Frost's offered cigarettes. He lit up for both of them. She inhaled deeply and held the smoke in her lungs for a while before exhaling, a look of bliss on her face. A woman after Frost's own heart. 'I shouldn't really be smoking. Those health warnings on the packets frighten the life out of me.'

'It's not a very good sales pitch, is it?' smiled Frost. 'So what can you tell us?'

Mrs Glisson turned to her daughter. 'Go on, Audrey. Tell the inspector.'

'Mum!' protested the girl, shaking her head. 'I don't want to.'

'Tell the detective why you stopped going to sleepovers at Debbie's house – go on, tell him.'

Audrey lowered her head and talked to the tabletop. 'It was her dad. He used to keep bursting in on us when we were getting undressed for bed. Never knocked or anything. And when I was in the shower, he'd charge in saying, "Oops, sorry, didn't know you were there." But he knew. He'd taken the bolt off the door – said it was broken.'

'Did he touch you – interfere with you?'

'No. I made sure I wasn't alone when he was about.'

'He's a dirty bastard,' said her mother.

'What did Debbie say about this?' Frost asked.

'She seemed embarrassed . . . wouldn't talk about it. She started to tell me something about him once, then clammed up.'

'If you ask me, he's been abusing his own daughter,' offered Mrs Glisson, flipping ash on the floor. 'If Debbie's gone missing, Audrey reckons she's either run away from her father or the sod's done her in.'

'Oh, Mum!' protested Audrey. 'I told you not to tell anyone.'

'Debbie's gone missing,' insisted her mother. 'You shouldn't hide these things. It could be serious.'

'It may not be that bad,' Frost told them. 'She could have run off with her boyfriend.'

'What, Tom Harris?' asked Audrey. 'She might

have done. She said they were going to get up to larks round his house this week while his mum and dad were away.'

'They're not round the parents' house,' Frost told her. 'We've checked.' Then he remembered. 'Debbie took her new bikini with her. Any idea why?'

'I know she and Tom used to go skinny dipping in that lake in the woods. She might have gone there.'

Skinny dipping? thought Frost. *Bloody hell. What a lucky bastard that Tom is. In my day, if you caught sight of a girl's bare knee you had to have a cold shower. But you wouldn't take a bikini if you were going skinny dipping.*

He stubbed out his cigarette and stood up. 'Anything else you can tell me?'

The girl and her mother both shook their heads.

'Well, thanks for the information. If you think of anything else that might help, let me know.' He scribbled his name and phone number on a piece of paper and handed it to the mother. 'We'll see ourselves out.'

'What do you reckon, Inspector?' Simms asked when they were outside

Frost frowned thoughtfully. 'The father definitely sounds like a dirty bastard. He might be interfering with his daughter, but we've got no proof. His wife knows something, but I don't think she'd tell. When Debbie turns up we can see if she wants to make a complaint, but we've got to find her first.' He stuck his hands in his pockets and stared across to the dark shape of Denton Woods. 'Skinny bloody dipping? A bit too flaming cold for that, surely. Just to be on the safe side, after you drop me off, go and have a look round the lake. It's deep enough to drown in and you could easily get cramp swimming when it's cold. See if their bikes are there.' In his pocket, his hand found a piece of paper. The building-society account number given by the blackmailer. Shit, he'd forgotten about it . . . and he still had the cheque to pay in . . . and he also hadn't checked to see if the account details were genuine.

His mobile played its little tune. It was Bill Wells.

'Jack, Mr Mullett's going spare. He wants to see you right now.'

'I think he fancies me,' said Frost. 'Tell him I'm on my way. And Bill, would you contact the Fortress Building Society and see who, if anyone, has an account number FDZ32432.'

Mullett slid the heavy glass ashtray across just too late to stop Frost's cigarette dropping a cylinder of ash on his desk. 'His *daughter*,' he said, 'missing since last night and you tell him you have no intention of organising a search?'

'Not at this stage,' said Frost. 'I'm more or less convinced she's done a runner with her boyfriend . . .' His voice tailed off. Doing his usual trick of reading upside-down memos in Mullett's in-tray, he spotted one from Head

Office with his name at the top. He carefully moved his chair forward so he could read what it was about, but Mullett forestalled him, quickly pulling the in-tray away and dropping some other papers on top. Frost's eyes narrowed. *Hello, what's the slimy bastard up to?*

'Don't you realise who you are dealing with, Frost? Clark is a very important man. He has the Chief Constable's ear.'

'I don't care if he has the Chief Constable's dick,' replied Frost. 'There's no way I'm organising a full-scale search yet.'

Mullett reddened as he shot a glance at his office door to make sure the Chief Constable wasn't suddenly within earshot. 'Less of that sort of talk, Inspector. You may not know how to handle these matters, but I do. I have told Mr Clark I am authorising a full-scale search immediately for his daughter.'

'I admire you, Super,' beamed Frost approvingly. 'Even though you know it will be expensive and a complete waste of time, will put us way over budget and we haven't got the men to do it, you are still prepared to stick your neck out and risk all that for a friend of the Chief Constable. I'll get on to outlying divisions right away and tell them you have agreed to stand the cost of the search on Denton's budget.'

'Other divisions?' spluttered Mullett, realising he should have made some checks before committing himself to Clark. 'Why do we need to involve other divisions?'

'Because we haven't the faintest idea where

they went,' explained Frost. 'They both went out on bikes. They could be twenty, thirty, forty miles away for all we know. They could even be in London by now. The girl didn't take any money, but the boy might well have done. Still, if you've committed yourself, Super, I'll put it in hand right away.' He made to stand up.

'Wait!' Mullett weakly waggled a restraining hand. 'What did you intend to do?'

'Put out an All Divisions Missing Persons, make a few local inquiries and wait for them to come slinking back, the girl with her knickers in her handbag and a satisfied smile on her face. If they haven't turned up by tonight, then I'll think about a more thorough search.'

'A token search now,' pleaded Mullett. 'Just a token search, so I can assure Mr Clark we have it well in hand?'

'Don't worry, Super, I'll fiddle it for you,' beamed Frost. 'I might need you to do me a favour one day.'

DC Morgan was waiting for him in his office. 'I've got a DNA sample from that bloke, Guv,' he announced proudly.

'Great,' said Frost. 'Any problems?'

'It wasn't easy. First he denied being anywhere near the car park last night. Flatly denied it. When I told him we had CCTV footage he changed his story and said yes, now he came to think of it he might have been there.'

'He'd forgotten where he was the night

before?' asked Frost. 'What is he – a doddery old sod or a Welshman?'

'No, Guv . . . in his early forties, I'd say. Anyway, I asked for a DNA sample. I told him he had every right to refuse, but if he did refuse I'd arrest him on suspicion of assault and rape. In the end he agreed. He's the rapist, Guv, I'm positive. It's him.'

'I wish you weren't so bloody sure, Taff,' muttered Frost. 'You're always flaming well wrong.' He thoughtfully fingered the scar that lined his cheek. 'Do you think he might do a bunk?'

'Nice house, nice wife, two kids and a dog, Guv. I can't see him doing a runner.'

'Play safe. Make an excuse to keep going back, Taff, and make sure he's still there. And tell Forensic I want that DNA sample tested right away. We're short staffed and the flaming cases keep piling up. Be great if we could get this one tied up sharpish.'

The door crashed open, banging against the wall, and an angry-looking Chief Inspector Skinner burst in. He glared at Frost. 'You've let that Sadie tart go?'

Frost started to explain about the blackmailer and the baby milk powder, but Skinner cut him short.

'Whatever the reason, in future you tell me first, not let me find out by walking into an empty cell.'

'Good point,' nodded Frost approvingly, as if praising Skinner for raising it.

'Another thing. I've called a meeting for all station staff, four o'clock this afternoon in the main Incident Room. I'm briefing everyone on the way I'm going to run things here in future. Make sure you are there.'

'Wouldn't miss it for the world,' cooed Frost.

Skinner stared at him. Like Mullett, he was never sure when Frost was being sincere or was taking the pee. He turned his attention to Morgan. 'What are you doing here?'

Morgan told him about the DNA sample.

Skinner grunted and turned his attention back to Frost. 'Right. For the moment, this is your case, Frost, but if the DNA is positive and it looks like we're going to get a result, then I take over . . . *comprende*?'

You bastard, thought Frost. *We do the hard work, you take the credit.* But he nodded. '*Comprende, signora*.'

Again Skinner glowered at Frost. Was the man being insolent or didn't he know what *signora* meant? No way of knowing for sure, but the fool's days in Denton were numbered, so there was no point making a scene now. He spun on his heel and barged out of the office, leaving the door wide open.

Morgan closed it carefully. 'I've heard about Skinner from my old division, Guv. He makes everyone else do the hard graft, then he steps in and takes the credit.'

'I know,' nodded Frost. 'It's like sweating away on the foreplay, then some other sod gets his leg over.' His internal phone rang. PC Lambert from Control.

'PC Jordan wants you to get over to Denton Lake right away, Inspector. They've found something.'

Frost's heart skipped a beat. 'The girl?' he whispered. *God, not the girl.*

'No, Inspector. Another piece of that chopped-off leg.'

'Shit!' said Frost.

3

Frost, DC Taffy Morgan at his side, gazed down gloomily at the muddy, evil-smelling piece of flesh, half-hidden in long, straggling, rain-beaten grass. Jordan and Simms looked on like two puppies wagging their tails at finding the ball for their master. *Pity you didn't chuck the flaming thing in the lake and say nothing*, thought Frost. *More flaming paperwork to no avail.*

'It's a bit of leg,' said Jordan.

'I know,' sniffed Frost. 'I'm a leg man, but it doesn't turn me on. There's probably more choice bits lurking about for some silly sod to find, but we haven't the time or the resources to look for them. Bag it up. See what Forensic make of it.' He was still hoping this was some medical student's idea of a joke, but had the growing suspicion that it was going to turn out to be something a lot more sinister.

He took a deep drag on his cigarette and looked around. They were on the outskirts of the lake which had been a magnet for dead bodies so many times in the past. He mooched over to the water's edge and stared down into the green, slimy water which was being rippled by the cutting wind. At the far end a duck squawked and flapped its wings as it skimmed across the surface. He shivered. It was flaming cold standing here. No way Debbie would risk her brand-new bikini in this slimy muck.

Another possibility kick-started – something he hadn't considered before. Supposing the boy had done away with Debbie, then roared off in panic. She could have told him she was pregnant and would name him as the father. Possible . . . but the unsubstantiated thought wasn't getting him anywhere. Where the hell was she and where the hell was the boy? She would have come back for her birthday if she could. He kept trying to kid himself she wouldn't, but . . . He stared again over the lake and shivered, this time not from the cold. He had one of his doom-laden premonitions.

He nodded at the lake. 'I think she's in there,' he said flatly. He knew he would never get Mullett's permission to call the underwater search team out just on the strength of one of his nasty feelings, when their past record had such a low success rate. But he felt strongly this time.

He turned to Morgan and indicated a dilapidated rowing boat, half in, half out of the lake, its bottom awash with muddy water. 'Feel like a row, Taff?'

Morgan stared at the boat in dismay. 'Flaming

heck, Guv, look at the holes in the bottom. It's like a sieve. I can't swim.'

'I can't play the violin,' said Frost, 'but I don't moan about it.' He signalled to Jordan. 'Push the boat out. Have a prod around with Taffy. She might be in there.'

Jordan was equally unenthusiastic and surveyed the leaky rowing boat with apprehension. 'Is that an order, Inspector?'

Frost shook his head. 'Of course not, son. You've both volunteered.'

He sat in the car with the heater going full blast, sucking at a cigarette as he listened to the local news on the radio.

> . . . Denton Police are appealing for help in tracing the whereabouts of two teenagers, Debbie Clark and Thomas Harris, who did not return home after a cycle ride yesterday evening. Anyone with information . . .

Bleeding Mullett, jumping the gun. Appeals to the public always brought an abundant crop of false sightings which some poor sod had to follow through. *And I'll be that poor sod*, he thought ruefully.

His head jerked up. What was that? It sounded like Jordan calling. He groaned. God, they'd found her. They'd found the girl. He clicked the radio off and flung open the car door. The cry was repeated. But it wasn't Jordan. It was the squawk of a flaming duck flying overhead. He sank back in his seat in relief. He didn't want them to find her. He wanted Debbie to be safe and well. But she was dead . . . He just knew it.

He started to fidget. Sitting, doing nothing, wasn't his way of working, so he mashed out the cigarette and climbed out of the car.

Another cry. But it wasn't the duck this time. It was Jordan. 'Inspector!' It was the urgent cry of someone who had found something nasty.

The two men were near the far side of the lake, the boat tilting over at an alarming angle as they both leant over one side to try to pull something out of the water. They were in grave danger of capsizing the rowing boat. They were dragging something out of the lake. Not a body. It was a red cycle, which didn't seem to have been in the water for very long.

Frost's heart sank. Debbie's bike was red. It had to be her bike.

For once, he didn't want his gut feeling to be proved correct. Then he heaved a sigh of relief. It wasn't Debbie's. It was a man's bike. And the boyfriend's bike was blue, so it couldn't be his.

'Chuck it back,' he called. 'It's a man's bike. Women's bikes don't have bars in case it snags their bloomers.'

'You're behind the times, Inspector,' yelled Jordan. 'Bikes are unisex now.'

Frost went cold. 'Are you sure?'

'Positive.'

With a final heave they hauled the dripping bike into the boat. Jordan bent and examined it.

'Same make and same serial number, Inspector. It's Debbie Clark's bike.'

Frost turned his back against the wind and lit up another cigarette. Shit and double shit. He waited impatiently while they rowed across, stepping back as they humped the bike out of the boat and laid it on the grass. He double-checked the serial number, but Jordan was right. He took another look at the murky, icy water. If her bike was there, the girl's body could be there, caught up in jettisoned debris somewhere – perhaps the boy's body as well. Why had he been so bloody cocksure in assuring the parents they'd soon be back home again, safe and sound. He shook his head to dispel the morbid thought. They'd found the bike, that was all. Debbie could still be alive and well, shacked up with the boy somewhere, miles away. But that didn't make sense. Why dump the bike? She'd need it to get home again. And why chuck it in the lake so it wouldn't be found? No. She had to be in that lake. There was enough evidence now for him to ask Mullett to call the police frogmen in and do a thorough search.

'Get it over to Forensic,' he told them. 'I doubt if any prints have survived submersion, but don't confuse them by adding your own.'

He pulled the mobile from his pocket and rang Mullett.

'I'm at Denton Woods, Super. We've just fished Debbie Clark's bike out of the lake. I think her body's in there. We're going to have to call the underwater search team in.'

* * *

He watched impassively. It was just a matter of time before they dragged the kid's body up. Her thirteenth bleeding birthday. All her cards waiting to be opened. He dreaded going back to the house and breaking the news. Not many bloody laughs in this job.

The underwater team waded out and plunged under the surface. His heart juddered and skipped a beat each time they hauled something up and dumped it in their rowing boat. As the boat filled it was rowed to the shore and its contents dumped. Soon the shore round the lake was littered with retrieved debris, including two supermarket trolleys, a DVD player and a video recorder whose serial numbers tallied with goods stolen during an ancient burglary, and a long-dead fox.

Morgan and Jordan, in the small rowing boat, were keeping well out of the way of the frogmen, and were prodding the bottom with a large pole. 'Over here,' called Morgan, waving frantically at the frogmen. 'I think it's a body . . .'

'Don't let it be,' pleaded Frost to himself. 'Please, don't let it be.'

He had to force himself to look as two of the frogmen broke the surface, hauling up a large, bulging dustbin liner, water streaming from holes in the bottom. With difficulty, Morgan and Jordan got it into the boat and rowed over to where Frost was waiting.

'Not heavy enough to be a body, Guv,' reported Morgan.

'Don't sound too bleeding disappointed,'

snapped Frost. The sack was tied with string, secured by tight knots. He slashed the string with his penknife, stepping back quickly as evil-smelling lake water belched out. 'You found it, Taff. To you the honour of looking inside.'

Very gingerly, Morgan slipped his hand inside and pulled out a sodden item of clothing. 'Men's trousers, Guv,' he announced.

'They're girls' slacks, you Welsh git. You're so busy pulling them down from the scrubbers you go out with, you don't notice they haven't got a fly opening.' But Debbie hadn't been wearing slacks when she left the previous night, so unless she'd changed somewhere . . .

Morgan delved inside again and pulled out more women's clothes: a sodden yellow sweater, a bra, black tights, and a pair of trainers with half a brick wedged inside to make the plastic sack sink.

Frost shook his head. 'These aren't Debbie's clothes.' He prodded the sodden sweater with his foot, then picked it up to examine it more closely. It was turned inside out as if it had been dragged off over the head. He then held up the bra. The fasteners were hanging by a thread as if the bra had been ripped off. This wasn't looking too happy. It looked as if the clothes had been forcibly removed.

'Any other girls reported missing recently, Guv?' asked Morgan.

'Girls are always being reported missing,' grunted Frost. 'And as far as "recently" goes, these clothes could have been dumped here months ago.' He dropped the sweater on top of the rest of the clothes. 'Stuff them back in the sack and let Forensic have a sniff. And when we get back to the station you can go through the records to see if the clothes match the description of any girl reported missing.'

'Inspector Frost!'

He turned round. One of the underwater team on the far side of the lake was splashing to the shore, holding something aloft in his hand. At first Frost couldn't make out what it was, then he cursed vehemently. 'Shit!'

It was another chunk of chopped-off foot.

An hour and four cigarettes later, the frogmen called off their search. 'Nothing else there, Inspector.'

'Good,' beamed Frost, nodding towards the debris that littered the ground. 'Put all this stuff back where you found it, then you can go home.'

The senior frogman grinned. 'Wouldn't want to do your chaps out of a job.' He made his way back to the van.

Frost kicked at a rusting petrol can. 'So where's the boy's flaming bike?' he muttered. 'He'll be our prime suspect if we find the girl's body.' He looked out again over the lake. Jordan and Morgan had retrieved the bike from somewhere in the middle. So how did it get there? It couldn't have been thrown that far. Of course! The flaming leaking rowing boat. There could be prints on the oars. But damn! Everyone had been using the boat. It would be smothered in prints by now, covering up the originals. A waste of time sending it to Forensic. Still, it would give the lazy sods something to do. 'And get the boat and oars over to Forensic,' he called.

His mobile chirped. Bill Wells from the station again. 'The girl's father has phoned, Jack. Wants to know the latest.'

'Knickers,' cursed Frost. 'He's bound to want to take me out and buy me a drink and I haven't got time. I'll go round and see him on my way back and tell him we've found his daughter's bike. Get the main Incident Room ready, Bill, I've got one of my nasty feelings about this.'

'You'd better tell Superintendent Mullett first. He hates to find these things out by accident.'

'I know, I know,' sighed Frost. 'As soon as I get the flaming time – bits of legs, blackmail at the supermarket, missing teenagers and that bloody rape. Where's Skinner? It's about time that fat sod did a bit of work.'

'He's in with Mullett. The red light's on . . . we mustn't disturb them.'

'Red light? They're having a love-in.'

Wells chuckled. 'Oh – something else, Jack. The boy's parents have returned from holiday. They've found your note and want to know what it's all about.'

Frost groaned again. 'Right, leave it to me.' He hung off and turned to DS Arthur Hanlon, who had just arrived. 'Job for you, Arthur. Go and see the boy's parents. Just tell them we think he's run away with the girl and we've got everyone out looking for them. Don't tell them we've found Debbie's bike. I'll be round with that news after I've seen the girl's father.'

'Right, Jack.'

'One other thing. Do a wee for me when you get the chance – I'm busting – and do one for yourself.'

Hanlon grinned and hurried off to his car.

As Frost slid into the driving seat of his own car, the flaming mobile rang yet again. It felt hot as he pressed it to his ear. It was an angry-sounding DCI Skinner.

'What's this about the Incident Room being prepared?' he barked.

Frost told him about the discovery of the bike.

'Then who gave you permission to turn it into a murder inquiry?' hissed Skinner. 'In future you make no decisions without checking with me first and obtaining my express permission. From now on, I do the murder cases. You're off this one. I'm taking over. *Comprende?*'

'*Jawohl, mein herr,*' said Frost, giving a Nazi salute as he clicked off the phone. One less case for him to sod up. He was thinking about the luxury of doing a wee and having something to eat when the flaming mobile rang again.

'Billy King!' said Wells as soon as Frost answered.

'Billy King?' echoed Frost, frowning. The name rang a distant bell. His brain riffled through its data bank and came up with scraps of information. 'Tubby little sod. Didn't I nick him years ago? House-breaking, petty larceny . . .'

'That's him,' said Wells.

'Then what about him?'

'You asked me to check with the building society about that account number. It belongs to Billy King.'

'Bloody hell!' exclaimed Frost happily. 'We don't often get luck like this. He's used his own flaming card. The man's a prat. I'll put my wee on hold and pay him a visit right now.'

'Before you do, Jack, DCI Skinner wants you to go round to the Clarks' and break the news that we've found Debbie's bike. He hasn't got time to do it now.'

'As long as he said "please",' said Frost sweetly, before ending the call and hurling obscenities into the air.

Clark glowered at him. 'What the hell do you want, Frost? I was told you were off this case.'

'I'm no longer in charge,' explained Frost, 'but Detective Chief Inspector Skinner asked me to call with the latest developments.'

'And they are?'

'I think I'd better come in,' said Frost.

He followed Clark into the lounge, where Mrs Clark sat huddled in an armchair. She looked up in alarm as Frost entered. 'It's bad news, isn't it?'

'I don't know,' replied Frost. 'It could mean nothing. I just don't know. We've found Debbie's bike.' He gave them the details.

'Why was her bike thrown in the lake?' shrieked Mrs Clark. 'Something's happened to her. I just know it.'

So do I, thought Frost, but he kept his face impassive. 'There could be all sorts of reasons,

Mrs Clark. She could have left the bike somewhere, someone stole it, rode off, then dumped it in the lake. That sort of thing often happens.'

'She could be drowned in that lake.'

'That's the only thing we're positive about at the moment. We've had the frogmen out. She isn't in the lake, that I promise you.'

'Then where the bloody hell is she?' demanded Clark.

'She could be holed up with the boy somewhere, too frightened to come home.'

'If she is, I'll wring that lad's neck,' snarled Clark.

Mrs Clark had buried her head in her hands and was sobbing convulsively. 'She's dead. I just know it. My little Debbie . . . she's dead.'

'We'll find her,' said Frost, hoping he sounded convincing. 'Try not to worry. We'll find her.'

Clark showed him out. 'You'd better bloody find her,' he snarled. 'And if your procrastination has caused my daughter any harm, you'll wish you'd never been born.'

Thank God that's over, thought Frost as he climbed into his car. *If we do find her body, I hope bloody Skinner is the one to break the news. So now for Billy King.*

Billy King's house was a shabby-looking, two-storey property, standing all on its own on disused farmland. Parked in front of the house was a dilapidated caravan, its flaking cream and green paint showing large patches of rust, the wheels sunk deep in muddied ruts.

PC Collier watched Frost pound on the front door with the flat of his hand and rattle the letter box. They could hear sounds from inside, but no one came to the door. Frost banged again, emphasising his knocking with a couple of hefty kicks.

At last the door was opened by a squat little double-chinned man in his shirtsleeves.

'Give us a flaming chance! Whatever you're selling, I don't want it!' Then recognition dawned. He poked a podgy finger at the inspector. 'Detective Sergeant Frost! Cor, haven't you aged?'

'Detective *Inspector*,' corrected Frost.

'Inspector?' gasped King incredulously. 'They've never made you a flaming inspector!' He turned to PC Collier. 'Frost was always a scream – a pleasure being arrested by him cos he always made you laugh!'

'Then this will make you flaming wet yourself,' Frost told him. 'I've got a warrant to search your premises.'

'Pull the other one,' giggled King. 'You think I don't know what this is all about? Come on in. I'll make you a cup of tea.' They followed him through to a small kitchen. 'Have you caught the sod yet?'

'What particular sod did you have in mind?' asked Frost.

'The burglar. The sod who pinched my stuff.'

Frost blinked at him. 'What are you talking about?'

'Don't you know what is going on in your own

flaming station? I was burgled, wasn't I? Sod broke in while we were away in the caravan on holiday. When I came back, the place had been done over. I'd been burgled.'

'Who'd burgle this bleeding place?' said Frost. 'You'd spend more on petrol driving here than you could nick. You're saying you had a burglary and you didn't report it?'

'Of course I flaming well reported it. A little fat bloke came round.'

'Detective Sergeant Hanlon?'

'That's him. And he was bloody useless. Nosed around, got some bloke to chuck fingerprint powder all over the place, then pissed off. That was the last I heard. I thought you were here to tell me you'd caught him.'

'You used to do a bit of burglary yourself, Bill. This sounds like an insurance fiddle to me.'

'Insurance fiddle? Don't talk to me about insurance companies. They're quick to take your flaming premium, but when you're unlucky enough to be robbed, they won't pay out. They want receipts. Who the hell keeps receipts?'

'Especially when you nicked the stuff in the first place,' said Frost, stuffing the search warrant back in his mac pocket. 'What was taken?'

'He turned the place over – made a right bleeding mess of it. Flaming amateur, if you ask me. All he took was an old wallet with a couple of quid in it.'

'And the wallet was all you claimed for on your insurance policy?'

Billy spread his hands and shrugged. 'All right,

Inspector Frost, I'll come clean as it's you. I might have exaggerated about the brand-new telly and DVD player and the wife's designer clothes, but all he took was the wallet with a couple of quid in it.'

'Was there anything else in the wallet apart from money?'

'Condoms, you mean? No, the wife has her own method of birth control. She bolts the bedroom door.' He wheezed heartily at his own joke.

'What about a cashpoint card for the Fortress Building Society?'

King screwed up his face in thought. 'Might have been. I haven't dealt with them for ages. I'm with the Woolwich now.' He frowned. 'Are you telling me the bastard took that as well?' He reached for the phone. 'I'm closing my account. There wasn't much left in it, but that bastard isn't going to have it.'

Frost knocked Billy's hand away from the phone. 'No, don't do anything. If he tries to use it, Billy, we can get him.' He pushed himself up from the chair. He'd check with Hanlon, but King's story had the ring of truth about it, and for all his faults, Billy wasn't the kind of bloke who would go around poisoning baby food. He paused as a thought struck him. The pin number. The blackmailer would be unable to withdraw money without the pin number. 'Was your pin number in the wallet?'

'Of course it was. Safest place for it. I wrote it on the back of the card.'

Frost smiled. 'What would crooks do without

prats like you, Billy?' He waved away the offer of a cup of tea and remembered his long-delayed wee. 'Do you think I could use your toilet?'

'But I haven't got a report of a flaming burglary,' said Frost, riffling once more through his overflowing in-tray. 'I felt a bigger prat than usual, going in there with a search warrant to find a card that had already been nicked.'

'I definitely sent you a copy, Jack,' insisted Hanlon. 'I gave it to that Welsh bloke.'

'Gave it to the Welsh bloke?' exploded Frost, pushing his in-tray away. 'You might just as well have flushed it down the flaming karzy.' He opened his office door and bellowed down the corridor. 'Lloyd flaming George. Come here!'

DC Morgan came trotting in, not knowing his offence, but wearing his hang-dog look of contrition, just in case. 'You wanted me, Guv?'

'No,' snapped Frost. 'I don't flaming want you, but I'm stuck with you. The crime report Hanlon gave you?'

Morgan looked blank for a moment, then brightened. 'All filed away, Guv.' He pulled open the drawer of the filing cabinet.

'You didn't think I should see it first – just in case I wanted to know what was going on?' He held his hand out for the report and skimmed through it. 'Smashed a back window to get in and cut his hand doing so. That rings a bell. Did we take a sample for DNA?'

'Not worth the expense, Jack,' Hanlon told

him. 'All he'd taken was a wallet with a few quid in it. SOCO found the odd print, but couldn't match them with anyone on record.'

'No, they wouldn't,' said Frost. 'This bloke is a rank amateur, like flaming Taffy here. Plenty of stuff he could have pinched, but he didn't touch it because he wouldn't know where to sell it. All he could handle was money and he was flaming lucky to find the wallet.'

'And you reckon this is the same bloke who's blackmailing the supermarket?'

'Yes. Now he's got the account details, he can have the hush money paid in.'

'But for all he knew, when Billy King realised it was pinched he'd have stopped it with the building society.'

'I doubt he thought that far ahead, Arthur. He probably tried the card out, found it worked and reckoned he was on to a winner. A flaming amateur trying for the big time. Shouldn't be hard to nab the sod. We'll pay Beazley's cheque in, then we'll watch all the cashpoints and when our blackmailer tries to make a withdrawal, we've got him.'

Frost stared again at the cheque with Beazley's signature scrawled along the bottom. He blew off the ash that had fallen from his cigarette and looked across the desk at DC Morgan. 'You know, Taff, with my forgery skills I reckon I could overwrite this with my name, cash it and do a bunk to somewhere exotic like Bangladesh or Basildon.'

Morgan grinned. 'But it wouldn't be honest, Guv.'

Frost nodded. 'Agreed, but that wouldn't stop me. It would be the fact that I would be letting that nice Mr Beazley down. I'd hate to think of his little, fat, greasy lower lip quivering with disappointment.' He held out the cheque and passbook. 'Nip across to the building society and give it to Mr Selby, the manager. He's expecting you. Tell him you're the dopey cop I told him about.' He pushed himself up from his chair. 'Right. Let's break the news to Hornrim Harry that his overtime bill is going to hit the roof tonight when we are out covering all the cash-points.' He made a mental list of all the things that could possibly go wrong with the operation and shuddered. 'This is going to be a complete balls-up, Taffy. I just know it.'

Morgan grinned. 'I have every faith in you, Guv.'

'That's because you're a prat, and a Welsh one at that,' said Frost, making his way to the old log cabin.

Mullett wasn't in his office. In fact the entire station seemed strangely deserted. Frost checked his watch, then he remembered. Bleeding hell! Fatty Arbuckle's meeting. The one he had promised not to be late for.

Frost hastened to the main Incident Room, pausing at the door to listen. Skinner's voice was booming out. He turned the door handle very carefully, hoping to slip in unobserved, but as he entered he received the full force of Skinner's blistering glare. All heads turned to look at him, including Hornrim Harry, who was seated alongside Skinner and was doing his 'frowning and tutting' disapproval act.

'Ah, Inspector Frost. Nice of you to join us,' sneered Skinner.

'No problem,' beamed Frost, completely unfazed. 'I didn't have anything else to do.' Sarcasm just bounced off him. He was relieved to see that his usual seat – back row, near the door – was vacant, so perhaps he could sneak out when things got boring.

Skinner exchanged glances with Mullett, as if to say, 'Don't worry, I'll soon get rid of this useless bastard for you.' Mullett nodded and smirked a tight smile of acknowledgement.

Frost was sitting next to the young WPC who had been with the rape victim in the hospital. He didn't know her name. His warm smile met with a blank stare.

'Right,' resumed Skinner. 'For the benefit of our late arrival I'll quickly repeat what I said before, as I am sure many of you haven't taken it in properly. I've only been in Denton division a few hours and already I've noticed slackness, slovenliness and laziness almost without exception. I hear moans about shortage of manpower. If you all put in a full day's work there would be no shortage.' He picked up a sheet of paper and fluttered it at arm's length. 'This, in case you haven't looked at it for some time, is your contract of employment. If you read it, you will be aware of the following points. Point number one: you are allowed one – repeat one – meal break of forty-five minutes per shift. It does not allow you half an hour of extra breaks, morning and afternoon, for tea, coffee, sandwiches and bleeding fairy cakes. I don't want to see anyone in the canteen outside the official forty-five minutes, unless they are off duty.'

Frost had mentally switched Skinner's voice off and it was just droning away in the background as he started to work out how many men he would need to stake out the various Fortress Building Society cashpoints. He looked up. Skinner didn't appear to be looking his way, so he decided this might be a good time to sneak out. He was just opening the door very carefully when Skinner spotted him.

'Going somewhere, Frost?'

'Just checking that the door was closed properly. Flaming draught,' said Frost, slamming it tight and giving the handle a few wiggles. He turned up his coat collar and faked a shiver, then slunk back in his seat. The fat bastard must have eyes in the back of his head.

'Now that Inspector Frost has checked the door for us,' continued Skinner, 'there are other time-wasting practices that I want rectified. Shift starting times are constantly delayed because officers are wasting time changing from civvies to police uniform and having a bloody good chat about last night's bleeding football while they do so. The man hours wasted by this would be enough to provide Denton division with three more officers.' He let his glance roam the faces in front of him as he repeated this to emphasise his point. 'Three new officers. And probably better flaming officers than we have got now. So in future, ladies and gentlemen, you will change into your police uniform *before* you leave home and will start your shift the minute you walk through the station doors.'

There was a rumble of discontent. Skinner looked up in mock surprise. 'Does that present a problem?'

Bill Wells raised a hand.

Skinner jabbed a finger at him. 'And you are . . .?'

'Wells – Sergeant Wells.'

Wells! thought Skinner. *Ah yes. The thicky who kept me hanging on the phone this morning. The thicky who thinks he deserves promotion. The thicky who had better watch his bloody step or he'll be following Frost out of Denton, if not leading the flaming way . . .*

'Yes, Sergeant Wells?' he cooed, knowing what was coming and primed to shoot the stupid git down.

'If I walk to the station in the morning wearing my uniform, people think I'm already on duty and they yell at me to solve their problems – domestic disputes, vandals, missing flaming cats – and all in my own time.'

'If you saw someone kicking his wife's teeth in, would you say, "Sorry, I'm not on duty yet"? A good policeman is always on duty.' He dismissed Wells with a derisive twitch of his hand. 'And, of course,' he continued, 'we will also gain man hours if, as I require, you finish your shift dead on time, not half an hour early so you can get changed. You will now leave your uniform on until you get back home.' He paused. That thicky sergeant had his hand up again. He sighed loudly and raised his eyes to the ceiling. 'Yes, Sergeant Wells?'

'Same point as before,' replied Wells. 'I've finished my shift, I'm walking home and, because I'm still in uniform, I'm going to get dragged into all sorts of things.'

'The same point, the same answer,' snapped Skinner. 'Nearly everyone in this station is not pulling their weight. I exclude Superintendent Mullett, of course.' Mullett beamed back his acknowledgement. 'Too many people are slacking, skiving, duty dodging, doing sloppy paperwork, not completing required returns.' Here he glowered meaningfully at Frost, but the man appeared to have fallen asleep with a lighted cigarette in his mouth. Skinner tightened his lips grimly. The inspector didn't know what was coming to him! 'None of this,' he went on, 'will be tolerated in future. Any deviation and I'll come down on you like a ton of bricks.' He turned to Mullett. 'Anything you'd like to add, sir?'

Mullett shook his head. 'No, Chief Inspector. I think you have covered all points admirably.'

Everyone except Frost stood as Mullett and Skinner gathered their papers and left the room, closing the door on a bubbling simmer of indignation and discontent.

A fuming Bill Wells made his way across to

Frost. 'What do you think of that, Jack?' he spluttered.

Frost beamed up at him. 'Skinner's all sweet talk now, but wait until he's been here a few weeks – he'll be a real right bastard.'

Skinner was with Mullett when Frost entered. He was seated alongside Mullett behind the desk and seemed to be pushing the superintendent out of position. Every now and then Mullett made a half-hearted attempt to move his chair back to centre, but Skinner didn't yield an inch. Mullett's expression indicated that he was starting to wonder whether he had made the right decision in accepting Skinner into Denton division. But the man had promised he would get rid of Frost quickly and painlessly, and that weighed heavily in Skinner's favour.

Mullett opened his mouth to ask Frost what he wanted, but Skinner beat him to it. 'What is it, Frost?'

Frost grabbed one of the two visitors' chairs and dragged it across the blue Wilton, leaving twin tracks of scuff marks. He plonked himself down and lit up. 'I'm going to need a hell of a lot of men on overtime for the next two nights,' he said.

Mullett was already shaking his head – the division was under attack from County for the size of its overtime bill – when Skinner asked, 'Why?'

Frost filled them in about the supermarket blackmailer. 'So we need to stake out the cashpoints and nab the sod when he tries to draw out his money.'

Skinner's eyes glinted. 'And you reckon you can catch him?'

How the bleeding hell do I know? thought Frost. Aloud he said, 'One hundred per cent sure.'

Skinner rubbed his chin in thought, then jabbed a finger at Frost. 'OK, I'm taking charge of this case. You carry out the stake-out – and you'd better give me a result. When you catch him, arrest him, then hand him over to me.'

'Right,' nodded Frost enthusiastically. If it meant getting the extra bodies on overtime, he didn't give a damn who was supposed to be in charge of the case. It meant someone else could take the flak for a change if the whole damn thing went pear-shaped, as most of Frost's fool-proof enterprises tended to.

'How many men will you need?'

'There are five Fortress cashpoints, two men on each—'

'Hold on,' interrupted Skinner. 'How do you know he'll use a Fortress cashpoint? He can use the card anywhere.'

'That's where our luck's in,' Frost told him. 'You can only use Fortress cards at their own cashpoints. They haven't joined Link yet. So all we'll need is two men on each of the five cash-points, with another man as back-up and an area car lurking in the background in case we have to chase the sod. I'm hoping he'll leave it until it's dark when there are fewer people about, so the main group will be covering from eight until, say, six the next morning – unless we catch him earlier, of course. And we'll need a skeleton surveillance team, with no back-up but able to call in reinforcements if necessary, during the day. They won't be on overtime, of course.'

Frost knew there was no way Mullett would authorise this in full, so he had upped the ante by asking for more men than he needed. He had asked Fortress Building Society to put two of their cashpoints out of action overnight, so they would only be watching three instead of five, but he didn't tell Mullett that.

'For how many days?' croaked Mullett, his brain whirling as he tried to calculate how much all this would cost.

'One or two at the most,' lied Frost. 'The minute he draws money out on the card, the building society will phone me. If our luck's in, we'll nab him tonight.' He oozed optimism, but Frost's luck was rarely in.

Mullett's head was already shaking when Skinner forestalled him again.

'I don't know about during the day. I want every man I can get my hands on to search the woods and other likely places for those missing kids. But you can have a maximum of five bodies for tonight – and let one of them be that dopey Welsh bloke. But if you sod this up . . .!' He let the threat hover like Damocles' sword over the inspector's head.

Frost put on his hurt look, as if sodding things up was inconceivable to him. He shot out of his chair and made for the door before they could change their minds.

'Hold it,' snapped Skinner. 'Don't forget. When you get him, you hand him over to me. I'll take it from there.'

Frost nodded. Always agree: that was his motto. You could always say you didn't understand afterwards.

'But remember, if you foul this up –' began Skinner, his mouth shutting with a snap when he realised he was talking to a slammed door. Frost had made his exit.

'When are you going to tell him he's being transferred out of Denton?' asked Mullett.

'Not yet,' replied Skinner, smiling maliciously. 'I don't want to dampen his enthusiasm for tonight's stake-out.'

4

A petulant wind rattled the windows of the Incident Room. It was a lousy night for a stake-out, but you couldn't pick your moment. Frost surveyed his team and was pleased to note that Bill Wells had included two WPCs, one the girl who had sat with the rape victim at Denton General, looking even younger out of uniform. This was good. A man and a woman in a shop doorway late at night would look far less conspicuous than a man on his own, and the blackmailer was sure to be edgy and ready to abort. Frost swilled down the dregs of his tea, lit up another cigarette from the stub of the old one, which he dumped in the mug, then clapped his hands for silence.

'Right. You all know what we're in for. A long, boring wait in the bleeding cold in the happy knowledge that Mullett begrudges paying you the overtime. We ought to catch the sod tonight, but as he can only withdraw a maximum of £500 a day, we'll have plenty of other chances. All the indications are that he's a rank amateur, but a dangerous one. He laced Supersaves own-brand wine with bleach – the fact that most of the customers thought it tasted better that way isn't the point. He also put a lethal dose of salt in babies' milk powder and nearly killed one. So we want him caught quickly.'

The young WPC put up her hand. 'You say he's a rank amateur, but this is a pretty ingenious way of getting his money.'

'You're right, love,' agreed Frost. 'It's bloody ingenious, but he didn't think of it himself – this is a copycat crime. A few years ago, back in London, an ex-cop – you can't trust the bastards – found a way of getting his blackmail money paid without risk. He opened up a building society account with a false name and address and got the money paid into that account. He then made withdrawals using his cashpoint card. Today, building societies won't let you open an account without the most vigorous of checks, so it shouldn't happen again. But our clever bastard amateur has found a way round that. He pinched a legitimate card on which the prat of an owner had written his pin number in large letters, just in case any crook should miss it. But for a change, we've got a bit of luck on our side. With the ex-cop, the Met had hundreds of cashpoints to cover. The Fortress Building Society has only got five cashpoints, so if our bloke wants to withdraw his money, his choice is limited. We've limited it even further by arranging with Fortress to put two of their cashpoints out of action, so we now have only three to watch.

'Detective Sergeant Hanlon has done a recce for us to find safe places where we can observe the cashpoints and not be seen. We will cover them by lurking in shop doorways, and I want a male and female officer together where possible. If anyone comes, go into a passionate embrace. That should both divert suspicion and give you a thrill. And you can take that dirty grin off your face, Taffy Morgan. We haven't got enough chastity belts to go round, so you will be with me, watching the main cashpoint in Market Square. No convenient shop doorways, so you and I will be in the car, round the corner. As soon as chummy withdraws the money, you will dash out and grab him.'

'How will we know that it's our bloke who's using the cashpoint?' Jordan asked.

'The Fortress technical staff are monitoring their main computer. As soon as chummy sticks his card in the slot, they will phone me and I'll phone you.' He checked his watch. Eight forty-five p.m. 'Right, just time for a quick wee, then off to your assigned stake-out positions. Hold it –' He looked up as Bill Wells came in and beckoned him over.

'Slight change of plan, Jack.'

'Oh?' said Frost warily.

'Skinner's just phoned. Mullett has talked him into cutting the overtime men by half.'

'Sod that!' exclaimed Frost. 'We're working to the barest minimum as it is.'

'He told me to tell you it's not a request, it's an order. He's going to need the extra men for the search of the woods for those two missing kids tomorrow morning.'

'Sod him!' repeated Frost vehemently. 'Tell him you couldn't find me.'

'Then he will expect me to phone or radio you.'

Frost took his mobile from his pocket and switched it off. 'My phone battery needs charging and my radio is on the blink.'

'He won't believe you, Jack.'

'The bastard doesn't believe me when I'm telling the truth, so what's the difference?'

Frost sat slumped in the passenger seat of his car, coat collar turned up, his scarf wound tightly round his neck against the cold. Parked down a side street, they didn't have the cashpoint in view, but would be able to reach it at a sprint in a few seconds. He shivered. 'I thought I told you to get this heater fixed.'

'I've booked it in for tomorrow, Guv,' lied Morgan, who had forgotten all about it.

'Lying Welsh bastard,' grunted Frost. He rubbed his hands together, then checked his watch. Coming up to midnight and no sign of the sod. He felt his stomach rumble. 'There's a chippy round the corner. Get me a cod and chips and put salt and vinegar on it. You can buy your own if you like.' He passed over a five-pound note. 'And I'm going to count the change.'

'Right, Guv.' Glad of the chance to stretch his legs, Morgan slid out of the car and disappeared round the corner. Frost sank lower in his seat.

This was going to be a sodding waste of time, he just knew it. He was stuck in a freezing-cold car and the blackmailing bastard was probably tucked up snug in a nice warm bed. He might as well have given Skinner those extra men he wanted. There'd be hell to pay tomorrow if he didn't get a result.

The radio buzzed. 'PC Jordan to Inspector Frost. Come in please. Urgent.'

'Yes?' said Frost, popping a cigarette in his mouth.

'We've just arrested a junkie trying to pinch money from people using the cash machine. He grabbed fifty quid from this old dear. We're going to have to take him back to the station.'

'Bloody hell,' moaned Frost. 'Now everyone will know that the fuzz is in the vicinity.'

'We had to arrest him, Inspector. We couldn't let him get away with it – the old dear was screaming blue murder.'

'All right,' sighed Frost. 'Take him back, book him in, then get back here. Our bloke hasn't turned up yet. And check with Sergeant Wells about that poor cow who had her handbag nicked earlier today. This might be the same man.'

A tapping at the side window made him look up. Someone was standing there. He wound the window down and a blast of cheap scent hit him in the face.

'Looking for a bit of fun, handsome?'

'Piss off,' groaned Frost, flashing his warrant card at the hard-faced, cheap-fake-leather-coated woman in her late forties with an equally fake smile.

'Bloody hell. It's the flaming filth!'

'Exactly,' said Frost. 'Now sling your hook, darling, before I run you in for offering goods past their sell-by date.'

She jerked two fingers at him and wandered off into the night, swinging her handbag like a gladiator's chain. A burble of conversation floated from round the corner, then Taffy slid into the car clutching two greasy packages.

'Just bumped into a cracking bit of stuff, Guv. I reckon I could have had her.'

'Only if you had the 50p to pay her,' grunted Frost, checking his change before slipping it into his mac pocket. 'I hope you didn't let her touch my chips. I shudder to think what else she's been fingering tonight.' He opened the package, broke off a chunk of fish and looked up angrily. 'This is haddock.'

'They didn't have cod,' lied Morgan, who had forgotten what Frost had asked for.

Frost reached for the door handle. 'Do you want me to go back there and check?'

Morgan looked shamefaced. 'Sorry, Guv. Actually, I forgot.'

Frost had just settled back in his seat when the sound of angry voices floated across the square. He wound down the window, but couldn't make out what was going on. 'Nip over and check that, Taff.'

A couple of minutes later, Morgan was back.

'It's that tom, Guv. The punter has only got thirty quid and she wants forty.'

'Not for her bleeding body, surely?' grunted Frost. 'She must be throwing in her car as well. So what's the hold-up?'

'The machine keeps rejecting his card. They're both getting stroppy.'

'This isn't going to be my night,' gloomed Frost. 'I'm in the excrement with fat-guts Skinner, arrests we don't want are cropping up all over the bleeding place, and you bought me haddock instead of cod.' He snatched his mobile up at the first ring. 'Frost?' It was Fortress Building Society. He listened. 'What? . . . Where? . . .Thanks.' He chucked the mobile up in the air with delight, but missed catching it so had to scrabble for it on the floor. 'Foot down, Taffy. He's bitten the bait. The card is currently being used to withdraw cash in Minton Street.' He groaned. The cashpoint Jordan had had to leave unwatched.

Morgan couldn't get the engine to fire and kept fiddling frantically with the ignition. 'If we're out of flaming petrol—' began Frost, but was cut short as the engine spluttered then suddenly roared to life with a jerk, sending his haddock and chips flying all over the car.

He brushed chips from his mac as the car sped round to the main road. He was right. The bloke must be a rank amateur. Surely he might have guessed that the police would be watching all the cashpoints. And Frost couldn't believe his luck. Catching the sod on the very first night of the stake-out. Minton Street was only a couple of minutes away, but just to be on the safe side he radioed through to Jordan, who with any luck should be on his way back now and approaching from the opposite direction. If chummy wasn't still at the till, they would stop and search any pedestrian or motorists in the vicinity. There would be very few people around at this time of night.

As they turned the corner into Minton Street, Frost scrubbed the windscreen with the sleeve of his mac. 'I can see him. The bastard is still there.'

The dimly lit area around the cashpoint showed a man checking some notes, then stuffing them into his pocket. Seemingly unaware of the approaching car, he turned down a side street.

'Left, left,' screamed Frost as Morgan missed the turn and had to brake sharply and skid the car round. There was a sickening crash and the tinkle of broken glass. Morgan had hit one of the parked cars. 'It was his fault,' yelled Frost. 'Drive on.' As they turned into the side street they could see the rear lights of a car driving off into the night.

'Tally ho!' cried Frost. He snatched up the radio handset and alerted Jordan that the suspect was heading his way. At the T-junction Taffy slowed as Frost, eyes squinted, scoured left and right. 'There!' Tiny pinpricks of red in the distance, then the sound of a police siren. Jordan had spotted the car and was in pursuit. The pinprick of red was followed by a flashing blue light.

'He's slowing,' radioed Jordan triumphantly. 'He's stopped . . . he's bloody stopped!'

Frost punched the air in delight. 'We've got him, Taff!' He screwed up the greasy chip bag and hurled it through the car window as they drove towards the flashing blue light of a parked Allegro. Jordan was opening the door as Frost's car pulled up behind.

'What the flaming hell is this all about, officer?' demanded a man's voice. 'I wasn't speeding and I'm not bloody drunk. You got a quota of arrests to make?'

Frost stopped dead in his tracks. He recognised that flaming voice. He was out of the car and over in a flash. 'Hello, hello, hello. Where have you been all the day, Billy Boy?' he beamed. The driver was Billy King, the man who claimed his building society card had been stolen.

King's face fell when he saw Frost. 'Twice in one flaming day! I must have run over a black cat or something. What am I supposed to have done now?'

Frost flashed a smug, self-satisfied smile. On the passenger seat next to Billy was a Fortress Building Society passbook, poking out from which was a cashpoint card. 'Been making a little withdrawal, Billy?'

'It's not a flaming crime, is it?'

'It's too cold standing here talking, Billy. Let's get you down to the nice, warm station so we can rough you up a bit. First of all, where's the money?'

'What flaming money?'

Frost sighed. 'Search him, Taffy.'

King shrunk back. 'Oh no. Not with them greasy fish-and-chip fingers. Let the other bloke do it.' He raised his arms as Jordan patted his pockets then withdrew a wallet from inside his jacket. Jordan opened it and pulled out a couple of notes.

'Twenty quid, Inspector, that's all,' reported Jordan.

'And there had still better be twenty quid in there when I get the wallet back,' sniffed King. 'I know what sticky-fingered bastards you coppers are.'

'Where's the rest, Billy?' asked Frost.

'I don't know what you're talking about.'

'It's in the car somewhere,' said Frost. 'Too bleeding cold to search here. We'll do it back at the station.' He took King's arm. 'Come on, sunshine. Let's go to the nice cop shop. My Welsh colleague will drive your car back.'

'He'd better take care of it,' scowled King. 'I ain't paid for it yet.'

'He'll treat it as if it were his own, Billy,' Frost assured him. 'He wrote his off yesterday.' He radioed through to the stake-out team and told them they could go home, but to book an extra hour for their trouble.

Frost dribbled smoke through his nose and watched King through the haze, on the other side of the table in the Interview Room.

Billy squirmed in his chair. 'I don't know what this is all about, Inspector. You're setting me up, aren't you? You're flaming well setting me up.'

Frost puffed out a smoke ring and watched it writhe its way up to the nicotine-stained ceiling. 'I have a strict code of ethics, Billy. I only set people up if I can't beat a confession out of them.' He was feeling pleased with himself. He never expected such a quick result. He was just waiting for Morgan and Jordan to return from their search of Billy's car bearing the five hundred quid.

'How much longer before you tell me what this is all about?' asked King. 'My old lady will be worried sick.'

'Not long, Billy,' said Frost. 'Ah!' He could hear approaching footsteps. Jordan and Morgan came in. In reply to his questioning gaze, they shook their heads. They had searched the car and found nothing.

Frost groaned and scrubbed his face with his hands. This was going to take longer than he had hoped. 'Give us a clue, Billy. Where have you hidden the money? Have you swallowed it? Shall we get out the syrup of figs or the enema we use for our horses?'

'You give me a clue, Inspector Frost. What money are you talking about?'

'The money you withdrew from the building society.'

'It's in my bloody wallet, if that copper hasn't nicked it.'

'There was only twenty quid in there, Billy.'
'So? That's all I had in my account. I told you.'
'You also told us, Billy, you had your cashpoint card stolen.' He flashed the plastic under Billy's nose. 'So what is this?'
'That's my wife's card. It's a joint account. Mine was pinched, so I used hers. So how about telling me what this is all about, or is it a flaming state secret?'
Frost's heart took a nosedive. He looked at the card. It was in joint names. 'You didn't bloody tell me it was a joint account.'
'You didn't bloody ask!'
Frost just stared at him. His mobile phone rang. Still looking at Billy he fumbled for the phone and put it to his ear.
'Frost,' he grunted.
As he listened, his heart nosedived even further into the depths of his stomach. Vindictive fate was kneeing him in the privates. 'Shit! Thanks for telling me.' He clicked off, shifted his gaze from Billy and stared in disbelief at his phone, then spun the chair round to face Jordan and Morgan. 'You want the bad news or the bad news? That was the Fortress Building Society. While we've been wasting our time with this prat, someone has used the stolen card to withdraw four hundred and eighty quid from the Minton Street cashpoint.'
'Four hundred and eighty?' queried Jordan.
'That was all the machine would let him have. Apparently twenty quid had been withdrawn earlier.'

Billy King smirked. 'That was me. Will you believe me now?'

Jordan moved to the door. 'Shall I get over there?'

Frost shook his head. 'It's too flaming late. He'll be miles away by now.' He buried his face in his hands. 'It's not my bleeding night.'

'It's even more of a rotten night for you now, Inspector Frost,' smirked Billy. 'I'm having you up for false arrest.' He stood and scooped up the stuff taken from his pockets, which was on the table between them.

Frost's hand shot out to grab King's wrist.

'Hold on, Billy, it might not be your bleeding night either.' He hooked a keyring on his index finger and spun it so it flashed in the light. 'I meant to ask you about this before, but there's an awful lot of keys here for just one small-time crook's crappy house.'

The smile faded from Billy's face. 'Oh – they're old keys, Inspector. I've never got around to throwing them away.' He held out his hand. 'If I could have them . . .'

Frost whirled the keys around.

King stared at them as if hypnotised.

'You used to rob old ladies, didn't you, Billy? Nick their handbags, pinch their money and then use their door key to sneak into their houses when they were out.'

'That was a long time ago. I don't do things like that any more.'

Frost gave him a long, hard stare, remembering how worried the man had seemed when the wallet was first taken away from him. Frost had only done a quick flip through, looking for the money, and Billy had seemed quite relieved when the wallet was put down again. Frost held out his hand. 'Show me your wallet again, Billy.'

An even more worried look. 'What for? You've seen it once.'

'I've got a looking-inside-wallets fetish,' said Frost, thrusting his open hand forward. 'Give it to me.'

Reluctantly, King pulled the wallet from his pocket and handed it over, watching apprehensively as Frost flipped it open. There were two credit cards inside. One was in Billy's name, but the other . . .

Frost smiled. 'What a coincidence, Billykins. We had an old lady in here earlier complaining some toe-rag had nicked her handbag. Now, her name is exactly the same as the name on this credit card and you're a toe-rag. Isn't that a coincidence?'

'I found it in the gutter, Inspector. I was going to hand it in, but what with you trying to stitch me up on a false charge . . .'

'She identified you, Billy,' continued Frost. 'We showed her the mugshots and she picked you out. "That's him – that fat little sod," she said.'

'You're lying. Any mugshot of me must be years old.'

'Policemen don't lie, Billy – unless they want to get a conviction. You know that.'

'I still think you're lying, Inspector.'

Frost opened the Interview Room door and yelled down the corridor to Sergeant Wells. 'Sergeant, was Bill King's mugshot in those photos we showed the old dear this morning?'

'Yes,' shouted back Wells.

'And did she pick him out as the bastard who robbed her?'

'You know she did!' yelled Wells.

Frost shut the door quickly, in case Wells decided to qualify his statement by adding that she identified every flaming face she saw. He sat down, put on his disarming smile and pushed his packet of cigarettes across the table. 'It's late, Billy, we're all shagged out and we want to go home. Now we can either bang you up for the night, sharing a cell with a frustrated, seventeen-stone raging queer, or you can cough the lot, give us a statement and we'll let you go home on police bail.'

'You're a bastard,' said Billy.

'So people keep telling me,' said Frost, 'but I don't see it myself.'

Frost stood by his office window to watch Billy climb into his car, slam the door angrily and drive off.

'We should have searched his house, Guv,' said Morgan. 'I bet we'd have found a whole pile of loot.'

'It's too flaming late for those larks,' yawned Frost, passing his cigarettes around. For a while they smoked in silence.

'Not entirely a wasted evening then, Guv,' offered Taffy.

Frost shrugged. 'It could have been a damn sight better. Still, what is it Rhett Butler says in *Gone with the Wind*?'

'Something like "Quite frankly, I don't give a monkey's"?' suggested Jordan.

'No,' said Frost. 'Something like "Tomorrow is another bleeding day." '

'Scarlett O'Hara says that,' said Morgan.

'Whatever her bleeding colour, she was flaming right,' said Frost. 'So we missed him tonight. There's other nights. He can only draw out five hundred quid at a time, so he's got to do it again and again. Even someone as stupid as me won't be able to continually sod up catching him.' He stood up and crushed his cigarette underfoot. An unmade bed in a cold house wasn't much of an attraction, but he was dead on his feet. 'Right, we try again tomorrow.'

His mobile rang. He frowned. Who the hell would be calling him at this flaming hour? Late-night – or early-morning – phone calls always spelled trouble.

'Frost . . . What? . . . Bloody *what*?' He collapsed back in his chair. 'Then how the flaming hell . . .?' He glanced up at the wall clock. 'Shit! Thanks for telling me.' He clicked off the phone and rammed it back in his pocket. 'Tomorrow isn't another bleeding day. It's tomorrow already. The bastard's withdrawn another five hundred quid.'

'I thought he couldn't withdraw more than five hundred a day,' said Jordan.

'He can't. But it's gone midnight. It's

tomorrow. He's a cleverer bastard than I thought. Still, he can't take out any more until Wednesday, so we've tomorrow night off. And now we know what time he usually makes withdrawals, we can concentrate our efforts.'

'Providing he follows the same pattern,' said Jordan.

'Oh, he must,' yawned Frost. 'He knows I'm relying on him.' He turned to Morgan. 'Don't they have CCTV cameras covering those cashpoints?'

'On some, Guv, not all.'

'Then let's hope this is one of them. First thing tomorrow – or today, rather – nip down to the building society and use your slimy Welsh charm to get hold of the tape.' He tipped the contents of his ashtray into the waste-paper bin. 'Let's go home.'

They didn't make it. As he reached the door, his phone rang again. It was Lambert from Control.

'Another girl's gone missing, Inspector. Jan O'Brien, thirteen years old.'

'Shit!' said Frost.

'May have nothing to do with it, Inspector, but at 23.52 we had a phone call from a man using the public phone box in the town square. He sounded drunk, but insisted he had just heard a girl screaming round the back of the multi-storey car park – where that other girl was raped. He hung up without giving any more. I sent an area car round there, they're touring the area, but there's no sign of anything yet.'

'Double shit,' said Frost.

* * *

'She hasn't gone missing, you stupid cow,' yelled the man.

'How can you be so bloody complacent?' shrieked his wife. 'It's two o'clock in the morning. She left Kathy's house at ten o'clock – that's four hours ago. She should be here by now.'

'She's been late before.'

'Not this bloody late, she hasn't.'

Frost, sitting between the couple in their tiny dining room, his head moving from side to side like the audience at a tennis match, raised a weary hand. 'Shut it, you two. Let's have a few facts.'

'You give him the bloody facts,' snarled the man to his wife. 'You brought the bleeding police in. When she comes waltzing back and saying she's sorry, we'll be a bloody laughing stock.'

'I'd rather be a bloody laughing stock than the mother of a raped and murdered girl.'

'Rape? That little madam is more likely to rape the boy. She comes and goes as she damn well pleases and does what she likes. If you want to make a fool of yourself to the police, good luck – count me out!' With a slam of the door he was gone, only to reappear almost immediately to shake a finger at his wife. 'Tell that copper how many other times she's come in late when I've been tramping the flaming streets looking for her. "Sorry, Dad, I should have phoned." Little cow! And what about the time she didn't come home until the next afternoon? Tell him that. I'm going to bed.' The door slammed behind him again, making Taffy Morgan, who was nearly asleep in the chair next to Frost, open his eyes with a start.

Mrs O'Brien jumped up, opened the door and yelled up the stairs, 'Good riddance, you bastard!' The bedroom door slammed.

Frost, whose head had started to throb, winced at each door slam and lit up another cigarette. 'Perhaps we could have a few details, Mrs O'Brien. You've checked with her friends?'

'Yes. She left Kathy's house at ten o'clock. No one has seen her since.'

'Your husband suggested this isn't the first time Jan has been out very late?'

'That was last year. She hasn't done it since. I had a talk with her and she promised she would always let me know if she was going to be delayed.' She wiped her eyes and sniffed. 'Something's happened to her, I know it has.'

'And the time she stayed out all night?' Frost asked.

'An all-night party at her friend's house. She said she'd be back by eleven, without fail. We gave her the money for a cab. The next morning her bed hadn't been slept in. Sid raised the flaming roof. She was still round at her friend's. She said she phoned for a cab, but it never came, so she thought it was safer to stay the night.'

Frost sucked down a lungful of smoke as he absorbed this. 'Your husband suggested she was sexually precocious.'

'She's physically developed for her age. But that's not her fault, is it? And she puts on make-up when she goes out with her friends and wears tight T-shirts, but all kids do that. Sid says she's a tart, but she's not. She's a little innocent. Don't you think I know my own daughter?'

Frost nodded, as if in agreement, and studied the photograph of the ponytailed Jan given to him by her mother. The kid looked like a right little goer to him. 'Has she got a mobile phone?'

'We've tried it. It's switched off. She always leaves it on.'

'Have you checked her room to see if she's left a note, or taken any clothes or anything?'

She jumped up. 'No. I'll do it now.'

'We'll come with you,' said Frost, nudging Taffy Morgan awake and following her up the stairs.

A typical young girl's bedroom. Pop posters, a hi-fi with twin speakers and a fourteen-inch TV. A single bed, unmade, pyjamas and school clothes on the floor, and a chest of drawers with two of the drawers pulled out. 'She's so untidy,' said Mrs O'Brien, picking the pyjamas up, folding them and laying them on the bed. She opened the wardrobe and riffled through the clothes swinging on their hangers. 'All her things seem to be here.' She looked around the room. 'And no sign of a note.'

'Does she have a bank book?'

Mrs O'Brien opened a drawer, rummaged around and pulled out the bank book.

Frost nodded gloomily. It was too much to expect that this would be a nice, simple run-away-from-home, with missing clothes and a note on the mantelpiece. 'She's probably with a friend,' he said, trying to sound reassuring. 'I'll get our patrol cars to keep a look-out for her, and if she hasn't come home by tomorrow, we'll start a full-scale search. But my bet is she'll be back full of apologies.' *Some flaming bet!* he told himself. 'Try not to worry.' Empty bleeding words. 'You said she had gone round her friend Kathy's house. Where does Kathy live?'

'Moorland Avenue.'

Shit, thought Frost. *Jan would have had to go round the back of the multi-storey car park, where we got that report of a girl screaming. But what credence could you put on it? A bloody drunk phoning! Let's hope and pray the kid's home by morning.* He looked round for Taffy Morgan, who was studying a photo of the girl in a skimpy swimsuit. He took it from him and jerked his head. 'We're going . . . and you're dribbling.' He turned to the mother. 'If your daughter comes back, phone the station – but I'll be sending someone round tomorrow anyway.'

She saw them out and stood at the open door watching until the car drove away and disappeared round the corner.

'What do you reckon, Guv?' asked Taffy.

'I reckon you ask too many stupid bleeding questions,' said Frost. Another thirteen-year-old girl was missing. Anything or nothing could have happened to her. But he was worried. Bloody worried. There was a rapist on the loose. The kid was sexually precocious, the sort of girl who'd attract the wrong sort of dirty bastard and Denton was full of dirty bastards. Yes, he was bloody worried.

The trip back to the station to collect Morgan's car took them past Denton Woods and along the road past the house of the other missing girl, Debbie Clark. The lights were still on. The poor mother was probably sitting by the phone, willing it to ring with good news. A black Mercedes Estate roared past them and turned into the drive.

'Hello, that's Debbie's father,' said Frost. 'What the hell is he doing out at this time of night?' He looked at his watch. Half past three. The wee small hours of the flaming morning.

Back at the station car park, Frost slid into the driving seat vacated by Morgan and yawned.

'What time tomorrow, Guv?' asked Taffy hopefully.

'You can have a lie-in, Taff,' said Frost. 'As long as you're here, excreting Welsh charm, by nine on the dot. I want you to go straight to Fortress and collect their CCTV tapes.' He looked again at the photo of ponytailed Jan O'Brien. 'And if Jan hasn't phoned her mum to say she's safe and sexually satisfied, we're going to have to make an early start with that one.' He screwed up his face and slowly shook his head from side to side. 'But somehow, Taff, I don't think that's going to happen. I've got one of my nasty feelings . . . the same sort of feeling I had when they dumped you on us. "This Welsh git's going to be a real right prat," I said, and I was right.'

Morgan grinned. 'You know you really love me, Guv.'

'Only because it's great to have someone who's a bigger prat than me,' said Frost. 'I didn't think it possible. Anyway, pleasant dreams.'

'Pleasant dreams, Guv,' echoed Taff, walking over to his car.

As Frost turned the key in the ignition, his mobile rang. It was Lambert from Control again.

'That call from the drunk – I sent Evans and Howe out in the area car to check. They've found Jan O'Brien's mobile phone.'

'Where?' asked Frost.

'In the gutter, just outside the car park – where the drunk said he heard someone screaming.'

'Excrement!' Frost drummed his fingers on the steering wheel and shook his head vigorously to wake himself up. It was nearly four o'clock in the morning. A bit flaming late to do much. If the parents hadn't reported the girl's return first thing in the morning, he'd make media appeals for the drunk to contact Denton police. At the moment they had sod all to go on. And it was too late to check her girlfriend to find out what time Jan actually left. If the drunk heard her around midnight she either left her friend's house much later than stated, or she went somewhere else first . . .

'Are you still there, Inspector?' asked Lambert.

'Yes . . . sorry . . . I was thinking. The mobile phone – it's probably been mauled about enough already, but don't let anyone else touch it without gloves. I want it checked for prints. If she was attacked, she might have tried to use the phone and the bloke snatched it from her and chucked it. If our luck's in for a change, it could have his dabs.'

'Right, Inspector. Anything else?'

There was something else, but what the hell was it? He lit up a cigarette he didn't want to help him think. 'Yes. Check with the mobile-phone company. I want to know all the calls she made on it tonight.'

'The parents?'

'We tell the parents sod all at this stage. If the kid hasn't turned up by morning, then I'll speak to them.'

'Right. Is that all, Inspector?'

Frost yawned. 'That's all I can think of.' He snatched the cigarette from his mouth and hurled it out of the car window. 'I don't want any more calls. Not unless it's a regicide or something funny like Mullett topping himself.'

'OK, Inspector. Good night.'

'Good night,' said Frost. He fired the engine and headed for home.

5

The ringing woke him, slowly dragging him by the scruff of his neck out of a deep sleep and shaking him back to semi-consciousness.

Frost opened his eyes. It was still pitch dark and the ringing was boring into his ears. What bleeding time was it? He fumbled for the alarm clock on the bedside cabinet and succeeded in sending it crashing to the floor. The ringing went on.

Cursing, he climbed out of bed and snatched up the sodding alarm, bringing it up close to his sleep-fuddled eyes, trying to make out the time. Six flaming past seven on a dark and freezing-cold morning. He'd had barely two hours' sleep. And why was the flaming thing ringing? He was sure he hadn't set it before flopping into the unmade bed last night. He tried to switch it off, but the ringing didn't stop – it was the downstairs phone in the hall. Shit! Phone calls at this hour of the morning were always bad news.

He padded in his bare feet across the cold lino and went to the bathroom to splash cold water on his face. He shivered as he headed downstairs. The central heating hadn't fired up yet and he was still in his pyjamas and a draught roared under the front door. He picked up the phone and basked for a few seconds in the resulting non-ringing silence.

'Frost,' he growled.

'Jack,' said Sergeant Wells. 'The mother's been on the blower. Her daughter hasn't returned home.'

What mother? What daughter? His sleep-deprived brain wasn't functioning properly. Then he remembered, and suddenly he was fully awake. Jan O'Brien. The teenager who hadn't come home. The teenager whose mobile phone was found near the spot where the drunk claimed he heard a girl screaming. He knew this was going to be a bad one. He just knew it. 'Shit!' he hissed.

'Sorry?' asked Wells, not hearing.

'I said I'll be right over.'

In fifteen minutes he had washed, dressed and shaved and was on his second cigarette of the day. His hand was turning the front-door latch when he paused, suddenly dreading having to face Mrs O'Brien, telling her about the reported screams, the finding of the phone. But sod this self-bleeding-pity. This was one of the joys of the bloody job, just one step down from the joy of having to tell a mother they'd found her child's body: a task he'd performed time without number since he joined the force. And it got worse, not easier.

* * *

It was as bad as he feared. The mother was hysterical and screaming, the father angry and belligerent, wanting to know why they hadn't been told all this last night, as if it would have eased their pain one iota.

'You will find her, won't you?' pleaded Mrs O'Brien.

'We'll find her,' Frost assured her, the same hollow words he always used. 'Don't worry, love. We'll find her.'

Back in the car, he tuned in to Denton FM, the local radio, as he drove back to the station.

> Denton Police are anxious to contact the person who phoned them last night reporting hearing screams in the vicinity of the multi-storey car park . . .

He hoped the sod hadn't been too flaming drunk to remember what he had heard.

Jordan was waiting for him as he pushed open the door of his office. 'We've been round to that girl Kathy, Inspector.'

Frost frowned. 'Who the hell is Kathy?'

'Jan O'Brien's friend – the girl she was with last night. She lied to Jan's mother – didn't want to get Jan into trouble. Jan was still there when the mother phoned and didn't leave to go home until nearly midnight.'

'Kathy lives at Moorland Avenue, doesn't she?'

'That's right, Inspector.'

Frost spun round in his chair to check the wall map and jabbed a finger on Moorland Avenue. 'So that could put her smack in the vicinity of the multi-storey when our friendly neighbourhood drunk heard the screams.'

Jordan nodded. 'Yes, Inspector.'

'Right,' said Frost, ramming a cigarette in his mouth. 'Then we need that bloody drunk.' His hand was hovering over the phone, ready to call Bill Wells, when the station sergeant came in and forestalled him.

'That drunk's been on the blower again, Jack. He heard the radio appeal, but wouldn't give his name. He says he can't help. He heard screaming, but saw sod all. He phoned from a call box again.'

'Sod it,' snarled Frost. 'I want him. He might have seen a car or something later. Another appeal, Bill. Would the prat who phoned the police phone us again, please. And I'll need all the men you can spare. We're going to have to put a search in hand.'

'I can't spare anyone, Jack. Mr Skinner's got them all looking for Debbie Clark and the boy.'

'Then he'll have to make it a combined search,' said Frost. 'Is he in yet?'

Wells looked past Frost, out of the office window. 'His car's just pulling in now.' He gritted his teeth and winced at the sound of an anguished squeal of brakes and a rubber-ripping skid. Wells gasped. 'Bloody hell, Jack. Taffy Morgan's nearly rammed into the back of Skinner's car.'

'Stupid Welsh git,' said Frost. 'I've told him a hundred times: "You'll never kill Skinner by ramming his car. You've got to wait until he gets out, then drive over him."' There was a burble of angry voices outside. 'Now what?'

'Skinner's having a quiet word with Taffy,' grinned Wells.

Doors slammed and thudding footsteps approached, then the office door crashed open and an angry Detective Chief Inspector Skinner marched in. He jabbed a finger at Wells. 'I've just driven past two of our men on their way to work still in civvies. I made it clear enough yesterday, even for you Denton thickies, that I want them in uniform before they clock on. I want to see them the minute they come in.'

'Right,' nodded Wells.

'And I want to see you, too,' snarled Skinner, stabbing a finger at Frost. 'Five minutes.' He slammed the door as he left and the windows rattled.

'And good morning to you too, you fat sod,' said Frost, jerking two fingers at the closed door. To his alarm, the door opened again and he thought Skinner had heard him and was coming back – but it was Taffy Morgan.

'Skinner's a bit touchy this morning,' said Taffy, flopping down in the chair behind his desk and taking the *Daily Mirror* from his pocket.

'I don't think he likes people ramming the back of his car,' said Frost. 'Now put that flaming paper away, I've got jobs for you. I want CCTV footage from the building society cash machine and I want CCTV footage of the area around the multi-storey for around midnight last night. If Jan O'Brien was abducted, let's see what cars were about at that time of night.'

'Right, Guv.' With a quick glance at the picture of a half-naked girl on page three, Taffy tucked the morning paper under his arm and left the office.

Frost's internal phone rang. It was Skinner.

'OK,' acknowledged Frost, giving the phone another two-fingered salute as he hung up. He pushed back his chair and stood up. 'Is "Get your effing arse in here" the same as saying "Would you kindly come into my office"?' he asked Bill Wells.

As he approached Skinner's office after a quick cup of tea in the canteen, Frost could clearly hear the DCI's angry voice bellowing from behind the closed door, which then opened to allow two sheepish-looking, out-of-uniform, PCs to emerge. 'And the next time I spot you on the way to work, but out of uniform, I'll have your flaming guts for garters,' roared Skinner, speeding them on their way.

'Little tip,' whispered Frost. 'He likes you to be wearing your uniform before you start duty – he might have been too shy to have mentioned it. I'm going in for my bollocking now.' He gave the door a half-hearted tap and entered.

A smouldering Skinner glowered at him from behind his desk. Much of the office had been stripped bare, ready for complete refurbishment.

If Mullett could raid the maintenance budget for a tarted-up, wooden-panelled office, then Skinner was not going to put up with this tatty affair. He slashed a finger at a chair and grunted, 'Sit!'

Woof, woof, thought Frost. *Are we going for walkies?* He flopped down in the chair. Skinner didn't look very well. His skin had a greenish pallor and there were beads of sweat on his forehead.

'You look rough,' said Frost.

Skinner rubbed his stomach. 'Superintendent Mullett took me out to dinner at his club last night. I think the oysters were off.'

'I hate oysters,' said Frost. 'They taste like salted snot.'

Skinner looked as if he was going to throw up. 'Never mind about me. A complete and utter balls-up last night.'

'The meal wasn't a success then?' asked Frost.

'You know damn well what I mean. The cash-point stake-out. All those men. All that bloody overtime and you let the sod get away with a thousand quid.'

'We made an arrest,' protested Frost.

'Oh yes,' sneered Skinner, 'a flaming handbag-snatcher. All that overtime and a flaming handbag-snatcher. I hear we have another bloody missing girl?'

Frost filled Skinner in.

Skinner tapped his teeth with his pencil. 'Do you think there's any link with the other two missing kids?'

'Possible, but I doubt it. I think our friendly neighbourhood rapist has got her.'

A ripple of pain made Skinner wince and rub his stomach. 'Bleeding oysters. Right. I'm on my way now to brief the search teams. I'll get them to look for Jan O'Brien as well. If you get any results from the CCTV footage, follow it through, but keep me posted. And if you get near to making an arrest, I take over – *comprende*?'

'*Buenas noches*,' agreed Frost, pushing himself out of the chair and beating a hasty retreat.

Back in his office, he wearily dragged his overflowing in-tray towards him. He skimmed through the memos and forms, then dragged the waste-paper bin over so he could discard all the tricky stuff and deny he had ever received it. Whatever they were, he didn't have the time to waste on them. He looked round as Taffy Morgan came in, a batch of videotapes in his hand.

'Sorry I've been so long, Guv,' said Taff, dropping wearily into his chair.

'Don't apologise, Taff,' said Frost. 'Things always seem to go a lot smoother when you're not here. So you've got the cashpoint and CCTV footage?'

'Yes, Guv.'

'Right. Take them into the Incident Room and run them through. Get Collier to help you.'

'Shall I have my breakfast first, Guv?' asked

Morgan hopefully. 'I've already ordered the big fry-up.'

'All you think about is your dick and your flaming stomach,' snorted Frost. 'No. Get cracking on those videotapes, they're more important. Don't worry about your breakfast – I'll eat it for you. And stop sulking – put your flaming lower lip in!'

When he returned from the canteen, his phone was ringing. Didn't the bleeding thing ever stay quiet for a few minutes? He answered it.

'Frost.'

It was Beazley, the owner of Supersaves. 'What the hell happened last night? Did you catch him?'

Shit, thought Frost. He'd forgotten about Beazley. 'Ah, Mr Beazley. I was just on my way over to you. We didn't catch him, but we've got some people on video footage you might be able to identify.' He thought it best not to mention the withdrawn thousand pounds at this stage, and hoped and prayed Morgan would turn something up.

'Then make it bloody snappy. My time is precious.'

'Fifteen minutes at the outside,' promised Frost, hanging up and making his way to the Incident Room, where Morgan and Collier were staring at a TV monitor showing juddering footage of late-night traffic.

'Does it take two of you to look at one tape?'

asked Frost. 'Have you done the building society cashpoint tape, yet?'

'It's next on the list, Guv.'

'Do it now. Beazley's shitting bricks.' Frost looked at the cassette they were slotting into the video player with misgiving. It was old and battered and the tape looked almost white from constant recording and replaying. In the interests of economy, the building society used the same tape over and over again, even when it was past its best. He drummed his fingers impatiently on the desk as Morgan switched the video player on and fast-forwarded to the previous night. 'Just before and just after midnight,' Frost reminded him as blurred black-and-white images raced across the screen and a digital clock at the top right-hand corner sped through the time.

Morgan jammed the Stop button. 'We're here, Guv.' He pressed Play.

The clock said 23.50. The out-of-focus shape appeared of a woman withdrawing cash. The image was blurred and almost unrecognisable, but Frost felt sure it was the tom who had approached him in the car. He made a mental note to get her picked up in case she had seen whoever had used the cashpoint after her.

'This is it, Guv!' exclaimed Morgan.

Frost groaned. The next image was unrecognisable. Probably a man in a dark coat with the collar up, his head bent low.

The figure moved off and the screen briefly went blank – the CCTV was programmed only to record when someone was at the cashpoint.

Then, with the clock showing 00.03, the same figure reappeared, face kept well down. The money was withdrawn and the figure moved off into the dark.

'I think it's the Pope,' offered Frost. 'Get Interpol on the phone. We'd better arrest him, just in case.' He leant back in his chair. 'Bleeding building society and its false economies.' He turned to Collier, who was hovering behind him. 'Any chance we could get the pictures enhanced?'

'I doubt it, Inspector,' Collier told him. 'There's hardly anything on the tape to enhance, and in any case, all we'd get would be an enhanced man with his face completely covered.'

'Try it anyway,' said Frost. 'And find out the address of that tom. She might be our only hope.' He rewound a few seconds and watched the man withdrawing cash again. 'Why do they bother with CCTV, and then put in cheap flaming cameras with dirty lenses, not enough light and a clapped-out tape?' He stood up. 'Get a couple of stills printed out. I've got to have something to show Beazley, even if it's flaming useless.' He wasn't going to enjoy that meeting.

As he made for the door, Bill Wells came in. 'Skinner wants to see you, Jack, and says it's urgent.'

Skinner, his face still green and sweaty, jabbed a finger at a chair, instructing Frost to sit. In front of him on the desk was an opened, ancient-looking folder bulging with photographs and yellowing, dog-eared pages of typescripts. 'I'm still feeling rough, so I'm off home to get my head down for a couple of hours. Keep a watching brief on the search.'

'Right,' said Frost, standing to go.

A finger wagged him back to the chair. 'I haven't finished. I want you to arrest a bloke for me. Just arrest him and get him banged up. I'll do the rest when I come back.' Skinner slid a forensic report across the desk. 'Graham Fielding, your suspected rapist. They've done a DNA on the sperm sample from Sally Marsden and it wasn't him. He's in the clear.'

'Shit!' snorted Frost. 'He was my odds-on favourite.'

Skinner pushed the file over and Frost found himself staring at a black-and-white photograph of a young girl's body, naked, her wide sightless eyes staring up into the sky, lying on her back amid long, straggling grass rimed with hoar frost.

Frost stared and shivered. He felt cold. Freezing cold. He was back in time, a cutting wind sawing through his clothes as he stood looking down at the girl's naked body . . . Deep in his brain a piercing bell was ringing, insisting that he knew who she was. But the name just wouldn't come. 'Who is she?'

'Casey Turner. Fifteen years old. Raped, strangled and dumped in the old St Martin's cemetery back in 1977.'

Frost whistled softly as the memory flash-flooded back. Casey Turner. Of course.

Fifteen-year-old Casey Turner. 'It was Christmas Day,' he said, half to himself. 'The poor little bitch was killed on Christmas Day. I was on the case – still a sergeant then, of course. Bert Williams was in charge, but we never got anywhere. No suspects . . . nothing.'

'I've got a suspect now,' smirked Skinner. 'A red-hot, bloody one hundred per cent cast-iron suspect.' He pulled a report from an envelope and gave it to Frost.

'*DNA Test Result*,' read Frost. He looked puzzled and checked the date at the top of the form. 'It's a recent sample. What's it got to do with an ancient murder?'

Skinner leant back in his chair and gave a smug smile. 'It's got everything to do with it. When the lab tests DNA samples, they compare them with their database of old DNA material to see if they can match it. It cleared your suspect of rape, but it matched the DNA from sperm samples and flecks of skin from under Casey Turner's fingernails where she clawed her killer some thirty years ago.'

Frost shook his head in wonder. 'Flaming hell. After all this bleeding time Fielding must have thought he'd got away with it.' He looked again at the photograph. Details of the case were charging back fast and furious. The girl's grief-stricken mother had had a complete nervous breakdown. One bitterly cold night she'd cleaned the house from top to bottom, cut her husband's sandwiches for the next morning and put them on the kitchen table ready for him to take to work, then, in only a thin frock and no coat, had wandered out to chuck herself off the top level of the multi-storey car park in town. Frost had had to go and break the news to the husband that he had now lost a wife as well as a daughter.

His thoughts were interrupted by Skinner, who was grimacing and rubbing his stomach. 'I'm off home. Now just bring him in. Don't question him – this is my case, not yours.'

'Right,' nodded Frost, tucking the folder under his arm.

'And don't sod it up!' barked Skinner.

'I'll make a note of that,' said Frost, pulling a pen from his pocket and scribbling on a scrap of paper. 'I always forget I'm not supposed to sod things up.'

He left Skinner scowling after him. 'You think you're so bleeding clever, sunshine, but just wait until tomorrow. Your days in Denton are numbered.'

Back at his desk, Frost opened the file and flipped through the yellowing pages of typescript. It was all coming back. His brain started churning over the events of that awful Christmas morning, all those years ago . . .

They'd only been married a few months and it should have been their first Christmas together, but at eight o'clock on Christmas morning the phone rang. Frank Gibson, the DS who had drawn the short straw for Christmas Day, had been rushed off to hospital with suspected appendicitis and Frost, as standby, was called in to fill the gap. When he told his wife, her fury knew no bounds. Their first Christmas together was going to be ruined. In tears, she threatened to chuck the Christmas dinner she had planned for so long in the dustbin.

She had one hell of a temper. By God, she was a feisty firebrand in those days and a little cracker to boot. Absolutely beautiful, and she adored him as much as he was crazy about her. So how did it all go wrong? How did the poor cow end up dying in that pokey hospital room, her only visitor a man she had long since fallen out of love with?

Much of it was his fault. Too much time spent on the job and not enough with her. And the promotion she had dreamt of for him had not happened until it was too late . . . until she was dying in that lousy hospital. He rubbed his scar. Until that toe-rag fired the bullet at him and he'd been given a George Cross and promoted to inspector. But by then the cancer was too far gone and when he tried to tell her his news, she couldn't take it in. He felt his eyes misting over and lit up a cigarette. He smoked and stared out of the window as memories came flooding back.

The station was dead and yawningly empty, the phones were quiet and the flaming heating wasn't working properly. He had phoned home a couple of times, trying to make the peace, but she had slammed the phone down on him. And then a phone bell suddenly ripped through the silence. Some drunk with enough fright in his voice to sound genuine was saying,

'There's a stone-dead naked tart in St Mary's churchyard.' Before Frost could answer, the man had hung up. There was no one else to send and it was probably warmer outside than in this freezing station, so he wound his scarf around his neck and went out to check. Let it be a bloody hoax, he kept telling himself. Let it be a bloody hoax. But it wasn't.

Lying in the straggling overgrown grass of the old churchyard, amongst the lop-sided, moss-covered headstones of the long dead, was a recent dead, a very recent dead, a young girl, cold as ice, stark naked, a crumpled dress at her feet, staring wide-eyed up at a clear Christmas sky. Somewhere in the distance church bells were ringing.

Bert Williams, the DI in charge of the case, was a dead loss; drunk most of the time and always letting others do all the work. Williams was out of his depth with the Casey Turner murder, although even a good copper wouldn't have had any luck solving it. They had no suspects. Nothing. And all their leads fizzled out.

The DI couldn't face breaking the news to the family, not that they would have appreciated a man unsteady on his feet, reeking of whisky. Williams had taken another swig from his hip flask behind a crumbling stone angel in the hope that it would bolster his courage to face the dead girl's family. But it didn't. 'You do it, Jack. You're so much better at this sort of thing than I am . . .'

Frost sensed someone looking over his shoulder. Taffy Morgan.

'That's an ancient case, Guv.' He picked up the photograph of the body and shook his head sadly. 'She's only a kid.'

Frost took the photograph back. 'Christmas morning. Christmas bloody morning. Get your coat, Taff. We're going to arrest the bastard who killed her.'

He let Morgan do the driving, his brain still in the past.

Reinforcements were still being drafted in, so he had to make the call to the girl's house on his own. He had parked outside, in the road, for some fifteen minutes, smoking to delay the moment when he would have to knock at the door. Get it bloody well over and done with. He snatched the cigarette from his mouth and hurled it out of the window, stepped out of the car and knocked at the front door.

From inside the house came the sound of cheerful music on the radio – Frank Sinatra singing 'Have Yourself a Merry Little Christmas' . . . Casey's mother opened the door, looking happy and excited . . .

'That's the house, Guv.' Morgan's voice snatched him roughly back to the present and he had to shake his head to get rid of the ghosts of the past. It was like waking from a realistic nightmare.

Taffy parked the car in front of the driveway. Frost studied the house. A nice-looking, three-bedroomed property, no more than ten years old, fronted by a small, neat lawn, in the centre of which an incongruous palm tree flourished. In honour of the palm tree, the house was called *The Oasis*.

As they scrunched up the gravelled path, a dog barked frantically inside. Frost stood back and let Taffy thumb the doorbell. The dog sounded hungry.

From inside the house a child's voice yelled at the dog to shut up. The door opened. A dark-haired boy, about ten years old, frowned up at them.

'Who is it?' called a man from upstairs.

'Is that Mr Fielding? Could we have a word, please?' called back Frost. 'Denton police.'

A dark-haired man in his late forties thudded down the stairs. 'Police? Who am I supposed to have raped now?' he grinned.

'Casey Turner,' said Frost.

A puzzled frown, then the man's head snapped back as if he had been hit. His jaw dropped and his eyes widened in shock. He shook his head as if to compose himself, his tongue flicking over dry lips. 'Who?' he croaked, trying to keep his voice steady.

'Might be a good idea if we came inside for a few minutes,' answered Frost. 'Rape isn't something you discuss on the doorstep.'

'Yes, of course, but I don't know what the hell you are talking about.'

'Who's at the door, Graham?' called a woman from the back of the house.

'It's the police, Mum,' the boy answered before Fielding could stop him. 'They say Daddy raped a girl.'

'It's all right, dear,' cut in Fielding hurriedly. 'Just that old business again.'

'But they cleared you of that,' she called.

'I know,' he replied. 'They're just tidying up

the paperwork. Just routine.' He snapped at his son, 'Go out and play – now!' He waited as the boy sullenly shuffled off, then beckoned the two detectives into the lounge and firmly shut the door. 'Now, perhaps you'll tell me what the hell this is all about.'

'You know what it's all about, don't you, son?' purred Frost, giving his deceptively friendly smile. He took the black-and-white photograph from his mac pocket and held it up to Fielding's face. 'Casey Turner, fifteen. Never got her Christmas presents. You stripped her, raped her, beat her up and killed her. Christmas Day, thirty years ago.'

'This is preposterous. Me? You're trying to make out I killed this girl?' blustered Fielding, pushing the photograph away. 'I don't know her. I've never seen her.'

Frost sank down into one of the armchairs. 'Before you tell us any more porkies, let me tell you what we've got.' He balanced the photograph on the arm of the chair, then pulled out a photostat of the DNA test report. 'As you know, you very kindly gave my Welsh colleague here a DNA sample following that rape in the car park.'

'And I was cleared. The test said it wasn't me.'

Frost nodded. 'Very true. But we're pugnacious bastards, I'm afraid. We compared your sample with an old semen sample taken from the body of Casey. It matched perfectly.' He proffered the DNA test result. 'Here it is, if you don't believe me.'

Fielding stared at the sheet, then dropped down in the armchair opposite Frost. 'I never raped her. I never killed her. It was so long ago.'

'Look on the bright side, son,' said Frost. 'You've had thirty years of freedom. Take that as a bonus you didn't bleeding well deserve. And now I'm going to take you down to the station for further questioning.'

The man remained in the chair. He bowed his head and spoke to the floor. 'We had sex. She was alive when I left her. Someone else must have killed her.'

Frost shook his head sadly. 'I'm pretty gullible, but even I can't swallow that. Still, don't waste time explaining to me. It isn't my case, thank God. I'm just here to take you to the station.' He stood up. 'Graham Fielding, I'm arresting you on suspicion of the rape and murder of Casey Turner on the twenty-fifth of December 1977.' He jerked his head to Morgan, who intoned the standard caution. Frost still hadn't got the hang of the new wording.

There was a hesitant tap at the door. Fielding's wife, an attractive woman with chestnut hair carrying a baby in her arms, came in. She looked at the three men and felt the tension in the air. 'Graham – what's wrong?'

Fielding looked up at Frost. 'Could I have a few words with my wife in private, please, Inspector? In the kitchen?'

'Of course,' said Frost.

When they left, he let his eyes travel round the room. There were wedding photos, family photos, holiday photos, baby photos: everyone smiling, everyone happy. He picked up a picture of Fielding's wife in a very brief bikini and nodded admiringly. 'The poor cow's in for a shock.' He carefully replaced the photograph on the shelf. 'I bet he's cursing the day they invented DNA.'

'I almost feel sorry for him,' said Morgan.

'Feel sorry for the poor girl he raped and killed on Christmas bleeding Day,' said Frost. 'Feel sorry for her mother, who was so grief-stricken she chucked herself off the top of the multi-storey car park. Her father only lived a couple of years after that. The entire family, dead, and all because of that shit-bag.'

'How the hell is he going to explain it to his wife?' asked Morgan. ' "Sorry, love. I raped and murdered a girl umpteen years ago and I'll probably go to prison for life. Sorry I haven't mentioned it before." '

'If he'd confessed at the time, he'd be out by now,' said Frost. Yells and cries from the back of the house made him look up. 'I think he's making a run for it, Taff. Go and give Collier a hand.' He lit up a cigarette and waited. After a few minutes the door opened and PC Collier led in a handcuffed Graham Fielding, followed by DC Morgan.

'I forgot to tell you, son,' said Frost. 'Us cops are not very trusting, so I had a PC waiting round the back just in case you wanted to leg it.'

From the kitchen came the heart-rending sound of a woman sobbing bitterly and trying to comfort a crying baby. The dog, sensing something was wrong, was barking ceaselessly. Fielding, white-faced, looked as if he too was ready to burst into tears at any minute.

Frost sighed. There were times when this bloody job wasn't a bundle of laughs. He wound his scarf round his neck and chucked his cigarette end into the empty grate. 'Come on. Let's get out of here.'

Fielding paced up and down the holding cell. 'I want bail,' he told Frost. 'I'm self-employed. If I don't work the family get no money. I can't let my customers down. I need bail.'

'The magistrate might grant you bail, but I doubt it,' Frost told him. 'You rarely get bail in a murder case, even one as old as this.'

'I never killed her,' insisted Fielding.

'I'm not the jury, son, just your bog-standard "don't believe a word the bastard is saying" common or garden cop. Anyway, like I told you, this isn't my case. Detective Chief Inspector Skinner should be here shortly. You can tell him you didn't do it. He's a miserable sod and could do with a good laugh.'

As he was closing the cell door, he thought of the man's wife and kids. 'Get a solicitor, son. He might wangle bail for you.'

Fielding, who had slumped down on the bunk bed, looked up, his face a picture of despair. 'I can't afford a solicitor.'

'If you ask for one, we'll get you one free,' Frost told him. 'We've got a whole list of dead-beat lawyers who don't mind losing a hopeless case just to gain experience.' Fielding's abject expression almost made him feel pity for the man. 'Only joking, son. They're all quite good. Just ask for one.'

He was mounting the stairs to the canteen when Wells came running after him.

'Jack!'

'Unless it's a multiple murder or some big-busted tart streaking, it can wait. I'm having my dinner,' said Frost.

'More important than both of them, Jack. Beazley's phoned about eight times. He's doing his nut.'

Frost stopped in his tracks. 'Shit!' He had forgotten all about Beazley. With a wistful glance at the canteen door, Frost turned and descended the stairs. 'Let's go and break the good news that I let his blackmailer get away with a thousand quid.'

Beazley leant back in his chair and stared at Frost, wide eyed, mouth gaping in disbelief. 'Am I hearing you right or do I need to get my bleeding ears syringed? You let the bastard get away with a thousand quid of my money? A thousand bloody quid? You don't do a flaming thing right. That Fortress cheque you asked for – it would have taken four days to clear so I had to transfer the money electronically. You never told me that, did you?"

'I'm sorry, Mr Beazley.'

'No, I'm the one who's flaming sorry for listening to you in the first place. You were supposed to be watching the cashpoints. Where the hell were you?'

'As I explained, Mr Beazley—' began Frost.

Beazley cut him short. 'I don't want your bloody explanations. That's not going to get my flaming money back, is it?'

'As I explained,' repeated Frost patiently, 'the man whose card had been stolen had a spare card which he hadn't told us about. When we got the message that the card was being used, we naturally went after him.'

'He was probably a bloody decoy,' said Beazley, 'and you fell for it.'

'No, Mr Beazley. It was just our rotten luck this stupid sod presented his card a few minutes before the blackmailer.'

'Talking of stupid sods, what are you going to do about it?'

Before Frost could answer, there was a timid tap at the door.

Beazley scowled and grunted, 'Yes?'

A grey-haired lady wearing steel-rimmed glasses and carrying a shorthand notebook came in. Beazley completely ignored her. 'So what are you going to do about it?' he repeated.

'We're resuming the stake-out tomorrow night. We'll get him this time.'

'Tomorrow night? What about tonight? Are you just going to let him help himself to more of my money?'

'He's already collected today's five hundred

pounds so he's got to wait until tomorrow.'

Beazley glared at Frost and tugged his lower lip. 'No. I'm pulling out. I've no faith in you. Get the rest of my money back.' Then he realised the woman was standing there. 'What the hell do you want?'

'You asked me to come in for dictation at twelve, Mr Beazley.'

'How can I give you dictation when I've got the bleeding plod here, you stupid cow? Piss off!'

As she left and Beazley turned his attention back to the DI, Frost's mobile rang.

'You asked me to ring you, Guv,' whispered Morgan.

'Bloody hell!' Frost exclaimed loudly for Beazley's benefit. 'I'm on my way.' He clicked off. 'Sorry, Mr Beazley, we'll have to talk about this later. We've got a paedophile on the loose.'

'If you're after him, it's his lucky day. He's as safe as bloody houses,' sniffed Beazley. 'And I want my money back.'

But Frost had gone.

In the outer office, the grey-haired lady was hammering away at a keyboard. She paused and smiled up at Frost as he was passing through. The door to Beazley's office crashed open and Beazley jabbed a finger at the woman. 'You, Fanny. In here. I want you.' He glared at Frost. 'And stop wasting my staff's time. She's here to work, not to listen to your rubbish.' The door slammed.

'I keep getting the urge to smash your boss in the kisser,' Frost told the woman.

She gathered up her shorthand notebook and smiled sweetly. 'In the kisser, Inspector? What's wrong with in the goolies?'

He clattered down the stairs to the car park. His stomach was rumbling. A foot-down drive back to the station and up to the canteen for dinner.

He was opening the car door when his mobile rang again. It was Taffy Morgan. 'It's all right, Taff,' he said. 'It worked. I'm on my way back to the station.'

'No, it's something else, Guv,' said Taffy, sounding serious. 'The embankment next to the railway tunnel just before Denton station. A bloke's just phoned in. He reckons he's found a body.'

6

The man who had found the body – sharp-nosed, in his late fifties and wearing a scruffy railway-company jacket and cap – was waiting for them at the side of the road on the bridge crossing the railway line. He flagged them down. 'Are you the police? I'm Fred Daniels. It's down there.' He pointed over the side of the bridge, down to the overgrown railway embankment that hugged the railway line. He was excited, anxious to make the most of his moment of fame. 'As soon as I opened my eyes this morning, I knew something awful was going to happen, I just knew.'

I don't want your bleeding life story, thought Frost, shutting his ears and staring down at the track. He shuddered. He was sharply reminded of an earlier occasion when he'd clambered down this very embankment to view a woman's decapitated body, and the farce of having to call the police surgeon in to certify death. They never found the head. It must have been pulverised by the engine. He couldn't remember any other details – one of so many cases – but the picture of that mangled, headless body was embedded in his brain.

'You all right, Guv?' Taffy Morgan was looking at him anxiously.

'Yes.' Frost turned to Daniels. 'So where is the body?'

'I'll show you.' The man scrabbled over the bridge wall and dropped down to the embankment on the other side. 'Follow me.'

Frost left Morgan to wait for the rest of the team and heaved himself over the wall.

'This way,' urged the man eagerly. 'And be careful. It's very steep. You could slide down to the railway line if you don't watch it.' He slithered down the incline, stopping at a clump of bushes and pointing. 'Behind there.'

Frost didn't need any further guidance. His nostrils twitched and he felt the first stirring of a protesting stomach. A too familiar smell: the rancid, cloying, decaying reek of death. Gingerly he made his way round the bushes. The smell hit him hard, making him gasp. He lit up a cigarette, but the smoke tasted of decomposed flesh. He tore the cigarette from his mouth and hurled it down on to the railway line.

The body was almost hidden by the overgrown vegetation. The smell was unbearable. Frost held his breath and parted the grass to look down on rotting slime that once was flesh. Human, but too decomposed to immediately ascertain the sex. It had been there some time so, thank God, it wasn't Debbie Clark or

Jan O'Brien. It wasn't easy to make out if the body had both feet, but it looked too decayed for the bits they had been finding to have come from it.

Stepping back, he yelled up to DC Morgan, who was in animated conversation with a young woman who seemed anxious to know what was going on. 'I don't want any bloody sightseers, Taffy. Get rid of her and come on down here.' He switched on his mobile and called the station. 'Seren-bleeding-dipity,' he told Sergeant Wells. 'When you look for one body, you find a different one. It's neither of our missing girls. Get the duty doc and the full murder team down here – and tell them an empty stomach is advisable.'

He turned his attention to the railway worker. 'It's well hidden. How come you spotted it?'

'I'm working on the line down there. I wanted a slash so I nipped up here to do it behind the bushes and that's when I found it. Flaming heck. It was the last thing I expected.' His nose quivered and he screwed his face up in disgust. 'When the wind changes, you can't half smell it, can you?'

'Smell what – your pee?'

'No – the body.'

'Right. Thank you, Mr Daniels,' said Frost, anxious to get rid of him. 'When you get a chance, would you call in at Denton police station and give us a written statement – just for the record.'

'My pleasure,' said Daniels enthusiastically. 'I'll do it now. If they think I'm coming into work after this, they're flaming well mistaken. Shaken me up rotten, this has. Like the time I tripped over a flaming body at the side of the line. Three trains had gone over it and the drivers hadn't noticed . . . How could they bleeding miss it?' He glanced at the bushes. 'At least this one is in one piece and not all mashed up in bits.'

'Yes, there's always a bright side,' agreed Frost.

A blue plastic marquee – erected with some difficulty because of the sharp slope of the embankment – had been set up over the body. Frost stuck his head inside and withdrew it quickly. The rotting-flesh smell was now concentrated inside the enclosed space. He turned his attention to the team from Forensic, backs bent, white-overalled, painstakingly doing a fingertip search of the surrounding area and coming up with masses of junk . . . spent matches, scraps of paper, rusty tin cans, plastic carrier bags. All absolutely useless, but all would have to be logged and grid-referenced. All a complete waste of bleeding time.

'Jack!' Dr Mackenzie, the duty police surgeon, was making his way down the slope with much difficulty. Frost steadied him as he slid to a halt outside the marquee. 'What have you got for me?'

'I've got a body with no nose,' said Frost.

Mackenzie had heard this chestnut many times before, but he went along with it. 'No nose? How does it smell?'

'Bloody horrible,' said Frost, cackling at the ancient joke.

'You'll have to get yourself some new material,' said the doctor, as Frost stood to one side to let him enter the tent first.

'This job's full of laughs,' said Frost, filling his lungs with fresh air before following Mackenzie in. 'I don't need new material.' He nodded at the body. 'It's not in tip-top condition, so I want to know if it's male or female, age, cause of death, and how long, to the nearest minute, it has been dead.'

Mackenzie, his handkerchief clapped over his mouth, took a quick look at the body. 'If you think I'm going to touch that for the sort of money the police pay me, Jack, you've got another thing coming. It's dead . . .' He bent and peered at it. 'I think it's female, probably young, but I'm not prodding about to find the cause of death. Let Drysdale enjoy himself doing that.' Drysdale was the Home Office pathologist, very much disliked by Mackenzie.

'Has she got two feet, Doc?' asked Frost.

Mackenzie blinked in astonishment. 'Eh?'

'We've been finding bits of a chopped-off foot. I want to know if it came from her.'

Mackenzie parted the overgrown grass and peered down. 'She's been chewed about by more animals than you can shake a stick at, but both feet seem to be there.'

'How long has she been dead?' asked Frost.

Mackenzie shrugged and spread his hands. 'Weeks, months – you tell me.' He looked down again. 'There's no clothing on the body. It could have been torn off by animals or stripped before being dumped, but I'd guess he or she was stripped before being dumped here. Drysdale will tell you.'

He stepped out of the marquee and took a deep breath. 'God! Doesn't fresh air taste good? I'll send in my bill, and make certain they pay it promptly this time. They made me wait weeks for the last cheque.' He clambered up the embankment to his car.

Harding from Forensic, who was in charge of the fingertip search, approached Frost. 'We've thoroughly searched the area up to the bridge, Inspector. We've found plenty of junk, but not a scrap of clothing. Do you want us to widen the search area?'

Frost tugged at his lower lip, then shook his head. 'No. It's my gut feeling she – if it is a she, Mackenzie wouldn't say for sure – was stripped naked before she was dumped here. My other gut feeling is that the clothes we found in the lake belong to this poor cow.' He shook a cigarette from the packet and lit up. 'Drysdale should be able to give us some idea as to how big she was and we can see if the clothing would fit.'

'I think Drysdale's retired or cutting down his hours,' Harding told him.

Frost brightened up. 'Ah well, not all bad news then.' He would have to let Dr Mackenzie know. He beckoned Morgan down.

The detective constable slithered down the

embankment. 'Do you want me to get you something to eat, Guv?'

Frost nodded at the open flap of the tent. 'Stick your nose in there, Taff, and tell me if you feel like eating.' He looked up. A plumpish woman in her early forties, wearing slacks and a thick windcheater, had clambered over the bridge wall and was cautiously making her way down. 'Who the bleeding hell is that, Taffy? You're supposed to be up there, stopping any fat tart who feels like it from coming down for a sniff.'

'You told me to come down here,' protested Morgan.

'I don't care what I said – get rid of her.'

Morgan clawed his way up to head her off, but to Frost's annoyance soon made his way down again with the woman in tow.

'I thought I told you to get rid of her,' hissed Frost.

'You don't know who she is, Guv. She's the new Home Office pathologist.'

Frost gaped. 'Flaming heck, Taff. There is a God after all!' He introduced himself to the woman. 'Detective Inspector Frost.'

She flashed a smile, showing perfect teeth. 'Dr Ridley. What have you got for me, Inspector?'

'We'd better look at the body first,' said Frost with a giggle. He hesitated at the flap. 'It's a bit whiffy in there.'

She opened her bag and took out a gauze mask that covered her mouth and nose, then stepped inside, her forehead wrinkling in distaste as she saw the body. At first she seemed as reluctant as Mackenzie to actually touch it. 'Not much I can tell you until I get her on the autopsy table.'

'She?' queried Frost. 'Definitely female?'

'Yes, female. She's been dead anything up to a month, could be more. Animals have had a good old go at her.'

'Any idea of age?' asked Frost.

The pathologist shook her head. 'She's in too poor a condition – you can just about tell the sex. I'd guess she's in her late teens or early twenties, but it's only a guess at this stage. Don't ask cause of death, because again, I don't know yet.'

'Sexually assaulted?' asked Frost.

'The state the body's in, we will probably never know, but again, wait for the autopsy. Any ID?'

Frost shook his head. 'We retrieved a dustbin sack full of girl's clothes from the lake in the woods yesterday. I'm hoping they tie in with the corpse.'

'Get them over to the autopsy room. I'll try to match them up with the body.' She took a last look at the remains. 'Nothing more I can do here.' She straightened up, snapped her bag shut and squeezed through the tent flap to the fresh air outside. She tore off her mask and sucked in gulps of air. 'Some pathologists take it in their stride, but I can never get used to it.'

She dictated a few brief notes into a small cassette recorder, then dropped it in her pocket and zipped up her windcheater. 'Where do we do the post-mortems?'

'The mortuary at Denton General,' Frost told

her. 'Meet me at Denton nick first and I'll take you there.'

'No need. I've got a map.' She consulted her wristwatch. 'Too late to do it now. Tomorrow afternoon – say one o'clock.'

'I'll be there,' called Frost, admiring her plump little bottom which was wiggling provocatively as she walked away.

'Cor. I couldn't half give her one,' whispered Morgan.

'That's because you're a randy Welsh git,' snapped Frost. 'And in any case, I saw her first so it's droit de seigneur, my little leek-muncher.' He returned the wave she gave him as she clambered over the bridge wall, then called Harding over.

'The pathologist's doing the PM tomorrow afternoon. Get the body to the morgue as soon as you've done your stuff. We might have to get the Maggot Man in to tell us how long she's been lying there, so bring the creepy crawlies as well. Did you get any DNA from those clothes we found in the lake?'

'Yes,' Harding told him.

'Good. Let's hope we can match it up with the body. But get them over to the morgue. The pathologist might be able to tell us if they would fit.'

'Did she give any indication as to the cause of death?' asked Harding.

'No. Hopefully the autopsy will tell us.'

'So at this stage, for all we know, it could be natural causes?'

'The poor cow's naked. You don't take off all your clothes, lie down on a railway embankment and die of natural causes.'

'There's chunks of her missing, Inspector. Animals could have torn her clothes off.'

'If you find bits of clothes underneath her when we shift the body, then it's possible. But if animals had done it there'd be shreds of clothing in the vicinity and you didn't find any. It's her clothes we fished out of the lake. I just know it.'

His mobile trilled. 'I'm busy – what is it?' he snapped.

'Is that you, Frost?'

Bloody hell! It was Mullett. 'Yes, Super, but I'm rather busy . . .'

'What on earth is going on? I've had Debbie Clark's father on the phone threatening to go to the Chief Constable. This is intolerable . . . absolutely unforgivable!'

'Sorry about that, Super,' breezed Frost, apologising on autopilot while trying to work out what the hell he was supposed to have done now.

'Sorry? Being sorry isn't good enough,' spluttered Mullett.

Then I'm not flaming sorry, thought Frost, still wondering what it was all about.

'His daughter is dead and he has to find out from a third party. Even by your standards, this is disgraceful.'

Frost frowned. What was the prat on about? 'Dead? Debbie Clark dead? Flaming heck, Super, I didn't know that.'

'Didn't know? What are you talking about?

You find her body, but you tell the press before you tell the family? The first they know of it is when a reporter from the *Denton Echo* hammers on their doorstep to ask for a photograph of their dead daughter—'

'Hold on, Super,' cut in Frost. 'We haven't found his daughter's body. The poor cow we've found is maggot-ridden. She's been dead for at least a month.'

'Then why tell the press it was Debbie Clark?'

'I never told the press.'

'Don't try and get out of it, Frost. I've checked. Even for you this seemed unbelievable, so I phoned the *Denton Echo* myself. They assured me that their reporter was informed by the police that it was Debbie . . .'

'Then he's a bleeding liar,' said Frost. 'I'll ring you back.' He cut Mullett off, dialled the *Denton Echo* and asked to be put through to the editor.

'What the hell are you playing at, Sandy,' he demanded, 'sending one of your reporters round to the Clarks and telling them we'd found their daughter's body?'

'What's wrong with that?' Lane asked.

'We haven't found her bleeding body, that's what's wrong with that.'

'Balls, Jack. She checked with one of your men and was told categorically you had found Debbie Clark's body. I'm running the story under her byline now.'

'She? It's a bloody she?'

'Yes, Jack. A new girl, very keen. She'll go far.'

'Not bleeding far enough, if I get hold of her.

If she says she's checked with one of my men, she's lying.'

'Jack,' insisted Lane, 'she may be new but she knows the ropes. She would never go ahead with a story like that if she hadn't been given the facts.'

'Sandy, I and another officer viewed the body, which definitely wasn't Debbie Clark, and we certainly didn't speak to a reporter.'

'I'm sorry, Jack. She spoke to one of your men.'

'None of my men would be so stupid,' began Frost – then he remembered that Taffy Morgan had been chatting up a young woman as Frost was slithering down to view the body. He went cold. 'I'll call you back, Sandy.' He dropped the phone in his pocket and yelled for Morgan to come over.

'Press, Guv?' said Morgan. 'No, I haven't spoken to the press.'

'Well, some silly sod has and you're the only silly sod around here.'

'Not guilty this time, Guv.'

'Did you speak to anyone?'

'No, Guv. Definitely not.'

'Someone with big tits, perhaps?'

Morgan opened his mouth, then shut it again as his eyes widened 'Ah . . .'

'Ah bleeding what?' asked Frost.

'There was this girl, Guv . . . a right little cracker . . .'

'With big tits?'

'Now you come to mention it, Guv . . . and she had this tight sweater on.'

'I don't want to know how the cow was dressed. What happened after you dribbled all over her dugs?'

'She asked if the body was Debbie Clark.'

'And what was your negative reply?'

Morgan pursed his lips and shrugged. 'I just said something vague.'

'Something vague? Like "Yes it is, no bloody doubt about it"?'

'Of course not, Guv. I just said something like . . .' His voice dropped to a mumble. 'Something like, "Yes, we believe it is."'

'*We believe it is!*' echoed Frost shrilly. 'You gave that reply to a reporter who thought she was talking to a bona fide member of the police instead of to a stupid Welsh prat?'

'Reporter? I didn't know she was a reporter, Guv.'

'Why not? Because she wasn't carrying a Speed Graphic camera and you thought the word "Press" on her sweater was an invitation?'

Morgan shuffled his feet and put on his whipped-puppy look.

Frost sighed in exasperation. 'In future, keep your bloody Welsh mouth shut, Taffy. Madam flaming Big Tits went straight round to the Clarks' house and asked for a photograph of their dead daughter so she could splash it all over the front page.'

Morgan stared down at his feet. 'Sorry, Guv.'

'You don't know how bleeding sorry you're going to be,' snarled Frost. 'I've got to go round there now and squirm and apologise to Debbie's mum and dad for causing them this flaming grief and get a bollocking from her loud-mouthed father. You stay here and give no more exclusive interviews to the press.'

'You can rely on me, Guv,' said Morgan.

'You're the last person I can bleeding well rely on,' retorted Frost.

The front door crashed open as soon as his car pulled up in the drive. Clark, his face crimson with rage, bellowed at Frost. 'You! I might have bloody guessed. Detective flaming Inefficiency. Thanks to you, my wife is in a state of collapse.'

'I'm sorry,' said Frost. 'The reporter had no business coming to you.'

'No bloody business,' shrieked Clark. 'She was told by the police that they had found my daughter's body.'

'She made a false assumption.'

'She said she was told by the police, and was surprised you lot hadn't been to us first.'

'She made a false assumption,' insisted Frost again.

Clark slammed the front door shut behind the inspector. 'Don't try to bluff your way out of this. She said she was categorically told this by the police.'

'She asked one of my colleagues, who had not yet seen the body, if it was Debbie. My colleague said, "We think so." She knew he hadn't seen the body so this was conjecture, not fact.'

'This is not bloody good enough, Detective Inspector whatever your bloody name is. If he didn't know, he should have told the reporter he didn't know. My wife is having hysterics. Nothing I do or say can convince her that it was a police balls-up.'

'I can only express my regrets,' mumbled Frost, mentally disembowelling Taffy Morgan.

'*Regrets?* You're going to have cause to regret this. I'm making an issue of it. Now go and put things right with my wife.'

He stamped up the stairs, followed by Frost, and opened the door to a darkened bedroom in which Frost could dimly make out the figure of Mrs Clark lying on the bed. She shot up as the two men entered the room and screamed at her husband, 'Get out! I don't want you near me.'

'The policeman in charge of the investigation is here.' He pushed Frost forward.

Her tear-stained face crumpled as she stared at Frost. 'You've come to tell me she's dead, haven't you? My lovely daughter . . . my baby . . . she's dead. That woman told me . . .'

'I'm not here to tell you that, Mrs Clark,' said Frost gently. 'We haven't found your daughter. We are still looking.'

'But that reporter said . . .'

'We have found a body, but it is definitely not Debbie.'

She shook her head. 'You're just saying that.'

'This body has been dead for at least a month, Mrs Clark. There is no way it can be Debbie. I'm afraid the reporter jumped to the wrong conclusion.'

She expelled a breath and started to cry again. 'Thank God . . . Thank God . . .'

Clark stepped forward. 'Now you've made your pathetic apology, Inspector, I will insist you are never allowed to have any dealings with this or any other serious case again. Now get out!' He flung the door open.

'Why are you so keen for him to go, Harold?' demanded his wife. 'Are you afraid he will discover the truth about your lies?'

Frost looked at Clark. 'What is this about, Mr Clark?'

'Nothing. My wife isn't well.'

'Nothing?' his wife screamed. 'Nothing? He lusted after his daughter . . . his own daughter . . . did you know that?'

'Please, Anne,' said Clark. 'You're not well . . .'

'You're the one who's not well. He threatened to kill that boy, Inspector . . . and he lied to you. He said he was indoors the evening Debbie went missing. He wasn't. He was out. He was out for over an hour. Did you know that, Inspector?'

Clark grabbed Frost's arm and steered him outside, shutting the bedroom door firmly behind them.

'I did not go out, Inspector. My wife is not well. She has mental problems and often imagines things that haven't happened.'

'Are you sure they haven't happened?' asked Frost. 'Lying to the police is a very serious matter.'

'How dare you adopt that threatening tone with me?' snapped Clark. 'My wife's GP is Dr

Cauldwell. Check with him – he will confirm what I've told you. Now get out.' He propelled Frost to the front door, pushed him outside and slammed the door shut.

'I will bloody check,' muttered Frost.

Back in the car, his stomach rumbled to remind him that he hadn't had his dinner yet. He hoped fish and chips would still be on by the time he got back to the station.

'Mackerel salad!' echoed Frost in disbelief. 'What sort of dinner is mackerel salad?'

'It's all we've got left,' said the woman.

'Of course it's all you've got left. No one flaming wants it.'

'Superintendent Mullett always asks for it.'

'I'm talking about normal people. Give me a baked-bean-and-bacon toasted sandwich.'

The Tannoy called him, so he took his sandwich down to the lobby.

'Jordan's brought in that tom you wanted to see,' Wells told him.

Frost frowned. 'What tom?'

'Maggie Dixon. The tom who was hovering round Market Square last night.'

'Oh, her!' He took a bite of his sandwich. 'That cow in the canteen said they'd only got mackerel salad.'

'Sounds fishy to me,' said Wells.

'Ha bloody ha,' said Frost, taking his sandwich and mug of tea to the Interview Room.

Maggie looked distinctly unappetising in the harsh light of day: thick lipstick and mascara and a heavily powdered face gave her an almost clown-like appearance. Her straw-blonde, bleached hair added its twopenn'orth to her unattractiveness. She was none too pleased to have been hauled in at this unearthly hour and stood, arms folded, glaring at Jordan. She transferred her glare to Frost as he entered.

'What's the bleeding idea, dragging me in here? I've got to get ready to go out and earn the rent.'

'Won't take long, Maggie,' soothed Frost. 'Sit down.'

She plonked herself down in a chair, still scowling.

'I'm hoping you can do something for me, Maggie.'

'I don't give policemen freebies, you know.'

Frost shuddered. 'Is that a promise?' He offered her a cigarette, which she snatched from the packet and rammed in her mouth, then she leant over the table to accept a light. Frost lit his too and sucked down smoke. 'You were near a Fortress Building Society cashpoint last night.'

Her eyes narrowed suspiciously. 'Who says so?'

'I bleeding say so. I saw you. Now don't drag this out, Maggie, there's a good tart. The quicker we get this over, the quicker you can be off your feet and on your back, keeping the landlord happy. Now, you were in the vicinity of that cashpoint last night while your client was trying to take money out so he could put his dick in.'

'What if I was? Is it a crime?'

'All I want to know is, did you see anyone use it?'

'Yeah.'

Frost fired off a salvo of smoke rings. 'Now we're getting somewhere. Describe him.'

'It wasn't a him, it was a her.'

Frost's mouth dropped open. A half-formed smoke ring dissipated.

'Are you sure?'

'Of course I'm sure. They don't have to have their dicks hanging out for me to know if it's a man or a woman.'

'Can you describe her?'

'Getting on a bit, dark coat, kept her head down.'

'Can't you tell us more than that?'

'You want a lot for one bleeding fag. I've told you all I know. As soon as I saw she was a woman, I switched off. I don't earn money from women. And talking of earning money, can I go now?'

Frost nodded. 'Take the lady back to where you found her, Jordan, but try not to succumb to her charms on the way.'

'I'll try,' grinned Jordan, 'but I'm only human.'

When they had left, Frost pushed the rest of his toasted sandwich in his mouth and flushed it down with a swig of tea. A woman? He wiped his mouth on the back of his hand and made his way to the Incident Room.

'Let's see the CCTV video of the blackmailer again,' he said to Collier.

Again the blurred, indistinct image shuddered across the screen.

'Could be a man, a woman, or even a bleeding

giraffe for all the good this flaming thing is,' he muttered.

As he passed through the lobby on the way back to his office, Bill Wells waylaid him. 'Graham Fielding wants to make a statement, Jack.'

'Bloody prisoners. Just because they've raped and murdered someone, they think they can make statements any flaming hour of the day or night. He's Skinner's prisoner, not mine. Skinner should be back tomorrow.'

'If a prisoner wants to make a statement, he's entitled to make one, Jack.'

'Stall him. I've been warned to keep my dirty hands off this one and you know how I always obey orders.'

DC Morgan was engrossed in the *Daily Mirror* when Frost returned to the office. He pushed it away hurriedly. 'We managed to get the body over to the morgue more or less in one piece, Guv. The undertaker says you owe him one. Oh – and Mr Harding said to tell you there were no traces of clothing under the body, so he reckons she was stripped before she was dumped.'

'That figures. It makes me more and more certain those clothes we fished out of the lake were hers. As soon as we get some idea from the pathologist as to age, height, how long dead, and so on, we'll try and find out who the hell she is. We've already put out an all-stations request on the clothes, but sod all so far.'

Someone had dumped a wad of papers in his in-tray. He gave the covering memo a cursory glance.

It was from Mullett: *Frost: this is urgent. Pl. attend. SCN Divisional Commander.* Without bothering to see what it was about, he chucked it over to Morgan. He had enough on his plate without any of Mullett's rubbish. 'Get this done, Taff.'

'What is it, Guv?'

'I don't know, but Mullett says it's urgent. Read it and chuck it in the waste bin – not necessarily in that order.'

Morgan turned to the front page, then let out a low whistle. 'It's from the FBI – the Federal Bureau of Investigation.'

'The FBI? They're not investigating my flaming car expenses, are they?'

Morgan grinned. 'No.' He read for a while, then looked up. 'The FBI have cracked a big paedophile ring operating on the internet. They've got the names of people paying by credit card for pornographic images of kids to be downloaded to their computers.' He flipped through the next two pages. 'And some of them live in Denton.'

'Anyone we know?' asked Frost.

Morgan carefully studied the pages before replying. 'No, Guv.' He turned a page. 'Lots of small fry, but there's a bloke from Denton here who's supposed to be a lay preacher – he's spent a packet on child porn over the last few months – well over a thousand quid.'

'Right, Taff,' said Frost. 'See Sergeant Wells. Get search warrants, get a computer expert and a couple of uniforms to assist and bring the bastards in.'

As Taffy left, Frost's phone rang. Mullett wanted to see him.

'What's happening about that paedophile ring?' asked Mullett.

'Being dealt with even as we speak, Super. I gave it top priority as you requested.'

'Good,' nodded Mullett. 'DCI Skinner won't be back today. Some form of stomach upset.'

'Yes, I heard you treated him to a meal,' said Frost. 'You have to be very careful what you eat in these transport cafés – some of them just have buckets for toilets.'

'I took him to my club,' retorted Mullett indignantly, 'as you know damn well, Frost. Anyway, he wants you to keep an eye on his cases, but take no action without consulting him first.'

'Wouldn't dream of it,' said Frost.

As he passed through the outer office, Ida Smith, Mullett's secretary, was hammering away at her keyboard at finger-blurring speed.

'Poor old Skinner,' said Frost. 'He swallowed a bad winkle. Have you ever had a bad winkle stuck inside you, Ida?'

She affected not to hear him. The man was foul-mouthed, uncouth and insufferable. She pretended to be concentrating on her work and typed even faster.

Frost's phone was ringing incessantly as he came back to his desk. *No bleeding peace for the wicked*, he thought as he picked up the handset.

'Jack,' said Sergeant Wells, 'Fielding's brief is here. He wants bail.'

* * *

The solicitor was a young woman in her early twenties, severely dressed, with a big nose, no chest and horn-rimmed glasses.

'I want police bail for my client,' she told Frost. 'He is happily married, runs a courier business which needs his presence and has a full answer to this accusation.'

Frost scraped a chair across the brown lino, dumped the case file on the table and sat down facing them. 'I'm standing in for my colleague, Detective Chief Inspector Skinner. There's no way we can grant bail.'

Fielding leapt up. 'I must have bail. I can't stay locked up here. I've got a business to run.'

His solicitor waved him down. 'Leave this to me, Mr Fielding.' She turned to Frost: 'I understand you have DNA evidence from semen found on the victim's clothes.'

'That's right,' nodded Frost. 'On her dress.'

'My client now admits that he did have sexual intercourse with this girl, but on an earlier occasion. The semen could well have come from that occasion – after thirty years there is no way you can prove otherwise.'

'A good point,' agreed Frost. 'I wish I'd thought of that. Trouble is, she wore that dress for the first time on Christmas Eve – she bought it for a party, so there's no way the semen could have got on it earlier. And to sod your client up even further, the scrapings of flesh from under her fingernails match your client's DNA too.'

She stared at Frost, then at her client, who

wouldn't meet her gaze. She shuffled through her papers to give herself time to think. She had never been presented with a situation such as this at law school. With a last glare at her client, she took a deep breath. 'I might have misunderstood my client's instructions, Inspector. Might I have a few words with him in private?'

'Be my guest,' said Frost grandly, gathering up the file and leaving them to it.

'How's it going?' asked Wells as he passed Frost, who was leaning on the wall in the passage outside the Interview Room, sucking at a cigarette.

'Him and Fanny are concocting a new storyline to prove he didn't do it. I think she raped herself, then strangled herself. How's the paedophile thing going?'

'We got the search warrant you wanted and they're on their way now. Do you think you can trust Morgan with this?'

'By the law of averages he must do something right now and again,' said Frost. 'But I'll poke my nose in as soon as I get Skinner's ancient murder out of the way. Ah!' The door opened and the solicitor beckoned him in.

'We're ready, Inspector.'

He stubbed out his cigarette and followed her back in. 'I'm all ears,' he said, dumping the file on the table and dropping down into his chair.

The woman nodded for her client to begin.

'All right, Inspector,' said Fielding. 'I'll tell you the truth. I was afraid to say it before as it looked bad for me. Yes, I was with her on Christmas Eve. Yes, we had sex, but she was alive when I left her. I swear by my baby's life, she was alive when I left her. I didn't beat her up. I didn't kill her. When I heard she was dead, I panicked. I didn't come forward.'

'Are you saying she willingly submitted to sex?' asked Frost.

'Yes.'

'That doesn't add up, I'm afraid, son. The poor little cow must have been terrified. She fought off her attacker . . . fought like mad. Like I told you, there was skin under her fingernails where she had scratched him. And it was your skin, son. The DNA test proves that conclusively.'

'I'd been with her a couple of times before, Inspector. At her climax she liked to rake your bare back with her nails. It gave her pleasure. It gave me a bit of pleasure at the time too, but it bloody well hurt afterwards. Some women are like that.'

'Yes, some like to bite your dick off, but I've never met any, thank God. So where did you have this back-lacerating sex?'

'Denton Woods.'

'Where in the woods?'

'By the lake.'

'Right, so what happened after you disentangled your lacerated body?'

'I dropped her off just outside Denton and we arranged to meet on Boxing Day.'

'Why didn't you take her home?'

'She said she had to meet someone and they'd give her a lift back.'

'Who?'

'I can't remember, Inspector. It was a long time ago.'

'It's a long time ago now, son, but it wasn't then. When you heard she'd been murdered, why didn't you tell the police the name of this bloke she was meeting?'

'I don't know, Inspector. I think she muttered a name which meant nothing to me and I could hardly make out what she was saying. Perhaps I didn't ask her . . . it was a bloody long time ago . . .'

'All right. Let's say I'm stupid enough to believe you. The next day, Christmas Day, she is found stripped naked, beaten up, raped, strangled, and dumped in a churchyard. The police put out appeals for help. Her parents are crying their bleeding eyes out. Why didn't you come forward then?'

'Because I was bloody scared. I was only seventeen. You don't believe me now. I'd have been lynched if I'd gone to the cops then. They were screaming for blood.'

'I was on duty at the time,' Frost told him. 'I had to break the news to the girl's parents. I'd have lynched you my bloody self. So you're trying to tell me that you had willing sex, had your back torn to ribbons, dropped her off and someone else murdered her?'

'Yes. That's exactly what I'm saying.'

Frost shook his head sadly. 'If I were you, son,

I'd make sure you get yourself a bloody good lawyer.'

Fielding scowled. 'You don't believe me?'

'It's not my job to believe you, that's the jury's job. But if I were on the jury, I wouldn't have to retire to find you guilty.'

'It's true,' Fielding shouted, banging his fist on the table.

'Then be prepared for a gross miscarriage of justice,' said Frost, 'because you will certainly go down for life.'

'My client's story sounds perfectly plausible to me,' said the solicitor. 'I intend to demand bail.'

'My colleague, Detective Chief Inspector Skinner, will be back tomorrow. He will question your client, take a statement and formally charge him. You can then ask the magistrate for bail.'

'I didn't do it,' insisted Fielding.

'Most of the people I arrest say that,' Frost told him. 'Funnily enough, the ones who confess are usually lying.'

He was in the car, driving to Denton Woods to check on the search team, when his mobile rang. It was Taffy Morgan.

'Guv, I'm outside that paedophile's house. We're just about to serve the search warrant.'

'I didn't ask for a flaming running commentary – just serve the flaming warrant.'

'You should hear this, Guv, it's important.'

'It had better be flaming important,' cut in Frost. 'I'm driving and on my mobile. It's against the law. I might have to arrest myself.'

'You'll like this, Guv. Guess who's just gone into the house?'

'Prince Philip?'

'No – better than him.' He paused for effect. 'Harold Clark – Debbie Clark's father.'

Frost rammed his foot on the brake and swung the car into a screeching U-turn. 'Stay put. Don't do anything, Taff. I'm on my way . . .'

7

The lay preacher's house was tucked down a quiet, tree-lined side road. It was an imposing dwelling, ivy clad and with a stone wall running round the perimeter. Clark's car was parked in the driveway by the front door.

Frost drove slowly past, then spotted DC Morgan's car tucked down an adjoining side street. He nosed the Ford in behind it and waited while Morgan and a bespectacled, worried-looking man, whom Frost took to be the computer expert, climbed into the back.

Morgan made the introductions. 'This is Harry Edwards, the computer man, Guv. Clark's still inside. It's that big house round the corner.'

'I saw it,' grunted Frost, holding his hand out for the search warrant to check Taffy hadn't made one of his par-for-the-course sod-ups. All seemed to be in order. He opened the car door. 'Right. Let's frighten the shit out of them.'

Frost switched on his charming smile as the front door was opened by a middle-aged man in a brown tweedy jacket, who blinked in surprise to find three strangers on his doorstep. 'Can I help you, gentlemen?' he asked.

'I wonder if you would mind reading this, Mr Alman,' said Frost sweetly. 'We're police officers and this is a warrant to search your premises.'

The man stared at the search warrant, then looked up at the inspector and shook his head in horrified disbelief. 'I don't understand. There must be some mistake.'

'Could be,' agreed Frost, 'but we have to check it out. The FBI seem to think that someone from this address, with your name and your credit-card details, has been buying and downloading pornographic images of children from the internet.'

The blood drained from Alman's face. He attempted a dismissive laugh and failed. 'It is a mistake, officer. I don't even have a computer.'

'Fair enough,' purred Frost. 'We'll just come in and take a look at the computer you haven't got, then we'll turn your place upside-down, and if we don't find what we're looking for, you won't believe the profuseness of our apologies.' He pushed past Alman into the house, followed by Morgan and Harry Edwards.

'This is preposterous,' spluttered Alman, trying to head them off. 'I'm a lay preacher. I'm about to hold a Bible class.' When he realised that Frost was ignoring him, he raised his voice almost to a shout. 'It's the police, with a warrant to search the house.'

From a room at the far end of the hall came a thud of footsteps, then a lock clicked as someone inside turned the key. Frost rattled the handle. It didn't budge. He turned to Alman. 'It seems to have suddenly locked itself from the inside. Do you have a key?'

Alman made a pretence of trying the handle. 'Oh dear. It often does that – the wind slams it shut and the lock clicks. I'm afraid I haven't got a key – but there's nothing in there.'

'Why do I get the feeling you're not telling the truth?' asked Frost. He stepped back and nodded to Morgan. 'Kick it in.'

Alman moved in front of the DC. 'You've no right to do this!' he shouted.

'Then I'm exceeding my authority,' snapped Frost, pushing him out of the way. 'Give it some boot, Taff.'

Morgan swung an ineffectual kick at the hinge side of the door, then leapt back, clutching his leg in pain.

'Prat!' hissed Frost, kicking hard just under the lock. There was a splintering of wood and the door crashed open.

They plunged into the room, where a semi-circle of empty chairs faced a computer. Debbie Clark's father was bent over the keyboard. On the screen, lists of names were rapidly vanishing. Harry Edwards pushed past Frost and clicked the computer off.

Clark shot a smug, knowing nod to Alman. 'I don't know how I did it,' he said, trying to sound apologetic, 'but I think I've accidentally erased everything on the hard drive. I'm terribly sorry.'

'These things happen,' said Alman. He

stepped back and waved an expansive hand at Frost. 'If you'd like to search this room, Inspector . . .'

Frost groaned inwardly and turned appealingly to Edwards, who beamed back a reassuring smile.

'It's a lot harder to delete things on a computer than one would think,' said Edwards, sitting down and switching the computer back on. He frowned impatiently at the monitor as the computer seemed to be taking forever to boot up. 'Come on, come on,' he urged. At last the 'Welcome' screen appeared, but repeated clicking of the mouse brought nothing else up.

'You need the password,' Alman told him. 'But in all this excitement and upset, I'm afraid I've completely forgotten it.'

'No need to apologise,' said Edwards. 'Nearly everyone seems to forget their password when I'm around. Now let's see if we can jog its memory and make everyone happy.' His fingers blurred over the keyboard as Frost held his breath. Lines of text flashed across the screen, only to vanish and be replaced by more text. Frost hadn't the faintest idea what was going on, but hoped Edwards did. It was taking so long, he was beginning to lose hope. Alman seemed to be sighing with relief, but his optimism was short-lived.

At last Edwards stopped, and pushed the chair back from the screen. 'I've got it all back, Inspector,' he announced.

'What do you want – applause?' grunted

Frost. 'If you've got it, let's flaming well see it.'

Edwards slid the mouse across its pad and clicked away. The screen rapidly filled up with postage-stamp-sized coloured images with text underneath, all too small for Frost to make out what they were. One small picture was selected, a magnifying-glass icon was clicked and the image filled the screen.

Frost screwed up his face in disgust at the photograph of a naked, hairy man forcing a naked child of no more than seven or eight on to a bed. The child was terrified and tearful.

Frost swung round to Alman in disgust. 'So what's your text for today, Father Alman? "Suffer the little children to come unto me"?'

Alman flushed deep red, but said nothing. Clark, pretending to be disinterested, was edging towards the door.

'That's one of the milder ones,' Edwards told him. 'Take a look at this.' He brought up another image.

'Leave it,' cried Frost. 'It might give these two bastards a sexual thrill, but I'm ready to throw up. I've seen enough.' He turned to Alman. 'You, sunshine, are under arrest.'

Clark cleared his throat. 'Look, Inspector, this has got nothing to do with me. I just popped in to visit a friend. I know nothing about these images, so if you will excuse me . . .' He scooped up his briefcase and moved towards the door, but Frost blocked his path and held out a hand. 'I'd like to see what you have in your briefcase, Mr Clark, if you don't mind.'

'I'm afraid I do mind, Inspector,' said Clark. 'This has absolutely nothing to do with me. I came here for a Bible class. I had no idea Alman was involved in anything like this. You may have a search warrant to search this house, but not the property of innocent people who are only visiting.'

'I'm afraid that's where you're wrong,' Frost told him. 'The search warrant covers everyone and everything that happens to be in the house at the time.' He spoke with all the conviction he could muster, but wasn't sure of the facts himself and hoped he was right. The bleeding law was so tricky, but he didn't have time to mug it up. Again he extended his hand. 'Your briefcase, please.'

With a snarl, Clark hurled the briefcase at Frost and looked away as if isolating himself from its contents. Frost opened it. Inside was a laptop computer.

'I wonder what we're going to find on here?' beamed Frost. 'I'm all agog.' He passed the laptop over to Edwards.

The computer man cleared a small table of papers and positioned the laptop. He opened the lid, pressed some keys and little coloured lights flashed. It took less time to boot up than the desktop model. He stroked the touchpad, clicked on an icon and the screen filled with thumbnail images similar to those on the desktop. He enlarged one. Another small child being abused.

Frost waved an agitated hand in disgust.

'Switch the bleeding thing off.' He turned to the two men. 'Well, well, well. Two dirty bastards for the price of one. No Bible class for you, I'm afraid, Mr Clark – I'm arresting you as well. I hope your friends in high places won't get too upset.'

Alman shook off Morgan's hand. 'This is outrageous! We've done no harm. These were bought for our private and personal use. Think we are perverted if you like, but we have harmed no one.'

Frost jabbed a finger at the desktop computer. 'Done no harm? If bastards like you weren't prepared to pay through the nose for this filth, bastards like that hairy sod wouldn't be putting kids through such torment.'

The doorbell rang. Alman and Clark exchanged worried glances. Frost twitched the curtain and looked out. A thin, middle-aged man clutching a laptop-sized briefcase was waiting on the doorstep. 'Another student for the Bible class,' said Frost. 'Show the gentleman in, Taff.' He peeked through the curtains again. Another car pulled up outside and another man, also holding a briefcase, got out and made for the house.

Frost beamed with delight. 'This is like shooting fish in a barrel. I'll have to get some more back-up. I think this is going to be our lucky day.'

Sergeant Wells slammed the cell door shut and turned the key. 'We're going to run out of cells at this rate, Jack,' he moaned.

'The price you have to pay for my brilliant success,' said Frost. 'Five of the bastards. All we had to do was wait for them to ring the doorbell and then run them in.'

'Inspector Frost!' Clark was calling from the end cell. 'Can I have a word?'

Wells unlocked the door and Frost went in. Clark was sitting on the bed, looked deflated and dejected.

'What is it?' asked Frost.

'I know what you must think of me, but I'm still a father. Any news of Debbie?'

'We've got teams out searching now, but nothing so far. As soon as there's any news, you'll be informed.'

Clark's head sank. 'Thank you,' he mumbled, knuckling tears from his eyes. 'Thank you so much.'

Wells closed the cell door and locked it again, then raised an eyebrow at Frost.

'Crocodile tears,' Frost told him. 'Clark is my number-one, prime bleeding suspect. When we find his daughter she'll be dead, and that bastard will have killed her.'

He looked in on the Incident Room, where Harry Edwards was now checking and printing out the contents of the confiscated computers.

'Lots of duplicates, Inspector,' he said. 'They obviously swapped the goodies around.'

Frost had a sudden thought. He unpinned a photograph from the pinboard and gave it to him. 'If she's in any of the downloads, let me know.'

Edwards studied the photo and laid it on the desk. 'Lovely little kid. Who is it?'

'Clark's missing daughter, Debbie.'

The man looked at the photo again. 'But she's only about six or seven. I thought the missing girl was in her early teens?'

'It's the only photo we have of her,' said Frost. 'Her doting father had a thing about her being photographed in case dirty bastards other than himself drooled over her. There might be early photos of her on the computer.'

'I'll see what I can find.' Edwards pinched his nose and rubbed his eyes. 'Some of these are the nastiest I've seen, and I've seen some bloody filth in my time. There's a couple with kids and dogs.'

'Rather you than me,' said Frost.

Morgan was waiting for him when he got back to his office.

'We've turned Alman's place over, Guv. Nothing else, but a few more addresses we can check.'

'We've got enough on our hands with the bodies we picked up today,' said Frost. 'The rest will have to wait.'

'One of them is a doctor,' said Morgan.

'Show me!' Frost took the list and whistled softly. 'Dr Cauldwell! Mrs Clark's GP. The one Clark invited me to contact to confirm his wife imagined things about him lusting after his daughter. Hardly an unbiased confirmation, then. We'll check that sod out first.' He flopped into his chair and fished out his cigarettes. 'Anything else?'

'You'd better see this, Guv,' said Morgan. 'They were under our noses and we nearly missed them.'

Frost took the sheet of bright-green A4 paper. It was the weekly announcement of Alman's Bible classes. He skimmed through it and handed it back. 'So?'

'Look at Sundays, Guv,' insisted Morgan.

Frost took back the sheet and looked again. He went cold. His mouth dropped open and the unlighted cigarette fell to the floor. 'Shit, shit and double shit.' He read it again in disbelief. *Sundays, 2.30 – 3.30. Children's Bible Class.* 'Children! The bastard has kids in there.' He pushed Morgan out of the way and marched down to the holding area, yelling for Bill Wells to unlock Alman's cell.

'We never touched the children,' blurted Alman, white-faced. 'On my word of honour, we never laid a finger on those kids.'

'Your bleeding word of honour isn't worth shit,' roared Frost.

'Look, Inspector,' pleaded Alman in a 'let's be reasonable' voice, 'I'm a lay preacher. My Sunday School is all above board. Yes, I liked being with children. It gave me pleasure, but that is as far as it went. I might have wanted to do things, but I didn't.' He spread his hands. 'Don't you see? If I tried anything and they reported it, I'd be finished. I wouldn't dare risk that.'

'You'd better be telling me the truth,' snarled Frost, 'otherwise I'll personally come in here, ruin my career and castrate you with my bare bleeding teeth.' He stepped back and signalled for Wells to slam shut the door and lock it.

'Do you think he's been interfering with those kids?' asked Wells.

'My gut reaction is that he likes dribbling over photos, but hasn't got the guts to do anything else. But we can't take any chances. I want the names and addresses of all those kids, then I want a team to call on the parents.'

'Where are we going to get this team from, Jack? I've got most of the lads out searching for Debbie Clark and her boyfriend.'

'Scrape the bottom of the barrel . . . use Taffy – and that young WPC, the new girl – what's her name, by the way?'

'Kate Holby. And you can't have her. Skinner's got her correlating the past five years' crime statistics.'

'That's a bleeding waste of time, and soul destroying.'

'I know. That's why Skinner gave it to her, Jack. He seems to have it in for her.'

'Why?'

Wells shrugged. 'I don't know. All I know is he's trying to get her to jack the job in, so he's giving her all the shitty jobs he can find. He had her on a cot death yesterday, and you know how everyone fights shy of them.'

Frost nodded grimly. He'd had his share, so he knew only too well. Parents crying, the mother in hysterics clutching the dead baby, defying anyone to try and take it from her.

'He sent her on her own? We always send two officers.'

'Skinner said he didn't give a monkey's what we always did – she went on her own. As you know, we have to treat all cot deaths as suspicious, so Kate had to get the baby from the mother, and strip it so she could examine it for signs of injury or abuse. Nineteen bleeding years old. She was shaken rigid when she came back. Skinner's a real right bastard.'

'What's he got against her?'

'I don't know, Jack. There's something, but she won't say. Anyway, you can't have her.'

'Yes I bleeding can. She can stuff Skinner's crime statistics. I want her and Taffy to interview the parents. They mustn't mention the word "paedophile" or suggest the kids might have been sexually abused. They can tell the parents that one or two Bible Class pupils think they had stuff stolen, so have their kids lost anything? If the parents have any suspicions at all, I reckon they're bound to tell a cop calling on them.'

Frost looked up as Taffy Morgan and Kate Holby returned to his office.

'Covered most of the parents, Guv,' reported Morgan. 'None of them gave any hint. A couple reckoned their kids had lost money and now think it could have been pinched, but that's all.'

Frost grunted his approval. This was what he had hoped for.

'I'd better get back to DCI Skinner's work,' said Kate.

'Hold it, love,' said Frost. 'I've got something better you can do. You were on the last Fortress Building Society stake-out, weren't you?'

She nodded.

'Then you're on another one tonight. It'll be an all-night job, so go home, get a bit of kip and report back at eleven o'clock for some overtime.'

'But DCI Skinner said—'

'I'm overriding him. He'll take it out on me, love, not you, so don't worry. Now off you go.'

She smiled a loin-tingling smile. 'Thank you.'

He watched her go. 'Cor,' he purred. 'If I was thirty years younger, and a dirty bastard like Taffy.'

But Wells was looking puzzled. 'What's this about a stake-out? I've got no authorisation for overtime.'

'Skinner's left me in charge, so I'm giving you the authorisation,' replied Frost. 'The same team as before.'

'But the blackmailer's already taken the five hundred quid for today.'

'So he'll come just after midnight. Trust me, Bill, I've got one of my feelings.'

'You'll be in the shit if you authorise all that overtime and he doesn't turn up, Jack.'

'He'll turn up,' said Frost. But even as he said it the doubts began piling up and up . . .

* * *

Quarter past eleven. The Incident Room was warm and no one was looking forward to huddling in shop doorways on the off chance that the blackmailer might do Frost a favour and get himself arrested in the act of taking some more money from the building-society account. But the overtime money would come in handy and had to be grabbed while it was going. The red-hot rumour was that Skinner was going to cut overtime to the bone.

Frost gloomily sipped his mug of tea as he surveyed his team. His feeling that tonight would be the night they caught the blackmailer had long since evaporated and he suspected this was going to be another expensive waste of time. Too late to call it off now, though. But they were spread too thinly. Bill Wells had only managed to rake up Simms, Jordan and Collier. Everyone else was involved in the search for the missing teenagers and there was no way they could be expected to stay alert all night, then start the search again at seven the next morning.

Also there, of course, was Taffy Morgan, with WPC Kate Holby, who looked stunning and vulnerable, wearing a fleece jacket over a tight-fitting grey turtleneck sweater and slacks. *She doesn't look more than sixteen*, thought Frost. *Just a kid – who we'll soon be sending out on her own into pubs to break up fights between knife-wielding drunken skinheads, or to scrape road-accident victims' bodies off the road. Just a bleeding kid!*

He glanced quickly at the clock. Twenty past

eleven. 'Right. You know where you'll be stationed. Go and take up your positions, but do it in dribs and drabs. I don't want a coach-load of the Old Bill all turning up at the same time. And remember, we're only there for the stake-out. We turn a blind eye to muggings, rapes, peeing in shop doorways and flashers. We leave them to on-duty uniforms to handle. We don't touch them – understood?'

A murmur of assent.

'Right. If you want to do a wee, do it now, and off you go. If we catch him tonight, I'll buy us all an Indian . . .'

Frost retreated further into the shop doorway as a squall of wind blew splashes of rain in his face. It had been threatening to rain all day, but there had only been the odd drizzle so far. He shivered. It was flaming cold. He looked quickly round Market Square to make sure Taffy Morgan was well concealed. He had given the DC the cashpoint the blackmailer had used before on the principle that lightning wouldn't strike in the same place twice and Morgan was the one most likely to sod things up.

He checked his watch. Six minutes to one. The bastard wasn't coming. He knew it. If he was going to come he'd have been here just after midnight. He'd give it another hour, then call it off. He tried to concentrate on watching the cashpoint, but his mind was whirling with thoughts of the missing teenagers. Three missing and no flaming idea where they were. Were the disappearances associated or was it just a coincidence?

His mobile bleeped. He fished it out of his mac pocket. It was Taffy Morgan.

'No sign of anyone, Guv,' moaned Morgan.

'Then I don't bloody well want to know,' snapped Frost.

'It's freezing cold,' added Morgan.

'We're having a heatwave over here,' said Frost, ending the call and dropping the phone back in his pocket.

He heard footsteps approaching and peeked out. A man with his head down against the driving wind was approaching. Frost stiffened, his hand on his mobile ready to summon aid. The man put his hand in his pocket, took out a handkerchief, blew his nose, then went on his way. *Shit!* thought Frost, dropping the mobile back in his mac. He looked again at his watch. Two minutes to one. *Come on, you bastard*, he urged. *Don't you know we're all cold and flaming fed up waiting for you?*

Running footsteps and a squeal of female laughter. Two men and two women, all giggling, passed by. One of the women spotted Frost in his doorway and made some comment which was greeted by howls of laughter.

Flaming hell, thought Frost. *When did I last have a woman? This flaming job is like a chastity belt – makes you want it, but won't let you have it.* He badly wanted a smoke, but feared that the glow of a burning cigarette would draw attention to the fact that he was skulking in a shop doorway.

Somewhere in the distance a church clock chimed a solitary one. Frost was cold, stiff and fed up. He didn't care a sod if the blackmailer turned up or not. He could have Beazley's sodding money. He just wanted to get back to the station and thaw out. The thought of a hot sausage sandwich was much more alluring than the prospect of capturing a flaming blackmailer. Sod it! If the blackmailer intended to come, he'd have been here by now.

Frost phoned Taffy, who took ages to answer. 'Wake up, you Welsh git. I'm calling it a night. Jordan's going to pick you up – stay awake until then.' Then he called Jordan and Collier and told them to pick everyone up and take them back to the station. 'There's a bottle of Johnnie Walker in my desk drawer,' he said. 'We can kill it while we watch Mullett's overtime bill mount up.' Bloody hell. The thought gave him a clout. The soaring overtime bill and nothing to show for it. He shrugged. He'd face that when it came. Tomorrow, as Scarlett O'Hara said after Clark Gable legged it, was another bleeding day.

The Rest Room was warm and cosy, a welcome contrast to shivering in shop doorways. They sat sprawled out sipping mugs of whisky, half an eye on the television screen with the sound turned off. Kate Holby had taken a sip, screwed up her nose and decided she didn't like it.

'We'll have some coffee soon,' Frost told her. 'I hope you enjoyed your stake-out. They're not all as exciting as this. Sometimes you just stand in doorways for hours and get bleeding cold and sod all happens . . .'

The microwave pinged. Collier took out the first two curries and carried one over to Frost, then slapped a couple more in.

'Well,' grunted Frost, peeling the film top from the plastic container. 'A bollocking from Mullett and Fatso tomorrow, a hefty bleeding overtime bill and sod all to show for it, but at least I'll have about three hours' sleep before that happens.' He dug out a spoonful of curry.

The phone rang.

He paused, the spoonful of hot curry quivering near his lips. He raised an eyebrow to the wall clock. Three twenty-five. Who the hell would be phoning at this godforsaken time? He tried to ignore it but it kept on ringing.

'Would someone who doesn't sound half-pissed answer that bloody thing?' he said. 'It might be Mullett enquiring about our welfare, or Tom Champagne telling me I've won the Reader's Digest prize draw.'

'I'd better do it,' smiled Kate. She picked up the phone. 'It's Fortress Building Society computer control,' she told Frost.

He pushed himself out of his chair. 'Don't tell me the bastard waited until we had all left.' He took the phone. 'Frost.'

'Sorry we've been so long getting through to you, Inspector,' said the voice at the other end of the line. 'But it's been panic stations here. All our computers went down. We've only just got them back up again. Did you get him?'

Frost's heart nosedived to the pit of his stomach. 'Get who?' But he knew bloody well who. Sod and double sod.

'Your blackmailer. He withdrew another five hundred pounds.'

Frost's drink-befuddled brain switched falteringly in and out of focus. 'Which cashpoint?'

'The one in Market Square. The same one as before.'

'What time?'

'Four minutes past one. You did catch him, didn't you?'

'I'll get back to you,' said Frost, slamming the phone down. 'If we'd caught him, I'd have bleeding said so, wouldn't I, you stupid prat,' he yelled at the handset.

The team had gone silent, all eyes on Frost, realising something had gone badly wrong. Frost spun round in his chair. 'He took another five hundred quid from the till in Market Square about a minute after we pulled out. The bastard must have known we were there. Where's Taffy Morgan? He was supposed to be watching that cashpoint.'

They looked blankly at each other.

'He never came back with us,' said Collier after a pause.

Frost turned to Jordan. 'I thought you were picking him up?'

'He wasn't there. I assumed he'd gone with Collier.'

Collier shook his head. 'He didn't come with me, Inspector.'

Frost fished out his mobile and keyed in Morgan's number. 'I bet the bastard's fallen asleep and is snoring his head off in the shop doorway.' The whisky was making him sweat. He wanted to go into the washroom and stick his head under the tap. Morgan's mobile was ringing. 'Come on, come on, you Welsh git,' urged Frost. But it just went on ringing. He clicked off and beckoned Jordan over. 'You sober enough to drive?'

Jordan nodded. 'Just about.'

'Go and look for him. Wake him up gently. A knee in the goolies should do.'

'Shall I check his digs?' asked Simms.

He looked flushed, but in slightly better shape than Jordan.

Before Frost could answer, the phone rang. 'This will be him,' he said, picking up the handset ready to give the DC an earful.

'Inspector Frost? PC Wilson here from Traffic. I'm calling from Denton General Hospital. We've followed up an ambulance 999 call. Bloke found unconscious in the gutter. No identification. We thought it was a hit and run.'

'There's a point to this, I hope,' said Frost, wedging the phone between his head and shoulder as he poked a cigarette in his mouth and reached for his lighter.

'Yes, there is a point, Inspector. When we got to the hospital we recognised the victim. It's DC Morgan.'

'Morgan?' echoed Frost.

'Yes. He was unconscious when they brought him in. The doctor reckons he's been clouted on the head with something heavy.'

'Is he all right?'

'Nothing broken, according to the X-rays, but they want to keep an eye on him overnight in case of complications.'

'And you said there was no ID on him?'

'That's right. Whoever whammed him must have taken his wallet.'

'Thanks,' said Frost. 'You can get back to booking motorists. I'll be right over.'

He replaced the phone and raised his eyes to the ceiling. 'The end of a perfect bleeding night. Unauthorised overtime, the money taken anyway, Morgan knocked unconscious and robbed and I've got a splitting bleeding headache.' He looked across at Kate Holby. 'You're the only sober one here, love. You'd better drive me to the hospital.'

He followed the young nurse through a darkened ward to a curtained bed at the far end. Somewhere in the background a feeble voice kept calling, 'Nurse . . . nurse,' but she took no notice.

'Shouldn't someone see to him?' asked Frost.

She shook her head. 'He only wants to know the time, then when you tell him, five minutes later he wants to know again.' She opened the curtains so Frost could enter.

Morgan lay in the bed, eyes closed, a white bandage round his head.

'Someone to see you, Mr Morgan,' said the nurse.

Morgan's eyelids fluttered as he turned his head. 'Hello, Guv.'

'Not too long,' said the nurse.

'Most girls think it's long enough,' nodded Frost, dragging a chair to the side of the bed. He unhooked the chart from the foot of the bed and flipped through it. 'What does "*Do Not Resuscitate*" mean?'

Morgan grinned, wincing as the effort hurt his head. 'What do you reckon to that young nurse, Guv? I wouldn't mind a bit of that in bed with me.'

'No chance, Taff,' said Frost, pretending to read from the chart. 'It says here "*Nil by Dick*".' He tossed the chart on the bed. 'So what happened?'

'I'm sorry, Guv,' Morgan murmured, putting on his shame-faced expression. 'I let you down.'

'Déjà flaming vu,' said Frost. 'I get the impression you've said that a few times before. So what happened tonight?'

'It was him, Guv. The blackmailer.'

Frost's head shot up. 'What? Are you sure?'

'I nearly had him – I nearly bloody had him. I tried to stop him, but he had something in his hand.'

'His dick?'

'No, Guv. Something heavy. One of those long torches, I think. He welted me round the head and I went out like a light. Next thing I knew I was in hospital and that lovely nurse was leaning over me. I thought I was in heaven, Guv.'

'You're sex mad,' said Frost. 'A couple of tits stuck up your nose and you're away. Now, start from the beginning.'

'Right, Guv. I see him approach the cashpoint.'

'What time was this?'

Just after you phoned me to say you was jacking it in. Anyway, he walks past, looks up and down, then goes back. I press right back in the doorway so he can't see me. He takes the card from his pocket, bungs it in the machine, takes out the cash. Another quick look up and down and away he goes.'

'In what direction?'

'The left, Guv. Towards the car park. As he turns the corner, I go after him. I grab his arm and yell, "I'm a police officer." There was this flash of silver – must have been the torch. My flaming head splits open. I see red flashes, then black . . .'

'Then a pair of nurse's tits,' snorted Frost. 'You should have called in for some flaming back-up before going after him.'

'I know, Guv. But I thought I could handle him.'

Frost heaved a deep sigh. 'I've told you before, Taff. Never rely on your own flaming judgement. Describe him.'

'About five foot eight or nine, dark zip-up jacket, dark trousers, balaclava and a cap, so you couldn't see his face or hair.'

'Marvellous, Taffy. That narrows our prime

suspects down to around fifteen million. He went through your pockets and pinched your wallet. Did you know that?'

'No, Guv. Wasn't much money in it.'

'He was probably after your condoms.' Frost heaved himself up out of the chair. 'I'll look in to see you tomorrow if you last the night.'

His footsteps clattered down the darkened ward. He waved goodbye to the young nurse, who was at a desk writing up some notes. 'He said he's ready for his enema now, nurse.'

In the background the same man's voice whined on and on, 'Nurse . . . nurse . . .'

WPC Kate Holby made coffee as soon as they got back to the station. She seemed brighter and much happier than Frost had previously seen her, clearly glad to be involved and part of a team. He gratefully accepted the mug and savoured the steaming aroma. Most of the team still looked the worse for wear, but were slowly sobering up. They had killed a bottle of whisky between them.

Frost tipped sugar from a packet into his mug and stirred the coffee with his pencil. 'Well,' he said, taking a sip, 'let's look on the bright side. Thanks to Taffy we've now got a bloody good excuse why the bloke got away with the money. And if Taffy dies, we get the sympathy vote as well. First thing tomorrow I want all the CCTV footage you can get. If – which is bloody doubtful – the building society have put in a new tape and cleaned the tape head, we might get a clearer picture of a bloke in a balaclava and a cap, which will do us no sodding good at all. Now I'm banking on him coming to collect the dosh by car. He's not going to risk walking the streets with five hundred nicker in his pocket.'

'He could have come by cab,' suggested Simms.

'I don't think he'd be that stupid,' said Frost, 'but check out all the cab firms anyway. I want details of everyone they picked up from, say, eleven thirty to half past one. One of you do that now.'

Jordan drained his coffee and stood up. 'I'll do it, Inspector.'

Frost grunted his thanks. 'I'll hang on here until you get back.' He turned back to the rest of the team. 'First thing tomorrow, I want CCTV tapes covering all roads in and out of Denton. There won't be much traffic about at that time of night, so I want every vehicle checked out. We're looking for vehicles coming into and leaving Denton at the right times.' He took another sip of his coffee and scratched his head with the pencil. 'Can't think of anything else you should do, but if you think of it, do it! Go and get some kip. We'll start bright and early tomorrow.'

Jordan shook him awake at half past four. No cab firm had any customers during the specified time span apart from a couple of prostitutes and their clients. Frost blinked gritty eyes as he took this in, then decided he was far too drowsy to attempt the drive home. He would sleep in his office and be ready for the CCTV tapes in the morning.

'Get someone to wake me at eight,' he yawned.

8

Frost woke up suddenly and reached out for an alarm clock that wasn't there, his hand flapping in empty space. Where the hell was he? His paper-strewn office desk juddered into blurry focus and he remembered the abortive stake-out of the night before. Gawd. He'd have to face Mullett and Godzilla Skinner about that – and flaming Beazley, of course. He'd forgotten that Beazley would be spitting blood at the news that another five hundred pounds of his money had found its way into the blackmailer's pocket in spite of a police stake-out which was intended to prevent any possibility of such a thing happening.

He shuddered at the thought, then winced as his splitting headache went into overdrive. He had a stiff neck and it hurt him to move his head. The perfect start to the day.

From the corridor outside came the persistent sound of clanging buckets as the cleaners sloshed their mops down the corridor, making the station reek of bleach and pine disinfectant, punctuated by the yells of the drunks in the cells demanding to be let out on bail, and Bill Wells yelling for them to shut up.

'The Denton-nick flaming dawn chorus,' he muttered to himself as he stood up and stretched to relieve the aches and pains in his back. Then he staggered out to the washroom, where he splashed cold water over his face and gave his chin a quick buzz with the electric razor. He studied the dishevelled, crumpled face that peered back at him from the steamed-up mirror and rubbed an easily satisfied hand over his chin. 'Close enough for jazz,' he muttered.

Passing the door of the Incident Room, he could hear the buzz of many voices inside. He opened it a crack and peeked in. Skinner was addressing the assembled search party. He closed it quickly before he was spotted and hurried to the lobby, where Bill Wells, bringing his logbook up to date, looked up and nodded a greeting. 'How did it go last night?'

'A bleeding disaster,' said Frost. 'Taffy Morgan got clonked and taken to hospital, but that was the only laugh we had.'

'Skinner's been screaming blue murder, Jack. He wants to see you about unauthorised overtime and taking the new girl away from the job he gave her.'

Frost sniffed. The siren aroma of sizzling sausages and bacon was fighting its way through pine disinfectant and bleach, trying to lure him up to the canteen for breakfast, but he thought he'd better make a move and get away before

Skinner's briefing ended. He was a bit too fragile to face Skinner at this unearthly hour of the morning.

'I'm off out,' he told Wells, speeding back to his office.

He was winding his maroon scarf round his neck when he heard the clatter of many footsteps down the corridor. The morning briefing was over. The search party was making its way to the car park to resume the hunt for the two missing girls and the boy. He was glad it wasn't his case any more. He doubted Debbie, for one, would still be alive. If she had run off with her boyfriend, she would have let her mother know by now, just to reassure her. He was glad Skinner would be the one to have to break the news to the parents when the bodies were found. The parents. This reminded him that Debbie's father and the other paedophiles were waiting to be questioned, Again, thank God it was Skinner's case. And then there was Graham Fielding, the Christmas killer. But they were all Skinner's concerns, not his. Fatso had some uses, after all.

He opened his office door and his heart sank as he came face to face with Godzilla.

'My office,' snapped Skinner, turning on his heel, not even checking if Frost was following or not.

Skinner's office was sparsely furnished; most of the furniture had been removed, ready for the decorators. Frost sat down opposite a simmering detective chief inspector.

'What the bloody hell do you think you were

up to, Frost? You don't bloody authorise overtime – I do. And what do we get for our overtime money? We get a bloody fiasco of a stake-out and chummy gets the five hundred quid anyway. You let that Welsh twit watch the most likely cashpoint and he gets himself knocked unconscious, but not unconscious enough for us to be spared his bleeding useless company for long . . .'

Frost did his usual trick in such circumstances. He switched off his ears and let his eyes wander over the contents of Skinner's in-tray. He was extremely interested in the 'Request for Transfer' form which lay on the top of the heap of papers. It was the second such form he had seen in so many days. Who the hell was requesting a transfer? Was it the new girl? Had Skinner succeeded in driving the poor cow out of Denton? He shifted his position so he was nearer the in-tray and able to read the details, but Skinner forestalled him by pulling the form from the tray and sliding it into his desk drawer, which he locked. *What's so bloody secret about a 'Request for Transfer' form?* thought Frost.

'You are listening to me, I hope?' barked Skinner.

'Every word,' said Frost, 'and I agree with you all the way.'

He hoped this was the right response.

Skinner stared hard at him. 'And you don't take that girl away from doing my work, do you hear?'

'Loud and clear,' nodded Frost. His policy was to agree with everything, then go his own way.

He slid his chair back and stood up. 'If that's all . . .'

'That's not bloody all,' snarled Skinner, his hand waving Frost back to his seat. But he'd run out of steam. His mouth opened and closed as he tried to think of something else, but he had covered everything in the tirade Frost had closed his ears to. 'Just make sure you obey my orders to the letter in future. *Comprende?*'

'*Absolument pas*,' said Frost.

He stuck his head round the door of the Incident Room to find Collier seated in front of a monitor, watching CCTV footage of late-night traffic the previous night. Collier pressed the Stop button when Frost came in.

'More traffic about last night than we thought, Inspector,' he reported, showing Frost the list of registration numbers he had noted down.

'What do "L" and "V" mean?' asked Frost.

'That means it's a lorry or a van, Inspector. All the rest are private cars.'

'He won't have come in a lorry or a van,' said Frost. 'Concentrate on the cars. We got the tape from the building society yet?'

'There isn't a tape, Inspector.'

Frost gaped. 'Why not?'

'We took the CCTV tape out yesterday for examination. They didn't replace it.'

'You are bloody joking?' croaked Frost.

Collier shook his head. 'I'm not joking. They didn't replace the tape.'

Frost stared at him incredulously. 'The stupid

bleeding sods.' He shrugged. 'Nothing we can do about it except swear, I suppose, and that's not my style. Carry on, son.'

Collier returned to the monitor and started the video again. A mustard-coloured Volkswagen Beetle sped across the screen. Frost's eyes dimmed as he remembered . . . He'd had a mustard Beetle before he was married. He used to take his young wife-to-be out into the depths of Denton Woods. The larks they had got up to in that old car. They were mad about each other then, so what went wrong? Why did it all go sour? Why did she die hating him? Why? . . . Why? . . . It must have been his flaming fault. Couldn't he do anything bloody right?

'You all right, Inspector?' asked Collier, concerned.

'I'm fine, son,' grunted Frost. 'Just fine.'

He told Bill Wells about the 'Request for Transfer' form on Skinner's desk. 'It's not Kate Holby, is it?' he asked.

'Not as far as I know,' said Wells. 'It would have come through me first, surely?'

'Yes,' nodded Frost. 'And why would he lock it in his drawer if it was her?' A sudden thought occurred to him. 'It must be him – Skinner. Perhaps there is a God after all, and he's not staying.'

'He's been on the blower to the decorators, chasing them up to do his office. He wouldn't do that if he was leaving.'

Frost shrugged and shook his head. He'd

exhausted all possibilities. He picked up Wells's phone. 'I'd better ring the hospital to see how Taffy is. I want to find out if I can spend his wreath money.' He dialled. 'Hello, Nurse. Is that the morgue? Do you have the body of a Welshman – little bloke, big dick? You've got lots of little men? Right, I'll hold on while you check the other bit.'

Wells looked concerned, then grinned when he saw that Frost still had the phone rest down. 'You nearly had me going there, Jack.'

Frost dialled the hospital and spoke to the Ward Sister. 'He's being discharged as we speak,' he told Wells. 'I'll go and pick him up.'

He was driving Taffy – who was rabbiting away about one of the young nurses on the ward – back to the station when the radio paged him. It was PC Lambert from Control.

'Inspector, Mr Beazley from the supermarket has phoned. He's heard about – his words – the balls-up last night. Leaving out the swear words, he wants to see you right away. He says if you're not there in fifteen minutes he's getting his money back from the building society and suing the police for the rest.'

'All right,' sighed Frost. 'As he's asked nicely, I'm on my way.'

The customer car park was filling up so he drove round the back to the staff car park. 'Try and look as if you're at death's door, Taff,' he said. 'I want to get a bit of sympathy.'

Morgan stepped out of the car and surveyed the staff car park, then nudged Frost and pointed. 'Cor. Look at that, Guv. I had one of those years ago. Smashing little cars – mine was pillar-box red.'

Frost looked where Morgan was pointing. He stopped dead. It was a mustard-coloured VW Beetle.

He slipped back into the driving seat. 'Hold on a minute, Taff.' He radioed the station. 'Tell Collier I want the registration number of that bilious yellow VW Beetle we picked up on CCTV last night.' He waited, then nodded. 'Thanks.' It was the same car.

'That car, Taff, was logged coming into and leaving the town centre at the time the money was taken last night. If our luck's in, we've found the bloke who clouted you round the head. Let's find out whose it is.'

The brown-overalled delivery man humping empty boxes down the stairs was most helpful. 'The Beetle? Yeah . . . I had one years ago. Great little cars. That one belongs to Miss Fowler – Beazley's secretary.'

Frost's eyes glinted. He was getting excited now. 'A woman, Taff, not a man. That tom said she saw a woman at the Fortress cashpoint. I had an idea it was an inside job and someone who hated Beazley, and that's her to a flaming T. He's always yelling at the poor cow. And come to think of it, she was there when I told Beazley we wouldn't be doing a stake-out last night . . . that's why she took a chance.'

'You need more than a car to prove it's her, Guv,' said Morgan. 'She could have had all sorts of reasons for driving at night.'

Frost bowed his head in thought, then took out his mobile phone. 'If I'd taken that amount of money out, Taff, I wouldn't want to be caught with it on me. You know what I'd do?'

Morgan blinked, thought for a second, then shrugged. 'No idea, Guv.'

'Then I'll tell you, my little Welsh sexpot. You can pay money into those cashpoints as well as taking it out. I'd withdraw Beazley's five hundred quid and I'd immediately pay it into my own Fortress account. Then if I was stopped by a little Welsh prat, I'd have nothing on me.' He dialled his contact at the building society. A quick conversation was followed by a thumbs up. 'She paid a thousand quid into her account just after midnight, last night, Taffy. So who's a clever boy then?'

Morgan frowned, blinked and shrugged. 'I've no idea, Guv.'

Miss Fowler looked up from her typing and smiled a greeting. 'Mr Beazley is most anxious to see you, Inspector Frost.'

'Not half as anxious as I am not to see him,' said Frost. 'But actually, Miss Fowler, it's you we've come to see, and I think you know what it's about.'

'Oh?' Her tight little smile did nothing to hide her concern. 'I can't think what you mean, I'm afraid, Inspector.'

Frost switched on his deceptively friendly smile. 'It's about Mr Beazley's money, love. You were seen at the Fortress Building Society cash-point just after midnight last night, and the night before.'

The smile flickered weakly. She found her keyboard of great interest. Then she straightened up and shook her head sadly, managing a brave smile. 'I knew. I just knew.'

'Knew what, love?' asked Frost.

'I knew you'd be the one to find me out. The minute you walked through that door, I knew it would be you.'

Frost looked around the typing pool. The other secretaries were straining their ears to pick up what was going on. 'Is there somewhere we could go? Somewhere more private?'

'Of course.' She took her handbag from the desk drawer and snapped it shut, but not before Frost spotted the Fortress Building Society pass-book. She nodded towards a frosted-glass door. 'That office is empty. We won't be disturbed.' She stood up and beckoned one of the typists. 'If Mr Beazley buzzes, Lynn, would you see what he wants? I'll be with these gentlemen.'

'How long will you be?' asked Lynn.

Five to ten years at least, thought Frost.

He sat at the empty desk in the office. Miss Fowler sat facing him, while Morgan stood by the window.

For a while she was silent, shoulders sunk, head bowed, staring at the top of the desk. Frost said nothing, waiting for her to speak.

At last she looked up. 'It was to pay that bastard back for all the years of humiliation I've suffered from him. I was loyal to him, but he didn't give a damn about how he hurt people. He's a sadistic swine. I didn't even want the money. I gave it all away. I've given him years of loyal service. You've seen how he treats me . . .'

Frost sighed deeply. 'If there was any justice in this world, love, the court would award you thousands of quid from the poor box for what you did, but there ain't no justice.'

'What will happen to me? Will I go to prison?'

'I don't see how it can be avoided, love,' said Frost. 'The courts don't take kindly to blackmailers. They hate them almost as much as they hate people who smack armed burglars.'

She stared at him, then leant back in her chair and blinked in bewilderment. 'Blackmail? What blackmail?'

'Please don't play silly buggers,' pleaded Frost. 'You know bloody well what blackmail.'

She stared again. Then the light dawned. 'You don't think it's me who's been poisoning the food? You surely don't think it's me?'

It was Frost's turn to look puzzled. 'What money are we talking about, then? You paid a thousand pounds into the cashpoint last night . . .' His eyes widened. 'Don't tell me you've been fiddling the books?'

She bowed her head.

'How much?'

She didn't answer. Her body shook as she broke down and sobbed.

Frost took his handkerchief from his pocket, saw the state of it and hurriedly put it back. 'How much?' he repeated.

She just shook her head.

Frost turned to Taffy Morgan. 'Wait outside for a minute.'

Morgan frowned. 'Outside?'

'Yes,' snapped Frost, pointing. 'The other side of the flaming door. Out!'

He waited until a puzzled Morgan left, then turned back to the woman. His voice softened. 'All right, love. How much did you pinch?'

She wiped a hand over her face to dry the tears. 'I don't know. It's been over years. Something like ten . . . fifteen thousand pounds.'

'Can you get it back without anyone knowing?'

She blinked at him, not comprehending. 'Put it back?'

He leant across the desk and lowered his voice. 'Listen, love, there's only you and me here. If you can get the money back without anyone knowing, I'm prepared to forget all about it.'

She sniffed back the tears and shook her head. 'I've given it all away . . . animal charities, Help the Aged, Cancer Research . . .'

'You got any savings, love, or is there anyone who would lend you the dosh?'

'My savings!' She gave a bitter laugh. 'They would nowhere cover that, and there's no one who would lend me that sort of money. I couldn't repay it anyway.'

'Could you borrow it from a bank?'

'With what security? I don't own my own house. Mr Beazley does not believe in paying lavish salaries.'

Frost slumped back in the chair and shook his head sadly. 'That, love, as we say in the trade, is a sod. I can't help you. I've got to make it official.'

She rummaged in the depths of her handbag and found a ridiculously small handkerchief, which became quickly sodden as she dried her eyes. 'What will happen to me?'

'You'll be charged, then, more than likely, released on bail until the trial.'

'And will I have to go to prison?'

'I'd be lying if I didn't say it was a distinct possibility.'

She let the handkerchief fall into the waste-paper basket. 'I couldn't face prison. I'd rather die – I'd rather kill myself than go to prison.'

Frost kept quiet. What could he say? That it wasn't as bad as people made out? Because it bloody well was, especially for a woman like her.

'There's always a chance Mr Beazley won't press charges,' he said. But even as he said it, he knew it was a forlorn hope. Beazley would delight in putting the poor cow through the hoop. 'Come what may, he's got to know, love.'

He pushed himself up from the chair, pausing on his way to the door to look out of the window at the cars, like toys, in the car park down below. The VW screamed out at him. A less unusual colour and she might have got away with it, at least for a while. Looking down at the Beetle, it once again churned up memories of early days with his young wife. If he had acted differently, or if they had had a kid . . . He shook away the thought, opened the door and called Morgan in. 'Keep the lady company, Taff. I'm off to see Beazley.'

Beazley's lower lip dropped in amazement. 'Pinching my bloody money? Over ten thousand bleeding quid? The bitch! You try and be a good employer . . .' He took an enormous cigar from his desk drawer, bit off the end which he spat in his waste bin, then lit up. 'Well, that's her bloody lot. The mealy-mouthed bleeding cow. Always so high and flaming mighty, and all the time she's been sticking her grubby hands in my till.'

'I take it you are going to press charges?'

Beazley pulled the cigar from his mouth and studied the glowing end. Frost noted it was still connected to his mouth by a thread of spittle, reminding him of the umbilical cord joining a space walker to his spaceship. Beazley stuck the cigar back in his mouth and let a writhing smoke ring drift lazily across the office. 'Press charges? That won't get my bleeding money back, will it? And giving other members of staff time off to testify in court? No bloody fear. She's out on her arse.' He gave a smug grin. 'Ten thousand quid? It would have cost more than that to make the cow redundant. She's out of here – and she can think herself bloody lucky.' A worried frown deepened as a sudden thought struck him. He picked up his phone and stabbed a few keys. 'If I sack someone for misconduct, can we avoid paying them their staff pension? What? Shit!! That's a rule we're going to have to get changed.' He banged the phone down, then ground his cigar into his ashtray and glared at Frost. 'Can you believe that? The bitch robs me and walks out of here with a flaming pension. Get her off my premises now. I don't want to see her miserable face again.'

Frost pushed himself out of his chair and hurried to the door. He was doubly pleased. First, because Miss Fowler wasn't going to prison, and second because, in all the excitement, Beazley had forgotten all about the latest withdrawal of five hundred quid.

A terrible scream interrupted his thoughts.

He dashed to the window. Six storeys down, in between the toy cars, lay a crumpled figure. People were running towards it.

There was red. Lots of red.

He sensed Beazley standing behind him, staring down in disbelief at the scene below.

Frost ran to the vacant office where he had left Miss Fowler, crashing into Morgan on the way. The DC was carrying a glass of water and seemed completely oblivious to the commotion outside. Frost barged him out of the way and flung the office door open. The room was empty. The window was wide open, the blind flapping. Behind him, Morgan was looking round the empty room, puzzled. 'Where is she, Guv?'

'Get an ambulance, you silly sod,' screamed Frost. 'Get a bloody ambulance . . .'

The ambulance took the body straight to the morgue.

Frost sat slumped in the passenger seat, listening to Morgan saying for the umpteenth time how sorry he was. 'She said she felt faint, Guv. She asked for a drink of water. I had no idea—'

'You *never* leave a prisoner unattended,' snapped Frost. 'You should know that. Now bloody shut up!' *Why the hell am I taking it out on Taffy?* he thought. *If she'd told me she felt faint, I'd have done exactly the same thing. I should have warned Taffy. She said she'd rather die than go to prison. If she'd only waited a couple of minutes . . .*

'I'm sorry, Guv,' said Morgan yet again.

'For Pete's sake, shut up.' Frost rammed a cigarette in his mouth. This had all the makings of another lousy day.

'How did it go, Jack?' asked Wells as Frost crashed through the lobby doors.

'Don't bleeding ask!' he snarled.

In his office he thudded down in his chair and looked for something to hurl at the wall to give vent to his burning fury. She said she'd rather die than go to prison, so why didn't he warn Taffy to be on his guard?

He looked up as Wells came in.

'Morgan's told me what happened, Jack. You can't blame yourself.'

'I do blame my bloody self.' He shook a

cigarette from the pack, stuck it in his mouth and passed another one over to Wells. 'I expect there'll be a bleeding inquiry.'

'Bound to be, Jack, but they can't blame you. You hadn't charged her or arrested her, so she wasn't in police custody. They can't blame you.'

'Maybe they can't blame me, but I flaming well do. She said she'd rather die. I should have been on my guard.'

'All right, so she said she would rather die. You had no reason to think she meant there and then. But if there is an inquiry, Jack, I wouldn't mention that if I were you.'

Before Frost could answer, the door swung open and Skinner burst in. He glowered at the two men. 'What's this – a flaming mothers' meeting?' He jabbed a finger at Wells. 'The lobby's unattended. Why aren't you there? And take that bloody cigarette out of your mouth.'

'Just going,' mumbled Wells, snatching at the cigarette and squeezing past Skinner, who watched him scurry down the corridor.

'Bloody useless,' he snarled, before turning to Frost.

'Another of your sod-ups, I understand? A prisoner killed herself in police custody?'

'She wasn't a prisoner and she wasn't in custody,' Frost told him. 'She hadn't been arrested or charged.'

'Hmmph,' sniffed Skinner, as if it made no difference. 'I've got some things to sort out with Superintendent Mullett this afternoon, so I won't be able to attend the post-mortem of that body you found on the railway embankment. I want you to attend on my behalf and give me a report. And try not to balls it up, for a change.' He spun on his heel and left the office.

Skinner was closing the door behind him when the sound of a soft, wet, juicy raspberry followed him out. He immediately charged back into the office to find Frost apparently deeply engrossed in paperwork. Frost looked up, eyebrows raised, as if surprised at the DCI's return.

All right, sunshine, thought Skinner grimly. *You'll be laughing on the other side of your face soon.* He closed the door, waited a minute or two, his hand hovering over the door handle, in case of a repetition, then made his way back to his own office.

Frost was on his way to drag Taffy Morgan from the canteen when Wells called after him, 'Hold on, Jack.'

'I'm in a hurry,' he replied. 'I'm late for the autopsy.'

'It's about the autopsy. Skinner wants the new WPC to attend.'

'No bleeding way,' replied Frost. 'This is going to be a stomach-heaver. What's left of the body stinks to high heaven – it's almost liquid. It would be enough to put anyone off the force, let alone a nineteen-year-old probationer.'

'That's what Skinner wants, I reckon. He's finding all the shitty jobs for her. Oh, and he said to get that stupid Welsh prat to do the archive collation in her place.'

'Stupid Welsh prat?' echoed Frost. 'Mullett isn't Welsh.'

Wells grinned. 'You know what prat he means, Jack. And about the girl – you'll have to take her. You can't ignore an order.'

'All right, I'll take her, but she can wait in the car outside. There's no way she's being subjected to this.'

There were three cars outside the mortuary. Frost parked behind a blue Citroën and Kate Holby made to get out.

'Hold on, love. Sit down a minute.' He handed her his mobile phone. 'I want you to wait out here and take any phone messages.'

'DCI Skinner said—'

'I know what Skinner said, love. Have you ever attended an autopsy?'

She shook her head.

'They're super-shitty at the best of times, but this one is super-shitty de-luxe, which is why Skinner has ducked out of going and sent me instead. You don't want to see it, I promise you.'

She stuck her chin out defiantly. 'I don't want favours shown to me just because I'm a girl. I want to be a good cop.'

'Listen, love, I'll tell you what a good cop does. He does all the lousy stinking jobs that have to be done, but if he can get out of doing them, he bloody well gets out of doing them. I've seen strong men faint at post-mortems which were Mills and Boon stuff compared to this. I've come near to crashing out once or twice and I've seen hundreds. Skinner would love for you to go out cold. Well, I'm not going to let it happen. A good cop can lie his head off when it's necessary. I shall tell him you watched it all the way without turning a hair. His disappointment will make my day.'

'I still want to come inside,' she said stubbornly.

'Then I'm ordering you to stay in the car.'

'You can't do that.'

'I know I can't, love, so I'm saying "please".' He put on his appealing, heartfelt expression, which had never failed him before. It didn't fail him this time. She stayed in the car.

The first thing that hit him when he pushed open the door of the autopsy room was the thudding sound of pop music. Bending over the autopsy table, a green-gowned, plump bottom was jiggling in time to the music. *Flaming hell!* thought Frost. *A bit of a change from misery-guts Drysdale.*

The second thing that hit him was the stench of putrefying flesh, a sickly smell that lingered for days and clung to your clothing and hair, no matter how much you scrubbed. There could be no doubt which body she was examining. Overhead the extractor fans were going full blast, but they were fighting a losing battle. Leaning against the tiled wall, looking as green as his gown, was the forensic photographer.

The pathologist turned at his approach. 'Hardly Chanel No. 5,' she shouted over the din of the music. When she saw that he couldn't hear her, she turned the volume down and said it again. She pointed to a ball of cotton wool and a jar of Vicks VapoRub. 'Stick it where you think it will do the most good.'

He grinned, pulled a couple of plugs of cotton wool, dunked them in the Vicks jar and gratefully inserted them in his nostrils. The pungent aroma made his eyes water, but mercifully overpowered the smell of decaying flesh.

'I started without you – I hope you don't mind,' she said.

'With this one you can finish without me,' he told her. The body on the slab was a disgusting mess. He wondered how she could possibly glean anything from it.

'My name's Carol,' she said.

'Jack,' he told her. First-name bleeding terms now!

The scalpel slashed a path in the neck. 'Hard to believe it, but I reckon she was a pretty girl once,' she said.

Frost nodded. 'I can believe it.' He had seen the rotting bodies of too many pretty girls in his time with Denton CID. 'Can you tell me anything we don't know?'

She gave him a knowing grin and lowered her voice so the photographer couldn't hear. 'I'm free tonight, did you know that?'

Bloody hell! thought Frost. *A sex-starved pathologist propositioning me over a rotting corpse. I'll be dating the undertaker's daughter next.* 'I'll pick you up at seven,' he said. 'But what about the body?'

'Female, eighteen to twenty-three, about five foot four. She probably had quite a good figure. Been dead some four to five weeks, perhaps a little longer. The entomologist should be more precise. She looked after her teeth, so you'll be able to identify her from her dental records and then get a positive ID from her DNA.'

'Cause of death?' asked Frost.

Carol pointed to the neck section she had opened with the scalpel to expose bone. 'Look!'

Frost didn't want to look that closely, but bent forward. Putrescence and slime. He was glad of the nose plugs. Then he saw what she meant and nodded. 'The cicoid?'

'Yes – it's fractured. It would take quite a bit of pressure to do that. Mind you, a karate chop would do it, but the fracturing would be different. It's invariably damaged with strangulation. I'd say manual strangulation, in this case. Even with a cadaver in this condition I'd expect to see ligature grooving, but there doesn't seem to be any.' She shrugged. 'If the body was in any sort of decent shape, I'd be certain, but in this condition I can only say more than likely.'

She beckoned the photographer over and they stepped back so he could take photographs of the splintered neck bone.

The photographer finished and returned to his wall position. Frost and the pathologist moved back to the body. She pointed. 'The neck has been chewed and ripped – probably by a fox – which doesn't help much.'

'Was she sexually assaulted?'

Again she shrugged. 'No way of knowing. I can't even tell you if she was a virgin. She was naked when you found her, but I can't say if she was stripped before or after death.'

'No remnants of clothing under the body when we moved it,' Frost told her.

'Then almost definitely she was naked when she was dumped. The odds are she was sexually assaulted, but I can't give you any proof.'

He tried not to watch as she cut, poked and probed the squelching tissue, but the body was a magnet for his eyes.

At last she straightened up. 'This is a waste of time. I can't tell you any more.' She dictated some notes into a small cassette recorder, then called for the mortuary attendant to remove the body.

Frost waited for the overhead fans to cleanse the air before pulling out his nose plugs. Carol peeled off her surgical gloves and dropped them in a waste bin. She then shrugged off the green gown. Under it she was wearing a grey sweater and black slacks. The sweater was well filled and for a brief moment Frost's thoughts were not of death and decay.

'Seven o'clock, then,' he whispered, feeling quite excited at the prospect.

She gave a conspiratorial nod. 'I'll be waiting.'

Outside, in the fresh air, he lit up a cigarette and inhaled a lungful of smoke. With a cry of disgust he snatched the cigarette out of his mouth and hurled it to the ground. The smoke tasted of Vicks VapoRub. He scrubbed his nose with his handkerchief, but to no avail. He could smell, he could taste, nothing but Vicks. Cursing loudly, he made his way to the car.

Kate was waiting for him. She looked up and smiled, glad her boring wait was over. 'How did it go?' she asked.

'Not as many laughs as I hoped,' said Frost.

The car radio was playing the local news:

> . . . hunt for the three missing teenagers has entered its third day. The officer in charge of the investigation, Detective Chief Inspector Skinner, says there is no obvious link between the disappearance of Jan O'Brien, and Debbie Clark and her boyfriend Thomas Harris, who have not been heard of since they left home three days ago . . .

'Switch it off,' said Frost. 'They're dead.'

Kate turned and looked at him, her eyebrows raised in query.

'Just a feeling,' he told her. 'One of my fallible intuitions. But I reckon they're dead. Stone-cold bleeding dead.' He had had enough of death. He was glad it wasn't his case any more.

'How did you get on with the new pathologist?' Wells asked as Frost passed through the lobby.

'As pathologists go, she's not a bad bit of crumpet,' Frost told him. 'I think she fancies me.'

'Well, after looking at decomposing bodies all day, I reckon even you might look tasty.'

'I'm taking her out to dinner tonight,' said Frost.

'Let's hope she washes her hands first,' grinned Wells.

'Frost!' Skinner's acidic bawl echoed down the corridor and a moment later he strode through the door. 'How is it you're always talking, never working, when I see you, Sergeant?' he snapped at Wells.

Wells quickly grabbed a pen and started totting up non-existent columns of figures.

'How did the new tart like the post-mortem?' Skinner asked.

'She was brilliant,' lied Frost. 'I was ready to pass out, but she never turned a hair – not even when she saw the maggots.'

Skinner's nose wrinkled in disgust. 'She can see a few more, then.' He looked at his watch. 'Mullett wants to see you in his office in half an hour. No excuses, Frost. You be there.'

'What's it about?' Frost asked.

Skinner's eyes glinted and he flashed a malevolent smile. 'That's what you're going to find out,' he replied as he marched back to his office.

'Why do I get the feeling it's not going to be something good?' said Frost.

'The bastard's up to something,' said Wells. 'He's been in and out of Mullett's office all morning. When I took some papers in to him he was on the phone. He cut the conversation stone dead when I came in and didn't start it again until I left.'

Frost remembered the transfer request he had seen in Skinner's in-tray.

'He's leaving. That's what it's about,' enthused Frost. 'The bastard is leaving Denton.'

9

Police Superintendent Mullett, Denton Divisional Commander, nervously drummed his fingers on the polished surface of his mahogany desk. This was the moment he had been looking forward to for so long, but there was no way he was going to face Frost on his own. Where was DCI Skinner? He had said he would be here.

A half-hearted tap at the door made Mullett's heart skip a beat. This had to be Frost, annoyingly prompt for once. The door was flung open before he could say 'Enter' and Frost shambled in, a cigarette drooping from his mouth, ash snowflaking down the front of his jacket and on to the newly vacuumed blue Wilton carpet.

'You wanted to see me, Super?' asked Frost, the waggling cigarette shedding more ash. What the hell was this all about? he wondered. Mullett looked even more shifty and devious than ever.

'Er – yes,' said Mullett, checking his watch. Where the devil was Skinner? 'Take a seat.' He indicated a hard-seated chair he had placed some way from his desk.

'Thanks,' grunted Frost, ignoring the offered chair and dragging a more comfortable visitor's chair from the wall over to Mullett's desk, positioning it next to the in-tray. Mullett hastily took a heavy glass ashtray from his drawer and slid it across, just too late to stop another shower of ash descending on his gleaming desktop.

'Sorry, Super,' grunted Frost, blowing the offending ash all over the place. He leant back in his chair. 'What did you want to see me about? Only I'm a bit pushed for time.'

Mullett fiddled with his fountain pen and patted some papers into shape to gain time. He wasn't ready to answer that question yet. It really was too bad of Skinner. Where on earth was he . . .?

A polite tap at the door made him sigh with relief. 'Enter,' he called and Detective Chief Inspector Skinner strode purposefully into the room, giving a smile to Mullett and a curt nod to Frost.

Mullett waved apologetically at the hard chair he had intended for Frost. Skinner dragged it behind Mullett's desk so he could sit next to the Superintendent, edging Mullett from the centre position.

'If you could kindly spare us a few moments of your valuable time, Inspector,' said Mullett sarcastically as Frost nudged the in-tray round, trying to read the name on the 'Request for

Transfer' form. A bit of gossip to share with Bill Wells.

'Sure,' said Frost graciously, tearing his eyes away. 'But if you could be quick – some of us have got work to do.' He stared pointedly at his watch, then beamed up at Mullett's bleak, worried smile and Skinner's grim frown. Then it was Frost's turn to frown. With a jolt he recognised the wad of papers Skinner was holding. Flaming heck! They were his monthly car expenses, which he assumed had already been passed and sent to County for payment. Today was the deadline. His mind raced. What the hell was Skinner doing with them?

'Are they my car expenses?' he asked. 'They've got to be at County today, otherwise I don't get paid until next month.'

Mullett shuffled some papers again and studied the top of his desk. He looked hopefully at Skinner, but Skinner was waiting for Mullett to reply. 'They're not going off to County, I'm afraid,' Mullett said eventually, carefully avoiding Frost's eyes.

'Oh? And why not?' demanded Frost.

This time Skinner answered. 'Because most of these receipts appear to have been falsified.' He spread them out on the desk in front of Frost.

'Falsified?' shrilled Frost in as indignant a tone as he could muster, while his brain raced through the data bank of his memory, wondering where the hell he had gone wrong. 'Don't tell me those lousy garages have been fiddling the amounts and I've missed it?'

'I very much doubt that it is the garages that have been doing the falsifying,' said Skinner, while Mullett, a smug smile on his face, nodded his agreement.

'And just what is that supposed to mean?' said Frost.

Skinner smashed a fist down on Mullett's desk and the glass ashtray leapt into the air, crashing down in another ash storm. 'Don't come the bloody innocent with me, Frost. You know damn well what I mean. The majority of these receipts have been altered in your favour. And I'm saying that you altered them.'

'If you think that, then flaming well prove it,' snapped Frost, hoping and praying that the fat sod couldn't.

Skinner leant back in his chair and smiled the smile of a fat sod who had four aces in his hand and a couple of kings to back them up. He took a receipt from the pile and waved it at Frost. 'I asked Forensic to examine this one. "20 litres" has been crudely altered to read "26 litres".'

Frost exhaled a sigh of relief. By sheer, undeserved good luck, Skinner had picked the one receipt that was genuine. It had already been altered, so he had been unable to alter it again. 'If you check with the garage, you will find that the cashier misread the pump reading and had to alter it afterwards.' He grabbed Mullett's phone and thrust it at the Chief Inspector. 'Go on. Phone them and ask.' He stood up. 'And when they confirm it, you can come to my office and apologise.' Attack, he knew, was the best form of defence.

He had hardly reached the door when Skinner roared, 'Sit down! I haven't finished with you yet. Then how do you explain this?'

Frost slumped back in his chair and looked at the petrol receipt pinned to the desktop by Skinner's finger. His heart sank. 'What about it?' he asked, knowing damn well that if the bastard had checked he would know too bloody well what it was about.

The bastard had checked. 'A bit off the beaten track, like most of the garages you choose to use, but I took a ride down there. The site was deserted. Elm Tree Garage has been closed for over two years.'

Frost's brain raced, churning this over. Sod it! He'd been getting too flaming careless. Mullett was so easy to fool, especially when he was caught on the hop and made to sign expense claims he didn't have time to check first. Sod, sod and double sod. He'd meant to throw those old blank receipt forms away ages ago. Stupid, stupid fool! 'I don't know how that happened,' he muttered. 'I must have tucked the receipt in my wallet ages ago and got it mixed up with the current ones.' He peered at Skinner to see how this was going down. It wasn't going anywhere!

Skinner was shaking his head. 'With a current date?'

'I probably noticed the date was wrong, so I put a new one in,' offered Frost, trying to suggest it was the most natural thing to do with an old receipt.

Smirking superciliously, and staring at Frost as

he did so, Skinner began to line up a series of petrol receipts on the desktop as if he was displaying a Royal Flush. 'And you did the same for these other five Elm Tree Garage receipts. How do you account for that?'

Frost wriggled uncomfortably in his chair. 'All right. So I lost some receipts and altered some others so I wouldn't lose out. Big deal!'

Skinner scooped up the receipts and put them back on the pile. 'If it had only happened once – or perhaps twice, or even in single figures – I might be disposed to believe you, Inspector Frost, but I've gone back six months and could go back even further. A sizeable number have been altered. By my calculations you've been making almost forty pounds a month from falsified car-expense claims.'

'And tax-free,' chimed in Mullett, who felt he was being left out of things.

'Yes,' agreed Skinner grimly. He turned to Mullett and nodded for him to take over.

Mullett had the grace not to look Frost in the eye. 'I won't tolerate dishonesty in my division.'

'Dishonesty?' exclaimed Frost incredulously. 'What bloody dishonesty? Half the overtime I can't be bothered to claim would wipe this out in a flash.'

Mullett turned in appeal to Skinner. He hadn't considered this aspect. Don't say Frost was going to wriggle out of it, as he always seemed able to do.

Skinner took over. 'You can't write off fiddling like that. Forgery is forgery. If you're too lazy to claim overtime, that's your look-out. You can't make up for it by fiddling.'

All right, thought Frost. *When you've lost, stop fighting.* 'So I might have made the odd mistake. Big deal. If it makes you happy, I'll pay it back.'

Skinner shook his head firmly and again turned to Mullett to take over. Mullett tried to look the other way. He wanted Skinner to continue with the unpleasant side of the business.

Skinner wasn't having any. 'Superintendent Mullett has something to say to you.'

'Oh yes,' mumbled Mullett. 'The, er, point is, Frost, I can't have people on my team who cheat. Paying back isn't good enough.'

'Then what the bleeding hell is good enough?' Frost demanded. 'Do you want me to disembowel my bleeding self?'

Mullett look pleadingly at Skinner, who stonewalled with a shake of the head. *This is up to you*, he signalled.

'This should be reported to County, Frost,' said Mullett at last. 'Much as I am always ready to lay my head on the block for my team, I have no option. It's my duty to report it and I imagine County will suspend you while they go through all your expense vouchers for the past five years or so to find out if there are other discrepancies.'

'They could do you for fraud,' added Skinner. 'Although they'd probably give you the opportunity of resigning instead. They don't like their dirty washing to be aired in public.'

Frost went cold. He could see the bastard was serious.

Mullett seemed to be finding something of interest out of the window, so Skinner picked up the reins again. 'However, you can count yourself bloody lucky that you've got such a kind and sympathetic Superintendent.' Mullett hung his head and brushed aside the compliment.

Frost stayed silent, waiting to see what the two scheming bastards had dreamed up for him.

'I would be extremely reluctant to terminate the career of one of my officers,' said Mullett, 'even though it would be fully justified. But by shutting my eyes to the offence I could get into serious trouble if the truth came out. However, if you are agreeable, there is a satisfactory way out.'

'Oh?' said Frost warily.

Again Mullett looked pleadingly at Skinner, who, fed up with the man's shilly-shallying, took over yet again.

'As it happens, Frost, there is an officer in my old division who would very much like to work in Denton. But that, of course, would require a vacancy here.'

'You want Superintendent Mullett to resign?' asked Frost innocently.

'You know bloody well I don't mean that,' snapped Skinner. 'I am suggesting that you are transferred to my old division, while the officer in question transfers to Denton.'

You lousy, stinking, conniving bastards, thought Frost. He took another drag at his cigarette and flicked the ash in the general direction of the heavy glass ashtray. He kept his face impassive. *Don't let the sods have the pleasure of seeing how much this is affecting me*. He pinched out the half-smoked cigarette and poked it in his pocket.

There was a pregnant pause.

'So what do you think?' asked Mullett at last.

I think you are a pair of shits, thought Frost. Aloud he said, 'I'll let you know tomorrow.'

'By tomorrow morning, first thing,' said Skinner. 'Otherwise Mullett will have no alternative but to report this matter to County and to the Inland Revenue.'

Mullett nodded his agreement, happy that he hadn't had to make the threat. 'That's all, Frost,' he said – but to an empty chair. The office door slammed and the glass ashtray did another dance on the desk as Frost took his departure.

'Well,' said Mullett. 'We handled that quite well, I thought.'

Skinner scooped up the petrol receipts. 'Bloody well,' he said. 'The sod didn't know what hit him.'

'Skinner's old division? Lexton?' said Wells, shaking his head sadly. 'It's a tip, and the Superintendent is a real right bastard.'

'Then I'll feel at home, won't I?' grunted Frost. 'But don't worry, I'm not going to let the sods get away with it.'

Wells looked at Frost anxiously. 'You're not going to do anything stupid, I hope?'

Frost affected surprise. 'When do I ever do anything stupid?'

'Every bleeding day,' said Wells.

'Yes . . . well, I meant apart from that. I've had

a word with Joe Henderson up at County. He says all the old car-expense vouchers are filed away in the basement storeroom. He reckons it shouldn't be too difficult for someone to sneak down there and bung them in the incinerator.'

Wells's eyes widened. 'You're not going to burn them?' he croaked. 'Supposing you get caught?'

'I won't get caught,' said Frost stubbornly. 'An old storeroom full of ancient expense claims. It isn't even locked.'

'But when they realise it's your file that's missing, they'll know damn well who took it.'

'Knowing and proving are two different things. Besides, I'll burn a couple of others as well.'

'But what about the vouchers Skinner showed you this afternoon?'

'They'll be locked in Mullett's filing cabinet. Once he's gone home for the night it won't take me five minutes to nick them.'

'But Jack—' spluttered Wells. The phone rang. He answered it and handed it to Frost. 'Your mate Henderson from County.'

Frost took the phone and listened. His face fell. 'The bastard. Thanks for telling me.' He banged the phone down. 'Skinner has requisitioned my old expenses file. It's being sent direct to him at the hotel he's staying at.'

Wells looked relieved. 'Well, at least it's stopped you from doing something stupid.'

'Yes,' agreed Frost sadly, ramming a cigarette in his mouth. He puffed smoke. 'Tell you what, though. I could get myself a can of petrol and burn his hotel down.'

'At last you're being sensible,' said Wells.

Frost sat slumped in his office chair, making paper darts from the contents of his in-tray and hurling them in the general direction of the waste-paper bin. His aim was poor and the floor was littered with crashed aircraft. Someone tapped at the door.

'Come in.'

Harding from Forensic entered, carrying a polythene evidence bag which he dumped on Frost's desk. It contained the various pieces of severed foot and leg so far recovered.

'I've had my lunch, thanks,' said Frost, giving it hardly a glance. Body parts were the least of his troubles.

There was a token smile from Harding, who was not a fan of Frost's tired humour. 'I thought you would be interested in our findings.'

'If it's from a medical student's dissecting room, I'm interested. Anything else, I'm bored stiff.'

Harding shook his head. 'If it had been smuggled out of a medical school we'd have expected evidence of preservatives. We found none.'

'Shit,' said Frost. 'Are you saying we're talking murder?'

'Not necessarily. It could have come from an amputation and a student took it away for a joke.'

'Terrific joke,' moaned Frost. 'I'm pissing myself. We don't know for sure, so we've got to assume it's murder and start looking for the rest of the bits.'

'I can tell you this,' Harding said. 'It's from a female, aged around thirty-five to forty, perhaps a bit older, and whoever sawed it off had some degree of medical knowledge. The way it's gone through the metatarsal suggests a proper bone-saw was probably used.'

'And how long would the owner have been dead,' asked Frost, 'assuming she isn't still walking around with half her foot missing, but hasn't bothered to report it because she knows the police are bleeding useless?'

'You'd better get the pathologist to answer that. At least a couple of weeks – possibly much more.'

Frost scratched his cheek. 'Give it to Skinner. I'm off all murder cases from now on.'

When Harding had left, Frost resumed his half-hearted paper-dart-throwing. He was dispirited and miserable – he could see no way of wriggling out of this. Lexton! A shit hole! He'd spent all his working life in Denton; he knew it like the back of his hand. He knew the people – the scumbags, the villains, everyone. He didn't want to start from scratch in a new division and, worst of all, he hated the thought that Skinner and Mullett had put one over on him. Why had he got so smug and bloody careless with the petrol claims? He hurled a paper dart savagely at the door, narrowly missing Taffy Morgan, who had burst in waving a sheet of A4.

'What's all this about, Guv?' Taffy thrust the page under Frost's nose. It was a circular from Mullett that Morgan had prised from the notice-board. It read:

Transfer of Detective Inspector Frost

As many of you may know, Detective Inspector Frost will be transferred to Lexton division from the first of next month. It is expected that his colleagues may wish to be associated with a suitable leaving present and your donations are invited.

The donation list was headed by the entry: *Supt. Mullett . . . £25.*

'Twenty-five lousy quid?' spluttered Frost. 'Is that all the lousy four-eyed git thinks I'm worth?' He snatched up his ballpoint pen and carefully altered the amount to read £125. 'Let the bastard try and wriggle out of that.'

Morgan took the sheet and read it again in disbelief.

'But you haven't applied for a transfer, Guv?'

'I didn't have to, Taffy. The bastards have kindly applied for me, and they're jumping the flaming gun.' He pushed himself up from his chair and unhooked his scarf and mac from the coat rack. 'I'm going out to get pissed. If anyone wants me, tell them to get stuffed.'

'But Guv—' pleaded Taffy to a slammed door.

Frost had gone.

* * *

Frost stared blearily at the ashtray overflowing with squashed cigarette ends, then moved his hand ever so carefully towards the glass in front of him, which seemed to be moving in and out of focus on the table. What was the point in getting pissed? It did no bleeding good and made him feel lousy. His head was throbbing and his mouth tasted foul. Pulling an unlit cigarette from his mouth, he laid it on the beer-wet pub table, then swallowed a shot of whisky in one gulp, shuddering as the raw spirit clawed its way down his throat. The rest of the pub was a blur and a babble of over-loud voices that hammered away at his headache. His nostrils twitched. Through the smell of stale spirits and cigarette smoke came a whiff of cheap perfume.

'All on our own, love?'

He raised his head and squinted at the out-of-focus outline of an orange-haired, over-made-up woman in a cheap fake-leather coat.

'Happy birthday Mr President,' she cooed, dragging up a chair and sitting next to him. 'Buy me a drink, love?'

'Piss off,' muttered Frost. He reached in his pocket and flashed his warrant card.

'Bloody hell!' She shot up from the chair and yelled across to the barman. 'Lowering the tone of the place, letting the filth in, aren't you, Fred?' Hitching the strap of her handbag over her shoulder, she marched to the door. The barman watched her leave, then made his way over to Frost.

'Can't you give some other pub a turn,

Inspector Frost?' he said. 'You're driving all my regulars away.'

'Soon,' slurred Frost. 'Very soon, Fred, my old son. Give me another whisky and a beer.' He produced a handful of loose change and squinted at it. 'Have I got enough?'

The barman waved the money away. 'If you promise to leave after I've served you, you can have it on the house.' He looked up and swore softly as two uniformed policemen came in. 'What is this? A flaming police convention?'

By concentrating hard, Frost made out the two men to be Jordan and Simms. He beckoned them over. 'Drinks on the house, lads.'

'No they bleeding well ain't,' snapped the barman as he turned to the uniformed officers. 'Can't you get him out of here?'

'We've been looking for you everywhere, Inspector,' said Simms, waving away the disgruntled barman.

'How did you find me?' Frost asked. 'I'd never have thought anyone would look in this place.'

'You've parked your car across two disabled parking spaces,' said Jordan. 'Someone phoned the station and complained. We recognised the registration number.'

'Tell you what,' said Frost, tapping the side of his nose conspiratorially. 'You go back to the station and tell them you couldn't find me. I won't split on you.'

Jordan shook his head. 'We need you, Inspector. A householder's stabbed a burglar to death.'

'Good for him,' slurred Frost. 'I bet he won't break into any more houses.' He retrieved his wet cigarette from the table and tried unsuccessfully to light it. 'Get Chief Inspector Fat-Guts to do it. He's supposed to be on duty tonight.'

'He's driven on to County to pick up some files. It's got to be you.'

'Excrement!' said Frost, chucking the cigarette away. He pushed himself up and stood unsteadily on his feet. 'Look at me. I'm in no fit state to take on a murder case.' He plonked heavily down in the seat again.

Simms beckoned the barman over. 'Make some coffee. Strong and black.'

'Coffee?' protested Fred. 'What do you think this is – the bleeding Ritz?'

'Just make some flaming coffee,' hissed Simms.

Frost lifted a hand in feeble protest. 'Forget it, lads. Like I told you, I'm in no fit state to take on a murder inquiry.' Then he shook his head and rubbed his face with his hands. 'Shit! When am I ever fit enough to take on a murder case? Skip the coffee. I can throw up just as well without it.' He rose to his feet again, put his hands on the table to steady himself, then pulled his car keys from his mac pocket. 'I'll be all right once I'm in the car.'

Simms prised the keys firmly from his hand. 'You're coming with us, Inspector. There's no way you're getting behind a steering wheel tonight.'

He sat in the back of the area car, being jolted

from side to side as it sped through the darkened streets. He had the window down, letting the slap of cold air try to clear his aching head.

'I hear you're being transferred to Lexton, Inspector,' said Jordan as they slowed down for traffic lights.

'Good news travels fast,' grunted Frost.

'The lads are up in arms about it. What's that all about?'

'I can't tell you,' replied Frost, wishing the pounding in his head would ease up. 'It would involve calling my superior officers fat, stinking, shitty, conniving bastards, and as you know, I don't make comments like that about our beloved superintendent and his fat-gutted side-kick.'

'We'll miss you, Inspector,' said Simms.

'I haven't gone yet,' Frost reminded him.

The traffic lights changed and the car sped on its way. Street lights blurred as the car raced through a shopping area, then more darkness as they turned down a side street, slowing to a stop outside a detached house with all lights blazing. Another police car and a Citroën estate were parked outside.

PC Collier opened the front door. 'The doctor's here,' he told them.

'Why? Is someone sick?' grunted Frost, following Collier down the hall into the kitchen, where PC Howe and Dr Mackenzie, the duty police surgeon, were looking down at the sprawled body of a man wearing dark ski goggles lying face-down on the floor. An open window above the sink made the curtains flap. The carpet around the body was wet with blood. At its side was a long-bladed knife, also stained with blood.

Mackenzie looked up as Frost came in. 'Dead,' he announced. He sniffed. 'You smell lovely, Jack. You didn't bring a bottle with you, by any chance?'

Frost grinned and bent down to lift the head of the corpse and pull back the goggles so he could see the face with its expression of open-eyed surprise. Frowning, he straightened up. 'I know this sod.'

'You should do, Inspector,' said Howe. 'Ronnie Knox, burglary, robbery, GBH. Came out of the nick after doing a three-year stretch last March. You sent him down.'

'Rumour had it he'd got a job and was going straight,' said Frost.

'You shouldn't believe rumours, Inspector,' said Simms.

Frost leant his head against the cool wall and half closed his eyes. The bloody headache kept pounding away relentlessly, like a bass beat at a disco. 'All right. So what happened?'

Mackenzie held up a hand. 'I'm not interested in what happened, Jack. I'll read all about it in the papers. I'm tired and I've got patients to kill tomorrow.' He took a chit from his bag. 'Just sign so I can claim my fee, then I'll be off.'

Frost took the form and the proffered pen and tried to focus on the details. He squinted at the time entered on the form, then at his wristwatch.

'You've put the wrong time down. It's half past eleven, not five past midnight.'

'I get paid an extra ten quid if I'm called out after midnight,' said the doctor.

Frost scrawled his signature and handed the chit back. 'You can get in trouble for making false claims, Doc.'

'Only if you're caught,' said Mackenzie, zipping up his case.

'That must have been where I went wrong,' said Frost bitterly.

The door closed behind the doctor and Frost again asked for details.

'The householder is a bloke called Gregson – John Gregson,' said Jordan.

Frost frowned, then stopped frowning because it made his headache worse. 'Hold on a minute. Gregson?' His memory raced through the database in his brain. 'Little fat bloke, bald head? He's got form – robbery with violence. I put him away five years ago. An ex-burglar is burgled. Poetic justice.' He nodded to Jordan. 'Carry on, son.'

'He's asleep in bed,' continued Jordan, 'when he hears a noise from the lounge. He creeps downstairs, clicks on the light and there's this bloke in goggles unplugging his video recorder.'

'Show me the lounge.'

'Through here,' said Jordan, leading Frost out of the kitchen and into a room leading off the hall. The heavy curtains in the lounge were drawn and a video recorder with trailing leads was on the carpet in front of the TV set. Frost gave the room a cursory glance, which didn't seem to provide him with any flashes of inspiration, so he returned with Jordan to the kitchen.

'Carry on, son.'

'Goggle man barges past him and makes for the kitchen, to get out through that window – the way he got in.'

Frost moved to the window. 'Doesn't seem to have been forced.'

'Gregson said he left it open. He'd brought an Indian in and the kitchen stank of curry.'

Frost stared out through the window on to the darkened back garden, to the rear of which was a tall wooden fence.

'He got over that fence, and through the conveniently open window,' continued Jordan.

Frost nodded. 'So he legs it to the kitchen. What next?'

'Gregson goes to grab him. The bloke suddenly starts flashing a knife – that knife –' He pointed to the knife by the body, 'and starts jabbing. He stabbed Gregson in the arm.'

Frost looked at the long-bladed, razor-sharp carving knife on the floor. 'That's a big bastard. You don't carry that just for getting stones out of horses' hooves.'

Jordan grinned. 'So to defend himself, Gregson grabs a kitchen knife from the worktop and gets his jab in. The burglar slumps to the floor, Gregson dials 999. The ambulance arrived shortly after we did, confirmed he was dead and left.'

'Where's the knife Gregson used?'

Howe held up a transparent plastic evidence bag containing a blooded kitchen knife.

Frost went to the tap and splashed cold water on his face. His head was still thumping and his stomach churning. He wasn't up to all this. He unbuttoned his mac and loosened his scarf. It was bloody hot in here, even with the window wide open. 'Let's have a word with . . .' He paused and blinked helplessly. He had forgotten the bloody bloke's name.

'Gregson,' Jordan told him and led him upstairs.

Gregson – fatter, balder and older than Frost remembered him, now in his fifties – was sitting on the bed, his head in his hands, sobbing quietly. He was still wearing his pyjamas, which were garish purple and bloodstained. His wrist bore a bloodstained bandage. Taffy Morgan, lolling in a chair next to him, jumped up as Frost entered. 'Mr Gregson, Guv,' he said, as if Frost didn't know.

Frost pulled up the chair Morgan had vacated and slumped down in it. 'We've got a dead body downstairs, Mr Gregson,' he said.

Gregson looked up and stared at Frost. 'I didn't mean to kill him. I just don't know how it happened. It was all so confused. I was dripping blood. I was just holding the knife to protect myself. He must have moved forward. I never even knew I'd stabbed him. He just looked at me, all sort of surprised, then slumped to the floor and there was blood – lots of blood.' He shook his head as if to try and erase the memory.

Frost listened patiently, trying to ignore the ominous churning in his stomach. He hoped the bathroom was next door. If it was downstairs he wasn't sure he'd make it. He suddenly realised that Gregson was looking at him, expecting an answer to an unheard question. 'Sorry, what was that again?'

'I said what is going to happen to me?'

Life imprisonment for you and £50,000 compensation for the burglar's family, the way our bleeding law is going, thought Frost. Aloud he said, 'Too early to say at this stage, Mr Gregson.' He sighed with relief as his stomach eased up a bit, then screwed up his face, trying to remember what Jordan had told him. 'He was unplugging your video when you spotted him?' Gregson nodded. Frost beckoned Morgan over. 'See if you can find chummy's car or van. It shouldn't be too far away.'

'His car?'

'He's not walking down the street in the small hours with a video recorder tucked under his arm like Anne Boleyn's bleeding head, now is he? Even our own PC Plods might find that a mite suspicious.'

'What sort of car has he got?' asked Morgan.

'How the bleeding hell would I know?' retorted Frost.

'Then I wouldn't know either, Guv, would I? If we knew where he lives, I could go to his house and ask.'

'No!' said Frost sharply. 'If he's married, or

living with someone, we're going to have to break the news that he's dead and I'm not up to that at the moment.' He could just see himself throwing up all over the bereaved. 'Forget the car for now.' He turned his attention back to Gregson. 'We're going to have to ask you to come to the station to make a statement, Mr Gregson. Put some clothes on and let the officer have your pyjamas. We'll need them for forensic examination.' He paused. What the hell was nagging him? The bed. Of course. It was a double bed.

'Are you married, Mr Gregson?'

Gregson kept his head bowed. 'Yes.'

'And where is your wife?'

Gregson stared blankly at Frost for a while before replying. His voice was flat. 'She left me over a month ago.'

'Oh! I'm sorry to hear that. And where is she now?'

'I don't know. I came home from work and there was a note on the table saying she'd left me and she wasn't coming back. I had no idea. There was no hint . . . I thought we had a perfect marriage.'

Frost shook his head sadly. 'Rotten luck. And now this . . .'

He told Morgan to take Gregson to the station, then trotted downstairs to join the four uniformed men who had made themselves mugs of instant coffee and were drinking, oblivious to the sprawled body on the floor. The window where the dead man had made his entrance was still wide open and the cold air was starting to clear Frost's head. He took the offered mug of coffee. 'Is there anything to eat in this house? I'm starving.'

Jordan looked in the fridge. 'Yoghurts?' he offered.

'Sod that,' said Frost. 'Find some bread and make us all some toast.'

While Jordan began feeding bread into the toaster, Frost filled them in on his conversation with Gregson. 'Probably a straightforward self-defence killing, but let's break all my rules and be thorough for a change. I get a feeling there's something not quite right here. He says his wife left him about a month ago – probably couldn't stand the sight of those bleeding purple pyjamas. Anyway, check that she's not buried in the garden. And knock up the neighbours. They might be able to throw some light on where she is.'

Simms consulted his wristwatch. 'A bit late to be knocking people up, Inspector.'

Frost squinted at his own watch, but his alcohol-blurred vision made it impossible to read, so he nodded. 'First thing in the morning then. And as soon as SOCO have finished, root around and try and trace where her parents live. They might know where to find her. Ah . . .' This as Jordan passed round a plate of buttered toast. For a while they munched quietly. 'Mind how you eat it,' warned Frost. 'I don't want toast crumbs all over the bleeding corpse. And someone wash up afterwards, otherwise the next time he kills a burglar he won't ask us back.' Supersaves own brand of washing-up liquid on the window ledge reminded him he was no further forward with the bloody blackmailer. Tomorrow . . . tomorrow . . . he'd think about what to do about that tomorrow. 'Any more of that toast left?'

Jordan was popping another load of bread in the toaster when the door crashed open. A furious-looking Detective Chief Inspector Skinner was framed in the doorway. 'What the bloody hell is going on here?'

'Bloody hell . . . the filth,' muttered Frost to himself. Aloud he said, 'We're just taking a meal break.'

'A meal break? Looks more like a bloody picnic – and all round the flaming corpse. If the press got hold of this . . .' He jerked his head at Frost. 'A word, Inspector.'

Frost followed him out to the hall, like a schoolboy summoned to the headmaster's study.

'Thank your lucky stars you're being transferred, otherwise I'd have had you demoted and back on the bloody beat,' snarled Skinner.

'I'm only here because they couldn't find you,' said Frost.

'That's no flaming excuse.' Skinner's nose twitched. 'And you're drunk.'

'I'm bloody not,' retorted Frost hotly, but he was conscious this lacked conviction as he was slurring his words and swaying slightly. He grabbed the door handle for support.

'Go home,' ordered Skinner. 'You're off this

bloody case. I'll take this up again with you tomorrow.'

Frost sat huddled in the back seat of the area car as Jordan drove him home. A thousand thoughts were spinning round his head, but he couldn't focus on any of them. There was something wrong, something nagging, and he couldn't think what it was. 'Pull over, son. Stop for a while. I want to have a think.'

Jordan slid the car into a side street and switched off the engine. He took the offered cigarette.

For a while they smoked, Frost's eyes half closed as he went over the events of the burglary. Then he said, 'I think I want to have a word with Gregson again, son. Take me back to the station.'

'Skinner ordered me to take you straight home, Inspector,' said Jordan.

'So who are you going to obey?' asked Frost. 'A fat-bellied sober chief inspector or a drunken sod like me?'

Jordan drove him to the station.

As he sat opposite Gregson in the Interview Room, he suddenly realised how dead tired he was. He stifled a yawn. 'A couple of things about this killing bother me,' he said, 'but I'm sure you can clear them up.' He shook a cigarette from the packet and offered one to Gregson, who declined with a wave of his hand. 'Ronnie Knox,' mused Frost as he lit up. 'He was a classy villain.' He shook out the match and dropped it in the ashtray, then looked up and beamed at Gregson. 'You used to do a spot of burglary yourself, didn't you? Not in Ronnie's class, of course.'

Gregson's head came up with a jolt as he vaguely recognised Frost. He pointed a querying finger.

'Yes,' nodded Frost. 'It was me who sent you down. I collared you and Ronnie. What about that for a coincidence?'

'I remember you now,' said Gregson. 'It was a long time ago. I learnt my lesson in jail and packed it in when I came out. Besides, I was getting too fat to climb through kitchen windows.'

Frost gave an understanding nod. 'But Ronnie kept himself in good nick. Like I said, he had class. He used to stake out these posh houses – usually when the owners were away – went in for jewellery, objets d'art, that sort of thing, not tuppence-ha'penny video recorders. And out of all the houses with rich pickings he could have chosen, why did he pick – if you'll pardon the expression – your shit hole of a place?'

'We used to look for easy access,' said Gregson. 'Like I told the other bloke, I'd left the window open – I guess it was an open invitation.'

'Ah,' nodded Frost knowingly. 'I hadn't thought of that. But there's one other thing. That dirty great knife he brought with him. It was far too big for his pockets and he'd need both hands free to climb over your fence, so where did he put it?'

'I expect he stuck it in the waistband of his trousers,' suggested Gregson.

'Flaming hell, no,' said Frost. 'Climbing the fence with that stuck down his trousers – he'd have cut his flaming dick off. And how the hell would he know your window was open? He couldn't have seen it until he climbed the fence.'

Gregson shrugged. 'I've no idea.'

'And another thing,' continued Frost. 'You said you switched on the light and found him unplugging your clapped-out video recorder? With the lights out and those heavy curtains drawn, it would have been pitch dark in there – and he didn't have a torch.' His headache started playing up again – he was wishing he hadn't started all this. It was Fatso Skinner's case anyway. 'If he climbed over your fence, we'll find wood fibres on his clothes, but I've got one of my funny feelings we won't find any. And once we trace your wife, I reckon she'll tell us that the knife Ronnie was supposed to have brought with him was in the house all the time – which would rather shoot your burglar story right up the arse. Might save us all a lot of time if you told us the truth, don't you think?'

Gregson buried his head in his hands. 'My wife . . . she left me for him.'

'What, for Ronnie Knox?'

Gregson nodded. 'He came round here to collect her things. They were going away together to Spain. He taunted me. The bastard taunted me. I lost my temper. The knife was on the worktop.'

'You killed him, then made out he'd broken in?' said Frost.

'I found an old pair of ski goggles of mine and put them on him. Then I slashed my arm with the knife, put his dabs on it and left it near the body.'

'You didn't stand a bleeding chance of getting away with it,' said Frost. 'As soon as we talked to your wife she'd have blown your story sky high.'

'A wife can't testify against her husband,' said Gregson.

Frost gave a scoffing laugh. 'If you believe that, you're a bigger prat than I thought.'

'What the bleeding hell is going on here, Frost?' Skinner, his face brick-red with rage, had crashed into the Interview Room.

'There were a couple of points—' began Frost, but Skinner wouldn't let him finish.

'Sod your couple of points. I told you to go home. This is my case. Now go . . . *now* . . .'

Frost waved goodbye as the area car drove away, then staggered into the house, dead tired. The little red light on his answerphone was flashing. He pressed the 'Play Message' button. A voice he didn't recognise. A shrill, angry voice. A woman's voice. 'You rotten, lousy, stinking bastard.' He shook his head as he clicked it off. Too tired to worry about it, he climbed the stairs to his bedroom.

He had been asleep barely an hour when he woke with a start. That woman on his answerphone. Of course! Of bloody course! It was Carol, the big-breasted, roly-poly pathologist.

His date. He had forgotten all about her. Sod, sod, and double sod. He groaned as he drifted back into a troubled sleep to dream fitfully of consummation with the naked pathologist, all warm and steaming, big-breasted and hungry-mouthed, hands exploring . . . A moment of bliss, shattered when bleeding Skinner burst in at the moment of penetration, waving those flaming forged car expenses . . . The alarm woke him.

10

'You look bloody rough, Jack,' grinned Wells as Frost made his pale-faced entrance. 'Drive you too hard, did she?'

Frost poked a cigarette in his parrot's cage of a mouth and lit up. The smoke sandpapered his raw throat as he sucked it down. 'The only body I got my hands on last night had a surprised expression on its face and a carving knife in its gut.'

'What – Ronnie Knox? Skinner's cock-a-hoop. He squeezed a confession out of Gregson. He's charged him with murder.'

'Now why didn't I think of that?' said Frost.

'Skinner wants to see you, Jack. The minute you got in, he said.'

'The bloody man's insatiable,' said Frost.

Skinner frowned angrily as Frost sauntered in and flopped heavily in a chair, showering cigarette ash everywhere.

'Please sit down,' he said sarcastically. 'Don't wait to be asked.'

'Thanks,' grunted Frost, the sarcasm just bouncing off him. 'You wanted to see me?'

Skinner pulled open a drawer and took out a blue form which he slid across the desk. 'Your request for a transfer. Just sign it at the bottom, would you?' Seeing Frost hesitate, he added, 'I got another batch of your expense claims from County last night. From a quick look through them it seems there are quite a few other items we could query if we really wanted to be sods.'

Frost withstood the urge to smash the bastard in the face and tried to look as if it was of no importance to him. *You've already got me, you bastards. Why turn the screw?* He scratched his signature at the bottom without bothering to read the form and slid it back to Skinner, who gave it a cursory glance and smiled with smug satisfaction as he replaced it in the desk drawer. Frost dragged down more smoke and mused over painful ways of slowly killing the sod.

'Good,' said Skinner, taking a key from his pocket and locking the drawer. 'Have you put your house on the market yet?'

Frost looked blank. 'Eh?'

'You should be starting in Lexton by the beginning of the month. You won't be able to flaming commute, will you? You'll have to move – buy yourself a place in Lexton.'

Frost tried to hide his dismay. Lexton was even more of a shit-house than Denton.

'To speed things up, I'm getting details of properties for sale sent to you. Nothing pricey – I've seen your place and you won't get much for it. And I've asked a couple of estate agents to contact you about selling.'

'That's very kind of you,' muttered Frost with all the insincerity he could muster. The bastard had him on the ropes, but his time would come.

'By the way, I got that case tied up last night.'

'Oh?'

'It was murder. Knox had run off with Gregson's wife and Gregson faked the burglary.'

'I wish I had your brilliance,' said Frost. 'That never occurred to me for one second.'

Skinner paused for a moment, but decided to accept this as a genuine compliment. 'Mind you, he wasn't very clever. When I went round to Knox's house to break the sad news, who do you think opened the door?'

'Camelia Parker-Bowles what was?' asked Frost.

'Gregson's wife. He didn't stand a chance of getting away with it.'

'You were too smart for him,' said Frost.

Again Skinner stared hard. Like Mullett, he was never sure when Frost was taking the piss. He again decided to give him the benefit of the doubt. 'Thanks.' He looked up as his office door opened, ready to snarl because no one had knocked first, but it was Mullett, who gave Frost his customary scowl, then beckoned Skinner to join him outside.

Jerking his head significantly at Frost, Skinner gave Mullett a quick thumbs-up sign to show that the dirty deed with the transfer form had been done. As the door closed behind them, Frost debated whether to press his ear against the door to find out what they were talking about, or take the opportunity to have a rummage through Skinner's in-tray. He settled for the rummage, but had hardly started when the detective chief inspector returned. Frost pretended he was blowing cigarette ash from the in-tray's papers.

'Superintendent Mullett has kindly invited me to join him at his club later for a celebratory lunch,' he told Frost, pulling the in-tray out of reach. 'And I'm steering clear of oysters.'

'What are you celebrating?' Frost asked, knowing damn well it was his signing of the transfer request.

Skinner hesitated, his mind whirling in search of an alternative reason. 'The . . . er . . . the way I tied up that stabbing case last night.'

'And without any help,' added Frost.

Skinner pretended not to hear. 'Keep an eye on things when I'm out. We still haven't found those missing teenagers and I'm getting bloody worried. Go and see how the search is going.'

'They're dead,' said Frost flatly.

'For once I agree with you,' said Skinner. 'As if we didn't have enough on our plates . . .'

Back in his office, Frost was getting ready to check up on the search parties when PC Lambert from Control came in waving two sheets of paper. 'The body on the railway embankment, Inspector. Manchester reckon it might be one of their missing teenagers.'

'Good. They can have her,' said Frost. 'Wrap her up and stick her in the post. Anyway, you want Skinner, not me.'

'Skinner's gone out. He said you'd attend to anything that might crop up while he was away.'

Frost took the papers. The first was a fax from Manchester Police.

> . . .The body of a girl – Unknown Corpse All Stations Request D107 – could be missing teenager Emily Roberts, 19, reported missing by her parents six weeks ago (Sept 22). Can you confirm time of death please? Photograph etc. following.

The other sheet was a colour printout of a young girl. Frost stared at it. There was no way he could associate the bloated, slimy, rotting body with this bubbling young girl, dark-haired and smiling, showing a perfect set of teeth. 'The teeth look as if they match,' he said, 'but there was nothing left of the rest of her to compare. We're waiting for the Maggot Man to give us an accurate time of death.'

He was halfway up the stairs to the canteen when Bill Wells called him back. He pretended not to hear, but the sergeant was persistent. 'Gentleman to see you, Jack.'

Frost sighed. 'I was going to get something to eat. Who is it?'

'The Forensic Entomologist.'

Frost blinked. 'Who?'

'The Maggot Man.'

'Shit,' said Frost.

Frost wasn't enjoying his meal, but the Maggot Man, bubbling over with his sole topic of conversation – detailed tit-bits about his profession – polished off his plateful with relish. 'When a body decomposes it releases volatile compounds and that's what attracts the flies.'

'Fascinating,' said Frost flatly, eyeing the piece of meat on his fork with distaste.

'Blowflies and maggots thrive on putrefying flesh.'

'Whatever turns them on,' muttered Frost, pushing his unfinished meal away.

'But,' continued the Maggot Man, 'when the odours of decomposition disappear, the flies leave the corpse, so by calculating the age of the maggots and the larvae and working back we can accurately pinpoint the precise date of death.'

'Did I tell you the joke about the bloke who drank the spittoon for a bet?' asked Frost.

'What's up with the Maggot Man?' asked Wells. 'He looked green when he left here.'

'I've no idea,' said Frost. 'He was all right until I told him my joke.'

'Not the spittoon joke – you didn't tell him the spittoon joke?' Wells was horrified.

'I was fed up with hearing about the sex life of blowflies. Who cares how a bluebottle gets its flaming leg over? Get on to Manchester and tell them that the six-weeks death date has been confirmed, so it looks as if we've got their missing teenager – and tell them not to send the parents down to identify her – there's nothing to bloody identify. Send us something for DNA matching.' He buttoned up his mac. 'I'd better go and give the search party my moral support.'

The sliding panel behind Wells slid open and Lambert called to Frost, 'Inspector, phone call from a farm worker – Flintwells Farm – he reckons he's found two bodies.'

Frost picked his way through a ten-acre field of corn, half of it cut and strewn with straw ready for bailing. A cloud of choking dust and the smell of diesel fumes hung over the area, through which he could dimly make out a combine harvester and a tractor towing a high-sided trailer alongside. He stepped gingerly through the stubble and approached the vehicles. A leathery-faced farmer in threadbare faded corduroys and a battered trilby hat was yelling at the driver of the combine harvester, who seemed unconcerned at the tirade.

'Couldn't you have waited until you'd finished the bloody field before phoning the police? We're never going to get it done now before it bloody rains.' He spun round at Frost's approach. 'Who are you?'

'Police,' announced Frost, flashing his warrant card.

'About bloody time,' moaned the farmer. 'Get these bloody bodies out of here so we can finish cutting the corn.' He pointed a thumb up at the darkening sky. 'If that lot comes down before we're finished, I lose the lot.'

'Tough,' said Frost unsympathetically. 'Was it you who phoned?'

'No, him.' The farmer jerked his head up at the combine-harvester driver towering above them both in the driving seat.

The driver, a ruddy-faced, dark-haired man in his mid-thirties, shouted down to Frost, 'You won't be able to see them from down there. You've got to be high up.' He pointed over the uncut corn to the far end of the field, where an embankment was heavily overgrown with bushes and shrubs and straggling grass. On top of the embankment, traffic roared past on the road to Denton. 'There's a naked body just behind that bush between the two trees. There's another body about ten yards to the right. Want me to show you?'

'No,' said Frost. 'You stay there.' The only way to reach the embankment was by trampling across the uncut corn.

'I want compensation for any damage,' called the farmer.

You wait until half the clod-hopping Denton police force come trampling through your corn. That's the time to talk about compensation, thought Frost as he headed over the field. *And a fat chance you'll have of getting any.*

He clambered up the embankment. *Why can't people dump bodies on level flaming ground?* he asked himself, looking back as the tractor-driver shouted and signalled that he should go more to the right.

He nearly tripped over the girl; she was well hidden in the long grass. It was Debbie Clark. She was on her back, naked, staring sightlessly at the rain clouds which were getting darker and darker. He gently touched her face. Icy cold and damp. So what the hell did he expect – warm, vibrant flesh? He shook his head in sadness. Twelve bleeding years old. 'What bastard did this to you, my love?' he muttered. He looked up at the road above, where traffic was speeding past. She had probably been chucked down here from a car or a van.

Pushing his way through the long dank grass which made his trousers wringing wet, he soon found the boy's body. Again, it would have been dropped from the road – it had rolled down and become wedged by the thick stem of a bush, intertwined with bramble. Thomas Harris, fully dressed, also was on his back. There was blood on his face, his trouser knees were jagged and torn, and the flesh beneath the holes was covered with bloody abrasions. His face was badly bruised and swollen. Frost looked up again at the road above. Traffic was still speeding past. No one looking down from the road would have been able to see the bodies – they would have been completely obscured by overgrown grass, brambles and bushes. They had both been dead for days.

He tugged out his mobile and called the station, requesting SOCO, Forensic and the full murder team. As he waited, smoking, the first heavy drops of rain plopped on his head. He shucked off his mac and draped it over the boy to stop the blood being washed away from his face. Within minutes he was drenched.

A thin line of police officers in yellow waterproofs, backs bent, were painstakingly carrying out a fingertip search of the area. The road above the embankment had been closed and more police were carefully searching through the grass verge. Frost, sitting in his car after having returned home to change out of his rain-soaked clothing, watched the forensic team erecting marquees to protect the bodies. He grudgingly admired the efficiency and thoroughness of the operation, but thought it a complete waste of manpower and time. Whoever dumped the bodies would have been in and out of the car or van in a matter of seconds and would hardly have left any impression on an area where junk, accumulated over the ages, was lying thick and plentiful. Rusty tin cans, spent matches, scraps of paper would all have to be logged and grid-referenced, then filed away unread. A waste of everyone's time.

At last the two blue plastic marquees had been erected. 'Starting to look like a bleeding camping site,' muttered Frost as he picked his way over the trampled corn. The forensic photographer was busy snapping in the marquee where the girl's body lay, so Frost moved to the other one, where Morgan, keeping out of the rain that was drumming on the tent roof, was looking at the body. 'No sign of his bike, Guv.

The girl's was in the lake, but no sign of his.'

'If we look for it, all we'll find is more bits of flaming chopped-up leg. Let's start looking for leg – we might find the bike,' grunted Frost, bending down over the body. He lifted a skin-scraped hand, then turned it over. The knuckles were badly bruised and bloody. He dropped the hand, then lifted the head by the hair to feel round the back of the skull. It was wet and sticky. His fingers came away dark with the boy's blood. He wiped them with a tissue. 'He's been hit hard round the back of his head. We're not supposed to touch the body, so try and look surprised when Drysdale tells us.'

'I thought Drysdale had retired, Guv,' said Morgan.

'You're right,' exclaimed Frost, brightening up. 'I'd forgotten about that.' Of course. It would be the roly-poly, bum-waggling Carol Ridley. He hoped he would be able to sweet-talk her into reinstating the promised leg-over.

The door flap opened and Dr Mackenzie, shaking rain from his trilby hat, pushed into the tent. 'You're getting to be my best customer, Jack.' Then he saw the body and his face softened. 'Is it the missing boy?'

'Yes,' said Frost. 'The girl's in the other marquee.'

The doctor shook his head sadly. 'When I see what these bastards do to kids, it always hits me, Jack. I suppose big-head Drysdale's on the way?' Mackenzie nursed a deep and well-nurtured hatred of Drysdale, the Home Office pathologist, who had once tried to discredit the doctor's evidence in court.

'It won't be Drysdale,' said Frost. 'He's retired. Just wait until you see who comes in his place. I'm on a promise of a bit of the other.'

Mackenzie grinned. 'About time they got shot of that big-mouthed bastard. I'd love to do a post-mortem on him – I wouldn't even bother to wait until he was dead.' He dumped his bag on the grass and bent to examine the body.

A voice interrupted from the tent flap. 'I'd be obliged, Inspector Frost, if you would not let any Tom, Dick or Harry maul the body before I've seen it.'

Frost turned his head and his heart sank. Drysdale, thin, austere and glowering, was standing by the tent opening.

Mackenzie stood up and glowered back. 'I don't consider myself to be any Tom, Dick or Harry.' He snapped his bag shut and turned to Frost. 'He's dead. That's all I'm paid to certify. I'll take a look at the girl now.' At the tent flap he paused. 'I don't envy you your bit of the other,' he said.

Drysdale frowned after him. 'What was that about?'

Frost shrugged. 'No idea, Doc.' He nodded a greeting to Drysdale's faded-blonde secretary, who followed the pathologist into the marquee, her mackintosh running with rain. As Drysdale started his examination, she kept well back to avoid being snapped at for dripping rain all over the corpse.

'You're lucky to get me,' Drysdale told Frost. 'I was just finishing an autopsy over at Lexford, otherwise you'd have got that overweight woman.'

'I don't deserve such luck,' muttered Frost bitterly.

'Killed elsewhere and deposited here,' dictated Drysdale to his secretary, her pen writhing over the loops and whirls of Pitman's shorthand. 'Probably thrown down from the road up there.'

Brilliant. Tell us something we don't flaming well know, thought Frost.

Drysdale ran his hands down the boy's trouser legs. 'Both legs broken.' He stared at the face. 'He's smashed up pretty badly. I'd say he's had a fall – and from quite a height.'

'You mean before he was dropped here?' asked Frost.

Drysdale grunted his agreement.

'And the fall killed him?'

'No. He was still alive after he fell.' Drysdale felt round the back of the head. 'His skull's caved in.'

'From when he fell?'

Drysdale shook his head. 'He fell face-down. Look at the abrasions, bruises and blood on the face and embedded grit.' He touched the nose with his forefinger. 'Broken. He fell face-down. He was hit on the head after he fell.'

'How can you be so sure?' Frost asked.

Drysdale pointed. 'See how the blood from the head wound has trickled down over the face and over the bruises and abrasions? The blow to the head was struck when he was face-down on the ground after the fall.'

Frost gave a grudging nod of approval. Drysdale might be a lousy, stuck-up bastard, but he knew his job.

The pathologist had now lifted the boy's arms. 'Both arms broken – from the fall, I imagine – he would have tried to save himself before he hit the ground.' He took the hands and studied them closely, front and back. 'Palms of hands badly bruised and abrased and embedded with particles of small stones or gravel. Arms broken, as I said.' He turned the hands over and stared again. 'Bad bruising across the knuckles and the back of the fingers. They've been hit hard – very hard, but the knuckles haven't broken – by a stick or rod of some kind.'

Frost leant over Drysdale's shoulder to get a closer look. 'Deliberately hit? That must have hurt, Doc.'

Drysdale winced at the 'Doc'. 'The pain would have been excruciating. Death occurred some forty-eight hours ago.'

Frost nodded. 'That ties in with the day he disappeared.' He filled the pathologist in on the details of the disappearances.

Drysdale straightened up. 'I'd like to see the girl now. When your people have finished you can remove this body to the mortuary.'

Frost led him to the other marquee, the secretary in hot pursuit. Drysdale snapped a finger at her in mute summons to provide a small sheet of plastic from his medical bag so he could kneel beside Debbie Clark's naked body on the damp grass. He felt the throat. 'Broken. Manual strangulation.'

Like the other poor cow, thought Frost.

Drysdale's hands travelled down the rest of her body. 'She's been sexually assaulted – brutally assaulted. No sign of semen. Her assailant must have used a condom. How old did you say she was?'

'Twelve,' Frost told him. 'A day off her thirteenth birthday. I'm going to get the bastard who did this if it's the last thing I do. The courts will probably fine him ten quid and endorse his driving licence.'

Drysdale gave a sour smile. 'Have photographs been taken of the body in this position?'

'Yes, Doc.'

'Would you turn her on her side, please. Her hands seem to be caught underneath her.'

Frost called in Morgan to help him and they turned the body on its side.

'Her hands are tied together,' said Drysdale.

'Eh?' Frost leant over. The girl's hands were bound together at the wrists with twine which had cut deeply into the flesh. 'Flaming hell!' hissed Frost. 'Look at her back!'

Her back was criss-crossed with blooded stripes.

'She's been beaten,' said Drysdale. 'With a thin cane or a riding crop.'

Drysdale took temperature readings, which weren't of much help. 'She's been dead some forty-eight hours or more, the same as the boy.' He stood up and held out his hands for his secretary to peel off his surgical gloves. 'Get the bodies formally identified and I'll do both autopsies at three. I've a very heavy schedule. It would be a welcome change if you were there on time.' He snapped his bag shut and, with a curt nod, padded after his secretary back to his car.

Frost followed him out, then clambered up the embankment to the road, where Harding from Forensic was beckoning. Harding, who was taking photographs of a section of the fencing, pointed to a small particle of black plastic sheeting which had snagged and torn off on the rough woodwork of the fence rail. It was dead in line with the spot where the girl's body had ended up.

'That's only been there for a couple of days, Inspector. I'll lay odds the girl was dropped down from here. The body would have been wrapped in black plastic sheeting while it was transported, then lifted from the car or van, laid on the top of the rail, the sheeting pulled away and the body rolled down.'

Frost chewed this over. 'If we managed to find the plastic sheeting, would you be able to say for sure that it was the one used?'

'Without a doubt,' said Harding.

'And there was me thinking you were bloody useless,' grunted Frost. 'There's bits of gravel embedded in the boy's hands. Take a sample. It might help us find where he fell.' He looked down at the lines of policemen searching painstakingly through the scrubland surrounding the bodies. 'Waste of bleeding time,' he muttered, deciding he was of no further use here. He yelled down to Morgan, 'Phone the morgue and get them to pick up the bodies. I'm off to the station.'

'Skinner wants you,' called Sergeant Wells as Frost passed through the lobby. 'He says it's urgent.'

'Right,' nodded Frost. He hoped Skinner would take over and attend Drysdale's post-mortem and would also volunteer to break the news to the kids' parents about finding the bodies, but he wouldn't be holding his breath. He was picking up his mac from the floor, after hurling it at the hook on the wall and missing, when the phone rang. It was Sandy Lane, the chief crime reporter from the *Denton Echo*.

'I understand you've found Debbie Clark's body.'

He obviously hadn't heard about the boy. Good. 'We've found *a* body,' replied Frost warily, 'but it hasn't been identified yet.'

'Is it Debbie Clark?'

'It hasn't been identified yet,' repeated Frost.

'Cause of death?'

'That will be determined when the post-mortem is carried out.'

'You're not giving much away,' moaned Sandy.

'The *Denton Echo* didn't give much away last Christmas,' Frost reminded him. 'A lousy Christmas card and a bleeding ballpoint pen that didn't work. So who got my whisky?'

'Times are hard, Jack. Our budget was slashed.'

'Talking of slashes, I've got to do one, so if you'll excuse me.' He banged down the phone and scratched a match on the desk to light up a cigarette. As he took a drag, Skinner crashed in.

'You were told I wanted to see you urgently.'

'I've only just got in. I haven't even done a wee yet.'

Skinner jerked his head for Frost to follow him back to his office, then nodded at a chair. 'You've found the bodies. Fill me in.'

Frost sat down and gave him the details. 'The post-mortem is at three.'

Skinner looked at his watch. 'I won't have time. I've got to get back to my old division to clear up some loose ends that the prats there don't seem able to handle. You go – and take that useless WPC tart. I won't have time to break the news to the families, so do that as well – and get the bodies identified.'

'Right,' said Frost, getting up out of the chair. 'As long as you don't think I'm creaming off all the plum jobs.'

Skinner ignored this. 'I've had all the newspaper boys on the phone so we'll have to give them an official briefing. Arrange a press conference for six o'clock.'

'You want me to do it?'

'No I bloody don't. This is my case, sunshine, not yours.'

It's your bleeding case when you're in the spotlight, thought Frost, *not when it comes to attending bloody post-mortems and telling people their kids are dead.*

'I'll be back in good time, so you can update me on the post-mortem results. You're just doing a watching brief.'

'I like watching briefs,' said Frost, 'especially on half-naked women.'

'You think you're so bloody funny, don't you?' snarled Skinner.

'I'm my greatest fan,' said Frost.

As he closed the door behind him, Frost paused. Identification of the bodies. Shit. Who the hell should he get for the girl? The mother was in no fit state and the father was banged up on paedophile charges. Sod it. It would have to be the father. Well, no point in delaying telling him his daughter was dead. But even though there was no point in delaying, he lit up another cigarette and sucked hard on it, before summoning up the resolve to break the news.

The cigarette dangling from his mouth, he looked into the Incident Room where Harry Edwards, the computer man, was printing out the downloaded photographs of child pornography recovered from the various houses of the prisoners. He looked up as Frost came in and shook his head in disgust. 'I don't know how much more of this I can take, Inspector. I've got kids of my own.'

Frost nodded sympathetically and idly picked up one of the printouts. It showed a young girl of around four or five, wearing only a vest, seated on a chair with her legs parted.

'How can anyone get a kick out of looking at an innocent kid like that?' asked Edwards bitterly.

Frost nodded. He was about to toss the photograph back on the pile when he paused and looked closer. Behind the child was a window with nursery-rhyme curtains. The curtains were open and the garden outside could be seen clearly. He had looked through that same window on to that same garden only two days ago. The nursery was now Debbie Clark's room. The four-year-old was her.

'They've all got one of those photos on their laptops,' said Edwards, noticing Frost's interest.

The bastard! seethed Frost to himself. *Drooling over his own four-year-old daughter with the rest of those dirty sods*. 'I'll borrow this,' he said, stuffing it into his pocket.

Clark, who had been sitting hunched up on his bunk, jumped up angrily as Frost came into the cell. 'When am I going to be let out of here?' he demanded.

'Depends on whether the magistrate grants you bail,' Frost told him, his hand closing on the photograph in his pocket. Not perhaps the time to bring it out. 'I'm afraid I've got some very bad news for you, Mr Clark.'

'Bad news?' shouted Clark, still angry. 'I . . .' He stopped and the colour seeped from his face. 'You mean . . .?' He forced himself to say it. 'Debbie?'

Frost nodded. He'd lost count of the number of times he had had to break news like this, but it never got any easier. 'We've found a body.'

Clark just stared, his mouth gaping open, then he began to shake his head vigorously. 'No . . . no . . . Please . . . no . . .'

'We're pretty certain it's Debbie, I'm afraid, but we need formal identification. Do you feel up to it?'

Clark collapsed on to the bunk, covering his face with his hands, his shoulders shaking. 'This will kill my wife.'

'Would you break the news to her?' asked Frost hopefully. *Please*, he silently pleaded. It was an ordeal he didn't want to have to go through.

Clark's head shake was emphatic. 'She hates me. She'll blame me . . . I couldn't . . .'

Shit! thought Frost. *That bastard Skinner* . . .

Clark raised a tear-stained face. 'How did she die?'

Again Frost's hand touched the print in his pocket. Were these crocodile tears? *Did you get the other dirty bastards to give you an alibi for the night she went missing? Did you kill your own daughter for fear she would tell people what you had been doing to her, and then the boy to keep his mouth shut?* 'We believe she was strangled. There will be a post-mortem.' He didn't want to disclose any other details at this stage. There was always a chance that Clark might blurt out something he shouldn't know about. Frost wound his scarf around his neck. 'So if you're ready, Mr Clark . . . ?'

He went to the cell door and yelled for Bill Wells to let them out.

The mortuary attendant, with skill born of much practice, surreptitiously parked his chewing gum under the desktop and slid his dog-eared copy of *Playboy* under some papers before opening the door to Frost and Clark.

They followed him through to the refrigerated section. He pulled open a newly labelled drawer, folded back the covering sheet and stepped respectfully back.

Clark steeled himself to look. He stared, bit his lip and shuddered, then nodded.

'Debbie?' whispered Frost.

Again Clark nodded. 'Yes.' He moved his hands to caress the face.

'Don't touch her,' yelled Frost, making the father start and jerk back. If this bastard had indeed killed his daughter, he didn't want evidence on the body to be jeopardised because Clark had mauled her. 'Don't touch her,' repeated Frost, more gently, but more firmly.

'I can't touch my own daughter?'

'Not at this stage,' said Frost, pulling him back and nodding for the attendant to close the drawer. He shivered at the burst of refrigerated air that was expelled as the drawer slid home.

Clark straightened up and shook Frost's hand off. 'Who did this? Who did this to my little girl?'

Frost stared back at him, hoping to see some vestige of guilt, but Clark wouldn't meet his gaze. 'We'll get the bastard who did this, Mr

Clark,' said Frost emphatically. 'I promise you. We'll get the bastard, whoever he may be.' The print in his mac pocket crackled. What should be his next Skinner-donated treat – to confront Clark with the photograph or break the news to the girl's mother? Breaking the news to the mother would be the greater hell, so he decided to get the worst over first.

Frost had taken Clark back to his cell and had been sitting outside the house for nearly half an hour, smoking cigarette after cigarette, trying to pluck up the courage to walk up that drive and knock on the door. '*I'm terribly sorry, Mrs Clark . . . I'm terribly sorry, Mrs Clark . . .*' He kept muttering the words to himself as if repetition would make them come out any easier. He had brought WPC Kate Holby with him, but was not setting her a good example. She sensed his anxiety and sat in the seat next to him, saying nothing. 'You never bloody get used to it,' said Frost. 'Sod it. It has to be done, so let's sodding well do it.' He snatched the cigarette from his mouth, crushed it and stepped out of the car. 'Here we go then. Over the bleeding top.'

It was even worse than he had feared. She screamed, she cried, she became hysterical, pounding him with her fists. Then she insisted on being taken to the mortuary to see the body, and when she saw it, her grief was uncontrollable and her body-racking sobs and screams echoed round the empty building. *Enough to wake the bleeding dead*, thought Frost. He could see that Kate Holby was even more shattered than he was and wished he hadn't asked her to accompany him, but the poor cow had to get used to the joys of policing in case she thought it was all bleeding fun and games. He tried to catch her eye, then decided a reassuring smile would be out of place. He felt so shattered, he wanted to get outside, away from the piercing screams that were drilling holes through his skull.

Mrs Clark's tears were now splashing down on the cold, white face of her daughter. Frost decided enough was enough. He put his arm around her and drew her back, motioning for the mortuary attendant to cover the face and close the drawer. 'Come on, love,' he soothed. 'Let's get you home.'

Angrily she shook his arm away. 'He killed her. That perverted bastard of a husband of mine killed her . . . his own daughter . . .'

'If he did, we'll get him,' said Frost.

'*If?*' she screamed. 'What do you mean, *if*? Of course he did it. He lusted after her. He took photographs . . .'

They managed to get her back to the car, where she resisted all the efforts of the WPC to comfort her. 'I'll kill him,' she kept muttering. 'If he comes near me, I'll kill him, so help me . . .'

They dropped her back home. She didn't want anyone with her. Her hands were shaking so much she couldn't get the key in the door. Frost took it from her and turned it in the lock. She barged past him, slamming the door shut on them without a word. He could still hear her screams and sobs as he walked back to the car. He slid into the passenger seat and told Kate to drive to the boy's parents' home. God, this was a sod of a day.

Drained and washed out, Frost staggered back to his office with a ham roll and a mug of tea from the canteen. Sandy Lane was in the visitors' chair, waiting for him; he pointed to two bottles of whisky on the desk. 'Merry last Christmas,' he said.

'If I had any strength of character, I'd refuse them,' said Frost, picking one up and surveying the label. 'I'll hide them away before anyone sees how cheaply I can be bought.' He pulled open a drawer and dropped them in. 'So what do you want to know?'

'Was it the missing girl – Debbie Clark?'

Frost nodded.

'Cause of death?'

'Some bastard raped her, flogged her and strangled her, but that's off the record until the post-mortem. You can say we're treating this as a murder inquiry.'

'And the boy?'

'Skull caved in, but that's not official until after the PM.'

'I'm told you've arrested Debbie's father.'

'On an entirely different matter, Sandy. Keep him out of it.'

'Are you going to charge him with possession of obscene photographs?'

'You've had all that two bottles of cheap whisky can buy. Be satisfied.'

'When will you be making the official press statement?'

'Skinner's doing that. It's laid on for six o'clock tonight, I think. Now clear off.'

Sandy rose from the chair. 'For those few meagre crumbs, my half-hearted thanks. Enjoy the whisky.'

'Whisky? What whisky?' asked Frost innocently, kneeing the drawer shut. As he took a bite of his ham roll, the phone rang. It was Mullett.

'I understand we've found two bodies, Frost – the boy and the girl.'

'That's right, Super.'

'Still no trace of the other girl?'

'Not a trace.'

'Right. I understand you've arranged a press conference for six o'clock tonight. I don't want you there. I'll be dealing with that.' There was no way he was going to let slummocky Frost appear on the nation's TV screens, with his scruffy mac and cigarette drooping from his lips, as a representative of Denton division.

Mullett clearly didn't know that Skinner intended doing the conference. Frost decided not to tell him. 'Right you are, Super.'

'Put all the details on my desk and ask my secretary to get my best uniform from the dry-cleaner's.'

No sooner had Frost banged the phone down than it rang again. This time it was Bill Wells.

'Drysdale's screaming blue murder down at the morgue, Jack. He seems to think you ought to be there.'

Frost looked at his watch and groaned. Ten past flaming three. Shit. 'Tell him I'm on my way.'

There was a tap at the door and an agitated WPC Holby looked in. 'We're going to be late for the autopsies, Inspector.'

Frost grimaced. He had forgotten that Skinner had ordered her to attend. 'Look, love, I know what Skinner said, but—'

She cut him short. 'I don't want to be molly-coddled. If it's part of the job, then I've got to do it.'

'All right, then,' sighed Frost. 'But if at any time you feel you want to walk out, do it – you won't be the first, or the last.'

'I won't walk out,' she said. 'I won't give him the satisfaction.'

'What's he got against you?' asked Frost.

She hesitated. 'My father was in the same division as DCI Skinner when they were both inspectors. He wanted my father to lie in court about some evidence supposed to have been found in a suspect's house. My father refused and the suspect got off. Skinner never forgets a grudge. Getting at me is his way of getting his own back on my father.'

'The man's a bastard,' said Frost. 'The trouble is, he's a bastard who's a chief inspector and you're only a probationer constable. He's got the edge. He could tell lies about you and he'd be believed; you could tell the truth about him and you wouldn't be.' God, he wished he wasn't going to be kicked out of Denton. He'd like to be able to stay and keep an eye on the girl, if only to spite Skinner. He had to find some way to foil the bastard. 'Look – why not apply for a transfer? Come with me to Lexton.'

She shook her head defiantly. 'There's no way I'm going to run away from him. He would consider that a victory.'

'It sometimes pays to run away, and come back and fight when the odds are better.' But he was wasting his breath. She was as stubborn as he was. He would never run away, even if it was the most sensible thing to do – sensible things to do weren't his style.

'I'm staying,' she said.

'Good for you, girl,' said Frost. Bloody hell, if a flaming nineteen-year-old kid could do it . . . 'If I can find a way to do the bastard down, I'm staying as well.'

11

Drysdale's frigid glare lowered the chill factor of the autopsy room by several degrees as Frost and WPC Holby entered. 'It would be an agreeable surprise if you were on time for once, Inspector.'

'I hate giving people surprises, Doc,' said Frost, pulling on the obligatory green gown. He rubbed his forehead. The cold of the room was making his scar ache.

Debbie, lying open-eyed and naked on the autopsy table, looked so small and vulnerable. Frost turned his head away as Drysdale selected a scalpel and made the first incision in the bluish-white flesh of the neck, muttering his standard running commentary to his green-gowned secretary, whose pen skimmed over her notebook, recording the words almost before Drysdale spoke them. This was just routine to them. It should have been routine for Frost, but he could never get used to it, especially when young kids were involved. His ears were still ringing from the mother's heart-wrenching screams of despair.

He let his eyes travel round the room: harsh neon lights burning down on the autopsy tables; green-tiled walls; the blue flicker of the electric insect-killers, of more use in hot weather than now. Somewhere a tap was dripping. There always seemed to be a dripping tap, plop-plop-plopping into a stainless-steel sink. Two autopsy tables. Two bodies. Two for the price of one. That tasteless thought reminded him of the supermarket and the blackmailer, now stuck on the back-burner. What the hell was he going to do about that? The thought was chopped short as he realised all eyes were on him. Drysdale, looking annoyed, had asked him something and was waiting for an answer.

'Sorry, Doc. I was miles away.'

Drysdale raised his eyes to the heavens and expelled a theatrical sigh. 'Sorry I'm not holding your attention, Inspector, but I ventured to ask if the bodies had been formally identified.'

'Yes, Doc. Both of them.'

'I asked because that specific section of the "Autopsy Request" form had been left blank and my mind-reading ability is not at its best today.'

'That's all right, Doc,' said Frost grandly. 'We all have our off-days.' He quickly filled in the form and handed it to Drysdale, who waved it towards his secretary, who took it and slipped it in a folder.

'Could the body be turned face-down, please,' requested Drysdale.

Frost moved back to let the photographer and

the mortuary attendant perform this task. One of the few perks of being an inspector was that you could get your subordinates to do the jobs you hated doing.

'Hands tied behind her back by ligatures around the wrists,' Drysdale intoned to his secretary. The clicking and purring of the camera was accompanied by the blinding glare of flash-guns as these details were recorded.

Frost moved forward so he could see better. Debbie's back was criss-crossed with angry bruises and red weals. Her wrists were tied with tough twine; blood had seeped where it had bitten deeply, cutting into the flesh and making it red raw. Debbie must have struggled frantically to free herself.

Harding from Forensic cut the twine free from the wrists, leaving the complicated knots intact. He held it up to be photographed before placing it carefully into an evidence bag. He then took scrapings from each of the fingernails while the pathologist tapped his foot and sucked air through his teeth impatiently.

Drysdale then carried out a careful examination of the girl's body, from the top of her head back down to her feet, stepping back and again waiting impatiently while Harding took swabs from the feet in case they yielded clues as to where she had been undressed and killed. He also took swabs from the weals on her back.

'Now lay her on her back, please,' said Drysdale, selecting another scalpel from the row of shining instruments laid out on a green cloth at the head of the autopsy table. He made a long, deep incision down the white flesh of the stomach. Again Frost turned his head away. After God knows how many post-mortems he had attended, he knew the routine off by heart. He knew the various stages without looking: the sounds, the scents, the whining and the burnt-flesh smell of the bone-saw as the whirring blade cut into the bone, the plopping noise, followed by the clang of the scales, as organs were weighed. He could never see the point of weighing the various organs. Drysdale's secretary leant forward to take the reading from the scales. It was like buying offal from a butcher.

The organs were transferred to a plastic container ready for the mortuary attendant to replace them and stitch up the body after the pathologist had walked away from the carnage of his autopsy. Frost shot a quick glance at Kate Holby to see how she was taking it. She was white-faced and was biting her lip hard, but didn't flinch when Drysdale's knife made a delicate cut so he could peel the flesh of the face away from the skull, like removing a Hallowe'en mask.

Drysdale now bent down and parted the girl's legs. 'Much bruising. Sexual penetration took place shortly before death. She was not a virgin.'

Frost's head shot up. Twelve years old and not a virgin? The boyfriend, who was now covered with a sheet on the other autopsy table, awaiting Drysdale's attention . . . or the crocodile-tear-dropping bastard of a father?

The pathologist was now gently scraping with a spatula. 'No trace of semen.' He permitted himself a wry smile. 'People know too much about DNA these days. It seems a condom was used.' Dropping the spatula into a stainless-steel kidney bowl, he examined the rest of the body, which yielded nothing that would help. 'Death by manual strangulation,' he told Frost, 'and she was brutally raped just before death.' He prised open the girl's mouth and shone a torch inside, the beam bouncing off perfect teeth. He then turned his attention to the eyes.

'Any sign that she was gagged, Doc?' asked Frost.

'If there was, Inspector, you can be sure I would have mentioned it in the hope you were paying attention,' sniffed the pathologist, as if explaining to a child.

'Check again, Doc. It's important.'

Drysdale stared at Frost. 'And why, pray, is it important?'

'When she was being raped, she'd have screamed her bleeding head off. If there was no gag, she must have been somewhere where there was no chance of her screams being heard.'

Drysdale's mouth twitched in annoyance, but he did a more thorough examination. 'Definitely no sign of a gag. Her killer could have clamped his hand over her mouth.'

'She'd have bitten the bastard's fingers off,' said Frost.

'It's for you to advance theories, not me,' sniffed the pathologist. 'I deal only with facts.

May I now continue with this autopsy, or do you want me to examine everything all over again?'

'No. You've been reasonably thorough, Doc,' conceded Frost. 'You carry on.'

Drysdale finished the examination of the girl without finding anything further that would help. They then moved to the boy on the other table.

'Arms broken, both legs broken. He's fallen or been dropped from a height of some twenty-four feet or so. His left leg would have been under him when he hit the ground and snapped at the ankle. Back of hands and knuckles badly bruised, two knuckles on right hand broken – they were hit hard with a stone of some sort. Grit embedded in palms. Back of skull caved in. A heavy, deliberate blow from a blunt instrument causing death.'

Drysdale took his fingernail scrapings and swabbed off some of the grit from the boy's hands.

At last the double autopsy was over and Drysdale was washing his hands at the sink.

Frost ambled over to Kate Holby, who was talking to the photographer. 'You all right, love?'

She smiled and nodded, but he could see her hands were shaking.

'I hate it when it's kids,' said Frost.

Frost perched himself on the corner of the desk in the Incident Room and surveyed his team, who looked as tired and worn out as he felt. They had been searching, hoping to find the two kids alive, and now fatigue had hit them. And still there was no sign of Jan O'Brien.

Frost swilled down his tea and lit up. 'As you know, we've found the missing girl, Debbie Clark –' He turned and jabbed a finger at the photograph on the pinboard. 'Stripped, beaten, raped and strangled. And Thomas Harris, arms and legs broken and his skull caved in. He'd fallen or been pushed from a height of some twenty feet or more on to gravel. We've got to find the site where he fell. We've come up with no CCTV footage of the kids cycling through the town, so they presumably went out of town somewhere. I'm guessing the site will be remote because the girl wasn't gagged and the poor little moo would have screamed her head off. So, somewhere remote, with a twenty-foot drop and surrounded by gravel. Start studying detailed maps and see if you come up with anything. We've got the girl's bike, we haven't got the boy's bike. I want it found. We covered a lot of places when we were searching for the bodies, so we can eliminate them.' He looked out of the window. 'It's peeing with rain and too flaming dark to start looking tonight, so we'll make an early start tomorrow. It should be light enough by seven, so meet here tomorrow morning at six thirty.' A groan from his audience. 'All right, if you don't think that's early enough, let's make it five o'clock.'

PC Collier's hand shot up. 'What about the stake-out at the building-society cashpoints?'

'Shit,' said Frost. He'd forgotten about it again. Anyway, it was low priority now. 'Thanks to our beloved commander showing County what a good boy he is by lending them more bodies than anyone else for the drugs bust, we now haven't got the manpower. Our blackmailer might do the decent thing and give it a miss tonight in view of the weather, but if he doesn't it's only five hundred quid and Beazley can easily afford that. If he moans, we'll have a whip-round for him.' He looked up as Bill Wells came in.

'Inspector, those bits of leg you keep finding.'

Frost groaned. 'Don't tell me some more has turned up.'

'No. Got a customer for you, Jack. He wants to give himself up. He used to be a butcher. He reckons he killed his wife and cut her up in little pieces.'

Frost stared at Wells, who didn't seem to be joking. 'Tell him to come back tomorrow, we're too shagged out tonight for confessions.'

'I've put him in Interview Room Number One,' said Wells.

'You're no fun any more,' said Frost, pushing himself up off the desk and scooping up his pack of cigarettes.

He followed Wells to the Interview Room.

The man didn't look anything like a typical butcher should. Far from being a fat, jolly, rosy-cheeked man in a striped apron and straw hat, he was thin and pale and in his late forties. Sitting hunched up at the table, he leapt to his feet when Frost and Wells came in.

Frost waved him down. 'Please sit down,

Mr . . . ?' He glanced at the report sheet Wells had filled in, which told him the man was Albert Lewis of 23 Victoria Street, Denton. 'Sit down, Mr Lewis.' Frost stared at the man, who looked vaguely familiar. He riffled through the disorganised filing cabinet of his memory, but details eluded him. 'Have we met before, Mr Lewis?'

Lewis shook his head. 'I don't think so.'

You're lying, you bastard, thought Frost. He excused himself and went out to the main desk where PC Collier was standing in for Wells. 'Check the computer, son. See if you can get anything on a Mr Albert Lewis, 23 Victoria Street, Denton. I'm in Interview Room Number One.'

Back with Lewis, he shook a cigarette from the packet and stuck it in his mouth.

'Please don't smoke,' said Lewis. 'It's a filthy habit. It spreads germs. Germs kill.'

Frost groaned inwardly. This was going to be a bundle of laughs. *You'd better have murdered your wife, mate*, he said to himself. *I hope I'm not sitting here fagless for one of those nutters who like to confess to all manner of crimes to get a bit of attention*. Lewis looked as if he lacked attention.

He stuck the cigarette back in its packet. 'I understand you're a butcher, Mr Lewis?'

'I was. Not now.'

'Oh?'

'For over twenty years I had a small shop in Ruckley Street. Quality meat. Good prices. People came from miles around. Then the bloody supermarkets started undercutting. I lost all my customers. I could barely scrape a living . . . couldn't pay the rent. I was evicted.'

'Sorry to hear that,' sympathised Frost. 'When was this?'

'Six – nine months ago. I didn't come here to talk about my shop.'

'Of course not. My sergeant tells me you've murdered your wife?'

'Yes,' said Lewis flatly, as if it was of minor interest.

Frost waited for details, but none came. 'And cut her up in little pieces?'

'Yes.'

'And when did this happen?'

Lewis wiped a hand over his face. 'I don't know – a week ago? I can't remember.'

'Not the sort of everyday incident that usually slips the mind,' suggested Frost, casting a despairing glance at Wells.

'We quarrelled. I lost my temper. I killed her.'

'What was the quarrel about?'

'I can't remember.'

There was a tap at the door and PC Collier came in with a computer printout. Frost skimmed through it and nodded his thanks. He turned back to Lewis. 'A quarrel so serious you killed her, but you don't remember it?'

Lewis stared blankly at the inspector. 'That's right.'

Frost yawned. This was all a bleeding waste of time; he was dying for a cigarette and the chance to get his head down. 'But you definitely remember killing her? Can you give me the odd detail?'

Lewis stared into space for a while before replying. 'Something snapped. We were in the kitchen. There was a rolling pin. I must have hit her and hit her. I don't remember doing it. There was screaming and suddenly there was silence and she was on the floor and there was blood all over her and blood on the rolling pin and blood on me. I couldn't believe I'd killed her.'

'You were sure she was dead?'

Lewis nodded slowly. 'Oh yes. Her skull was smashed. There was blood and brains . . .'

'Then what?'

'I dragged her body to the bathroom and managed to get her into the bath.'

'Why did you do that?'

Lewis screwed up his face as if in pain and shook his head to ease the memory. 'I had to dispose of the body. I had to cut her up.'

'You cut her up?' echoed Frost.

'I managed to undress her, then I got some sharp knives and a bone-saw. I used to be a butcher. I still had my tools. I sawed off her arms, then her legs . . . then her head.' Again he shuddered and winced at the memory. 'I can still hear the sound of the saw going through her bones.'

Frost winced too. It dragged back the memory of the post-mortem on the two kids. 'Right. So you cut her up into bite-sized chunks. Then what?'

'I turned on the bath taps to flush away the

blood. I put her remains in two plastic dustbin sacks and I disposed of them.'

'Where?'

Lewis dropped his head. 'I don't remember.'

Frost yawned again. 'I wonder how I guessed you were going to say that.'

'I said it because I don't remember,' retorted Lewis.

'You don't remember, Mr Lewis, because it never bloody well happened, did it? You're making all this up, aren't you?'

Lewis blinked rapidly in astonishment. 'What are you talking about? I'm telling you, I killed my wife.'

'The only crime you've committed is wasting police time,' Frost told him. He waved the computer printout. 'I thought I remembered you. Last year you came in here and said you'd murdered your wife. You said you'd strangled her with the flex from the electric iron.'

'And you didn't believe me.'

'I believed you – right until we went round to your house and your wife opened the door to us. Even someone as thick as me could work out that she wasn't dead then.'

'I was on medication then. I had depression after losing my business. I didn't know what I was doing. It's all different now. I really have killed her. I'll show you.' He plunged his hands under the table and brought up a plastic shopping bag. *Shit*, thought Frost, recoiling. *I hope the sod hasn't brought her bleeding head to show us.*

Lewis upturned the bag and shook it. A large meat cleaver thudded on to the table. 'That's what I used.'

Frost picked it up and ran his thumb along the cutting edge. It was razor sharp – definitely sharp enough to sever a head from a body. He moved it well away from Lewis. 'I can't see any blood on it.'

'I washed everything in the dishwasher, even the bone-saw.'

'Tell you what,' smiled Frost. 'Why don't we all go back to your house and take a look around. If your wife is there she can make us all a nice cup of tea.'

Lewis's house was a one-bedroomed bungalow down a quiet side street. Morgan parked the car outside and they pushed open the iron gate and scrunched up the gravel path to the front door. Lewis fumbled in his pocket and brought out a bunch of keys. He opened the front door, then stepped back.

'I don't want to go in,' he said.

'Sorry,' said Frost, gripping him by the arm and pushing him inside. 'I'm afraid I must insist.'

They stepped into a small hallway with a telephone on a side table against the wall. Frost shivered. There was a distinctly, hostile, unwelcoming atmosphere to the place. Everything was clean and cold to the point of sterility and reeked of furniture polish and pine disinfectant 'Mrs Lewis,' he called. 'Are you there?'

No answer. The house screamed emptiness.

'She can't answer you,' said Lewis. 'She's dead.'

A door to the right took them into the lounge, a prim and proper room with an uncomfortable-looking brown three-piece suite, and a long-unused coal fireplace with a gleaming brass fender and a beige, marble-tiled surround. At the side of the fireplace stood an old sixteen-inch television set. Frost imagined Lewis and his wife sitting stiffly side by side, frowning disapprovingly at the images on the tiny TV.

There was a photograph on the mantelpiece: A small boy sat grinning in a toy pedal car. Standing beside the boy, looking down proudly, was a younger version of Lewis, every inch the happy father. Frost picked up the photograph to examine it more closely. 'Your son, Mr Lewis?'

Lewis snatched it from Frost and clutched it tightly to his chest. 'Matthew,' he whispered. 'Little Matthew. He died . . . five years old . . . meningitis.'

'I'm sorry,' mumbled Frost, completely wrong-footed.

'Are you?' asked Lewis tonelessly, taking a long look at the photo before wiping Frost's fingerprints from the glass with a spotlessly clean handkerchief and carefully replacing it in the exact spot from where Frost had removed it. 'Please don't touch any photographs. Especially those of my son.'

'Where's the kitchen?' asked Frost.

Without a word, Lewis steered them through another door, which led to the dining room with its dark oak table, two chairs and sideboard. A door from this room took them into a small kitchen with an imitation-pine laminated floor, gleaming grey plastic worktops and a strong smell of bleach. Frost thought of Sadie's kitchen with its sinkful of dirty dishes and soiled washing everywhere – but even hers was more welcoming than this sterile cubicle.

'So this is where it all happened?' asked Frost.

'Yes,' said Lewis, wiping an offending speck of dirt off the worktop with his handkerchief. 'Germs get everywhere,' he muttered. 'They breed.'

'Dirty little sods,' said Frost. 'But back to your wife . . .'

'She was standing here when I hit her. She fell to the floor there.' He pointed.

'I see,' said Frost, who was dying for a cigarette, but knew there was no chance of having one in this operating theatre of a kitchen. 'So where is the bathroom?'

Lewis opened a door to the passage. A door to the left opened on to a small bathroom, tiled from floor to ceiling with blue and white tiles, reminding Frost appropriately, of a butcher's shop. The white bath glimmered, the plughole gleamed, as did the taps.

'What did you do with her clothes?'

'I burnt them.'

'You must have got blood all over yourself and your own clothes?'

'Yes. I had to burn my clothes as well, then I bathed and bathed and scrubbed and bathed.'

Frost scratched his chin. 'Right. Now we come to the crunch. What did you do with all the bits?'

'I took them to the car. It was night. No one could see me. I drove around and threw them away.'

'Where?'

Lewis shook his head 'I don't remember. I keep trying to remember. That night was just like a bad dream.'

'Where's your bedroom?' Frost asked. 'If your wife is fast asleep in there your bad dream could have a happy ending.'

Lewis pointed. 'First door on the left.' He leant over and turned on the cold tap, watching the water splash and gurgle down the plughole. Frost pulled his hand away and turned the tap off. 'Just in case you're telling us the truth, Mr Lewis, don't touch anything!'

There were two single beds in the bedroom, their sheets crisp and blindingly white like those in a hospital ward. Folded candy-striped pyjamas lay on the pillow of one, nothing on the other. Frost opened the wardrobe door: men's clothes on one side, women's on the other, all strictly segregated. Frost closed the door. What was he expecting to find – the wife's body swinging from a coat-hanger?

'What do you reckon, Guv?' asked Morgan.

'I don't know,' said Frost. 'This whole place is so bleeding clean it gives me the creeps. You feel you want to break wind just to give the place a homely atmosphere.'

They returned to the bathroom, where Lewis

had just finished blotting offending drops of cold water from the bath. 'I've just remembered something, Inspector. I think I buried the head in Denton Woods. I might be able to recognise the spot if you drove me there.'

'It's far too late for those larks, and it's peeing with rain,' Frost told him. 'We'll have a look tomorrow when we're all a bit more alert.'

'What's going to happen to me?' asked Lewis plaintively. 'I'm not staying here.'

'We'll find you a nice warm cell for tonight,' said Frost, 'then give your place a thorough going-over in the morning.'

'Find the gentleman a cell,' called Frost to Wells. 'Suspicion of murder.'

'I've only got one vacancy,' said Wells, leading them to the cells. 'Bookings have been heavy tonight.' He opened the door to a small cell with a bunk bed.

'Here you are, Mr Lewis,' said Frost. 'No single supplement. If you want anything, just yell and my sergeant here will tell you to shut up.'

Lewis looked around him with distaste. 'Could I have a mop, a bucket of hot water and some disinfectant, please? This place is full of germs.'

'Our germs won't hurt you,' said Wells.

Lewis looked pityingly at the sergeant, who obviously didn't understand. 'Germs kill. They killed my son . . . my five-year-old son.'

'Give them to him,' said Frost.

* * *

'Do you really think he's killed his wife?' asked Wells.

Frost sucked deeply at his cigarette and expelled a lungful of smoke. 'It's anyone's guess at this stage. He's capable of doing it. The poor sod is obviously mentally disturbed. He lost his kid, then his business – more than enough to push him over the edge. And if you wanted to kill someone and cut them up, you couldn't find a more suitable place than that abattoir of a house. But a couple of things niggle. He says he can't remember where he dumped the pieces, which I find bloody strange, because he remembers lots of other details. 'And . . .' He scratched his chin. 'This is trivial. You murder your wife, cut her up and scrub the place from top to bottom. But would you take her nightdress from the pillow and put it away?'

'That's right, Guv,' put in Morgan. 'Her nightdress wasn't there, was it?'

'Perhaps she slept in the nude?' suggested Wells.

'It's not the sort of house where anyone would sleep in the nude,' said Frost. 'The poor cow would die of frostbite.' He shrugged. 'If she walked out on him she'd take her nightdress with her and I reckon that's what has happened. He became impossible to live with, so she did a runner. Mind you, if we find her buttocks marinating in the deep freeze tomorrow, I'll admit I'm wrong.' He turned to Morgan. 'Our first job tomorrow, Taff, is to give that place a real going-over.'

'I thought we were supposed to start looking for the murder site,' said Morgan.

Frost clapped a hand to his brow. 'Shit! I forgot about that. All right, but take Lewis for a tour of Denton Woods first. He reckons he might remember where he got rid of some of the bits. And make sure you're back by seven.'

Morgan looked dismayed. 'But Guv, by the time I drop you off and get my head down, that would mean I'd only get three hours' sleep.'

Frost checked his watch and beamed. 'You're right, Taff. Your maths is impeccable. Don't be late.'

12

A bleary-eyed Morgan sat fuming in the office as Frost breezed in just after eight. 'Did I say seven?' asked Frost innocently. 'I could have sworn I said eight. There wouldn't have been enough people here at seven to do the search. Well, were the teddy bears having a picnic in the woods or did Lewis turn up trumps?'

'We tramped for miles, Guv. He says it all looks different and it was night time. He pointed out about five places it might have been, but it wasn't.'

'Never mind, Taff. Nip up to the canteen and get two sausage sandwiches and two mugs of tea and bring them to the Incident Room.'

On his way to the Incident Room, Frost was stopped by Johnny Johnson, the duty station sergeant.

'That bloke Beazley from the supermarket wants to know if you've caught the blackmailer.'

'Tell him I'm out on a murder inquiry and you don't know when I'll be back.'

'And two officers from Manchester CID are on

their way. Should be here later this morning.'

Frost screwed up his face as he tried to think why two officers from Manchester would be coming. He snapped his fingers. 'Oh – the decomposing body. I hope they take it back with them. Let Skinner see them – he should be here soon.'

The hot sausage had melted the butter, which was making the bread all soggy as Frost bit into it. He pushed the remains of the sandwich into his mouth, swilled it down with a mouthful of tea, then wiped his fingers on the front of his jacket. He had a small team assembled for the search of Lewis's bungalow: Norton from SOCO, Harding from Forensic, PC Jordan, Taffy and WPC Kate Holby.

He wiped his mouth with the back of his hand and fed in a cigarette. 'You all know what this is about. Lewis walked in here last night claiming he'd murdered his wife and cut her up into pieces, which he says he chucked, but can't remember where. He says he thinks he left her heart in San Francisco, but that might just be a song he remembers.' He grinned at the ripple of laughter. 'The poor sod hasn't got all his marbles, so this could all be in his mind. He had to give up his butcher's shop last year and his five-year-old kid died of meningitis a couple of years back. He reckons he killed his wife in the kitchen, then butchered her in the bath. That should mean a lot of blood. The place looks as if it has been scrubbed and disinfected from top to bottom, but even so, I'm hoping we can still find some. I want drains and waste pipes checked. I want the place searched thoroughly in case there's any bits of body lying around he might have missed.' He turned to Kate Holby. 'Check the wardrobes and drawers and things. If she's upped and left him, has she taken the sort of things you'd expect a woman to take, like a chastity belt or open-crotch knickers? Jordan, I want you to knock up the neighbours. See if they can throw any light on the missing woman. Did they see anything suspicious, like her husband sawing her arms and legs off without her permission?' He swivelled round to the cork board and pinned up a photograph. 'This is Mrs Lewis. If you find a head, make sure it's the right one, otherwise chuck it back. I want this to be thorough, but speedy. We've then got a murder site and a bike to find.' He looked out of the window. 'At least the rain's stopped.' He drained the dregs of his tea. 'All right. Let's go.'

Curtains twitched as the flotilla of police cars pulled up outside the bungalow. 'Plenty of nosy sods about,' Frost told Jordan, 'so start knocking on doors.'

He unlocked the front door with Lewis's key and winced as the cold, antiseptic atmosphere again hit him in the face. 'At least you can't smell rotting bodies,' he muttered, 'but even that would be preferable.' Somehow, even without Lewis being present, he couldn't bring himself to smoke inside, so went out into the garden to light up and watched Jordan going from house to house, knocking on doors. Clangings from the bathroom told him the waste pipes were being opened up. Behind him, Norton from SOCO was heaving up a manhole cover to inspect the drains. A cry from Taffy Morgan sent him flying back inside the bungalow.

'There's a loft, Guv, did you know?' Morgan pointed to a small trapdoor over the hall.

'Don't tell me about it,' snapped Frost. 'Get your Welsh butt up there and take a look.'

Morgan located a small stepladder in the garden shed and heaved himself up, his torch flashing around the tiny loft, which had insufficient headroom for anyone to stand. 'It's all clean and dusted up here, Guv,' he reported. 'Just a couple of suitcases and a kiddy's pedal car.'

'Chuck the suitcases down,' said Frost.

They were full of children's clothes, all ironed and neatly folded.

'Put them back where you found them,' Frost told him, 'and if he asks, we never touched them.'

The clang of the manhole cover being replaced sent him scurrying back outside. Norton wasn't optimistic. 'It's been scrubbed and disinfected, Inspector. I've taken samples but they're probably going to be pure carbolic. If there was ever any blood it's been well washed away.'

Frost nodded gloomily. 'More or less what I expected.'

Back inside, Kate Holby was waiting for him.

'I've checked the wardrobes, the dressing table and the coat racks, Inspector. No sign of a woman's coat, handbag or day-to-day shoes. I'd say she packed her bags and walked out on him.'

'Probably couldn't stand the smell of disinfectant,' said Frost. 'I can't say it turns me on. Thanks, love.' He looked up expectantly as Harding came out of the bathroom.

'That was a complete waste of time.'

'Why, are you constipated?' asked Frost.

A sour smile from Harding, who never found Frost's jokes funny. 'Everything has been disinfected and scrubbed clean. Even so, if he had dismembered a body in there I'd expect to find some traces of blood, but I can't.'

'Ah well,' said Frost philosophically, 'we had to check it out just to pretend we're thorough.' He raised enquiring eyebrows at Jordan, who had just returned from the neighbours. 'Anyone looking after bloodstained parcels for him?'

Jordan grinned. 'Not a lot of joy, Inspector. Mrs Lewis used to help out at the butcher's shop from time to time and they got on well with the neighbours. But when their kiddy died they were both absolutely devastated and hardly spoke to anyone. Lewis got more and more morose – even in the shop, which didn't help the business. They hardly saw him at all after he lost the tenancy, but they could hear flaming rows from time to time. No one saw the wife leave, but she hasn't been seen around for a week or so.'

'Did she have any family – anyone she might run to?'

'Parents died years ago. One brother in Australia.'

Frost grunted his thanks and called everyone together. 'OK, everyone. Back to the station, then I want you out looking for that bike and the murder site.' He jabbed a finger at Morgan. 'One more job for you, Taff. If she walked out on him, she's going to need money. Find out if she has a credit card and if it's been used recently. I'm busting for a pee, but that toilet looks so hygienic, I'm afraid to squeeze a drop out.'

'Skinner's screaming for you,' said Wells as Frost walked through the lobby.

'Why am I so irresistible to that man?' asked Frost. 'I'll see him in a minute. We're going to have to kick Lewis out.'

'No bits of body?'

'No bits of body, not even the odd nipple. I reckon she walked out on him.'

'Are you going to charge him with wasting police time?'

Frost shook his head. 'I reckon the poor sod really believes he did kill her. He can't face up to the fact that she's left him. He needs treatment, not being put away.'

'Frost!' Skinner's angry voice roared down the corridor. He was by his open office door and didn't look at all pleased. 'I want you.'

'Won't be two ticks,' called Frost.

'Now!' bellowed Skinner, disappearing into his office and slamming the door.

'It's good news,' Frost told Wells. 'I just know

it.' He lit up a cigarette and sauntered into Skinner's office.

Looking washed out, his skin a sickly green pallor, Skinner dropped two tablets in a glass of water and watched them fizz. 'Bleeding oysters at Mullett's club again,' he muttered. 'I should have learnt my flaming lesson after last time.' Without looking up, he pointed to his in-tray. 'What the hell is that?' It was Graham Fielding's typed statement, which his solicitor had insisted Frost should take.

Frost stared at it. 'It's your in-tray,' he said, scraping a chair to the desk and sitting down.

'Don't play silly buggers with me, Frost. You know damn well what I mean.' He stirred the contents of the glass with a pencil and swallowed it down. 'This!' He held aloft Fielding's typed statement. 'What the hell did you think you were doing?'

'He wanted to make a statement and his solicitor insisted, so I had to take it.'

'You had no flaming business to. I told you not to. I don't want statements saying he's innocent. I want statements saying he did it. This is my case, not yours.' He winced, then with a gasp of pain he clutched his stomach and clapped a hand over his mouth. 'I'll talk to you later,' he mumbled as he staggered to the door.

Hope you don't make it, thought Frost. He frisked through the in-tray, found nothing of interest, so returned to his own office, where DC Morgan was waiting for him.

'I've checked with the bank and the

credit-card company, Guv. She made two cash withdrawals of a hundred pounds from their joint account on two consecutive days last week.'

'Where from?'

'The cash machine at Tesco's supermarket, Catford, south London.'

'Right,' said Frost. 'That clinches it. Let's go and tell Lewis he's outstayed his welcome.'

Lewis blinked at Frost in disbelief. 'But I killed her. I told you, I killed her.'

Frost shook his head. 'I know you will find it hard to accept this, Mr Lewis, but we believe she walked out on you. She's in Catford and she's been drawing money from your account.'

Lewis stared open-mouthed at Frost in sheer disbelief. 'How can she withdraw money if she's dead?'

'Perhaps because she's not dead,' suggested Frost.

Lewis buried his head in his hands. 'You won't believe me, will you? If only I could remember where I put the pieces.' He looked up at Frost. 'Someone will find them. Someone's bound to find them.'

'If they do, I'll arrest you like a shot,' said Frost, 'and that's a promise. And if your wife comes back, you will let me know, won't you?'

'You're wrong,' said Lewis. 'You are absolutely wrong.'

'It won't be the first time,' said Frost, ushering him out of the cell. He watched Lewis go, a forlorn figure, shoulders hunched.

At the door, Lewis turned. 'It was the germs,' he said. 'The germs killed my son so I killed her because of the germs.'

Suddenly, for no reason he could think of, Frost began to have doubts. Grave doubts.

Station Sergeant Johnny Johnson looked up and switched on his 'How can I help you?' smile as the two men approached the inquiry desk in the lobby.

'Detective Superintendent Barrett and Detective Constable Fussell, Manchester CID,' announced the older of the two, a thick-set man in his late forties. 'Would you let DCI Skinner know we're here?'

'I'm afraid DCI Skinner is out with a search party at the moment, Superintendent,' Johnson told him. 'Could anyone else help?'

Barrett frowned. 'He knew we were coming and now he's bloody out?' He raised his eyes to the ceiling and gave a scoffing snort. 'Flaming typical. It's about the body you found – Emily Roberts.'

'Ah – Inspector Frost is handling that at the moment, sir.'

Barrett frowned again. 'Frost? Scruffy Herbert – always got a fag in his mouth?'

'Yes, the one with the George Cross,' said Johnson, unwilling to let this fat sod from Manchester bad-mouth Denton personnel. He picked up the phone and dialled. 'Inspector Frost, two officers from Manchester CID to see you.'

* * *

Frost took them to the Incident Room and showed them the clothes recovered from the lake in Denton Woods. Barrett examined them briefly, nodding as he did so. His DC was taking his time, checking each item carefully against a typed list. 'They look like the girl's clothes,' he admitted grudgingly.

'More than flaming "look like",' snapped Barrett. 'They *are* her bloody clothes.'

'But still no proof they came from the body.'

'What do you want, flaming jam on it? You're not the Crown bleeding Prosecution Service looking for ways not to prosecute, you're a detective flaming constable, and the way you're going on, you'll end your career in the force as a detective flaming constable. We've got a body that matches her description, we've got clothes that match those she was wearing. Of course they came from Emily Roberts. Give Inspector Frost the envelope.'

Fussell fished a plastic envelope from his briefcase and handed it to Frost. 'Hairs from her hairbrush.'

'For DNA testing,' said Barrett. 'Then no one can moan we've got the wrong body. We'd like to have a look at it, by the way.'

'You can take it home with you if you like,' said Frost. 'It's not a pretty sight. I'd rather look at Skinner than the body – that will tell you the sort of shape it's in.'

Barrett grinned. 'What do you think of your new DCI?'

‘Far be it for me to call a man a shitty bastard just because he is a shitty bastard,’ said Frost, ‘so I’ll keep my mouth shut.’ He unhooked his mac from the rack and slipped it on. ‘You might not feel like any lunch after this.’

Handkerchiefs clapped to their noses, the two Manchester detectives looked down at the remains. ‘And the pathologist reckons she was strangled?’ asked Barrett.

‘Yes,’ nodded Frost. ‘Broken bone in the throat, probably manual strangulation, but decomposition too advanced to see any ligature marks.’

‘Sexually assaulted?’

‘Again, decomposition too advanced to tell.’

‘I’ve seen enough,’ grunted Barrett. He turned to the DC. ‘Unless you want to make sure she’s dead?’

Fussell grinned. ‘If the pathologist says she’s dead, sir, I’ll take a chance.’

Frost signalled for the mortuary attendant to close the drawer. ‘Do you want to see where she was found?’

Barrett nodded. ‘Yeah. It won’t tell us much, but while we’re here let’s take a look.’

The blue marquee was still mounted on the railway embankment at the spot where the girl’s body had been located. It was guarded by a fed-up-looking, freezing-cold PC. ‘If you wanted warmth and excitement, son, you shouldn’t have joined the force,’ Frost told him. They stepped inside the marquee, where the smell of death and decay still clung tenaciously. They all stared at the marked area on the grass as if it could yield up some secret, then quickly backed outside. Frost's mobile chirped. Skinner was back and wanted to see the two Manchester men.

Skinner ushered them into his office, then, before Frost could follow them, stepped outside and shut the door.

'I know this Superintendent Barrett,' he said, keeping his voice down. 'He's a real right slimy bastard.'

Takes one to know one, thought Frost.

'He's going to try to dump this case on us,' Skinner continued, 'and we're not going to have it. We've got enough on our plates. She was killed on his patch and the body dumped here, so it's his case, not ours. We'll give them what assistance we can, when we can and if we can, which probably means bloody never, but our stuff takes priority. *Comprende*?'

'*Toute suite*,' nodded Frost.

They were in Skinner's office, seated round his desk drinking mugs of Sergeant Johnson's instant coffee. The atmosphere crackled and sizzled with the unconcealed animosity between Barrett and Skinner. Barrett had various maps and papers spread over the desktop. 'This is a more recent photograph. We found it in her digs.' He passed Skinner a colour photo of a girl in her teens, her fair hair in a ponytail. Skinner gave it barely a glance before flipping it across to Frost.

'Lovely-looking girl,' muttered Frost, finding it hard to eliminate from his mind the way she looked now.

'Emily Roberts,' intoned Barrett. 'Nineteen years old. Guess where she was born?'

'I don't play guessing games,' said Skinner.

'In the fair city of Denton,' smirked Barrett.

Skinner scowled. 'You kept that bloody quiet. Weren't we supposed to know?'

'We've only just found out ourselves. Her parents emigrated to Australia some six months ago and we've had one hell of a job trying to contact them. Emily didn't want to go. There was a family row and she stayed behind. She didn't keep any of their letters, so we didn't have an address. The Melbourne police managed to trace them and they are on their way over here. She was born in Denton. The family moved to Manchester some five years ago when she was fourteen. After her parents emigrated, she moved in with a girlfriend who had a flat. She worked in Tesco's on the check-out. The night she went missing she told her flatmate she was meeting her boyfriend at a local disco. She left at around seven thirty and that was the last anyone saw of her. The boyfriend said he waited all evening, but she never turned up. He left the disco with his mates around midnight and went straight home.'

'You checked his alibi, I hope?' asked Skinner.

Barrett whiplashed a 'Do you take me for a

complete prat?' look across the desk. He turned to his DC. 'No. We forgot to do that, didn't we, Constable?' Back to Skinner: 'Of course we bloody well checked it out. All his mates confirmed it and we checked out a lot of his movements on CCTV.'

'Any footage of the girl on CCTV?' asked Frost.

Barrett shook his head. 'We checked the area near the disco and the centre of town. No sign of her.'

'So how do you reckon she got to Denton?' asked Frost.

'Well she didn't go by train. There are CCTV cameras in the booking hall and on the platforms. We're working on the theory that she went by car, either voluntarily or she was abducted and taken to Denton, where she was assaulted and killed and the body was dumped.'

Skinner flapped a hand dismissively. 'Without evidence to the contrary, I'm working on the theory that she was killed on your patch and her body was brought to Denton and hidden where we found it. Denton was just the dumping ground – so it's your case, not ours. We'll see to the coroner's inquest, but from there on the rest is up to you.'

'Why should he kill her in Manchester then drive all the way to Denton to dump the body?' asked Barrett. 'It doesn't make sense.'

'I've no idea,' replied Skinner, 'but as it's your case, I'm not going to rack my brains to find out.'

'Perhaps the killer got her in his car, tried to have sex, she resisted, so he killed her, panicked and drove like the clappers to get the hell out of there until he could get rid of her,' offered Frost, sucking sugar from the end of the pencil he had used to stir his coffee.

'I'll go along with that,' said Skinner, rising from his chair. 'He killed her in Manchester and dumped her in Denton. So if you'll excuse me—'

'Mind you,' continued Frost, slipping the pencil back in his top pocket, 'whoever killed her probably came from Denton.'

Skinner glowered. If looks could kill, Frost's body would be the next one on the mortuary slab. 'And how do you make that out?' he hissed.

'You'd have to know Denton bloody well to find that bridge where he dumped the body – somewhere where it wouldn't be found for weeks. It's right off the beaten track.'

As Skinner opened his mouth to shoot Frost down, DC Fussell said, 'If he came from Denton, that makes it more than likely he took her to Denton to kill her.'

Skinner decided to vent his rage on the DC. Smiling sweetly, he said through clenched teeth, 'Forgive me, whatever your name is, but might I ask your rank?'

'Detective constable.'

'Detective constable?' echoed Skinner in mock surprise. 'The way you were airing your unsolicited views, I thought you were at least a chief inspector.'

Barrett leapt from his chair and thrust his face right up to Skinner's. 'If you've got sarcastic remarks to make, Skinner, make them to your own men. And if we're talking rank, remember I'm a superintendent and you are a chief inspector. DC Fussell's comment was valid and I agree with him. Wherever she was killed, the odds are she was killed by someone from Denton, as I will advise our chief constable. This will be a joint investigation and I expect – in fact, I demand – your fullest cooperation. And you will be up to your knees in shit if we don't get it.' He pushed various papers from his briefcase across to Skinner. 'I'm leaving these with you. Keep me informed as to the progress of your investigation. We'll do the same.' With a jerk of his head for DC Fussell to follow him, he swept out of the office.

Skinner gathered up the papers and thrust them into Frost's hands. 'You do not contradict me, do you hear? Next time, keep your bloody mouth shut,' he snapped, his face contorted with rage.

Frost smiled. One of the unforeseen bonuses of getting the boot from the division was that there were few other sanctions left that they could throw at him.

He dumped the papers on his office desk, sniffing as he detected the siren aroma of pork sausage, chips and beans wafting down from the canteen. He decided to take an early lunch.

'Inspector!' Sergeant Johnny Johnson was

waving excitedly, a leathery-faced man in a boiler-suit at his side. 'We've got the dead boy's bike.'

Frost hurried over. 'What? Where is it?'

'Out the back. In the exhibits shed!'

Frost frowned. 'You're not telling me it's been there all the bleeding time?'

'No,' grinned Johnson. 'This gentleman, Mr Harry Gibson, found it and brought it in for us.'

'He brought it in?' echoed Frost in disbelief. 'He didn't leave it untouched where it flaming well was?'

'I had to touch it to bring it in,' said Harry.

'Yes, silly me, of course,' said Frost. 'So where did you find it?'

'You know that big empty office block just off Denton Road?'

Frost nodded. He knew it. A speculative development company had plans for a business complex just outside Denton and the modern office block was to be its centrepiece. But the company ran out of money and went bust. The office block had remained empty ever since.

'That's where I found it.'

'So what were you doing there?'

'I'm a sort of caretaker for the liquidators. I repair broken windows when the kids chuck bricks, make certain the chain-link fencing is secure, cut back the undergrowth – that sort of thing.'

'I don't want a flaming job description,' said Frost. 'How did you find the bike?'

'The grass round the outside of the fence was

overgrown, so I decided to cut it back. I saw the bike and thought to myself, *That could be the bike the plods are looking for*, so I humped it on the van and drove it over here. I was wondering if there was any sort of reward?'

'In heaven,' grunted Frost, 'not down here.'

'It was very well hidden,' continued Harry. 'Whoever put it there didn't want it found.'

Frost chewed this over. 'Right. Hang on here a minute while I go and take a look at the bike, then I want you to take me to where you found it – the exact spot.' He jabbed a finger at Johnson. 'And get someone to take his fingerprints. I bet they're all over the flaming bike.'

'What do you want them for?' asked the caretaker. 'I ain't done nothing.'

'For elimination,' said Johnson. 'Now come with me.'

The bike was propped up against the wall in the exhibits shed undergoing examination by Norton from SOCO, who was on his knees, taking scrapings from the tyres. He straightened up and stretched as Frost approached. 'It's still wet from being left out in the open, Inspector. I'll dry it off with a hairdryer and see if I can get any decent prints from it.'

'It'll be smothered with prints from the git who found it,' said Frost. 'It's definitely the boy's bike?'

'No doubt about it, Inspector.'

Frost stared gloomily at the bike, which told

him nothing. 'Let me know if you come up with anything. I'm off to look at where he found it.'

It was only mid-afternoon but it was already getting dark. The office building, some ten storeys high, looked stark and desolate against the night sky. The wind blowing round the top created a cyclone effect at ground level, where bits of rubbish and scraps of paper were lapping the building. The wind had managed to uproot the LUXURY OFFICE UNITS TO LET sign, which now lay on the ground.

'Bleeding wind,' said Harry. 'As fast as I put it up, it gets blown down again.'

Frost kicked the sign to one side. The ground underneath was dry, the grass flattened and yellow. 'It doesn't look as if it has ever been put up again since it first fell down.'

Harry shrugged. 'What's the point? You put it up, the wind blows it down. It's like painting the flaming Forth Bridge.' He jerked his head. 'Round here.'

Frost, Morgan and Norton from SOCO followed him round the exterior of the chain-link fencing to the rear of the building, where some of the undergrowth had been cut back. 'That's where it was.' He pointed. The inspector's torch picked out a depression in the grass. If you wanted to keep a bike well hidden and the undergrowth was uncut, this was the place to put it.

Frost chewed thoughtfully at his fingernail. 'Why didn't they chuck this bike in the river with the girl's?' he wondered. He parted some brambles so he could look through the fencing. The beam of his torch crawled over grass on to a patio area which encircled the complex. He gazed up at the building; he could just make out the windows on each floor, with their balconies and window-boxes intended to take the starkness off the design. Alongside the balconies an ivy-entwined metal trellis crawled up the wall to the top floor.

He moved his gaze from the trellis and stabbed the beam of his torch at the stone-slabbed patio with its sunken, gravel-topped miniature gardens. He called Norton over. 'A pound to a pinch of nasty stuff that gravel matches the grit we found on the boy's body. Check it when we get inside.' He moved slightly to the left, where his torch had picked up a section of the chain-link fencing which bulged inwards where it had been detached from its base. He beckoned Taffy Morgan over. 'You're a fat little sod, Taff. See if you can crawl under there.'

Morgan looked doubtfully at the sodden grass. 'I'll get wet, Guv.'

Frost smiled sweetly. 'Only your clothes and your body . . . now get under there, fatty.'

With theatrical grunts and groans, Morgan managed to squeeze himself under the fence and emerged on the other side. He stood up, his clothes sodden, and stared ruefully at Frost from the other side.

'That's how the boy got in,' said Frost. 'You wait there. We're coming in the dry way through the gates.'

Frost and Norton walked with the caretaker to the main entrance, which Harry unlocked. They joined Morgan. Again Frost looked up at the metal trellis. 'Do you reckon you could shin up to one of those balconies, Taff?'

Morgan looked up and gaped. 'You're joking, Guv?'

'All right,' said Frost, 'forget it. I'm not paying 5p for a bleeding wreath if you fall.' He beckoned the caretaker over. 'I want to take a look inside.'

Harry checked his watch. 'Not tonight, Inspector. A time lock kicks in at four o'clock. We can't get in until the morning.'

Frost snorted. 'I haven't got time to sod about until then. This is a murder investigation. Find a brick, Taff. We'll smash one of those windows.'

'Hold on,' said Harry, alarmed. 'No need for drastic measures. We might be able to get in through the boiler house. We're supposed to bolt it on the inside, but we sometimes forget.'

His torch showing the way, he took them down stone steps, selected a key from a bunch and opened the door. 'Your luck's in, Inspector. I must have forgotten to bolt it.'

I bet you never bolt it, thought Frost. They stepped into a small cellar-like room which held a bank of electric switchboards and two commercial central-heating boilers which weren't operating. Passing through another door, they climbed some more stairs and were in the darkened lobby. Harry pressed a switch and fluorescent lights shimmered into life. A small reception desk stood alongside a lift.

'How many floors does this place have?' asked Frost.

'Ten.' He opened the lift doors. 'What floor do you want?'

'Let's start at the top.'

They stepped out of the lift into black emptiness. Harry found the switch and the lights clicked on to reveal a barren, empty floor with rows of windows on each side.

'If ever they rent this place out, the floors will be partitioned off into separate offices,' explained Harry.

There were plenty of radiators, all stone cold. The entire building was like an icebox. Their footsteps echoed eerily as they walked across the uncarpeted composition floor. Frost moved over to a window and looked out. Blackness was speckled with lights from distant Denton. So what else did he expect to see – Halley's flaming Comet?

The balcony door wasn't locked. Turning the handle, he pushed it open and stepped out, bracing himself and grabbing the iron rail tight against the force of the wind, his hair and tie streaming.

Frost looked down ten storeys into yawning blackness, then took the cigarette from his mouth and let it fall. It was like dropping a stone down a bottomless well. The red dot took ages before it shot out a miniature shower of sparks when it hit the ground and was swallowed up by the darkness. That was a bloody long way down. The boy couldn't have fallen from here. He'd have done more than break his legs. He would have been smashed to pieces when he hit the concrete of the patio. He must have fallen from one of the lower floors. But which one?

Frost stepped back from the balcony and closed the door, conscious that the others were looking at him, expecting him to come up with something. Well, they could bloody well expect. It felt warmer inside after his stint on the balcony, but it was still an icebox.

'Debbie Clark was here,' he said. 'Not on this floor, but she was here, in this building. It's too dark to do a proper search tonight. We'll get our team together and go over it inch by inch in the morning.' He stabbed a finger at Harry. 'When we leave, you stay out of here. This is now a crime scene. If we catch you inside I'll have you up for perverting the course of justice.'

'You try and bleeding help,' moaned Harry, 'and that's the bleeding thanks you get.'

13

Frost was woken up in the middle of the night by the insistent ringing of his mobile phone. He staggered out of bed and clicked on the light. Where the hell was the phone? The damn thing was in the room somewhere, but he couldn't remember where he had left it. He eventually located it under the bed.

'Frost.' It had better not be a flaming wrong number.

'Fortress Building Society, Inspector. Someone is withdrawing five hundred pounds from the cashpoint in Market Square right now. If you hurry, you can get him.'

'Thanks,' said Frost. 'For a minute I thought it was bad news.' He clicked off the phone and put it where he would forget it again.

Shit! Beazley would chew his privates off in the morning. He shrugged. There was sod all he could do about it, he'd just have to cross that bridge when he came to it. He lit up a cigarette and smoked for a while before crawling back into bed. He switched off the light, but was unable to sleep. His mind kept whirring round and round, reminding him of all the vital things he had to do and didn't have time for. Why wasn't flaming Skinner taking some of the load off his back?

He was still awake when the milkman rattled by at six and had just drifted off to sleep when the alarm went off at half past seven. It was still pitch dark outside.

Frost swept through the lobby on his way to the Briefing Room, yelling a greeting to Station Sergeant Johnny Johnson. 'How's it going, Johnny?'

Johnson slammed the incident book shut. 'Our paedophile prisoners are complaining about the standard of their accommodation. They want bail.'

'They want castrating,' said Frost. 'I thought Skinner was dealing with them.'

'He's had to go back to his old division.'

'I wish he'd bloody stay there. I think we'd better oppose bail for their own safety. Let's try and get them put on remand – oh, and when that nice Mr Beazley phones, you don't know where I am.'

He pushed through the swing doors and into the Briefing Room, where he gratefully accepted a mug of steaming hot tea from Collier. He stirred it with a pencil and wiped the sleep out of his eyes, then turned his attention to the search team.

'As you probably know, we've found the boy's bike. It was hidden in some shrubbery outside that big empty office block on Denton Road. I'm pretty certain that's where the boy was killed and that's probably where the girl was killed.'

He paused as Johnny Johnson came in and handed him a memo from Forensic. He scanned it, then waved it aloft. 'Forensic have confirmed it. The boy was killed there – the grit matches. There's a metal trellis running up the side of the window by the balconies. I reckon something was going on inside that the boy wanted to see, so he climbs up the trellis, gets a grip on the balcony rail and is hanging there, ready to haul himself over, when our friendly neighbourhood murderer hears him and smashes his knuckles with a stick, making the kid lose his grip and fall. The fall didn't kill him, so while he's lying there, moaning with pain, the bastard comes down and bashes the kid's skull in.'

'Why?' asked Jordan.

'Because the boy had seen something he should not have seen. He could have seen the girl being killed. There's no proof of that at the moment, but I'm bloody certain Debbie Clark was killed there.'

'So why didn't the killer chuck the boy's bike in the river along with the girl's?'

'Probably because he couldn't find it,' answered Frost. 'It's hard to spot in daylight – at night it would have been impossible. It was too well hidden. I'm banking on this sequence of events, but if anyone can come up with anything better, let me know. I'm not too proud to pinch it as my own.' He waved his cigarettes around, then lit up.

'I reckon Debbie Clark was going to meet someone and she was a bit worried about it – bloody rightly so, as it turned out – so she asked her boyfriend to follow and keep an eye on her. Whoever she meets takes her into the office block. Thomas hides outside, then sees lights come on at one of the floors, so he climbs up the trellis to get a closer look, and gets his head smashed in for his troubles. The first thing we're going to do is find out which floor he fell from. I want the patio on all four sides searched for traces of blood. The poor sod would have bled like mad, both when he hit the ground and when his brains were knocked out. When we find where he fell, we can then check the trellis for signs of him climbing – the greenery should be crushed or disturbed, which should lead us to the actual balcony he was hanging on to when he was helped down. We might find blood and prints on the rail. When we know the floor, we can search inside to see if there is any trace of the girl having been there. It's going to be a cold, back-breaking task and if you find anything, I'll take the credit, which Skinner will then take for himself. I also want the surrounding area searched to see if we can find the brain-splattered blunt instrument that finished off the boy.' He pinched out his cigarette and dropped it in his pocket. 'All right. Let's get going.'

It was PC Collier who found it. 'Inspector!'

Frost came running over. Not only was the gravel stained and flecked with blood, there were marks where the boy's body had been dragged before being lifted. Frost shouted for the others to stop the search. 'We've found it!'

They gathered round him as he moved over to the trellis. 'This is where he climbed up – look.' He pointed. 'You can see broken stems where he trod on them.' His eyes followed the ivy upwards. 'I reckon he made it to the fourth floor – the plants seem undamaged above that point.' He pointed to the blood marks. 'Get them covered up and radio Forensic. Now let's take a look inside.'

They clattered up the stairs to the fourth floor, a vast echoing barn of empty space stretching the entire width of the building. It was pitch dark – all the blinds had been closed. Frost jabbed a finger at Jordan. 'Get on to that caretaker and ask him if the blinds should be shut in an empty building.' He fumbled for the switches and clicked on the lights. 'Now open the bloody things.' He waited while the blinds were opened and daylight streamed into the barren area. Frost opened the door to the balcony and checked to confirm there were no more broken branches above this level. This had to be it. 'Get Norton up here to check for prints and blood.'

While Norton went to work, Frost struck a match on the NO SMOKING sign and dragged at a cigarette. He moved to the balcony to watch, then looked out over the distant houses to the outskirts of Denton. What a dump the place looked. But dump or not, he wasn't going to let the bastards chuck him out. But how was he going to stop them? Why the hell did he start fiddling his expenses? It wasn't as if he needed the money. His thoughts were cut short. Morgan was calling him.

'Guv!' The DC had found something and was holding it aloft triumphantly.

'Show me,' said Frost, holding out his hand. It was a spent match. 'I just used that to light my fag, you prat. Now make yourself useful for a change. Go downstairs and wait outside. I want to know if anyone would have been able to hear the poor cow when she screamed her bleeding head off, begging the bastard to stop.' He ordered the blinds to be shut again, as they would probably have deadened the sound on the night.

Minutes later, Morgan phoned to say he was positioned outside. Frost yelled, 'Mullett is a sod!' at the top of his voice. The sound echoed around the empty floor. He phoned Morgan. 'Well? Did you hear that?'

'No, Guv – and I was listening.'

'Without me telling you to,' said Frost. 'Get back up here.'

As he thought – from the double-glazed fourth floor, the poor girl could have screamed and screamed until the whole floor echoed to her pleas, and no one outside would have heard her, even if anyone was about in this remote area.

Norton reported marks on the rail, but no distinguishing prints. 'If he was gripping the rail, Inspector, and someone then cracked his knuckles, he would have released his grip, his hand would have slid open and smeared whatever prints were there.'

'No matter,' shrugged Frost. 'We know he was here, prints or not.'

'There's specks of blood. I'll get Forensic to match it.'

'If you want,' said Frost. 'We know whose blood it will be.'

Jordan reported back. 'The caretaker said the blinds are never shut, Inspector.'

'Then the killer shut these,' said Frost. 'That clinches it. The boy would have seen the lights come on and then the blinds close – that's why he shinned up here.'

The searchers, now at the far end of the floor, had found nothing, except for a few bits of ancient rubbish.

Frost dug his hands in his pockets. 'She was here. The poor little cow was stripped, beaten and raped. She screamed her bleeding head off and no one heard. All right, let's retrace our footsteps. Let's assume she came in by the main entrance . . .'

'She couldn't do that, Inspector,' Collier pointed out. 'The time lock. She wouldn't be able to get in after four and she left home at half seven.'

'Good point,' said Frost. 'Bloody good point. You've shot my theory right up the fundamental orifice, but . . .' He stopped. 'There must be some way of overriding the time switch. Supposing some silly sod got themselves locked inside the building and wanted to get out? Phone the caretaker and ask him. The rest of you, downstairs.'

As they clattered down the stairs, Frost yelled after them, 'Keep your grubby paws off the hand rail. If he had a spark of bleeding decency, our killer would have left prints.'

The lobby by the main entrance where Frost had been the previous night was the only part of the building that was fitted out. Its floor was covered with heavy-duty green carpeting and it was equipped with visitors' chairs. Frost nodded at the two ivory phones on the reception desk. 'Check them.'

'Wiped clean,' reported Norton. 'But the phones are dead, so they could have been cleaned months or more ago.'

'Right, now check the lift-summoning button and the button inside for the fourth floor.'

Norton checked and shook his head. 'Blurred prints all on top of each other. I reckon the caretaker uses it every day.'

'You're bleeding useless,' said Frost. 'Check the handrail to the fourth floor.'

Collier hurried down the stairs. 'The caretaker says you can set and un-set the time switch from the lobby. The switch box is under the reception desk.'

Frost bent and looked. There it was. A white switch box with buttons setting 'on' and 'off' times and days of the week. A green button was marked 'Emergency Override'.

Frost called Norton over. 'See if you can get any prints off that. The rest of you, search this place from top to bottom. See if you can find some trace – anything – that the girl was here or that something dodgy was going on, or can find the weapon that knocked the boy's brains out. I know she was bloody well here, but I can't bloody prove it . . . Apart from that, I've got this case tied up.' He shook his head. 'Whoever killed her knew this place. He knew how to get in – how to work the time lock. He knew he could do what he liked with her and she wouldn't be heard. But why did she come? It must have been someone she trusted . . . or thought she could trust. Her father? That bastard – he's involved in this somehow. We know he had it in for the boyfriend.'

'Perhaps Debbie saw her dad kill Thomas Harris and had to be silenced, Guv?' offered Morgan.

Frost rubbed his scar. The cold in the unheated building was making it ache. 'She wasn't just killed, Taff, she was beaten and raped.' Would a father kill his own daughter? The sort of bastard who could hand photographs of his young daughter in the nude to a gang of paedophiles would certainly be capable of it, and if he lusted after her, he might be capable of rape, but the beating? He hadn't faced Clark with the photograph yet. Something else on the long list of vital things he wasn't doing.

His mobile phone rang.

It was Bill Wells from the station.

'Jack, you've got to get this sod Beazley off my back. He's doing his nut. He wants you and he's blaming me for not getting you to contact him. He's taken my name, address and number and is going to report me to the Home Secretary, the Queen, the Prime Minister, Carol Vorderman, the bloody lot. He's not going to wait much longer.'

Frost groaned. Yet another addition to the long list of vital jobs he just didn't have time for.

'As soon as I can, Bill, I promise you. As soon as I can.' That was a bleeding lie for a start. He'd put it off as long as he could. He switched the phone off and dropped it back in his mac pocket, then yelled for PC Collier.

'Leave what you are doing, son, and come with me. We're going back to the nick. There was another withdrawal from the cashpoint last night. Pick up the CCTV footage from Fortress and get more CCTV videos of cars in the vicinity at the time. A common factor must show itself up.'

Frost waltzed through the doors of the station. 'Honey, I'm home,' he called to Bill Wells, who had now taken over from Johnny Johnson.

'Your dinner's in the oven and there's a gentleman here to see you,' said Wells, nodding to a man sitting on the bench opposite his desk.

Frost groaned. It was Lewis. 'I'm rather busy, Mr Lewis,' he began as the man rose to meet him.

'I want to be arrested,' said Lewis. 'I've killed my wife.'

'We've been through all this, Mr Lewis,' began Frost, edging for the door.

'You think I'm mad, don't you?'

'Of course not,' said Frost. 'Just absent-minded. As soon as you remember where you put the pieces, come and see me.' He put his hand on Lewis's arm and gently led him to the doors. 'You go home now, Mr Lewis.'

'She's dead,' said Lewis softly. 'I killed her.'

'I know,' nodded Frost. 'And you can't prove it. It's a sod, isn't it?' He propelled the man through the doors and firmly pushed them shut behind him. 'He's getting to be a bleeding nuisance,' he told Bill Wells.

'He might be telling the truth, Jack.'

'She's in London, drawing money out of the bank on her cash card. Bit difficult to do that when you're cut up in little pieces.'

'Someone's been drawing cash. It could be Lewis.'

'It could be Elvis bleeding Presley, but it isn't,' snapped Frost. 'It's her.' He said it as if he was convinced. Why were bleeding doubts still gnawing away?

'Have you seen Beazley yet?' asked Wells. 'I get palpitations each time the phone rings.'

The phone rang. Wells stepped back and looked at it apprehensively.

'You'd better answer it,' said Frost. 'It might be Tom Champagne.'

It was Beazley.

'He's on his way to you now, Mr Beazley,' croaked Wells. He moved the phone away from his ear as a stream of invective poured out. The tirade stopped. 'On his way now, Mr Beazley, I promise you.' He hung up quickly and looked appealingly at Frost. 'Please, Jack.'

'I want to have a word with Clark,' said Frost. All right – it was a delaying tactic. But he did have to talk to him.

'Why can't I have bail?' demanded Clark.

'Where would you go?' asked Frost. 'Your wife won't have you back with her.'

'The house is in my name,' said Clark. 'She'll do what she is damn well told.'

'You don't like people going against your wishes, do you?' said Frost.

'And what is that supposed to mean?'

'You told your daughter she wasn't to go out with Thomas Harris. She went against your wishes. Now she is dead and the boy is dead.'

Clark stared at Frost, eyes wide, mouth open. 'Are you suggesting I killed . . . killed my own daughter? I'm not saying another word unless my solicitor is present.'

Staring back at Clark, Frost took the childhood photograph of Debbie from his pocket and thrust it in Clark's face. 'Is this your daughter, Mr Clark?'

'You know damn well it is. Where the hell did you get it from?'

'It was on the computer of your paedophile chums. Did you share it around so they could all dribble over it?'

The colour drained from Clark's face. He took

the photograph and gaped at it in disbelief. 'Inspector, you've got to believe me . . . I never . . . I . . .' He shook his head. 'Wait . . . I did send it to one of our group. This was long before I knew of their . . . our special tastes. I was proud of her. I was just showing her off. This was years ago . . . I never dreamt . . .'

I don't believe you, you sod, thought Frost. *I don't flaming well believe you.* He took the photograph back. 'On the evening Debbie went missing, you told me you stayed in. Your wife tells me this is not true. You left the house shortly after Debbie did and didn't return until almost midnight.'

'I'm sorry,' said Clark. 'I lied. I was with some of our group.'

'You mean the paedophiles?'

Clark nodded. 'Some new photographs had been downloaded. We were to collect them. I couldn't tell you. They will vouch for me. I promise you, they will vouch for me.'

Yes, thought Frost. *All those lying bastards would stick together*. He yelled for Bill Wells to let him out. 'I'll speak to them, Mr Clark. Let's see if they can lie as well as you can.'

'Get them to confirm it later, Jack,' pleaded Wells. 'Beazley's going to be back on that phone any second.' The phone rang. 'I'll bring them in now, sir,' said Wells, hanging up and scooping up some papers. 'Mullett wants the overtime returns,' he said before dashing off.

While Frost waited, he glanced at the pages Wells had been working on. It was a list of keyholders for various properties to be updated. He was about to push it away when a name caught his eye. He snatched up the page and studied it closer. 'Bloody hell!' He waved the page at Wells when the sergeant came back.

'This keyholder. It's our flaming butcher. The one who reckons he turned his wife into mincemeat.'

Wells looked at the page and nodded. 'That's right. Why?'

'What is he the keyholder of?'

'His butcher's shop.'

But he was kicked out of there nearly a year ago.'

'He's still the keyholder. The landlord couldn't get anyone else and he just stayed on by default. Why?'

'Why didn't you bloody tell me this before? If I wanted to cut up my wife and dump her remains, what better place than an empty butcher's shop?'

Wells twitched his shoulders. 'Never gave it a thought, Jack. But you yourself said he was fantasising.'

'Because more bits of body than the odd foot or ankle would have turned up otherwise. He's dumped her in that bloody shop, Bill, I just know it. Do you have a spare set of keys here?'

Wells unlocked a drawer and pulled out a box full of labelled keys. 'Here you are.'

Frost snatched the keys and made for the door.

'Where are you going, Jack?'

'To take a bloody look.'

'But Mr Beazley . . .'

'He can bloody wait.'

As the door slammed behind him, the phone rang and rang . . .

As he drove to Lewis's old butcher's shop, his mind began whirring yet again as he went through all the things he had to do. Jan O'Brien, the other missing teenager: she was a pupil at the same school as Debbie Clark. Was it just a coincidence? Probably. It was the obvious school for Denton girls of her age to attend.

Had Jan run away from home, as she had done so many times before? Was she shacked up somewhere with a new boyfriend? Possibly, but that didn't explain her mobile phone found near where the drunk heard a girl screaming. No. She was in trouble somewhere, serious trouble, but they had no idea where the hell she was. She could be still in Denton, or miles away, or – and he shuddered at the thought – she could be dead. Could it be the same killer who murdered Debbie and Thomas? Another body to be slashed and sliced open on the autopsy slab?

But this was all speculation. He'd have to look in on her parents to see if there had been any contact. It was a forlorn hope, but people didn't always bother to tell the police when a missing person suddenly returned.

And God, he still had to tell Thomas Harris's parents that their son's bike had been found, before they read about it in the press. It was definitely the boy's, but he'd need a formal identification. But more importantly, he had to see Debbie's mother to find out if she knew of any reason why her daughter would go to that deserted office block. And then there was the dreaded visit to bloody Beazley.

A policeman's lot was not a flaming happy one. Why the bloody hell wasn't Skinner down here to help?

The butcher's! In chewing over all the other things he had to do, he had almost forgotten the flaming butcher's, his main reason for coming out in the first place. Where the hell was he? He had been driving on autopilot. An angry tooting of a horn snatched him away from his self-pitying thoughts and back to his driving. Shit! He had nearly driven straight through a red light and had narrowly missed crashing into a petrol tanker whose driver was mouthing obscenities at him. He pretended not to notice.

He jerked his head from left to right, trying to find a landmark, and realised he was near Thomas's parents' house – so that would be his first port of call.

The boy's parents were still numb from grief and shock. They sat side by side on a settee in the lounge, holding hands, staring into space. They seemed barely aware of Frost's presence and he had to repeat each question several times before he got an answer. No, they knew of no reason why their son would have gone to the office block. Yes, Mr Harris would come down to the station to identify the bike. There were long moments of silence. Eventually, Frost mumbled his goodbyes and let himself out.

Then he headed to Jan O'Brien's house. He didn't have to ask if they had heard from the girl. As soon as his car pulled up outside, the mother came running out to ask if there was any news. 'Not yet,' said Frost, 'but we're pulling out all the stops trying to find her.' That was a bloody lie. They'd looked everywhere while searching for the other two kids and that was it. Details had been circulated to all divisions with no results. The trail had gone cold and congealed. There was little more that could be done, especially with Denton's limited resources.

'She's dead,' sobbed Mrs O'Brien. 'Like that poor Debbie Clark. She's dead. I know it.'

'We'll find her,' soothed Frost, trying to sound convincing. 'Don't worry, love, we'll find her.' Another bloody lie, but what the hell? He couldn't tell her what he really thought.

Back in the car. Where next? Debbie Clark's mother. Gawd, he was dreading this. His mobile rang: it was Bill Wells.

'Jack, Beazley's going ballistic.'

'Soon, Bill. I've got Debbie's mother to see, then I'm going to check Lewis's old shop for pussy's pieces, then I'll see Beazley.'

'The mother? You told me you were going straight to the butcher's and that was your only call.'

'I lied, Bill. Get off my back. I'm having a sod of a morning.' He terminated the call and switched the phone off.

Outside the Clarks' house, Frost sat in the car and smoked. It was his usual delaying tactic and this was something he definitely wasn't looking forward to. Come to think of it, there was very little to look forward to these days. If Skinner got his way, which looked inevitable, Frost would be out of Denton in a matter of weeks. He'd have to see about selling his house and finding somewhere to live in Lexton. Lexton! A dump that made Denton look like Palm Springs. Bastard, bleeding Skinner. His mind skimmed over various painful deaths he could plan for the man, but none was drastic enough.

He yanked the cigarette from his mouth and hurled it through the car window. Debbie's mother might be able to come up with something – anything to reinforce the sod-all they already had.

She took ages answering the bell. He could hear shuffling footsteps, as if someone was dragging themselves along, and when she opened the door he was shocked at her appearance. Mrs Clark had aged ten years since he last saw her: grey-streaked, uncombed hair sprawled over her shoulders, her eyes were unfocused, a cigarette dangled from her lips and there was the reek of whisky on her breath. She squinted red-rimmed, tear-stained eyes at him, her face screwed up as she tried to remember who he was.

'Frost,' he said. 'Inspector Frost. How are you?' Stupid question. He could see how the poor cow was.

'How am I? On top of the effing world,' she snapped. 'How the bloody hell do you think I am?' She turned and shuffled back up the hall. Frost followed, closing the front door behind him.

The hall was littered with unopened letters that had dropped through the letter box. Frost scooped them up and took them into the lounge, where Mrs Clark had slumped in an armchair. He quickly shuffled through the post in case there was anything addressed to Debbie or anything from vindictive cranks who took delight in writing abusive letters to bereaved families. Nothing.

Mrs Clark was clutching a photograph of a younger Debbie and was rocking from side to side, silently sobbing. Frost felt overwhelmed with pity for her – he was determined to get the bastard who had ravaged and killed her only child. 'We think Debbie went to that deserted office block just outside Denton,' he said softly. 'Any idea why she would go there?'

She shook her head. 'Ask my husband. He killed them both. He lusted after his own daughter. If he couldn't have her, no one else could . . . that's why he killed my lovely baby.'

Frost stood up to go. He had heard all this before. 'We're looking into that, Mrs Clark.'

She thrust the photograph she was holding at him. 'I haven't even got an up-to-date photograph. This is all I have.' In the colour print, Debbie was no more than nine or ten. 'That bastard . . . She was so beautiful . . . She wanted to be a model, but he wouldn't let her.'

Frost sank down in the chair again. This was something new. 'A model?'

'She sent a photograph and they did a test. They wanted her. All he had to do was sign the consent form, but the bastard refused. He said models were involved in sex and drugs and he wasn't having his daughter mixed up with that . . . and this from a man lusting over pornographic pictures of young children. It was everything Debbie wanted and he refused. It broke her heart.'

'Twelve's a bit young to be a model,' said Frost, handing back the photograph.

'This was years ago when she was nine. It was for a mail-order catalogue for children's clothes. He wouldn't let her have any more photographs taken in case she applied again.' She clutched the picture to her chest. 'This is all I've got.'

'Do you remember the name of this model agency?'

She thought for a while. 'Dagmar – Digmar Child Modelling. Something like that. Why, is it important?'

'It probably isn't,' shrugged Frost, scribbling the name down on the back of an old envelope. Important or not, they had sod-all else to go on. 'You wouldn't have any papers about them – an address?'

'He threw them away. Tore them up in front of

her and threw them away in case she tried to go back to them. He threw everything away.'

'Where did Debbie go to get the photographs taken? Was it local?'

'It was somewhere not too far away, I think. She did it all without telling us and when the papers came for signature he tore them up.'

'And how did Debbie take all this?'

'I told you. It broke her heart. I tried to comfort her. I said, "Wait until you're sixteen, my love. You won't need his consent when you're sixteen." ' She covered her face with her hands and started sobbing again. 'She's never going to be sixteen. She's dead.'

Frost lit up a cigarette and dribbled smoke through his nose, waiting for her to calm down. This could be a lead or, more than likely, another blind alley, but it had to be investigated. 'And as far as you know, she never made contact with the agency again?'

'No. She was terrified of him . . . the way he screamed and shouted. The hypocritical bastard.' She pushed herself up and shuffled over to the sideboard to pour herself half a tumbler of Johnny Walker. 'Join me?'

'No thanks, love.' Frost stood up again. 'You shouldn't be on your own. You should have someone with you.'

'I should have my daughter with me, but she's dead.' She drained the whisky and hurled the glass into the empty grate. 'She's bloody dead.' Sobs racked her body.

'I know, love, I know,' said Frost sadly. 'I bloody know.'

Back in the car, he switched his mobile phone on and it buzzed angrily and flashed its lights.

'Yes, Bill?' said Frost, as if he didn't know what it was all about.

'Jack, what the hell are you playing at? Beazley's chewing my privates off. He's been on to Mullett so he's chewing his off as well. I said you were on your way.'

'I'm on my way to the butcher's shop, then I'll be straight back.' He cut the sergeant's protests short by clicking off the phone and dropping it in his mac pocket.

As he cut through the back streets to avoid traffic congestion, his mind started racing again over all he had to do and all his doubts and worries bubbled to the surface. It was getting too much and he wasn't up to it. He was a sergeant, bumped up to an inspector because some junkie pumped a bullet in his head. He rubbed the scar, which was aching again. Sod that bleeding medal. Without it he would still be a sergeant, and not a bleeding good sergeant at that, but other people would then be making the decisions he was having to make and would be doing a much better job of it. Too many flaming bodies and not a single flaming clue.

His radio crackled. 'Inspector Frost, come in please. You are required urgently at the station.'

Yes, so Mullett could give him a bollocking. He switched the radio off and coasted the car down a back street, past a row of boarded-up shops, their doors scrawled with ancient graffiti. The area was dead. Even the graffiti writers had stopped coming.

The butcher's shop was on a corner, its facade completely boarded up. The key clicked in the lock and turned easily. As he pushed open the door, the smell of death hit him like a wall. The sickly, cloying, stomach-churning stench of a long-dead body. He stepped back and closed the door. Shit. Just what he bloody feared. He took a lungful of fresh air, then pushed the door wide open, steeling himself before moving tentatively inside. With everything boarded up, the place was in pitch darkness. He fumbled for a light switch and clicked it on. Nothing. Of course, the supply would have been cut off long ago.

Scrabbling in his mac pocket, he located his torch. At first it wouldn't work – he'd been meaning to change the battery – but a couple of shakes and a bang made it flicker reluctantly to life and give out a feeble yellow beam which threatened to die at any minute. He steered the beam around the shop. The light bounced off white tiled walls, then picked out another partly open door which led to the refrigeration room. That was where the smell was coming from. He wished he still had some of that Vicks to shove up his nose, but all he had was an inadequate handkerchief which he clasped to his face. Gritting his teeth, he took a tentative step into the dark, watching the torchbeam creep across a blood-smeared, tiled floor, then his stomach heaved. In the corner was a heap of rotting, green, slimy putrescent flesh, crawling with maggots and dotted with bloated bluebottles.

He crashed his way outside and was violently sick, leaning against the wall of the shop as his stomach churned and churned. Even out in the open he could still smell and taste that stench. It was much worse than the first girl's body they had found. That had been out in the open. This was in a confined space. So he was right: Lewis was a nutter. He had killed his wife and cut her up as he would an animal carcass. He shakily lit a cigarette, but after one puff threw it away. The smoke reeked of death. Wiping his mouth with his handkerchief, he fished out his mobile to call the station. Let the boys from SOCO and Forensic throw up their dinners. Why should he have all the fun?

Bill Wells answered the phone. 'Flaming heck, Jack, where have you been? We've been calling and calling—'

Frost impatiently cut him short. 'I know, but—'

But Wells wouldn't listen. 'She's here, Jack.'

Frost frowned. 'Who? Who are you talking about?'

'Mrs Lewis. The butcher's wife. She's alive and well. The Met managed to trace her. She wants to talk to you.'

Frost stared at the phone in disbelief. 'Say that again.'

'Mrs Lewis isn't dead . . . and to prove it, she's here! She wants to see you about her husband.'

'On my way,' croaked Frost, his mind in a whirl. If she was alive, then who the hell was rotting away in the refrigeration room, stinking the place out? He lit up another cigarette to delay the moment when he would have to go back and take a closer look. He shuddered. Maggots. How he hated maggots.

This time the smell seemed even stronger and the beam from his torch even weaker. He had almost to stick his nose in the rotting mess to see what it was. A quick flick of the torch on to the heap told him. Stupid bloody fool!

He hurried out, slamming the refrigerator-room door firmly behind him and staggering out to the street to suck down lungfuls of fresh air. He shook his head and laughed at his flaming stupidity. He would have expected Morgan to make such a mistake – but not that he himself would have jumped to the wrong flaming conclusion. The remains weren't human. They were fly-blown animal carcasses – just what he should have bloody well expected from a butcher's shop that had been abruptly closed. A shiver ran down his back as he realised what a prat he would have looked had he called out the full murder team to look at a couple of dead pigs.

Even with the car windows open and the wind blowing through, he could still smell the reek of rotting meat on his clothes.

Mrs Lewis was overweight and in her late forties,

with dark-brown hair and a raw-meat complexion; she looked like a typical butcher's wife. Nicotine-stained fingers circled her third cup of police tea and the ashtray was full of cigarette stubs.

'What the hell is going on?' she demanded as Frost came in. 'Bloody police knocking on my door. The neighbours must think I'm a prostitute or something.'

Only if they need glasses, thought Frost. Aloud he said, 'Sorry about this, Mrs Lewis. Didn't the Met explain what it was all about?'

'No they bloody well didn't. Dumped me in a police car and drove me straight here.' She pushed her cup away. 'And after all that I'm left sitting here drinking cat's pee.' She snatched at the cigarette Frost offered her. 'I never used to smoke, but he drove me mad. So what the hell is this all about?'

Frost lit up for both of them. 'Your husband came in here and told us he had killed you and cut you up into little pieces.'

Her mouth sagged, the cigarette clinging to her lower lip. 'Again? And you bloody well believed him?'

'He was most insistent,' said Frost. 'Trouble was, he couldn't remember where he had dumped all the bits. We didn't believe him, but we had to take it seriously, just in case . . .'

'He's round the twist,' she said. 'He always was a bit weird, but he went right over the top when we lost our little boy.' Her voice faltered and she stared hard at the table top. 'My lovely little Matthew . . .' She shook her head, pulled a handkerchief from her handbag and dabbed her eyes. 'Might not have been quite so bad if I could have had any more kids, but I couldn't. I was as upset as he was, but I didn't get any comfort from him. He started blaming me for Matthew's death. Said I should never have let him go to the hospital. Meningitis – he had meningitis. So what was I supposed to do – leave him at home? He reckoned it was the hospital that killed him. All right, I know he loved Matthew – loved him a bit too much, if you ask me – but he was taking his death out on me. Then he started being rude to the few customers we had in the shop, and when the landlord kicked him out he really went weird . . . muttering to himself, sharpening his bloody knives over and over. I used to be friendly with the woman next door. She was a paediatric nurse and that was enough for him – he blamed nurses for Matthew's death. She soon stopped coming over, he frightened her so much.'

Frost nodded sympathetically. 'You've had it rough, love.'

She dropped her sodden handkerchief into her handbag and snapped it shut. 'Can I go now?'

Frost nodded. 'Yes. Thanks for coming.' He held the door open for her.

'So how do I get back to London?' she asked.

'See the nice sergeant in the lobby,' Frost told her. 'He'll either arrange a car or give you the money for your train fare.'

At the doorway she paused. 'I used to love him once. But he changed . . .'

Frost nodded. Hadn't this happened with his own wife? God, how they had loved each other at the beginning and how they had hated each other at the end. He shook his head and wiped his hand over his face. *It was all my fault*, he told himself. *If only* . . . He mentally compared the beautiful young cracker he had married with the drawn figure, her lovely dark hair now streaked with grey, dying in the hospital side ward, where she could be wheeled out on a trolley and taken down in the lift to the mortuary without alarming the other patients. *All my sodding fault.*

As he pushed his way through the swing doors, he could hear Bill Wells explaining to Mrs Lewis that he just didn't have the transport or the cash allocation to get her back to London, while she was explaining to Wells that that scruffy inspector had told her he would do it, so he had bloody well better do it, and bloody soon. Frost backed out and decided to use the rear exit.

Mullett's gleaming blue Porsche was parked by the exit, reminding Frost that he should have reported to Hornrim Harry ages ago. There was a gleaming pearl-grey Mercedes sprawled across two parking places next to the Jaguar, with the registration number BEA 001. Bloody hell. He must be here, chewing the privates off Mullett. Frost quickened his step. He nearly made it. He was climbing into his battered Ford when

Mullett's voice roared out from an open window: 'Frost! My office – now!'

Sod it!

Beazley, his face brick-red with anger, was chomping on one of his outsize cigars, and the corpses of two other cigars lay in Mullett's ashtray. The office reeked of cigar smoke.

Mullett was equally angry. 'I sent for you ages ago, Frost!'

'I was just about to come in when you called,' lied Frost, drawing himself up a chair as far from Beazley as possible. He lit up and flipped the spent match in the general direction of the ashtray.

'Coming to see me?' shrilled Mullett. 'You were getting into your car.'

'Just checking the mileage for my car expenses,' said Frost. 'You know I like them to be dead accurate.'

'Never mind your bleeding car expenses,' snarled Beazley. 'What happened to that brilliant suggestion of yours to catch the sod who's pinching my money? You said it was bleeding foolproof. Another five hundred quid up the Swanee last night. I might as well leave the bleeding money in the street for him to pick up.'

'I'm sorry, Mr Beazley,' said Frost. 'We now have other priorities. I've got three kids' bodies in the morgue and another teenager gone missing.'

'Sod your other bloody priorities,' roared

Beazley. '*I'm* your number-one priority. I want the blackmailer caught, I want all my money returned and I want it done now.' He poked a finger at Mullett. 'I'm holding you responsible as well, Superintendent. Your Chief Constable is in the same lodge as me and he'll be interested to learn how incompetent Denton Police Force is.'

Everyone seems to be chummy with our flaming Chief Constable, thought Frost, flicking ash on the carpet.

Mullett, white as a sheet, tried to calm the man down. 'No need for that, Mr Beazley. Inspector Frost will have a full surveillance team round those cashpoints tonight.'

'OK,' said Frost, pushing himself up from his chair. 'But I'll nip round and see the dead kids' parents first and tell them Mr Beazley wants priority over the search for their killer, and I'll try and talk them out of going to the press, because it would be bad publicity for Mr Beazley and his supermarket . . .'

Beazley leapt up, sending his chair flying. He mashed his cigar to death. 'If you dare—'

'*I* wouldn't dare,' cut in Frost, 'but I can't speak for the murdered teenagers' parents.'

The muscle at the side of Beazley's mouth kept twitching. He was breathing deeply, trying to contain himself. 'All right. I'll give you until the end of the week. If you haven't caught the sod by then I'll see both of you are kicked out of the force.' He stormed out of the office, slamming the door shut after him.

Mullett looked at Frost. 'I want the blackmailer caught, Frost.'

'Give me more men, more overtime.'

Mullett fluttered a hand. 'Anything . . . anything . . . only get him caught.' He flopped back in his chair and mopped his brow. 'This is all your fault, and he's blaming me as well.'

Frost beamed back at him. 'There ain't no justice, Super. I'll go and see about the extra men and overtime . . .'

Never any peace. There was always someone waiting in his office. This time it was PC Collier, clutching a computer printout.

'Whatever it is, bin it,' said Frost as he sat down. 'We're all on overtime tonight watching the cashpoints again.'

'It's that child-modelling agency you asked me to try and trace, Inspector. I think I've found it.'

Frost took the computer printout. 'Delmar Model Agency, 39 High Street, Melbridge.' He looked up at Collier and nodded. 'Well done, son. This could well be the one.'

'Turn the page, Inspector,' said Collier.

Frost flipped the sheet over and whistled softly. They used to have a studio in the office block on Denton Road. 'Bloody hell!' He unhooked his scarf and wound it round his neck. 'Come on, son, let's pay them a visit.'

'They went out of business a couple of years ago, Inspector. The owner died. No list of employees, no records anywhere.'

'Shit!' said Frost. He drummed his fingers on

his desk. 'Whoever worked there must have paid tax. Go to the tax office. Tell them it's a murder inquiry. They should have a list of employees somewhere.'

'They could be filed under name, Inspector, not workplace.'

'You're probably right, son, but ask them anyway.'

Leaving Collier, he nipped up to the canteen for a quick cup of coffee and a bacon roll and spotted DS Hanlon nursing a cup of tea at a table with other members of the search party that had been scouring Denton Woods for Jan O'Brien. They all looked tired and fed up. Frost dumped his tray on the table beside the sergeant. 'I take it you haven't found anything, Arthur? Any body – especially Skinner's – would be a bonus.'

Hanlon gave a weary grin. 'We've searched those flaming woods so many times, Jack. I know every blade of grass off by heart.'

Frost found it hard to swallow the bacon in his roll. It reminded him of the maggoty carcasses in the butcher's. He pushed the plate away, took a swig of tea and lit a cigarette. He filled his lungs with smoke, then slowly exhaled. 'She's not there, Arthur. We're wasting our time. Send most of the team home and let them have a kip. I'll be wanting volunteers to stake out the cashpoints again tonight.'

'You've got the overtime agreed, I hope?' asked Hanlon. 'Only last time . . .'

'Mullett's agreed,' nodded Frost. 'He's terrified Beazley's going to report him to his

Masonic buddies, so the sky's the limit.' Then he remembered the modelling agency. 'Go and see Jan's parents, Arthur. Ask them if their daughter ever wanted to be a model, or was ever contacted by the Delmar Model Agency. She went to the same school as Debbie Clark. Talk to the teachers, the kids . . . did she ever say anything about modelling or about a modelling agency?' He filled Hanlon in on the details. 'Not much of a lead, Arthur, but it's all I've got.'

Frost staggered up the stairs to bed just after three in the morning. The stake-out had been a complete waste of time. They had waited, shivering in the wind and rain until a couple of minutes before midnight, when the Fortress computer people phoned to say that five hundred pounds had just been withdrawn from a cashpoint at Frimley, a small town some three miles from Denton. Frost had phoned the Frimley police who sent a car round, but far too late. They had staked out the cashpoint in case the blackmailer returned after midnight to make a second withdrawal, while Frost and his team covered the Denton cashpoints. At two o'clock, cold and dispirited, he had decided to call it a night.

In his dream Frost was running for dear life. The figure chasing him had a knife. A long knife. He crashed through a door, heart pounding, and found himself inside the refrigerator room at the butcher's. The light was on, the white-tiled walls were smeared with fresh blood and crawling with maggots. On the floor were newly slaughtered lambs, their throats bleeding on to the white tiles. His pursuer was at the door. There was no way to lock it. He leant against it. The man outside started pounding at the door, which shook with the blows. The door crashed open . . .

He awoke, dripping with sweat and panting, his heart hammering. *Bloody hell, you can stick these sort of dreams*, he thought. *What about the ones with the naked nymphos, which have been missing from the agenda for far too long?* He clicked on the bedside lamp to check the time. Half past four in the morning. He had been asleep barely an hour.

Suddenly the pounding started again. He sat up in bed. It was coming from his front door.

He staggered from the bed to swish back the curtains and look out into the darkened street below. The blue light of an area police car was flashing. Shit! What the hell had happened now?

He padded down the stairs and opened the front door. He vaguely recognised the officer standing there – it was someone from Traffic, but he couldn't think of his name.

'Sorry to knock you up, Inspector, but your phone's off the hook.' He pointed to the hall table.

'So it is,' grunted Frost, replacing the phone on its base. 'So kind of you to wake me up at half past flaming four in the morning just to tell me that.'

The officer grinned. 'PC Lambert from Control is anxious to talk to you, Inspector. He says it's urgent.'

'At half past four it had better flaming well be,' snarled Frost.

It was cold in the hall. Frost slipped his mac over his pyjamas before phoning the station. 'This had better be good, Lambert,' he yawned into the mouthpiece. 'Who's dead, Mullett or Skinner? Please say it's both.'

'The charge nurse from Denton General Hospital has phoned, Inspector, worried about one of their nurses. She hasn't reported for duty.'

'Then tell them to sack her,' grunted Frost.

'She's always been conscientious, loves her job, this is the first time she hasn't turned up for night duty and she's not answering her phone. They sent someone round to her house – it was in darkness.'

'There's a surprise. At four o'clock in the morning I'd expect every bleeding light to be on.'

A token chuckle from Lambert, who pressed on. 'Three pints of milk on the doorstep and papers stuck in the letter box. They fear something might have happened to her.'

'Like she's gone off drinking milk and reading papers? Why the flaming hell did you wake me up to tell me this? It would be just as bleeding pointless at nine o'clock.'

'She lives next door to Lewis, the butcher,' said Lambert.

Frost's knuckles whitened as he gripped the phone tighter. 'A nurse?'

'Yes, Inspector.'

'A paediatric nurse?'

'Yes, Inspector.'

'Get back to the hospital and check if she was one of the nurses who looked after Lewis's kid.'

He sat on the stairs and smoked. Lambert was back in five minutes.

'Yes, Inspector, she was.'

A warning bell started tinkling softly in Frost's brain. 'It might be a coincidence, but I'd better check it out. Get on to Taffy Morgan. Drag him out of bed if necessary. Tell him to pick me up in ten flaming minutes or they'll be finding parts of his legs and dick all over Denton Woods.'

Apart from the odd porch-light, the street was in darkness. Morgan parked the car outside the nurse's house, then gave Frost a nudge to wake him. 'We're here, Guv.'

Frost shook himself awake, yawned, then climbed out of the car. 'Right. Let's take a look.' He gave a passing glance to the butcher's house next door, half expecting, even at that late hour, that the curtains would twitch.

There were three pints of milk on the doorstep and three morning papers protruding from the letter box, which Frost tugged out so he could poke his torch through. Its beam picked up a few letters strewn across the mat. He straightened up. 'Just so we don't make proper prats of ourselves . . .' He hammered the door knocker. They waited. Nothing.

'I don't think she's in, Guv,' offered Morgan.

'I wish I had your perceptive intuition,' grunted Frost. He walked across the front garden to the window and slashed his torchbeam through the gap in the curtains. An empty room. So what did he expect to see – a pile of body parts on top of a nurse's bloodstained uniform?

'I suppose there's no rear entrance to this place?'

'Back-to-back houses, Guv.'

Frost returned to the front door and knocked again. 'Never know your luck, she might have gone to the lavvy.' After a couple of seconds of silence, he stepped back and nodded at the glass door panel. 'Break the glass, Taff. We're going in this way.'

'What do I use, Guv?' Morgan asked.

Frost pointed to the step. 'One of the milk bottles.'

Morgan grabbed a milk bottle and used it as a club, smashing both the door panel and the bottle, which shattered, sending milk flying everywhere.

'. . . first pouring the milk out, of course,' said Frost mildly.

'Sorry, Guv,' said Morgan.

The door swung open as Frost stuck his hand through and turned the catch. He shone his torch on an expensive, milk-sodden carpet topped with milk-sodden letters. 'If we don't find a body, Taff, you're in deep trouble.' They skirted the mess and looked through all the rooms. Everything was as it should be.

'What do you think, Guv?' asked Morgan.

'I think I'm a prat for letting Lambert talk me into this. We're either going to have to pay for the smashed door, the ruined carpet and the bottle of milk you poured all over the bloody place, or lie our bloody heads off and say it was like this when we came.'

'That last bit sounds good to me, Guv,' said Morgan.

'The first bit never stood a chance,' said Frost.

It was gone five when Morgan dropped him off. The damn phone started ringing the minute he opened the front door. 'Dr Shipman's surgery,' he grunted. 'Do you want a house call?'

'Too early in the morning for flaming jokes,' said Station Sergeant Johnny Johnson. 'The hospital have phoned again, Jack. They're still worried about that nurse.'

'Then book her in as a missing person. She's only been gone a couple of days.'

'It's longer than that, Jack.'

'There were only three bottles of milk on the step and there was nothing suspicious in the house.'

'She was supposed to have gone off on holiday for two weeks, sharing an apartment with a nurse from another hospital. They've managed to get hold of the other nurse. Our one never turned up. She'd paid for the holiday and she never turned up. She was mad keen to go. All she'd been talking about was this flaming holiday and she never turned up.'

Frost tipped back in his chair and stared up at the ceiling. 'I agree with you, Johnny, it don't sound too good. Bloody hell. We've got enough to flaming well do without this. Well, we can't do any more tonight. I'll send Taffy over to the hospital first thing tomorrow to get details.' He hung up and trudged upstairs to bed.

He couldn't sleep. He tossed and turned, smoked innumerable cigarettes, then gave the pillow a couple of punches and tried to concentrate on drifting off. It didn't work. He kept thinking about the missing nurse. Supposing she didn't know Lewis's wife had left him? Supposing she drifted over one evening for a cup of coffee and a chat and Lewis and his bleeding butcher's knife were waiting for her? He shook the thought out of his head. It was all conjecture.

He tried to focus on something more pleasant – that fat pathologist, for a start. He cursed himself for missing his flaming chance there – he bet she was hot stuff under the sheets. His attempt to conjure up a picture of the naked pathologist failed . . . all he kept getting was a bloodstained, maggot-ridden corpse.

He sat up straight in bed. Something was nagging away. Something important. Something he had missed.

Maggots! Why were there bloody maggots? The Maggot Man had said flies wouldn't touch a long-dead body. The meat in the refrigeration room had been rotting for months, so why were there maggots?

He squirmed back on to the pillow and pulled the bedclothes over him. Whatever the reason it could wait until morning. He sat up again. Sod it.

It couldn't wait, not if he wanted to get any sleep. Another look at the alarm clock. Twenty-two minutes past five, pitch black and cold outside. If he got up and nosed around the butcher's shop now, it would be too late to go back to bed after he'd found it was all a bleeding waste of time.

He swung his feet on to the floor and dragged on his clothes.

Please let it be a bleeding waste of time.

14

Even the lamp-post had been vandalised: a jumble of coloured wires dangled forlornly from the switch box. The Council had obviously seen no need to spend money on repairing it in a deserted street, so the road was in total darkness as his car slithered to a halt outside the boarded-up butcher's shop. His headlights picked up the shape of an abandoned car further up the road. That's all this place was now – a dumping ground for unwanted junk and, perhaps, unwanted bodies. It was a bitterly cold night, but warm inside the car with the heater going full blast. He leant back in his seat. Couldn't this wait until the morning?

Frost poked a cigarette in his mouth and smoked to delay making a decision. Sod it, he had no flaming choice. He'd come this far and he wouldn't be able to go back to sleep not knowing whether or not bite-sized chunks of the missing nurse were rotting away in there.

Chucking his cigarette away, he stepped out into the cold street. He patted his pocket. The key! Sod it, he'd forgotten the flaming key! The perfect excuse to go back home and leave it until the morning. But he'd opened countless doors before when he didn't have a key.

Clicking on the torch, he studied the lock. It didn't look too substantial. A couple of well-placed kicks might be the Open Sesame. He gave the handle a tentative turn, just in case, and to his surprise the door swung open, creaking like something from a Hammer horror film. Frost paused, screwing his face in thought, trying to remember if he had locked up when he was here earlier. He could swear he had. He seemed to remember turning the key, then trying the door to make sure it was properly locked. Well, it wasn't locked now, so he clearly hadn't. Pushing the door open further, he stepped into the foul-smelling, hostile dark.

Bang on cue, just when he needed it most, his torch gave a death rattle, flickered and died. Sod it! He knew it was on its last legs, so why the hell hadn't he changed the battery? Another good excuse for leaving the search until later – perhaps even sending Taffy Morgan in. He shook the thought away. One of the penalties of rank was that you didn't ask your subordinates to do things you wouldn't do yourself.

Frost gave the torch a couple of slaps against the side of his leg and frightened it into spitting out a feeble, quivering beam, which waited until he was inside the refrigeration room before cutting out completely. All his shakings and bangings failed to give it the kiss of life.

A clunk. The damn door had shut itself behind him, enclosing him in pitch blackness you could cut with a butcher's cleaver. His shoe slithered on something slimy and nasty and the smell in the enclosed space was making him gag. He fumbled in his pocket for his cigarette lighter and flicked it on, hoping the gas would last out. The flame threw out hardly any light, but at least he could now locate the heap of rotting meat. How the hell was he going to examine it? One thing was sure – he wasn't going to touch that heap of smouldering putrescent muck with his bare hands.

He gave a rotting carcass a tentative kick and it tottered to the floor with a squelch, exposing something white behind. What the hell was it? He bent and held the cigarette lighter closer, then his heart skipped a beat before hammering away at top speed. Marble-white and stained with blood.

It was a hand. A severed human hand.

Frost stepped back in horror and disgust, then suddenly he felt his feet give way from under him. As he tried to regain his balance, the lighter and the torch dropped from his grasp, landing with a squelch in the heap of putrid filth. There was a thud as his back hit the floor, then a louder thud as his head cracked on a tile. He was momentarily stunned. White dots did a frantic dance in the darkness. His hand, which he had automatically used to try to break his fall, was hurting like hell, firing up bursts of teeth-gritting pain. He must have broken his flaming wrist.

He tried to move his head but a stab of pain made him stop. It hurt. Bloody hell, how it flaming hurt, and his back wasn't much better. He was smothered in muck which stank to high heaven, and he was in agony. He couldn't see a bloody thing and he wasn't going to delve down blindly in the heap to try and find his lighter.

At first, pushing himself up with his good hand didn't work. His feet slithered from under him and he was once more on his back. The pain almost made him sick. His clothes were a sodden mess and he tried not to think of the fat, bloated maggots he had seen crawling over their food supply earlier that day, the sodding maggots that had made him return for another look. Why the bloody hell had he come back? More importantly, why the bloody hell had he come back on his own?

At last he managed to scramble unsteadily to his feet. His head spun. He had lost all sense of direction. Where the hell was the door? He wanted to get out bloody fast. The back of his head was still stabbing with pain. He touched it gingerly, but didn't know if the sticky mess he felt was from his own blood or the animal remains. A shake of the head to try and clear it made it ache even more.

Completely disorientated, he stretched an arm out in front of him and carefully moved forward, inch by inch, to avoid stepping on anything that would send him crashing down again, trying to locate the wall. Where the hell was it? It seemed miles away. Then his fingers touched cold tiles. The wall – but which way was the door? Pressing a sweat-soaked hand on the tiles, he followed the wall in a clockwise direction.

He stopped dead.

The hairs on the back of his neck prickled.

There was someone else in the pitch-dark room with him.

He couldn't see anything. He couldn't hear anything. But he knew. He just bloody knew . . .

That flaming car parked up the road. What a stupid prat he was. Of course the sodding thing wasn't abandoned. It was in too good nick to be abandoned . . . and the unlocked door . . .

Lewis! Who else would be lurking around at this time of night? It had to be Lewis, standing there in the dark, probably running a testing thumb along the blade of his butcher's knife to make sure it was sharp enough to chop up a nosy-parker, flat-footed copper.

Frost cleared his throat. 'I can see you. I'm a police officer . . . Let's have a bit of light, please.'

The tiled walls flung his words back. All he could hear was the hammering of his heart.

'Don't sod me about, Mr Lewis. I know it's you. Let's get out into the open and talk about this.'

Nothing . . . unless . . . Breathing – he thought he could hear breathing . . .

He held his breath until his lungs ached and listened, ears straining to detect the slightest sound . . . Nothing. There was no one there. His bleeding imagination was playing tricks again.

He expelled his breath in a sigh of relief and gulped down a lungful of fetid air. Frost slid his sweaty hand along the tiles, still seeking the elusive door that would let him out of this stinking hell hole and into the fresh air.

Then the blinding beam of a torch hit him in the face.

He couldn't move. The shock made him freeze. He tried to say something. The words wouldn't come.

A voice broke the silence. 'What are you doing here?'

Frost screwed his eyes up against the blinding glare. Through half-closed eyes, with torchlight bouncing off the wall, he could just about make out the figure of Lewis. And his worst fear was realised – the bastard had a knife in his other hand.

'We had a report someone was trying to break in, Mr Lewis. They sent me to check it out.' He tried to sound convincing.

The torchbeam shifted from his face over to the heap of carrion in the corner. It lit up the severed hand before flashing back to Frost's face.

'She killed my son,' said Lewis sadly. 'You've seen too much.'

'Don't do anything stupid,' said Frost. 'I've already phoned for back-up. They're on their way now.'

'Liar!' said Lewis. 'You haven't used your phone since you've been in here.' Then he choked back a sob. 'Lies! Everyone lies to me. The hospital told me lies. My little boy never told lies.' Then he lunged at Frost with the knife. Frost side-stepped to avoid the blow, but felt his feet shoot from under him again and crashed to the floor. The impetus of the missed knife blow made Lewis plunge forward and lose his balance. As he thudded to the slippery tiled floor, his arm jerked up, sending his torch soaring in the air, to comet-tail down before hitting the floor. A tinkle of broken glass and the room was in complete darkness again.

Frost rolled desperately away from Lewis, who was struggling to get back on his feet and making chilling moaning noises.

As Frost rolled, his hand felt a gap . . . a space. Thank God! He'd found the bloody doorway. But as he staggered unsteadily to his feet, Lewis was at him again. The knife whistled past Frost's head, just nicking his ear – warm blood trickled down his ice-cold cheek. Scrabbling frantically, Frost located the door handle, but his blood-slippery hand couldn't get a grip. He snatched at his mac and wrapped that round the handle. It turned, but the door wouldn't budge. He charged it again and again with his shoulder. The pain was excruciating, but the door stayed firmly shut.

Sounds indicated that Lewis had regained his footing. Although Frost couldn't see him, he could hear the rasp of his breath. He hurled himself in the general direction, managing to hit Lewis in the chest and sending them both down to the floor again. They rolled, one on top of the other, Frost grunting with pain as their combined weights pressed on his injured wrist. He tried to grab the arm holding the knife, but again couldn't get a grip and Lewis easily managed to wrench his hand free. Frost was just able to roll to one side as the knife again cut through the darkness, this time slashing his cheek. Blood poured into his mouth. With a heave, he managed to send Lewis crashing back, giving himself time to stagger to his feet. He remembered where the door was, even after all the rolling about, threw himself towards it and again wrestled with the handle. It still wouldn't budge. He shook his head and tried to think. *Of course, you flaming fool! It opens inwards. The bloody door opens inwards.* He pulled and sighed with relief. It opened easily.

He charged through the gap as Lewis made one final lunge. Frost slammed the door shut behind him. He heard a sickening scrunching sound, a scream of agony and a clatter as the knife dropped to the floor.

'My hand – you're crushing my hand!' shrieked Lewis.

Frost opened the door and dragged Lewis out, kicking the knife well out of his reach. He winced as the pain from his injured wrist intensified.

In the early-morning light he could see that the butcher's hand was a mangled mess. 'As if we haven't got enough bleeding blood,' he muttered, fishing a pair of handcuffs from his pocket and locking Lewis's good wrist to his own good wrist. *A couple of bleeding walking wounded,* he thought. Everything hurt – his head, his back, his wrist – and blood was trickling down his face and neck from his slashed ear and cheek. He was totally exhausted. He didn't think he could make the journey across to his car without a rest. He slid down to the pavement and leant back against the shop front, sucking in lungfuls of clean air. The butcher was now sobbing softly.

'Is that how that nurse screamed when you cut her up?' asked Frost.

Lewis stopped sobbing. 'She killed my little boy,' he said, as if that explained everything.

'Let's get you to the car,' said Frost, pushing himself to his feet and bending as he tried to drag Lewis up. Suddenly, catching Frost off balance, Lewis plunged back into the shop, dragging Frost with him, and made a desperate lunge for the knife on the floor, almost toppling Frost as he grabbed it. One hand handcuffed, the other out of action, Frost swung out his foot, catching Lewis on the side of his head. Lewis went limp and the knife clattered to the ground. The butcher was out cold.

Totally drained, Frost slithered down beside the unmoving Lewis and rummaged in his pocket for a cigarette. Then he remembered that his lighter was buried amongst the offal. *Sod it.* His matches were in the car, so was his radio. He lifted one of Lewis's eyelids and just saw the whites of his eyes. The man was definitely unconscious. He unlocked the handcuffs, made it to the car and radioed for back-up.

* * *

The little Asian pharmacist in the twenty-four-hour chemist's was anxious to get Frost – and the smell of him – out of his shop as quickly as possible. 'Your wrist is not broken, only badly sprained,' he said, strapping it up tightly and selling Frost some extra-strong painkillers. 'Should be prescription only, but for you, Inspector Frost, I make an exception. Do not take more than six in any twenty-four hours.'

The pharmacist cleaned the cut on Frost's face with something that stung like mad, then slapped a sticking plaster on it. He held open the shop door and ushered Frost out, before hastily snatching an air-freshener from a shelf and spraying it liberally around.

The tablets, extra flaming strong or not, didn't seem to be having much effect on the pain; neither did a shower and change of clothes have much effect on the aroma. The smell of death clung tenaciously.

Frost got back in the car and drove to the butcher's to see how things were going. It was bloody painful driving, but it would be just as painful sitting behind his desk.

He parked behind the generating van that was pumping electricity to light up the inside of the butcher's so that Harding and his forensic team, plus SOCO, could see what they were doing and what it was they were smelling.

He'd had more than enough of the inside of the place so he stayed in the car and smoked, gritting his teeth against the throbbing agony of his sprained wrist. Bloody hell – it wouldn't have hurt as much as this if it had been broken.

After the second cigarette, Harding, the head of Forensic, staggered out, tearing the white filter mask from his face before being violently sick in the gutter.

'I hope you're going to clean that up before you go!' called Frost. 'Someone's dog might eat that!'

Harding raised a green, sweaty face and forced a grin, mopping his brow as he approached the car, talking to Frost through the open window.

'It's the body of a woman, Inspector – bits of one foot missing – almost certainly the bits you've been finding in Denton Woods. Throat cut, stab wounds all over her. Been dead a couple of weeks, I reckon.'

'That fits!' nodded Frost. 'It's the nurse who lived next door.' He turned his head at the lights of an approaching car, which slid to a halt behind him. Sandy Lane of the *Denton Echo* got out. 'Put a bit of rotting meat out and the bleeding vultures soon arrive,' muttered Frost as Lane approached the car.

'Understand you've found a body, Jack?' He sniffed and screwed up his face. 'What's that bloody awful smell?'

'It's my new aftershave,' said Frost. 'It stops randy reporters from putting their hand on my knee.'

'Well, it's working for me,' said Lane, flapping a hand in front of his nose. 'Who is it, Jack? Is it the other missing teenager?' He glanced at his wristwatch. 'Sod it. Too flaming late to make the London dailies.'

'If you'd given me some decent whisky,' replied Frost, 'I'd have kept the body on ice until a more convenient time.'

'But is it the missing girl?' insisted Lane.

Frost shrugged. 'She hasn't been identified yet.'

'Don't sod me about, Jack. I've been up all night and I'm tired.'

Frost smiled up at him. 'That whisky you gave me was like cat's pee.'

'All right,' sighed Lane. 'Two bottles of Johnnie Walker.'

'It's not the missing schoolgirl,' said Frost. 'We are working on the possibility that it may be connected with our investigations into a nurse reported missing from Denton General Hospital.'

'Cause of death?'

'Off the record, multiple stab wounds. For the record, we are awaiting the result of the post-mortem, but suspicious sods that we are, we suspect foul play.' After Taffy Morgan's foul-up with the press, Frost was treading on eggs.

'Was she raped?'

'The bit I saw wasn't raped,' answered Frost, 'but then it was only her hand.'

Lane's eyes widened. 'The bit you saw? You mean she was dismembered . . . cut into pieces?' He jerked a thumb. 'And in a butcher's shop?' His face brightened. 'Wow! We've got a terrific story here, Jack. The London papers would die for this. Give me some details?'

'That's all you're going to get for now, Sandy, but you can say that a forty-six-year-old man is helping us with our inquiries. We'll be issuing a press release after the autopsy and after we've had positive identification.'

'Three bottles of whisky, Jack?'

'Piss off.'

Lane grinned, waved his goodbyes and went back to his car. As he pulled out, a gleaming black Rolls Royce purred round the corner and filled Lane's vacated parking space. It was Drysdale, the Home Office pathologist. 'Where's my little fat roly poly?' muttered Frost to himself as he stepped out to meet him.

'Mucky one for you this time, Doc,' said Frost.

'Your ones usually are,' sniffed Drysdale. 'Lead the way, please.'

'Follow your nose,' said Frost, taking a deep breath as he bade a temporary goodbye to fresh air and led the way in, followed by the pathologist and his faded blonde secretary.

The harsh emergency lighting hammered off the white tiled walls. Seeing the mess made the smell seem stronger than ever. Frost found a cigarette and lit up, only to be stopped by Drysdale.

'Put that out, Inspector,' he snapped. 'I can't smell what I want to smell.'

'Whatever turns you on, Doc,' muttered Frost, spotting a box of face masks on a chopping block and slipping one on thankfully. Drysdale disdained the offer and his secretary, following her master's lead, shook her head, although she was looking distinctly green.

Even with the mask on, the smell seeped through. There were too many people inside the tiny room, making it hotter than ever. 'The bleeding place seemed twice the size in the dark,' muttered Frost to himself. 'Everyone wait outside,' he called. 'The doc can't appreciate the bouquet with all you sweaty sods in here.'

They needed no second bidding. With the lights streaming down, the scene looked even gorier than before. Forensic and SOCO had done a good job of sorting out the bloody pieces, which were laid out on green polythene sheeting like a macabre jigsaw puzzle. The head and limbs had been sawn from the trunk, which was naked. The hands and feet had been sawn from the limbs. Parts of the foot were missing – obviously the pieces that had been turning up in Denton Woods. The throat had been slashed, the stomach split and organs removed. It was like something out of Jack the Ripper.

'Is she dead, Doc?' asked Frost.

Drysdale, who didn't appreciate Frost's humour, gave him a cold glare and bent down to examine the carnage more closely. He prodded the trunk with his finger.

'She's been dead between one and two weeks.' His secretary briefly took away the handkerchief she had clasped to her nose and scribbled the great man's findings down in her shorthand notebook. 'Collect some of those maggots for the entomologist. He'll be more precise.'

Drysdale straightened up and consulted his

wristwatch. 'I can fit in a post-mortem at three this afternoon. Get the body to the mortuary, with the other bits of foot you tell me you have found. Stress to the attendant I do not want it washed or cleaned in any way until I say so.' He pointed to the tiled floor. 'And get samples of dried blood from all parts of the floor and walls . . . mark the location of each and take photographs. I need to confirm if any of it is human, which could mean she was killed in here.'

'Sure, Doc,' nodded Frost, hoping he could remember all this. 'So, for the record, cause of death?'

'She more than likely died from the many knife wounds – her throat's been cut, but I'll need to do the autopsy to determine if that was the prime cause. Three o'clock, Inspector. And I'd be obliged if, just for once, you weren't late.'

'Wouldn't miss it for the world,' said Frost.

Frost's cigarette was alight the minute his foot touched the pavement. The rest of the team were huddled in their cars, most of them smoking. He watched the rear lights of Drysdale's Rolls disappear round the corner, then called out, 'As you've been so good, I'm letting you go back inside again.' He issued Drysdale's instructions about getting the body over to the morgue, together with the other parts they had found previously. 'He wants the matching set. And the flaming prat wants maggots and blood samples from all over the walls and floor . . . and every bloodstain photographed. It would be easier to ask Lewis where he killed her, but Drysdale wants to do it the hard way.'

He beckoned DS Hanlon over. 'Arthur, get on to the Electricity people. I want the current restored to this place so we can get the refrigeration room operational. Drysdale's bound to discover one of her nipples is missing or something, and we'll have to send some poor sod back in to fish it out, so let's get it chilled down. And we'd better have a uniform guarding the doors in case souvenir hunters want a bit of ear-hole for their scrapbook.' He raised his voice to address the others. 'When you've finished, back to the station for breakfast – brains and liver on toast. And no pinching bits of meat for your dinner. It's been counted.'

'Superintendent Mullett wants to see you,' called Wells as Frost pushed through the swing doors.

'He can go and—' began Frost, then picking up the sergeant's urgent face-twitching signal that the superintendent was within earshot, hastily amended, 'He can be assured he's only got to ask.' He turned to see Mullett in the doorway. 'Oh hello, Super. Didn't see you there.'

'My office!' barked Mullett, spinning on his heels and marching back down the corridor.

'It's the third door from the end,' called Frost.

Mullett got up from his chair and opened a window wide as Frost entered.

'Yes, there is a funny smell in here, Super,'

said Frost, flopping in a chair. 'I noticed it the minute I came in.'

Mullett frowned. 'Hardly the time for cheap humour, Frost.' He looked the DI up and down, scowling his displeasure. 'You look a mess. You're dishevelled, unshaven, and those clothes have seen better days.'

'Sorry,' said Frost. 'Next time I fight for my life in the bleeding dark I'll put my best suit on.'

'Your sarcasm about the incident is misplaced, Frost. This should wipe that smile off your face. I have just had our local radio station on the phone, wanting me to confirm that a suspect arrested this morning is in intensive care with his fingers smashed and severe concussion following a savage kick in the head.' He repeated these last words to emphasise the seriousness. 'A kick, Frost . . . in the head.'

'Yes, I heard you the first time,' said Frost. 'I was defending myself. He came at me with a knife.'

'To kick a man in the head, he would have to be down on the floor, Frost. You hardly needed to defend yourself when your assailant was on the floor.'

'He was reaching for the bloody knife.'

'You could have kicked it out of the way. The press are going to have a field day over this, and you can't expect me to back you.'

'That's the last thing I would expect,' said Frost. 'I only had one free hand.' He held up the strapped wrist. 'This one was useless. I was groggy after hitting my head on the floor. This mad bastard had already taken a slice out of my ear and my cheek, just in case you think I cut myself shaving.' He touched the sticking plaster and wished it was bigger.

Mullett dismissed this with a wave of his hand. 'Excuses, excuses. If Lewis dies . . .'

His phone rang. Mullett frowned at it for daring to interrupt, then picked it up. 'Mullett!' The frown vanished. He straightened himself up in his chair, smoothing his hair and straightening an already immaculate tie. 'Good morning, Chief Constable. Yes, I've heard, sir.'

Mullett covered the mouthpiece with his hand and hissed to Frost, 'He's heard about your brutal arrest – I'm not going to cover up for you.' Then back instantly to the phone. 'Yes, sir. I'm dealing with that right now. I have Frost in the office with me . . . I—' He stopped dead. As if a switch had clicked, his expression changed. 'I couldn't agree with you more, sir . . . a very brave thing to do . . . tackling a man with a knife in the pitch dark . . . and he suffered minor injuries himself, did you know? Yes, sir . . . Funnily enough I was telling him that as you phoned . . . a credit to the Denton force.'

Frost leant back in his chair and smirked.

'One minor problem,' Mullett went on. 'I've had the local TV station on accusing us of police brutality . . . Yes, sir, I shall certainly put them in their place. As you know, sir, I back my men to the hilt.' He ignored Frost's exaggerated expression of disbelief. 'His transfer request? . . . I'm doing my best to talk him out of it, sir, but his mind seems to be made up . . . Yes, sir, I'll try again . . . I agree we need men like him in the division . . . Thank you, sir.' He hung up and shuffled some papers on his desk, trying to reassemble his thoughts.

'No need to talk me out of it, Super,' beamed Frost. 'To help you out, I'll stay.'

'The Chief Constable is unaware of your forgeries and your obtaining money by false pretences, Frost. If he found out, there would be no question of you staying anywhere in the force . . . you would be out on your ear and nothing I could do would stop it.'

'I'm sure of that,' said Frost. He stood up. 'Anything else?'

Mullett waved him back into his chair. 'There is something else, Frost. I've had DCI Skinner on the phone. He's still tying up loose ends in his old division, but he should be able to return to Denton permanently in a week or two. And when he does he wants to bring his own Detective Inspector with him. So we want you to be ready to move out instantly. What have you done about selling your house?'

'I've thought about it,' said Frost.

'You've got to do more than think about it. You'll need somewhere to live in Lexton. DCI Skinner has kindly given your details to estate agents there, who will be contacting you.'

'DCI Skinner's kindness overwhelms me at times,' said Frost. 'And there was me thinking he was a lousy bastard.'

'I shall pretend I didn't hear that,' said Mullett.

'As time is of the essence, Frost, I suggest you take the rest of the day off and get your house tidied up into a fit condition for estate agents to value it.'

Back in his office, Frost phoned Taffy Morgan at the hospital. 'How's Lewis?' he asked.

'He's all right, Guv. He was only stunned.'

'Oh dear. Mullett was hoping he'd die so he could boot me out. Are they keeping him in?'

'Only for another twenty-four hours for observation.'

'Right. I'll get Sergeant Wells to send you a relief. I need you down here.'

'The doctors are worried about his mental state.'

'That's funny, Taff. I'm worried about yours. What are they going to do about it?'

'They reckon they should get him sectioned.'

'Bloody good idea . . . he's not going to be fit to plead and it will get him off our backs. I'll get Bill Wells on to it.'

He hung up. His head was hurting. His wrist was hurting. It wasn't time for the next lot of painkillers, but he shook out a double dose and swallowed them dry. *Dangerous to exceed the stated dose*, it said. Well, he'd live dangerously. They weren't doing any bleeding good anyway. He yawned and scrubbed his face with his hands. Why was he so bloody tired? Was it the tablets? He read the manufacturer's warnings . . . the tablets could evidently cause everything from exploding eyeballs to heart failure . . . *Should you experience any of these symptoms, stop taking the medication instantly and consult your GP*. And yes, they could cause tiredness – *Do not drive or operate heavy machinery*.

He yawned again. Of course he was flaming tired. What with all the sodding about with Lewis, he'd barely had half an hour's sleep. Well, he wasn't fit for work in this state. He'd obey his thoughtful Divisional Commander and go home for a couple of hours and have a kip.

As he yawned his way through the lobby, Bill Wells called after him, 'Mullett wants you again, Jack.'

'He can bloody want,' said Frost.

The minute his head touched the pillow, thoughts started whirling round his brain – all the things he had to do, all the things he hadn't done – and he knew there was no chance of sleep. He lit a cigarette and lay there, staring upwards, watching the smoke writhe its way to the nicotine-stained ceiling. What was that song Peggy Lee used to sing – 'Don't Smoke In Bed'? There was supposed to be a danger of dropping off to sleep and burning yourself to death when the bedclothes caught fire. The worst thing about smoking in bed as far as he was concerned was that the ash kept falling on his chest. He brushed away the latest deposit, stubbed the cigarette out and shut his eyes, willing sleep to pay him a visit. He was just drifting off when . . .

The bloody hall phone rang.

He tried to ignore it, but it rang and rang and rang.

Cursing softly, he padded downstairs and snatched up the handset. 'Frost.'

'My name is Richard from Ripley's estate agent's. When would it be convenient to call to value your home?'

'What did you say your name was?' asked Frost sweetly.

'Richard.'

'Then piss off, Richard.' He slammed the phone down, making the hall table shake. Sod it. Sleep was impossible now. And he'd have to face up to the fact that, like it or not, they were going to boot him out of Denton and he'd have to sell this place. An estate agent would have to call and put a price on it. Prospective buyers would come to have a sniff around, shake their heads and say, 'We were looking for something bigger, cheaper, less scruffy, and in a better state of repair.'

As he turned to go back upstairs a package plopped through the letter box. A plastic sack from Oxfam, who were inviting householders to fill it with unwanted clothing.

If he was going to move into somewhere smaller he would have to chuck away a whole batch of stuff. The wardrobe was jam-packed with his late wife's clothes. They could all go for a start. He made a detour to the bathroom, where he splashed cold water over his face to chase away the last vestiges of tiredness, rubbed his chin and decided a shave could wait, then went back into the bedroom. There were so many dresses, coats, blouses, skirts, going back years. His wife had never thrown anything away. He shook them off their hangers and started stuffing them into the bag.

Then he came to the red dress. The red, short-sleeved, low-necked cocktail dress. The dress she had worn that Christmas . . .

The first Christmas after they had married. Their very first Christmas together in their own home, and it was all spoilt when the bloody phone rang and he was called back on duty because of the murdered girl – the girl Graham Fielding had raped and strangled.

That stinking row . . . her tears, her threats . . . 'If you leave me on Christmas Day I won't be here when you get back!' Nothing would console her . . . He remembered her tear-stained face . . . but he had been called out on duty. He had to leave her.

It was gone ten at night when he finally got back home, cold, tired, apprehensive and miserable. Their big day together ruined. The house seemed dark and empty. He called out her name. No reply. His heart sank. Had she gone to bed, or, worse still, had she carried out her threat and left him?

He walked down the passage to the kitchen, clicking on lights as he went. He steeled himself and pushed open the door. The warm smell of cooking hit him in the face.

The lights were off. His wife, in the red cocktail dress, was at the table, which she had laid with a red cloth, red serviettes and red candles, the reflected flames dancing on her skin. God, she was beautiful. He could see her now. Absolutely beautiful.

She rushed to meet him. They kissed. They both kept saying, 'I'm sorry, I'm sorry, I'm sorry . . .' They exchanged presents. She had bought him a super cigarette lighter, which he lost after a week and didn't dare tell her. He had bought her a sexy nightdress and another present. He called it a Marilyn Monroe nightdress as it was all she claimed to wear in bed . . . a bottle of Chanel No. 5, which had cost him a packet. 'That's the nightdress I'm going to wear tonight,' she told him.

The most wonderful Christmas night of his life. What happened? How did things go avalanching downhill? Why did such deep, passionate love change to cold, sullen hate? How did his beautiful, loving wife change into the bitter, grim-faced woman who he had to sit and watch die? It was all his fault. She had ambitions. She wanted him to go places, but he knew his limitations.

He realised he was crying. Hot tears coursed down his cheeks. He pressed his face into the red dress. The perfume – the Chanel. Was it his imagination or could he still smell the ghost of that perfume? God, what a night they had had . . .

He looked down at the sack, half filled with her clothes. No point in being sentimental. Everything had to go, even the red dress.

But he couldn't do it. He put the dress back on its hanger and returned it to the wardrobe. The rest of the clothes he crammed in, forcing them down to make room, then tied the sack.

He sat on the bed and smoked some more, and thought of all the good times. Bloody hell. He was supposed to be a cynical bastard. That knock on the head was making him all sentimental and flaming weepy. Chanel No. 5 in the tiniest of bottles. 'For that price I expected a pint at least,' he had told the sales girl when he bought it. It had cost him a packet. But she was worth it, every penny.

He caught sight of the alarm clock. Damn. If he didn't hurry he'd be late once again for Drysdale's post-mortem.

The pathologist straightened up from the autopsy table and stepped back to allow the photographers to take their photographs of the dismembered body, which had now been cleaned up slightly.

'She received a blow to the head which would have rendered her unconscious,' he told Frost. 'Then her throat was cut – the way animals are slaughtered, I suppose.' He peeled off his surgical gloves and dropped them in the disposal bin on top of his discarded plastic apron. 'The dismembering of the body was carried out immediately after death.'

Drysdale moved across to the sink and washed his hands, holding them out for the towel his faithful, ever-anticipating secretary had ready. 'Our suspect is a butcher, I believe?'

'Yes,' nodded Frost. 'I don't think he'll ever stand trial. His solicitor has got doctors to say he's unfit to plead and I don't think we're going to argue about that.'

Drysdale pushed his arms into the sleeves of the overcoat his secretary was holding out, then looked back at the body on the table and shook his head. 'In all my years as a pathologist, it never ceases to disgust me how people can do such things to fellow human beings.'

'His five-year-old son died in Denton Hospital,' said Frost. 'He doted on the kid and cracked up. He blamed the hospital and the nurses for the kid's death.' He rubbed his aching wrist. 'I almost feel sorry for the poor sod.'

Drysdale stared at Frost. 'You amaze me, Inspector.'

As soon as the pathologist had left, Frost tore off the green mortuary gown and hurried out to his car. He was thankful that Drysdale was satisfied they had recovered all the body parts and didn't want the shop searched again for a navel or an ear-hole or something equally obscure. Blood samples and maggots had been sent off to the appropriate experts, but he didn't give a sod about the result. Wherever and whenever she had been killed, the poor cow was dead and they had the killer, and if it didn't come to trial there would be a hell of a lot less paperwork.

Back in his office, a memo from Mullett glowered at him from his in-tray. Mullett was concerned at the amount of manpower being used in the search for the missing teenager, Jan O'Brien. When, he asked, would the officers involved be able to return to their normal duties?

'*As soon as possible*,' scrawled Frost across the neatly typed memo, which he winged across to his out-tray. Bloody hell. There was no flaming peace in this job. Wouldn't it be lovely if a couple of days went by without bodies turning up, girls going missing and bastards blackmailing the supermarket? How was he going to get through everything he had to do with Hornrim Harry screaming about costs and missing paperwork, and half the force out of Denton on special duties?

His phone buzzed. 'Mullett wants to see you now,' said Bill Wells.

'Tell him I'm out,' said Frost, grabbing his mac and making for his car.

He drove around aimlessly; his head was still throbbing and his flaming wrist was hurting like hell, and he was getting sleepy. He passed the turning leading to the butcher's, and wondered who Wells had given the lousy job of standing on guard outside – or inside, if they had a strong stomach. It was cold, windy and raining and he pitied whichever poor sod had drawn the short straw.

The poor sod in question was WPC Kate Holby, who was huddled up in the shop doorway sheltering from the driving rain. She quickly sprang to attention as Frost's car drew up.

'All right, love,' called Frost, turning up his mac collar as he joined her in the doorway. 'You don't have to impress me, I'm nobody. Sold much meat?'

She grinned. For a while they silently watched the rain drumming on the pavement and gurgling down the drain. 'You're looking a lot happier now, love,' said Frost. 'Settling in, are you?'

'It's been a lot better these last few days,' she said.

'That's because Skinner's not here, isn't it?'

She said nothing.

'Look, love. Our mutual friend Skinner is kicking me out to Lexton in a couple of weeks. You really should come with me. You could easily get a transfer. I might be able to get you into CID.' The thought of the kid stuck with Skinner and no one to stick up for her was something he didn't like to contemplate.

She shook her head. 'I'm not letting him drive me out. I'm not running away.'

'If you don't stand a chance of winning, it's often better to run,' said Frost. 'I'd run away from the bastard if I were you. Your time will come. You're bloody good, love, like your dad. You'll zoom up the ranks. You might even be Skinner's boss one day, then you can pay the bastard back.'

'He's not forcing me out,' she said stubbornly.

Frost shrugged. 'Fair enough. But if you ever change your mind . . .' He looked out into the rain again and noticed Lewis's car was still parked outside. It should have been taken back to the station. Something else he had forgotten about. 'Why aren't you waiting inside, out of the rain?' he asked.

'I haven't got the key,' she told him.

'Didn't the bastards let you have the key—' began Frost, stopping suddenly as he realised the key was in his pocket. He was about to hand it over, but dropped it back into his pocket again.

'Hell, why are we guarding this place? The autopsy's over, no bits are missing and if anyone wants to break in and pinch any of that meat, they're welcome. Hop in my car, I'll drive you back to the station, then I'm off home to get my head down for a couple of hours.'

As he slowed down and waited for the traffic lights to change, he looked at her out of the corner of his eye. Her face was reflecting the red glow of the stop signal . . . red like the dress his wife wore that Christmas. God, the kid was a cracker. A stubborn little cow, but a cracker. She reminded him of his wife when she was that age.

The lights turned green and the car jerked forward. *You're getting to be a bleeding maudlin old sod*, he told himself.

15

Detective Inspector Jack Frost walked into his office to find DS Arthur Hanlon on a chair doing something to the overhead light.

'Don't jump, Arthur – think of your wife and kids. Why make them happy?'

Hanlon clambered down to put a blown light bulb on the desk. 'I've changed the bulb. You couldn't do it with your poor hand.'

Frost grunted his thanks. 'If anyone says you're not a little sweetie, Arthur, send them to me. Now piss off. I've got to get my head down for a couple of hours, otherwise I'll be even more bleeding useless than usual.' He riffled through his in-tray: all the usual junk from Mullett – memos marked 'Urgent' with lots of underlinings in red ink. They could wait.

Hanlon grinned. 'Manchester CID have been on the blower, Jack. They want to know what progress we've made with the murdered girl.'

'Flaming heck,' snorted Frost. 'We've got enough on our plate with our own unsolved murders without trying to solve theirs.' He plonked down in his chair, dragged the Emily Roberts file from his in-tray and flipped through it. 'It suits them to work on the theory that the girl was picked up in Manchester and brought down here to be killed. Skinner wants her to have been killed in Manchester and the body dumped down here, so it's Manchester's pigeon. Between you and me, I'm inclined to go along with Manchester CID's version. If she was killed there, why dump her here?'

'They say you asked if she had done any modelling, or wanted to be a model. They can't turn anything up that would support this.'

'I was trying to tie her killing in with Debbie Clark. Both bodies on an embankment, both naked. And they both went to the same school in Denton, did you know that?'

Hanlon shook his head. 'So what am I going to tell them, Jack?'

Frost worried away at his scar, deep in thought. 'We've got sod all to go on, Arthur. A dumped body, that's all.' He rested his chin on his palm and chewed his little finger. 'If the killer came from Denton, why would he go to Manchester to pick up a girl? There's plenty of girls in Denton.'

Hanlon shrugged.

Frost held up a finger as a thought struck him. 'Try this out for size, Arthur, as the bishop said to the actress – the killer was going to Manchester anyway. When he was there, he saw his chance and took it.' He leant back in his chair. 'And I'll tell you something else, Arthur. If you were driving from Denton to Manchester you wouldn't want to go there and back in the same day. You'd stay overnight in a hotel or a B&B, and when you stay somewhere you've got to register – give your name and address. Hotels are required by law to keep the records for six months or so – I can't remember exactly how long. Get Manchester CID to check it out, see if anyone from Denton stayed in the area overnight the day the girl went missing. If we can find the name of anyone who worked for that modelling agency or worked in the office block, then bingo, two dicky birds with one stone.'

'There's a hell of a lot of hotels and B&Bs in Manchester, Jack. They won't be too pleased.'

'We're not in the business of pleasing them. They know the area where she went missing. They can start from there. If they have more luck than I usually do, it could be the first one they try.'

'Supposing he registered under a false name and address?'

'Many of these places ask for car registration numbers – we could trace him through that. And the odds are he paid by credit card, so he'd have to give his proper name. Do what I say, Arthur, there's a good boy. Get on to Manchester. It'll keep them off our backs for a while.'

As Hanlon left, Frost's phone rang. It was Marcus from the Crown Prosecution Service. 'We're taking Graham Fielding to court on Wednesday, Inspector. We understand his solicitor is going to ask for bail.'

'Bail? On a murder charge? He won't stand a chance.'

'I wouldn't be so sure. The courts sometimes use their discretion. The crime happened a long time ago.'

'That doesn't make the poor cow he killed any less dead, does it?'

'I suppose not,' said Marcus grudgingly. 'Do we oppose bail?'

'Of course we bleeding well oppose it,' said Frost. 'Who's our lawyer?'

'Mr Jefferson.'

'That useless prat! Well let's hope he doesn't sod this one up like he did the last one.' He slammed the phone down and was reaching for his mac when Bill Wells came in.

'Whatever it is, Bill, it will have to wait. I'm off home for a couple of hours.'

'Just received this package,' said Wells, dumping it on the desk. It measured about nine inches by five inches and was wrapped in brown paper and neatly sellotaped.

Frost picked it up and examined it. The typed label was addressed to: THE OFFICER IN CHARGE, DENTON POLICE STATION, DENTON

He looked up at Wells. 'So? Why haven't you opened it?'

'I don't like the look of it. It could be a bomb.'

Frost stared at him. 'Why should it be a bleeding bomb?'

'It's the same size as that package Flintwell division had the other week. That was a bomb.'

'It wasn't a flaming bomb,' said Frost. 'It was a hoax . . . it was full of talcum powder.'

'This may not be a hoax.'

'Then call the flaming bomb squad, or give it to Mullett. Let him lay his life down for his men.'

Wells hesitated, still trying to get Frost to take the package.

'Oh, give it here.' Frost snatched it from the sergeant, grabbed a paper knife and slit the sealed ends. 'Stand by for the explosion.'

Wells stepped back warily.

Frost held it down with his elbow and tore off the wrapping with his good hand. 'Bloody hell!' he cried. There was a shattering bang and bits of broken glass everywhere. Wells flung himself down on the ground.

'Sorry,' said Frost. 'I must have accidentally knocked that dud light bulb on the floor.'

A glowering Wells stood up, brushing pieces of broken light bulb from his uniform. 'You bastard, Jack. You did that on purpose.'

'That's either slander or libel,' said Frost. 'If I knew which it was I'd sue you.' He stripped the brown paper away. Inside was a video cassette. There was no covering note. He slid the package over to Wells. 'Get someone to play it. If there's anything I should see, let me know when I get back. If it blows up and kills someone, tell them I'm sorry.'

'Very funny,' sniffed Wells.

There was no way he was going to get the sleep he so desperately craved. As he turned the key in the lock, he could already hear his phone ringing.

It was Bill Wells.

'What the hell is it now?' snarled Frost.

'You switched your mobile off.'

'I know. Stupid bastards keep trying to phone me. So what is it?'

'That video, Jack. You've got to see it.'

'What's on it?'

'I think you'd better see it for yourself, Jack.'

'All right, I'll see it when I get back. Now let me get some sleep.'

'Now, Jack. You've got to see it now.'

Frost frowned. 'I'm dead on my flaming feet, Bill. This isn't a leg-pull, is it? Are you paying me back for the light bulb?'

'It's not a leg-pull, Jack; I wish it was. I'm deadly serious.' He sounded it.

'All right,' sighed Frost. 'I'm on my way.'

Mullett waylaid him as he hurried down the corridor. He'd checked Frost's in-tray and found all his memos untouched.

'My office, now, Frost.'

'Right away, Super,' said Frost on autopilot. He didn't follow Mullett. He branched off into the Incident Room, where DS Hanlon, Wells and PC Collier were waiting for him. They all looked shaken and grim-faced.

Frost stuck a cigarette in his mouth and sat himself down in the chair facing the monitor.

'The tape's loaded, Inspector,' Collier told him. 'Just press Play.'

Frost pressed Play.

Black-and-white flashes zipped across the screen, then a juddering picture of two people appeared, too fuzzy to make out, then the picture steadied. Something black moved from side to side – a black cloth covering something.

Frost fiddled with the volume control. 'What's happened to the sound?'

'There's no sound, Jack,' said Wells. 'Just watch.'

The video camera zoomed back. The black cloth was a hood, completely covering someone's head. It was shaking violently from side to side.

A hand snatched at the hood and pulled it off. A close-up of a pair of tear-stained eyes blinking at the light. The head twisted away from the camera. A blur as a hand passed in front of the face and jerked it back to face the camera, holding it firmly so it couldn't move. The camera zoomed back further. A young girl, terrified and crying.

The cigarette dropped from Frost's mouth. He stared in horrified disbelief. 'Good God . . .'

It was the tortured, pleading, crying face of Debbie Clark.

The picture blacked out. White snow shivered across the black screen.

Frost was still staring, frozen to his chair, open-mouthed. He went to switch off and rewind the tape. A restraining hand stopped him.

'There's more to come, Jack,' said Wells gently.

The snow juddered, then cleared to reveal a quivering picture of Debbie Clark's face.

Whoever was holding the camera was shaking violently. The picture steadied. The girl's head and bare shoulders filled the screen; Frost could just make out the dark shape of someone standing behind her. Debbie moved her head to one side. Hands grabbed her hair and roughly jerked her back.

The girl's lips were moving. She was saying something . . . pleading with whoever was operating the video camera.

Two hands moved up slowly from behind her and encircled her throat. She vainly shook her head from side to side, trying to shake them off, still screaming and pleading.

The hands tightened their grip on her throat.

Her face crumpled in agony.

Her eyes bulged. Blood trickled from her mouth.

The hands squeezed tighter, tighter, then released their grip.

The girl slid lifelessly to the floor, the camera following her down.

Keeping well out of the camera view, her killer dragged her up by her hair. Her head hung limply, tongue lolling.

She was dead.

The hands let go and she slumped back to the floor.

The picture ended abruptly and noisy, raw tape took over.

'Switch the bleeding thing off,' said Frost. He couldn't take his eyes off the monitor.

Collier leant across him and clicked off the video player.

Frost felt cold, he felt sick, he felt angry, he felt pity, and he felt bloody helpless.

He shook a cigarette from the packet and, with unsteady hands, poked it in his mouth.

'Bloody hell,' he croaked. 'They filmed the poor kid being strangled. The perverted bastards!'

The others said nothing. They were as affected as he was.

'I want everyone involved in this investigation to see that tape,' said Frost. 'We drop everything else and we concentrate on this one. We've got to get these bastards. I want copies of that tape made. I want the original to go over to Forensic with the wrapping paper and I want them to drop everything too. This is top priority.' He scrubbed his face with his hands. He had never felt so upset and shaken in all his life.

'Why film it? Why send us a copy?' asked Hanlon.

Frost shook his head. He didn't have any answers. He shunted his cigarettes around.

The Incident Room door opened and closed. No one looked round to see who it was.

'What is going on, Frost?' hissed Mullett. 'I specifically told you to come to my office. Instead I find you lolling and smoking in here.'

Frost didn't look up. He took a long drag at his cigarette and expelled a lungful of smoke. 'Something more important than a bollocking in your office came up,' he snapped.

Mullett's face went beetroot. 'And what could be more important than a summons from your divisional commander?' he snapped back.

'This!' said Frost, jerking a finger at the monitor and vacating the chair. He nodded to Collier. 'Play the tape for Superintendent Mullett, son.'

Mullett glanced at the screen impatiently. Then he froze. His face whitened and he dropped down into the chair, staring, as if hypnotised, at the images on the monitor. As it ended, he turned his head away and took off his glasses to pinch his nose and dab his eyes. 'My God!' he said.

'Came by post an hour ago,' Frost told him. 'London postmark.'

Mullett covered his face with his hands and shook his head. 'My God!' he said again. He blew his nose loudly, then stood up. 'Take all the men you want, Frost – from other divisions if necessary, but get these animals.'

Frost nodded his thanks. 'I want to keep this bottled up for the moment, Super. No one outside need know we've had this tape – especially the parents. Now is not the time.'

'Anything you say, Frost,' said Mullett, who then hurried back to his office.

'See,' said Frost. 'The bastard has a heart after all. Show him a video of a girl being strangled and he's putty in your hands.' He screwed up his eyes and shook his head in an attempt to erase the images he had just witnessed. 'Hanlon, get the video copied and send the original straight over to Forensic. And let's go back to my office. I've got some whisky.'

Frost sat in his office with Hanlon and Wells, all moodily drinking Sandy Lane's Scotch out of mugs. They were still shaken. Frost spat out a tea leaf. 'Right. Why did they send us the tape?'

Blank faces.

'You're a lot of bleeding help.'

'We know there's at least two of them,' said Hanlon. 'One to take the film, the other to kill the girl.'

'The camera could have been on a tripod,' suggested Wells.

Frost shook his head. 'No. It was jerking about too much – in any case, the girl was talking to whoever held the camera, pleading for her bleeding life.'

A tap on the door and Jordan, Simms and Kate Holby came in, all looking shattered. 'We've just seen the copy of the tape,' said Jordan.

'Then you'll need some of this,' said Frost, finding some battered polystyrene cups and slurping whisky in them. Even Kate didn't refuse, coughing as she sipped it. It was a tight squeeze in his tiny office; some were sitting on chairs, others on the corners of the desks. 'We keep this to ourselves,' said Frost for the benefit of the newcomers. 'No one outside the station must know about the tape. If the parents find out they'll want to see it and I'm not going through that. Anyone got any brilliant ideas to add to my own sod all?'

'It was definitely taken in that office block,' said Simms. 'The same walls.'

'Yes, I noticed that,' said Frost. He snapped his fingers as a thought struck him. 'She was sitting in a chair. They wouldn't have brought one with them, so they must have taken one from the lobby.' He jabbed a finger at Jordan and Simms. 'As soon as you've finished your booze, get over there. I want all the chairs collected and taken to Forensic. If our luck's in for a change, there might be prints.'

'The hands strangling her,' offered Hanlon, 'definitely a man – bare hairy arms.'

'The sod was probably naked and hairy all over,' said Frost. 'The poor cow had already been beaten and raped.' He drained his cup and decided against a refill. The room was hot, he was overtired and the drink was going to his head. It was important to keep a clear mind.

'Did you notice how he was keeping well to one side so as not to obstruct the view of the camera?' asked Kate.

'He wanted to make certain he couldn't be identified,' said Hanlon.

'How could we identify him? We only saw his hands. No, it was more than that,' said the WPC. 'He was making certain the camera got a clear view of the girl.'

Frost spun round in his chair. 'You're right, girl, you are bloody right. Let's take another look.' They drained their mugs and followed him into the Incident Room.

They crowded round the monitor. There was

silence as the tortured face of the girl appeared. Silence until the tape ended.

Frost turned to Kate. 'You're dead right, love. Everything is arranged so we get a clear view of the girl. Nothing else matters. There's a bit there where it judders and jerks. I reckon they stopped the camera because she moved her head, pulled it round to the camera again and restarted filming. I think we now know what's behind that.'

'Perhaps I'm a bit thick . . .' began Hanlon.

'Don't be so bleeding modest, Arthur,' said Frost. 'You're more than a bit thick, you're bleeding thick. I reckon those bastards were making a snuff movie.'

'What?' asked Wells.

'There are perverts, Bill, who get their kicks out of seeing people die – preferably painfully killed. They'd pay a bomb for a video if they were sure it was genuine. I reckon the whole point of the killing was to make a snuff movie, either for kicks, for money or for both.'

'Bloody hell,' hissed Wells.

'My sentiments exactly,' said Frost, picking up the phone on its first ring. It was Harding from Forensic.

Frost cradled the phone on his shoulder, wedging it with his chin as he lit up another cigarette. 'What have you got?' He listened, grunting from time to time. 'Yes . . . we bloody well knew that . . . Fingerprints?' His expression changed. He grabbed the phone and pressed it tighter to his ear. 'Are you sure? If anyone says you're flaming useless, tell them it's only most of the time.' He slammed the phone down and turned to the others, who were looking at him expectantly.

'Right. The videotape was brand new – never been used before. The bit we saw had been copied from the video-camera tape. It was copied with the audio lead out, either by accident or design. Harding agrees it had been stopped and started a couple of times, probably to re-arrange Debbie's face so the camera could get a clear look at what the poor cow was going through. He confirms the background is the wall of the office block on Denton Road, which we flaming well knew. He'll check it out, but is almost certain it's the floor the boy fell from. I don't think there's much flaming doubt about that either. Right, now we come to the fingerprints. There were two clear dabs on the cassette – Sergeant Wells and Collier, so I'm arresting them both on suspicion. Clearly whoever sent it wiped it clean before wrapping it up. After they wrapped it and sealed it down, they wiped it again. It's now smothered in dirty finger marks, but the odds are they came from the postal staff, plus Bill Wells who brought it to me, and me, who opened it. So far, so bleeding bad. But it looks as if they wiped off the prints after they stuck it down, so they couldn't get to the prints on the taped folds and couldn't wipe them off. Forensic have found two lovely clear dabs.'

'Too much to hope they are on record?' asked Hanlon.

'Yes, Arthur,' nodded Frost. 'Too much to hope. But thanks to Forensic it narrows the field down. Before this, we didn't have the faintest idea who did it, but now we can eliminate everyone who has got a criminal record!' He sighed, took a last drag at his cigarette and ground it underfoot. 'We're still no further forward. Why did they send us the tape? To brag about what they had done, or to torment us for being a load of twats? – as if we didn't know that already.' He sighed. 'Come on, let's kill that bottle of whisky.'

As Frost pushed himself up out of his chair, the door burst open and Sandy Lane came in. 'No one at the desk, so I let myself in,' he beamed. He pointed to the monitor. 'You been watching the videotape of the girl?'

Frost's jaw sagged. He stared at Lane, then dropped back into the chair. 'What videotape?' he asked. How the hell had Lane got wind of this? Had some bastard been blabbing to the press? He shot a suspicious look at Morgan.

'The tape of the dead girl – Debbie Clark,' replied Lane, as if it was obvious what tape he was talking about.

'I know nothing about any bleeding tape,' lied Frost. Who had told the sod?

Lane dragged up a spare chair and sat next to the inspector. 'Come off it, Jack. We've just had an anonymous phone call. A woman. She said, "If you want a scoop, ask the filth about the video we sent them. Ask them if they'd like a video of the other girl." As soon as she said filth, I thought of you.'

Frost leant back in his chair and stared at the reporter, his mind racing. 'What other girl?'

Lane shrugged. 'That's all she said before she hung up. I presume she meant that girl you found on the railway embankment.'

'Or she might have meant that other missing teenager, Jan O'Brien,' said Frost anxiously. 'You record all incoming calls, don't you?'

'Yes,' nodded Lane. He dug in his pocket and pulled out an audio cassette and held it aloft. 'But as you haven't received the video, there's no point in my giving you this.' He snatched his hand back as Frost tried to grab it. 'Come on, Jack. Give me a flaming break. A story like this – I could get it in all the London dailies with an exclusive byline.'

'Sod your bylines,' snarled Frost. 'My only concern is to nail these bastards. That other poor cow might still be alive. I want to find her before they do to her what they did to Debbie. I want that tape, Sandy!'

'No way,' said the reporter firmly.

Frost beckoned to Kate Holby. 'Run the video for him.'

As she fed the tape into the machine, he grabbed the reporter's sleeve. 'This is off the record, Sandy, strictly off the bleeding record. If you breathe a bloody word of it outside . . .' He let the threat hang.

But Lane was unaware of Frost. He was transfixed, staring at the screen. Towards the end he turned his head away. 'Christ!' he muttered as the tape flickered to a close. 'I've seen some shitty things in my time, Jack, but this . . .'

'We don't yet know why it was sent to us,'

Frost told him. 'But until we do, we're keeping shtum. They want us to acknowledge it, that's why they got on to you, but we're not going to. Nothing appears in the press, Sandy, and I want that audio cassette now.'

Without a word, Lane handed it over. Frost gave it to Kate, who loaded the cassette recorder.

A beeping sound, then a woman's voice:

'*I want to speak to the crime bloke.*'

'Speaking. Who is this, please?'

'*I ain't telling you who I am. You know that kid who was murdered – the school kid?*'

'What about her?'

'*Debbie. If you want a scoop, ask the filth about the video.*'

'What video?'

'*And ask them if they want a video of the other girl.*'

'But—'

A click, the dialling tone, then silence.

Frost worried away at his scar. 'Sounds like a real bit of low life.' He turned to Morgan. 'Not one of your girlfriends is she, Taff?'

Morgan grinned and shook his head.

'She called the girl "Debbie",' said Frost, half to himself. 'Almost as if she knew the kid personally.' He leant back in his chair and fired a salvo of smoke rings up to the ceiling, watching them slowly disperse. 'She wants publicity. She wants it in the press. Why?'

No one could come up with a reason.

'A snuff movie?' suggested Lane.

'We've already thought of that. If it's a snuff

movie and they're hoping to sell it, it's only worth anything if it's genuine.'

'There's no doubt it's genuine,' said Hanlon. 'That was Debbie Clark all right.'

Frost sat up as a thought struck him. 'Wait a minute . . . wait a flaming minute . . .' He turned to Sandy. 'The only photograph published in the press was that old school photo taken when she was about nine. Her father wouldn't let her have her photo taken after that. It wasn't a very good photo and it was nothing like the way she looked now.' He clicked his fingers. 'Of course! The sods want to be able to provide proof it is Debbie and not some tart acting and pretending to be Debbie. Well, they're not bloody well going to get proof from us.' He spun round to the reporter. 'She's bound to phone you again, Sandy. When she does, tell her you've been to the police and they deny ever receiving a video. She'll then have to send you – or us – another one, which might give us a bit more gen.' He stopped suddenly as another thought hit him. 'If I was them, I'd then send a copy of the video to the mother. There's no way that poor cow would keep quiet about it.' He jabbed a finger at Bill Wells. 'Get on to the post office. I want them to hold all her mail until we've examined it. And let's have someone on duty outside the house 24/7 in case they decide to deliver it personally. Mullett's okayed limitless overtime. It'd be rude not to take full advantage of it.'

Wells nodded. 'I'll put it in hand right now, Jack.' He scuttled out of the room.

'Well,' said Frost, 'we've got her fingerprints and her voice. If only we had her telephone number and knicker size.'

'I've got the phone number,' said Lane smugly. 'We've got caller ID. We hold the last ninety-nine calls dialled in to us.' He pulled a sheet of notepaper from his pocket and handed it to Frost. 'It's a Denton number. I dialled, but got no answer. I imagine it's a public call box. People are getting too smart these days. They know calls can be traced.'

Frost glanced briefly at the number, then handed the paper to Hanlon. 'Get on to BT, Arthur. I want to know whose number that is and I want to know now, so no sodding about.' He drummed his fingers impatiently as Hanlon made the call.

'Thank you,' said Hanlon, hanging up. 'Sandy is right, Jack. It's the public call box on the corner of Middleton Street.'

Frost spun round to Jordan. 'Pick up SOCO and nip down there. There could be prints on the phone.' But as Jordan reached the door, he called him back. 'Hold it. She might be a creature of habit and use the same phone box to call Sandy again. I want it under constant surveillance.' Back to Lane. 'I'll lend you one of our police radios, Sandy. If she sees there's nothing in the papers she might phone you again from the same phone box. If she does, radio through right away.'

'What if she doesn't use the same phone box?' asked Morgan.

'Then we won't bleeding catch her, will we?'

snapped Frost. 'Mullett's given us carte blanche so we'll have twenty-four-hour surveillance on every flaming call box in the area. But I still want dabs off that phone before someone else uses it. I want someone to get them who looks too much of a prat to be a policeman.'

All eyes swivelled to Morgan.

'OK, Guv,' said Morgan sheepishly. 'I'll do it.'

'No,' said Frost. 'Not only do you look too much of a prat, you *are* too much of a prat. I want someone with sense.' He turned to Kate Holby. 'Change into civvies, love, then get a fingerprint kit from SOCO and make sure no one sees you taking the prints.'

He rubbed his hands together. This was what he thrived on. Action. Getting things moving. Not sitting in a chair, twiddling his flaming thumbs. If their luck was in they'd get this cow. He stood up. 'Let's finish off that cat's pee Sandy calls whisky. It would be a pity to let it go bad in the bottle.'

It was a cold night with rain slashing against the window, but with everyone packed into Frost's tiny office, which was thick with cigarette smoke, and with a warm inner glow provided by the second bottle of Sandy Lane's whisky, Frost was sweating. He had called off the stake-out of the building-society cashpoints. Beazley could scream and shout as much as he liked, but the killing of the two teenagers was taking priority. All public phone boxes in the town were under observation, but there was no message yet from

Sandy Lane. Kate Holby had checked the phone the woman had used, but it had been wiped clean of prints.

A sudden mental image of Debbie Clark's tortured face sent a shudder through Frost's body. The silent scream. He banged his mug down and stood up. There had to be something on the tape that he had missed. He didn't want to go through the harrowing ordeal of watching it again, but he had to.

He stomped back to the Incident Room where Taffy Morgan, detailed to check through the list of cars captured on CCTV around the times of the blackmailer's withdrawals, quickly slid a newspaper under the computer printout.

'You're not fooling me one bit, you lazy Welsh git,' snapped Frost. 'Run that video again.'

He waited impatiently as Taffy opened and shut drawers before locating the cassette.

Frost steeled himself, but found himself wincing, shuddering, sharing the kid's pain and terror. 'Hold it, Taff. Go back to the bit just before she screams.' He moved closer to the monitor. She's saying something.'

'But we can't hear her,' said Taffy.

'You have a gift for stating the bloody obvious,' snarled Frost. 'Maybe we can't make out what she's saying, but I bet a flaming lip-reader could.' Frost buzzed Johnny Johnson, the night-duty station sergeant. 'Johnny, this is urgent. I want a lip-reader here, now.'

'Now?' echoed Johnson. 'You won't get anyone until the morning.'

'Morning? What flaming office hours do they work?'

'Jack,' said Johnson patiently. 'It's two o'clock in the morning.'

Frost focused bleary eyes on his wristwatch to check. 'Bloody hell. Doesn't time fly when you're enjoying yourself?'

His mobile rang. Sandy Lane.

'Yes, Sandy?' asked Frost excitedly.

'Don't get your knickers in a twist, Jack. She hasn't phoned. It's late. I'm going home.'

'All right,' sighed Frost. 'I can't see her phoning now.'

Back in his office, he killed the last drop of whisky, shrugged on his mac and walked unsteadily out to his car.

A traffic car stopped him on his way home.

'Your car's been lurching all over the road. I've reason to believe you've been drinking, sir.'

Frost smiled sweetly at him and slurred, 'Not only have I been drinking, officer, I have a funny feeling I'm pissed.'

The PC shone his torch. 'Oh, it's you, Inspector Frost.' He yelled back to his partner in the traffic car, 'Follow us, Charlie. I'm driving the Inspector home. Move over, sir.'

After three attempts to get the key in the lock, Frost eventually managed to open the front door. There were two messages on his mat from estate agents wanting to make appointments to view the house. He kicked at them but missed, then stumbled upstairs and flung himself, fully dressed, on the bed. He fell instantly asleep.

He dreamt he was watching the video again, but this time there was sound, ghastly sound. The girl's screams echoed and echoed round and round in his brain before turning into the shrill ringing of the alarm clock.

16

He was definitely not at his best when Sergeant Wells ushered in the lip-reader, a bird-like woman with a sharp nose and greying hair screwed back untidily into a bun. She sat uneasily in the offered chair, clutching a large handbag protectively to her chest, looking nervously at the liverish Frost, whose headache was giving him gyp. He palmed a couple of aspirins from a container and washed them down with the dregs of his tea. She declined the offer of a cup for herself, anxious to avoid anything that would delay her getting out of this dreadful place.

Frost forced a smile. 'We've got a pretty rotten job for you, I'm afraid, love.'

He received a sour smile in return. 'Miss Pelham, if you don't mind,' she corrected. 'I was told you wanted me to lip-read someone on a video tape without sound.'

'It's a pretty harrowing video,' Frost warned her.

'I'm not easily shocked, Inspector.'

Then I won't show you my dick, thought Frost. Aloud he said, 'Neither am I, but this shook me bloody rigid.' He briefly explained what was involved.

She went white and shook her head firmly. 'I'm sorry. I don't think I'm the right person for this, Inspector. There must be other people who can lip-read. I don't think I could bear to watch it.'

'Please,' wheedled Frost. 'Time is of the essence. We've got to catch the bastards who did this to a twelve-year-old kid. I wouldn't ask if it wasn't absolutely vital . . . Please . . .'

A reluctant nod. She stood up, still clutching her handbag, and followed him to the Incident Room.

Frost signalled to PC Collier, who switched the video player on and started the tape.

Miss Pelham gave a gasp of horror, turned her head away from the screen and stood up to go, inching towards the door. 'I'm sorry, I can't watch this . . . I can't . . .'

'Then we'll never catch the bastard,' said Frost. 'He'll get away with it. He'll be free to do this again to some other poor kid.'

She hesitated then sat down again, bit her lip tightly and nodded. 'All right.' She was shaking violently.

Collier restarted the tape. The woman's face went chalk-white as she stared at the screen, her lips moving in sync with the girl's. Frost, leaning over her shoulder, also watched, but even he had to turn his head away as the girl slumped to the floor.

The tape ended. Miss Pelham looked up at him. 'Would you run it through again, please?'

When it finished again, she fished a tiny handkerchief from her handbag and dabbed her eyes, then turned to the inspector. 'Most of the time she is crying and saying nothing, but just before she is . . .' She hesitated and forced herself to continue, '. . . strangled, she looks at whoever is filming and says, "*Please . . . something . . . stop him*." '

'*Something?*' snapped Frost. 'That's no bloody good.'

'Her head jerks away . . . it's difficult . . . Something like "Millie" or "Molly". It isn't clear.'

'Could it be Maggie or Minnie or Maisie?' asked Frost.

'No – I am almost certain it isn't any of them.'

' "*Please, Millie . . . stop him*," ' muttered Frost to himself. ' "*Please, Molly . . . stop him*." You're sure about that?'

'Of course I'm not sure. I can only say it's something like that, Inspector. I can't be definite. She moves her head away.'

'*Millie*, *Molly*,' mused Frost. 'Mandy? What about Mandy?'

She thought this over. 'It could be, but I don't think so. There's an "l" sound there. There's lots of strange names for girls now that I don't know, it could be any of them . . . but I still think it's Millie or Molly or something similar.'

A woman operating the camera, thought Frost. *Probably the same woman who made the phone call to*

Sandy Lane. He thanked her. 'Send in your bill, love. I'll see it's paid quickly.'

She paused at the door and shook her head. 'Just find the killer and lock him up for life, Inspector. That's all the payment I want.'

Frost paced up and down the Incident Room in front of his assembled team, voicing his thoughts out loud. 'Millie . . . Molly . . . first names. Someone she knew . . . someone she was on first-name terms with. Someone she bloody trusted and who was so flaming trustworthy she filmed Debbie being strangled.'

'Could it be one of the girls at school?' suggested DC Morgan.

'The voice on the tape last night wasn't that of a schoolgirl,' said Hanlon.

'Taffy might have a point,' said Frost. 'The caller might not be the only woman involved. And as far as the phone call is concerned, Forensic reckon the woman is disguising her voice and is not the low-life bitch she sounds like, so all of Taffy's girlfriends are out of the frame.' He sat on the corner of the desk and wished his head would stop aching. 'This is what we do. I want someone to get a book listing girls' names – they're usually books for mothers with babies. See if there are any more names that would fit. Then I want someone to go on the computer and print out a list of all the people called Millie and Molly or something similar who are on record. Then I want all of those women visited and questioned about where they were and what they were doing the night Debbie Clark went missing. Any cocky cows who don't answer, arrest them on any charge you can think of and bring them into the station. Sod civil bloody liberties. And someone go through the list of people who used to work at that office block and see if any of them have a name that matches.' He nodded at DS Hanlon. 'You organise that, Arthur. I'm going to get something to eat, then I'm off to Debbie's school to see if any of the girls there are called Molly or Millie.'

He made it to the canteen, but the smell of greasy fried food made his stomach churn so he decided to skip breakfast – lunch as well, probably.

'I'm off to the school,' he called out to Bill Wells.

Wells held up the telephone, waving it urgently. 'Mr Beazley's on the blower. Wants to talk to you urgently—'

He was talking to a swinging lobby door.

Miss Robins, the headteacher, a mannish, middle-aged woman in a tailored suit and sensible shoes, surveyed the dishevelled figure hunched up in the chair opposite her with frowning disapproval. 'What you are asking is impossible, Inspector. The Data Protection Act—'

Frost cut her short. 'All right. When we find another kid raped and strangled like Debbie Clark you can say, "Too bad – but at least I didn't violate the Data Protection Act."'

She flushed. 'That's moral blackmail, Inspector.'

'Yes,' snapped Frost. 'I'll use any means not to see another kid's body on a slab in the morgue. I'm even prepared to break into your lousy school tonight and steal the bleeding records.' He fumbled in his inside pocket. 'Would you like to see a photograph of how Debbie looked when we found her?' He didn't have the photograph on him, but the bluff worked.

She held up her hands in protest. 'No ... please. If you could tell me exactly why you want a computer printout of all our pupils.'

'We have good reason to believe that Debbie was going to meet someone called Millie, or Molly, or something similar the night she was killed. We want to trace that person and eliminate them from our inquiries. It could be a schoolfriend of Debbie's, we don't know, but we've got to check everyone, even if it means contravening the Data Protection Act.'

The headteacher pressed a key on her intercom. 'Janet, sorry to interrupt your free period, but do you think you could let me have a computer printout of the school roll?'

Frost tapped her arm. 'Let's have the rolls for the past five years as well. It could be someone who has already left school.'

'And rolls for the past five years,' added Miss Robins. 'And it is rather urgent.' She flipped the key up. 'A terrible business, Inspector.'

'Yes,' agreed Frost. Another thought struck

him. 'Have any of your teachers got a name like Millie or Molly?'

She wrinkled her brow in thought, then shook her head. 'No – none of them.'

'What about other workers here – dinner ladies, cleaners and so on?'

Again she shook her head. 'I don't think so, but I'm afraid I don't know all their names – some of them come and go so quickly.'

'Then let's have a list of staff as well as teachers,' said Frost. The number of possibilities was beginning to mount and he wasn't even sure if the mysterious Millie or Molly was someone from the school. The school was clearly a no-smoking area, a factor which made the craving for a fag greater than ever. *Hurry up with these flaming lists*, he silently urged.

A tap at the door. At last. A mousy-looking, buck-toothed woman in a brown cardigan with a goofy, jolly-hockey-sticks expression entered with a sheaf of computer printouts.

'Thank you, Janet,' said Miss Robins, passing the lists over to Frost. 'Janet Leigh is our computer expert – she was Debbie's form mistress.'

Frost nodded a brief greeting as he stuffed the printouts in his pocket. 'We're hoping to trace someone called Millie, or Molly, or something very similar who was friendly with Debbie. It's a slim chance, but it could lead somewhere. Any of your girls with names like that?'

'Millie . . . Molly?' The teacher shook her head. 'None in my form. Offhand, I can't think of any girls in the school with those names.'

'Dinner ladies, cleaners, anyone?'

Again she shook her head, then she waggled a triumphant finger at him. 'Bridget Malone. The cleaner.'

'Bridget?' frowned Frost. 'Perhaps I'm dim . . .'

'The children all called her Molly – Molly Malone. You know, "Cockles and Mussels, alive alive-oh." '

This sounded promising. 'I'd like to talk to her,' said Frost.

'She's not in today,' said the headteacher. 'She's got a stomach bug.'

'Give me her address,' said Frost. 'I might pop round and take her some grapes.'

'Guv,' called Morgan excitedly, 'we've struck gold. I've run Bridget Malone through the computer. She's got form!'

Frost grabbed the computer printout, skimmed through it and tossed it to one side. 'You got me going for a minute there, Taff. Pinching knickers from Marks and Sparks – hardly premium-league stuff.'

'There's something else, Guv, that should make your day.'

Frost's face brightened. 'You're going to resign, Taff? That's terrific news. Put me down for 3p towards your leaving present.'

Morgan grinned. 'This might be even better news for you, Guv.' He waved another computer printout. 'She's living with Patsy Kelly.'

Frost snatched the printout from him.

'Flaming hell, Taff. Don't resign until tomorrow. Patsy Kelly's a nasty, slimy bastard if ever there was one – he'd make Mullett look like a saint.' He flipped through the pages. 'I've put that bastard away a few times . . . GBH . . . Robbery with Violence . . . porno videos . . . obtaining money by menace, drug-dealing. That was his last one – drug-dealing – selling to school kids, by all accounts. I bet that's what little Bridget was doing when she was supposed to be Ajaxing out the lavatory pans. He's just the sort of bastard who'd kill a kid for money.' He was getting excited now.

'Shall we bring her in, Guv?'

Frost played a drum roll on the desktop with his fingers. 'We haven't got enough on her, Taff – just that the kids call her Molly, and Debbie might or might not have said Molly.' Another brief drum roll. 'Didn't you have to go to the school a few weeks back – stuff being pinched from the kids' lockers?'

Morgan nodded. 'Yes. Couldn't pin it on anyone, though.'

'If you couldn't crack the case, then no one could,' said Frost. 'She's got form. Wasn't she one of your suspects?'

'It could have been anyone in the school, Guv – most likely one of the kids. I didn't run them through the computer.'

'The kids call her Molly, and she's living with scumbag Patsy Kelly. Suspicion, but not a shred of proof. We need to turn their place over, but Kelly would never let us in without a search warrant. Who's the duty magistrate this week?'

Morgan consulted the list on the pinboard. 'Alison Miller, Guv.'

Frost's face fell. 'Shit!' he said.

Frost rubbed his hands together to get his circulation going. It was freezing cold in the back room where old mother Miller had parked him while she finished her meal. He took out his pack of cigarettes, but the clinically clean room hissed its frowning disapproval, so he hastily dropped them back in his pocket and fidgeted in the uncomfortable armchair, watching the hands of the clock on the mantelpiece crawl round. At last the door clicked open and Alison Miller, a heavily built, thick-eyebrowed, grim-looking woman in her late fifties came in to glare down at him.

'You do pick the most inconvenient times, Inspector Frost. I was in the middle of my meal.'

'Sorry, mum,' mumbled Frost. 'Murderers have no consideration for others.'

'Don't be flippant and don't call me "mum" – it's "ma'am", if you don't mind. And please sit in the other armchair – that one has just been re-upholstered after someone's cigarette burnt a hole in it.'

'Ah – yes. Sorry about that, I couldn't find an ashtray.'

'The reason you couldn't find an ashtray, Inspector Frost, was because I do not permit the filthy habit of smoking in this house. You may inform Superintendent Mullett that the bill for the re-upholstery will be forwarded to him for payment as soon as I receive it. So why are you here?'

Frost pulled the papers from his pocket. 'If you could just sign this, then you can get back to your nosh.'

She found her glasses in her pocket and studied the papers carefully. 'A search warrant, Inspector? Another one of your famous search warrants?'

'Yes,' said Frost anxiously. 'If you could just sign where I've marked it.'

'I know perfectly well where to sign search warrants, Inspector. Let me remind you that I do not sign these orders automatically. If I am to give the police powers to do a ham-fisted search of someone's house, probably dumping lighted cigarettes willy-nilly, then I want justification.'

'But of course—' began Frost.

A bony hand waved him to silence. 'The last two warrants you prevailed upon me to sign – at two o'clock in the morning, as I recall – were a red-hot, cast-iron tip-off from a 100 per cent reliable source and two houses jam-packed to the rafters with stolen goods, if I remember your words correctly. And what did you find?'

'Ah . . .' began Frost before the hand again cut him short.

'You found nothing, Inspector. Nothing at all. You promised faithfully that you would report back to me with the results of the searches, but you were obviously too ashamed to do so.'

'We were so busy . . .'

'A promise is a promise, Inspector. It was on that condition, and that condition only, that I signed the warrants in spite of my misgivings. And then there was that Warrington Road episode.'

Frost groaned. He knew the old cow would bring that up. Flaming Taffy Morgan getting the address wrong.

'A warrant, signed by me and made out for the wrong address. A perfectly respectable lady, a lay preacher, a member of the Church Council. And you broke into her house in the early hours looking for evidence that she was running a brothel. And you got me to sign the warrant.'

'That's all in the past—' began Frost.

'The very recent past, Inspector. It is no wonder I treat all your requests for search warrants with the greatest suspicion. Just because this woman is called Molly, you want to search her house in the hope that you can find something that will connect her with the murdered girl?'

'Yes,' nodded Frost.

'Just a name that the girl might or might not have said.' She folded up the warrant and handed it back to him. 'You might just as well put the names of every woman called Molly into a hat, pull one out and then expect me to sign a search warrant. No, Inspector Frost. You give me some solid evidence first.'

'They could have this other missing girl, Jan O'Brien. I want to get to them first.'

'Then come up with some proof. I'd like you to leave now, Inspector.'

* * *

Seething inwardly, Frost stomped out to the car, slamming the front door loudly behind him. He flopped into the front passenger seat. 'Back to the nick,' he barked to Morgan.

'Did she sign it, Guv?'

'Just shut your bleeding mouth and drive,' snarled Frost.

'I'll take that as a no,' grinned Morgan.

The Incident Room was hazy with cigarette smoke as Frost paced up and down, waiting for the call from PC Jordan, who was in an unmarked car keeping Kelly's house under observation.

Bill Wells came in with two mugs of tea. He looked around the room. 'Where is everyone?'

'It's best you don't know,' said Frost, taking one of the mugs.

Wells sat himself down. 'So she wouldn't sign the search warrant?'

'That fat, lousy, four-eyed cow . . .' began Frost.

'To be fair . . .' soothed Wells.

'I don't want to be bleeding fair,' snapped Frost. 'I'm trying to save the life of a missing schoolgirl, assuming the bastards haven't already done to her what they did to Debbie Clark – but she says there's not enough flaming evidence. Do we let a kid die just because there's not enough bleeding evidence?'

'There's nothing you can do about it, Jack,' said Wells.

'Oh yes there flaming is.'

'What?'

'You don't want to know – trust me, you don't want to know.' Frost plucked the cigarette from his mouth and ground it to death on the floor. 'If that cow won't sign a search warrant, I'll search the place without one.'

'Kelly would never agree to that.'

'I don't intend doing it while Kelly is there.'

Wells stared at him. 'You're not going to break into his house, Jack? You're not that bloody stupid?'

Frost sipped his tea and said nothing.

'Jack – Skinner's back. He phoned from his digs. He could well be coming into the station tonight. If he finds out – never mind kicking you out of Denton, he'd have you booted off the force.'

'Sod Skinner.'

'Jack,' pleaded Wells, now getting desperate. 'If you're caught in that house, any evidence you find will be slung out of court. They'll say you planted it.'

'I won't get caught,' said Frost stubbornly.

'You said you wouldn't get caught with your fiddled car expenses,' countered Wells.

'That's right,' snorted Frost. 'Hit me with bleeding common sense. It's stupid, it's daft, it's suicidal, but I'm going to do it. I've turned Kelly's house over enough times. I know my way around it blindfolded, and I know how to get in without leaving a trace.'

'But Jack—'

Frost waved him to silence. His radio, which was on the desk in front of him, was squawking. It was PC Jordan.

'Inspector, Kelly and the woman have just left 23 Dunn Street in a light-blue Citroën heading for the town centre.'

Frost glanced up at the wall clock. Ten thirty-four. 'They're going to the Blue Parrot. They go there every Friday night. Keep on their tail. Once they're inside, radio back and I'll send someone else to take over the surveillance for when they come out.'

'Roger.' The radio clicked off.

'What's this about, Jack?' demanded Wells. 'Jordan and Simms are supposed to be checking a suspected flasher at Flint Street.'

'This is more important than a flaming dick-dangler. Kelly and the tart go to the Blue Parrot every Friday night and stay until two o'clock in the morning. That gives me over three clear hours to turn their pad over.'

'You're mad, Jack. Stark, staring mad. You joined the force to uphold the law, not break it.'

'I didn't join the force to stand idly by when a kid's life could be in danger just because some fat cow of a magistrate won't sign a search warrant.' Frost unhooked his scarf and yelled down the corridor for Taffy Morgan.

'Yes, Guv?'

'Get your jemmy and a sack marked "Swag". We're going to do a spot of house-breaking.'

'You're taking Morgan with you?' asked Wells incredulously.

Frost nodded.

'Then it's doomed, Jack. It's flaming doomed.'

No lights were showing from the front of the house as the car cruised past. Frost tapped Morgan's arm. 'There's a road round the rear – next turning on the left. Let's make sure there's no sign of life round the back.'

Morgan drove round to the back street, where a high brick wall with wooden doors fastened on the inside provided a back entrance to the houses. Only one of the houses showed a light. Frost did a quick count: it wasn't Kelly's house. He double-checked. He'd be a real right prat if he broke into the wrong house. 'One last check, Taff,' he muttered, pulling his mobile phone from his pocket and dialling Kelly's number. He let it ring and ring before clicking off. 'No one at home,' he reported. 'Park here, Taff, and switch off the lights.' He looked up at a starless sky. 'A burglar's moon. Just what we want.'

Morgan didn't share the inspector's enthusiasm. 'I don't like this, Guv.'

Before Frost could reply, PC Jordan radioed in. 'I'm at the Blue Parrot, Inspector. Kelly's parked the car. They're entering the club now.'

'Keep the car under continuous observation. They shouldn't be out until gone two, but if they emerge any bleeding earlier, don't keep it to yourself. Let me know right away. I'll send someone to relieve you in a couple of hours.'

Frost lit up a cigarette and noticed that his hand was shaking. His sprained wrist was aching like mad – it was not in an ideal condition for climbing over brick walls, but it was now or never. He rubbed it to ease the pain. An icy blast of chilling premonition that things were going to go badly wrong rippled through his body. 'Right, Taff, it's over-the-top time.'

'Do you want me to come with you, Guv?' asked Morgan, praying for a 'no'.

'No, Taff. For two reasons. If it all goes pear-shaped it's better that one silly sod is caught instead of two, and secondly, if you come with me you're bound to sod things up. Stay in the car with the engine running, and if I come charging out with people screaming behind me, don't say "What's going on, Guv?" – just put your foot down and drive the flaming heck out of here – making sure I'm in the bleeding car first.'

'Right, Guv,' nodded Morgan.

Frost pinched out his cigarette and dropped it back in the packet. 'Come on, Taff. Give me a leg up so I can get over the wall, then I'll unbolt the back door ready for a speedy withdrawal, or coitus interruptus as we call it in the trade.'

Morgan, too nervous even to grin, heaved the inspector up to the top of the wall. Frost pulled himself to the top, wincing at the pain from his wrist, when—

'*Shit!*'

A security light flashed on, flooding the back garden with light. Frost hugged the top of the wall, trying to bury himself into the bricks. Then he gave a sigh of relief as something scuttled along the ground below him. The security light was in the garden of the house next door and had been set off by a cat. Heart hammering, he pressed harder against the top of the wall, waiting for the neighbours to come out to see what had triggered the security light. He waited. Nothing happened. The cat had probably caught them out many times before.

Sliding over, he dropped down into Kelly's garden, narrowly missing the cucumber frame that Taffy Morgan would have hit spot on, then he quietly unbolted the back gate and opened it. 'Back in the car, Taff,' he said to Morgan. 'Engine running and ready to get the hell out of here.'

Morgan nodded and returned to the security of the car.

Leaving the back gate slightly ajar, Frost made his way up the path towards the rear of the house. It was dark. There were tall wooden fences on each side which meant the chances of him being seen were limited. Crouching down, he hurried to the back door and, ever the optimist, tried the handle. It was locked.

The old Victorian house had sash windows, which were usually a sod to open quietly. He hoped the catch inside wasn't on. He managed to get his fingernails under the frame, then his fingers. For a change, his luck was in. The window slid upwards, but in the silence of the night the creaking sound screamed out. Someone must surely hear that. He paused, listening, ready to run – but nothing.

The beam of his torch travelled around an

expensive fitted kitchen in charcoal grey with solid teak worktops. A knee up on the sill and he was inside.

Again he paused, ears strained. The silence was broken only by the ticking of a clock somewhere in the room and the thudding of his heart.

He headed to the large, double-doored, American-style fridge-freezer, which was crammed with all sorts of expensive foods and bottles of wine. He helped himself to a strawberry, then went straight for the chiller compartment. Nestling next to the tomatoes and salad stuff was a roll of greasy banknotes, just where he expected to find them. Kelly was nothing if not consistent. He riffled through the wad – about six thousand quid. Crime was definitely paying for Kelly. He replaced the notes where he found them and pushed through a door into the dining room, walking across deep-piled, expensive fitted carpet to a massive oak sideboard.

Frost pulled open a couple of drawers and made a half-hearted search, but his gut feeling was that whatever Kelly had to hide, he wouldn't keep it in such an obvious place. His gut feeling also told him the missing girl wasn't in the house. That would be too much to hope for.

He gave the lounge a quick going-over – a massive forty-two-inch plasma screen dominated the room and there were surround-sound speakers all over the place. A flashy figured-walnut cocktail cabinet bulged with wines and spirits.

He followed his torchbeam up the stairs. First stop the bathroom, where he lifted the ceramic top of the lavatory cistern and took out a waterproof bag. Five thousand pounds or more in used banknotes and about twenty small polythene packets of white powder – drugs of some kind. Not what he was looking for. He put them back in the cistern and replaced the lid.

A car horn sounded. He stiffened. God, was it Taffy? Was Kelly back early? But no, Morgan wasn't that subtle. He'd jam his thumb on the horn and wake up the whole bleeding street. He held his breath and listened. The sound wasn't repeated. He expelled his held breath and fished out a screwdriver from his mac pocket, then turned his attention to the panels on the side of the bath, another favourite hiding place of Kelly's. Tunelessly humming to himself, he began to turn the screws holding the panel in place.

Back at the Blue Parrot, Jordan yawned and looked again at his watch. He hated surveillance duty, especially when you were on your own. Nothing to do but stare out of the windscreen. You daren't pick up a paper or a magazine for a quick read – something always happened the minute you took your eyes away. Friday was a busy night – cars kept driving in and out; shrieking, shouting passengers alighted or embarked. Everyone but him seemed to be having a great time. He yawned again and shivered. It was cold in the car, but he couldn't put the heat on in case it sent him to sleep. He took a swig from his flask of coffee. He had smoked too much. His fingers were oily with nicotine and his mouth tasted foul. The last thing in the world he wanted was another cigarette, but there was nothing else to do. He lit one up and stared out again at the light-blue Citroën parked on the other side of the car park.

Frost had to resist the temptation to smoke. Kelly was a non-smoker and the absence of ash-trays suggested the woman was also. They would detect the smell of cigarette smoke the minute they entered the house.

The screws were proving obstinate, but at last he got the panel off and poked his torch inside. Nothing. Absolutely sod all! Not like the last time he did the place over, when it was jam-packed with expensive fax machines and DVD recorders, and Kelly had expressed utter hammy astonishment as to how they had come to be there. 'God's truth, Inspector, someone's trying to frame me.'

He tried to replace the panel, but the damn thing wouldn't go back in the space it had come out of so easily. He banged it with his fist and the hollow sound echoed round the empty house. Shit. He froze, hoping no one had heard. He tried again. Still the stupid bleeding thing wouldn't cooperate, in spite of being helped with his knee. Double shit. If he couldn't get the flaming thing back it would be a dead give away. He had a sudden thought and turned the panel upside-down and tried again. This time it purred into place. Hands sweating, he replaced the screws, noting that he had managed to chew the heads of a couple of them. He rubbed in some grime from the soles of his shoes to disguise the shiny scratches and hoped they wouldn't be noticed. A cigarette. He'd give his bloody right arm for a cigarette. Wiping his sweaty palms down the sides of his trousers, he made his way into the main bedroom.

Nothing in the bedroom. Not a bloody thing! Doubts began chewing away at his insides. He wasn't going to find anything. Everything would go wrong. He'd be caught red-handed in the flaming house and Mullett would think Christmas had come early. What had he got? Sod all, really. Just a name the poor kid may or may not have called out and someone with a nick-name that matched. He went to the window and peered out at the back alley just to make sure Taffy hadn't decided to nip off and get himself some fish and chips. The car was still there and Taffy was in the driving seat, looking more or less awake. Why had he come here? Bill Wells was right. He was stark, staring, flaming mad.

He left the bedroom and stood on the landing looking up at the ceiling. There was a trapdoor leading to the loft. There wouldn't be anything in the loft. He knew it. There never was and Kelly was a creature of habit, but he had to look. It was his last hope. A quick flash of his torch on his wristwatch. Flaming hell. He'd been here over an hour and still hadn't finished. He hoped

Kelly and Molly Malone were enjoying themselves.

Jordan shook his head and reached out again for the flask of coffee. It was supposed to help keep you awake, but all it did was make him want to pee. He was bursting. He nipped out for a quick slash behind the car, then climbed back into the uncomfortable driving seat. He looked at his watch. Only an hour had passed. It seemed like flaming years. Where was the relief Frost was supposed to be sending?

There was a gentle tapping on the side window. Good old Frost, for once he hadn't forgotten. Jordan opened the car door so that WPC Kate Holby could slide into the seat beside him. He filled her in, pointing out the location of the Citroën. She was about to leave for her own car when—

'Jordan! What the hell are you doing here?'

Shit! Detective Chief Inspector Skinner was all tarted up in a smart suit, stinking of beer and with a nasty 'I'm looking for trouble' glint in his eye.

Jordan's mouth opened and closed. He couldn't think of a damn thing to say.

'I asked you what the hell you were doing here, both of you?'

'Surveillance, sir,' Jordan choked out at last.

'Surveillance?' Skinner checked his watch. 'At this time of the bloody night. Who authorised it?'

'Inspector Frost, sir.'

'And where is Inspector Frost?'

'Back at the station, I think, sir.'

'And what, Constable, are you supposed to be surveillancing?'

'Suspect is a chap called Kelly, sir. Receiver of stolen goods.'

'And he's inside the club?'

'Yes, sir.'

'With his arms full of stolen goods?'

Jordan thought quickly. 'He sometimes seeks orders for stolen goods from contacts in the club, sir. We want to follow him to find out where he's got them stashed.'

Skinner gave Jordan a cold, hard stare, then turned his attention to Kate Holby.

'And what do you think you're doing here?'

The girl flushed. 'I'm relieving PC Jordan.'

'You're doing surveillance as well? Who the hell gave you permission to do surveillance? Have you finished compiling those lists that I gave you?'

'No, sir.'

'Didn't I say you were to do no other duties until you'd finished everything I'd allocated you?'

'Yes, but Inspector Frost—'

'You don't take orders from Inspector Frost, you take them from me. This is a bloody waste of time. I'm the only one who authorises surveillance overtime and this is unauthorised. Clear out of here right now, the pair of you, and tell Inspector Frost I want to see him first thing tomorrow morning.'

'Yes, Chief Inspector,' mumbled Jordan.

'Now!' yelled Skinner. 'Clear out of here now!' He waited for Kate Holby to return to her car and for Jordan to reverse and leave the car park. As Jordan did so, he noticed a flashily dressed woman in Skinner's car, obviously waiting to be taken into the club. He doubted she was Skinner's wife. No wonder he wanted the surveillance discontinued.

Jordan was backing out when, to his horror, he saw Kelly and Malone leaving the club and making for the Citroën. Kelly had his arm round the woman, who didn't seem very well. This was confirmed when she turned her head and vomited all over the tarmac.

'Shit! They're leaving early.' He snatched up his mobile to warn Frost.

The loft was tightly crammed with junk and looked as if it hadn't been disturbed for years. The floorboards were crumbling with dry rot and Frost nearly put his foot through to the ceiling below. A quick flash around with his torch revealed nothing. He climbed down and brushed dust and cobwebs from his coat. He checked his watch. One thirty. Plenty of time. Kelly never left the club until two at the earliest.

Jordan had lost Kelly's car. He was so sure Kelly was heading for home that he had overtaken him in case he saw he was being followed. He tucked into a lay-by and waited. And waited. Shit! They must have turned off down one of the side roads, but where the hell would they be going at half one in the flaming morning? Hoping and praying Skinner wasn't listening in, he radioed all area cars asking them to keep a look-out for Kelly and to report back as soon as they saw him.

He had tried to ring Inspector Frost on his mobile phone to warn him, but all he got was a recorded message that the person called was not available and would he like to leave a message. Typical! Frost had switched the damn thing off. He tried Frost's radio. 'Inspector Frost, come in please . . . Please . . . come in . . .'

Why Frost suddenly decided to look in the airing cupboard was a complete mystery to him. His experience of his own airing cupboard was that when you opened the door the contents cascaded out all over the floor and had to be rammed back with much swearing. He tentatively opened the door, his torchbeam crawling over neatly folded towels and sheets. On the bottom shelf lay a pile of assorted items in a cardboard box. He pulled it out and examined the contents. Creditcards, chequebooks, cheque-guarantee cards, all in different names – clearly the spoils of theft.

As he was pushing the box back, he spotted another one at the back of the shelf. He pulled it out half-heartedly and lifted the lid. Wrist-watches, cheap jewellery, assorted credit cards and . . . His heart stopped. At the bottom of the box was a phone. A Nokia mobile phone. The same make, model and colour as Debbie Clark's missing mobile.

* * *

Taffy Morgan had just finished off a packet of salt and vinegar crisps and was chucking the screwed-up bag out of the window when he suddenly heard a muffled voice.

'Inspector Frost, come in please . . .'

Where the hell was it coming from? The glove compartment. He opened it and there was the pocket radio Frost should have taken with him. Morgan pulled it out and answered the call.

'For Pete's sake, get hold of Inspector Frost!' yelled Jordan. 'Kelly's left the club. We think he's on his way home.'

Hands trembling, Frost carefully wrapped a handkerchief around the mobile, took it out and examined it more closely under the light of his torch. It was switched off, so he clicked it on. What next? There was no indication of the phone's number. On his own mobile there was a way to bring the owner's number up on the screen, but he couldn't remember how it was done and didn't want to press keys randomly in case it messed things up. He brought up the menu. The battery level was very low – it looked ready to die at any minute. He switched it off quickly. If the phone was dead there was no way he could find out if it was Debbie's.

Think, think, think! How could he check? There was a way. There had to be. Right. He had Debbie's mobile number on him somewhere. If he phoned the number and the mobile rang, that would prove it was her phone and he had the bastards. He rummaged through his pockets to find the scrap of paper with the number scribbled down, then scuttled back to the bedroom to use the bedside phone. As his hand went to pick it up, it rang.

Jordan's radio spluttered. 'Charlie Baker calling. We've just spotted Kelly and the woman driving away from the twenty-four-hour chemist in Market Square. Do we follow?'

'Don't follow,' said Jordan. 'See if you can get to the house before them. Park round the back behind Taffy Morgan. I'll let you know if I want any more help.'

He drove as quickly as he could to Kelly's house, still trying to work out how to warn Frost, who hadn't got his radio or mobile. He braked sharply at a public telephone box with a couple of yellowing, tattered phone directories dangling from a chain. He dashed in. The kiosk stank of urine and the floor was littered with stale, damp papers and takeaway containers. Most of the pages had been torn out of the directory, but he hoped Kelly's number was there. It was! He rammed 20p in the slot and dialled Kelly's number. It rang and rang. 'Answer the flaming thing,' hissed Jordan. 'You've got to get your arse out of there bloody quick.'

Frost froze. The shrill ringing of the phone sounded as if it could be heard halfway down the street. 'Stop, you sod, stop,' he muttered angrily. But the damn thing went on and on and on . . .

* * *

'The bloody fool's not going to answer!' cursed Jordan, slamming down the phone. Charlie Baker wouldn't be there yet and the minutes were ticking away. There was nothing for it, desperate measures were called for. He'd have to involve accident-prone Taffy Morgan.

The ringing stopped. The subsequent silence screamed. Frost waited for a couple of seconds, then lifted the receiver. He shone his torch on the girl's number and dialled. A pause. He waited, holding his breath. A woman's voice announced, '*The person you are calling is unavailable. If you would like to leave a—*' Damn. Of course. He'd switched the damn thing off to conserve the battery. He hung up, switched on the mobile and waited for it to register. He dialled again. '*The number you are calling has not been recognised . . .*'

Double shit. He flicked his torch at the scrap of paper. Damn, he'd transposed the last two numbers. He drew a deep breath and, carefully checking each digit, slowly and deliberately he dialled again. One digit to go when . . .

Banging, crashing, then footsteps thudding up the stairs.

Bleeding hell! Kelly was back and no one had warned him. He clicked off the torch and stood stock still, holding his breath, his heart going ballistic, in the dark.

The footsteps stopped outside the bedroom door.

'Guv . . . Where are you? It's me – Morgan!'

Frost sighed with relief. Taffy bloody Morgan! 'You frightened the shit out of me, you Welsh sod. What are you doing here?'

'Get out quick, Guv. They left early. They'll be here any minute.'

'So why didn't you phone me?'

'Your phone is switched off. Come on, Guv.' He tugged at Frost's sleeve to hurry him up.

A car drew up outside.

Frost twitched back the curtains and took a quick peek at the street below. Flaming arseholes! Kelly's car was reversing into the drive.

'The back way,' hissed Frost. 'It's our only chance.'

The sound of a key turning in the lock downstairs.

Frost froze. Too bloody late. There was no way they could get down the stairs and out without being seen.

'Guv,' bleated Morgan.

Frost flapped a hand to silence him. 'Keep bleeding quiet and pray.' What excuse could he use . . . they'd heard a burglar so they broke into the house the back way? Sod it. Might as well be hung for a sheep as for a flaming lamb. He dialled the last digit. And nothing happened. He'd risked everything for sod all.

They stood in the dark, waiting to be caught red-handed. For a brief moment there was screaming silence. No – not silence!

Very faintly, powered by the dying breath of a failing battery, the mobile was ringing. He had dialled Debbie's number and it was ringing. It was Debbie's phone!

They had to get out unseen. Once out he would get a search warrant, turn the house over and 'find' the phone. If they were caught inside the house, Kelly's brief could claim the evidence was planted.

Downstairs the front door opened. Footsteps pounded up the stairs. The toilet door opened and closed. The sound of someone being violently sick. One in the toilet, but where was the other one?

Kelly's voice called, 'Are you all right up there?' He began ascending the stairs.

This is it, thought Frost. *We've bloody had it.*

Then there was a hammering at the front door. 'Police. Open up.'

Kelly paused on the stairs. 'Police?' he echoed. 'What the hell do you want?'

Footsteps retreated down the stairs. The door unlatched and opened.

PC Simms's voice announced, 'Sorry to bother you, sir. Is that your car on the forecourt?'

'What if it bloody is? Is it an offence to park your own bloody car on your own bloody forecourt?'

'We'd like you to check it, sir. We just spotted someone trying to break into the boot.'

'The bastard. Did you get him?'

'I'm afraid not, sir.'

'Typical, bloody typical.'

Footsteps crunched on the gravel outside.

Frost could hear muffled voices. Kelly was on the forecourt.

I owe you one, Simms, thought Frost.

He listened to more sounds of retching from the toilet. 'Come on, Taff. We're going!' They tiptoed down the stairs. Halfway across the living room, Frost stopped dead. 'Shit.'

He was still holding Debbie's bleeding mobile!

Prat, prat, stupid flaming prat! If he couldn't get the damn thing back before Kelly returned it would be curtains. There would be no way they could use the phone as evidence – assuming he hadn't been booted out of the force long before then.

'What's up, Guv? Why have we stopped?'

'Don't ask flaming questions. Wait for me in the car.'

'But Guv—'

'For Pete's sake, Taffy – go! And if I'm not out in a couple of minutes, leave me, get the hell out of here.'

'But Guv—'

'Don't argue, Taffy, just bloody do it!' He shoved Morgan out of the way and spun on his heel to charge back up the stairs. He knew he was making a noise, but hoped vomiting Vera in the karzy would be too preoccupied with throwing up to notice.

The muffled voices from outside suddenly died. Flaming heck. Was Kelly coming back in? 'Please, Simms,' he prayed, 'keep him out there for another minute – fifty seconds, anything . . .'

He replaced the mobile in the airing cupboard with fumbling fingers. As he dashed back down the stairs, the voices outside started up again. Reprieved, but for how long?

Through the living room into the kitchen, out into the garden, running like hell. Halfway up the garden he heard the car starting up. *No Taffy – please, no!*

Slamming the back gate behind him, he saw the rear lights of the car moving off.

Sod making a noise. 'Taffy!' he yelled.

Thank God! The Welsh git had heard him. The car stopped and backed at speed, then screamed to a stop. Frost hurled himself in and lay speechless, panting at Taffy's side, sucking in air and rubbing the stitch in his side.

'Drive,' he gasped.

As they sped round the corner, they could see the area car with two uniformed men walking round Kelly's Citroën. The driver's window had been smashed. 'Good old Simms,' said Frost. He leaned over and punched the horn as they passed. Behind Kelly's back, Simms fluttered a hand of acknowledgement.

'Can we go home now, Guv?' yawned Morgan. 'It's been a long day.'

'No we flaming can't,' said Frost. 'But to compensate, tomorrow's going to be a short day because I doubt you'll be in bed much before noon.'

17

Alison Miller wrapped her sensible brown tweedy dressing gown more tightly round her flannelette nightdress and glared angrily at the two detectives who had banged on her door at this unearthly hour. 'This had better be extremely important,' she said. 'Do you know what time it is?'

Frost glanced at his watch. 'It's three o'clock, mum,' he said cheerfully. 'Sorry to disturb your beauty sleep. I know how much you need it.'

She gave him a hard stare, never knowing whether he was being deliberately rude or not. Frost's innocent expression made her decide, reluctantly, to give him the benefit of the doubt. She glanced at the warrant, then at him. 'What are you playing at? This is the same address as before.'

'You've got a marvellous memory, mum,' said Frost. She winced each time the wretched man called her 'mum'.

'Ma'am,' she snapped icily.

'Sorry, mum,' said Frost. 'Yes, the same

address, but this time I've cast-iron information from a very reliable source that items belonging to the dead girl, Debbie Clark, are in the house.'

'And might I know the name of this reliable source?'

'I had to give him an assurance that his name wouldn't be revealed and I know you wouldn't want me to break my word. As soon as you sign this warrant, we're going straight to the house and I am 200 per cent certain that, thanks to your cooperation, we will find the evidence we are looking for to convict the poor girl's killer.'

She looked at the warrant again and shook her head. 'I don't like this, Inspector, I don't like it one little bit.'

'It does you credit, mum,' said Frost, 'that even though you don't like it, you realise that catching the murderers of two schoolkids overrides any doubts you may have.'

She pursed her lips, still reluctant to do anything to help someone who dragged her out of bed at three in the morning. But it was cold standing at the front door in her dressing gown and her warm bed was beckoning and she was too tired to argue. She took Frost's offered Bic and scrawled her signature.

She blinked and realised she was standing alone, empty-handed, without a word of thanks, hearing the sound of a car roaring off at speed. 'Not even a thank-you,' she sniffed as she made her way upstairs to bed.

The lights were still on in Kelly's house. Frost

sent Jordan and Simms round the back to block that escape route, then nodded for Morgan to hammer at the knocker and jam his finger on the doorbell. 'Open up. Police,' he bawled.

Footsteps rang down the hall, a chain slipped on and the door opened a fraction. 'What the hell is it this time?'

Frost waved the warrant at the partially open door. 'Open up, Kelly. I've got a warrant to search these premises.'

'A warrant?' The warrant was snatched through. 'Wait a minute . . .' The footsteps retreated up the hall.

'He's going to flush his drugs down the karzy,' said Frost. 'Smash the door in.' He stepped back as Lambert swung the ram at the door. At the second blow the door crashed open and they charged in. Kelly was at the top of the stairs with an armful of polythene packets, hammering frantically at the bathroom door. 'Open up, you silly cow. The cops are here!'

From inside came the sound of retching.

Frost strode up the stairs, his hand outstretched.

'Are those packets for me, Patsy?' he smirked, then nodded at the bathroom door as the sound of vomiting continued. 'Morning sickness? Congratulations. Call him Jack after your favourite cop.'

'You think you're so bloody funny,' snarled Kelly, peering down the stairs as the sound of crashing and banging came from below. 'What are they looking for?'

'Other illicit substances you might have overlooked, Patsy.' Frost ripped open one of the packets. 'And what have we here?' He dabbed a finger into the powder and licked it. 'I don't think it's sherbet. I do believe it's coke.' He turned to PC Lambert. 'That's against the law, isn't it, Constable, or am I thinking of parking on a yellow line?'

'I've never seen these packets before in my life,' said Kelly, moving slightly to one side to block the airing-cupboard door.

'I spy with my little eye an airing cupboard,' said Frost, pushing him out of the way. 'What have you got in there that you don't want me to see?' He shoved Kelly to one side and flung open the door. Then he did a double take and his heart sank. The box containing the phone – it wasn't there! He knew where he had left it and it wasn't there. There were two other boxes that hadn't been there before. He pulled them out and lifted the lids. More packets of coke – Kelly's visits to the Blue Parrot were clearly made to collect fresh supplies. Sod the drugs – what had Kelly done with the bloody phone? Had the bastard forestalled him? Had he moved it?

A stack of folded tea towels had toppled over. Had it fallen on the box containing the phone when he hurriedly rammed it back earlier? It had to be that. It just had to be.

Holding his breath, he lifted up the tea towels. He breathed again. The box was there! He pulled it out. 'What's in here then, Patsy?'

Kelly gave it half a glance and shrugged.

'No idea. Something you've planted, I expect.'

Frost shook his head in mock sadness. 'Come now, Patsy. We only do things like that as a last resort.' He riffled through the contents, leaving the phone until last. 'Watches, credit cards, debit cards . . . all sorts of flaming cards, but none in your name. I wonder why that is? Flaming credit-card companies – they never seem to get your name right.' He held one aloft. 'This one's made out to Susan Carter.'

'I've never seen them before in my life,' repeated Kelly.

'I must be a mind-reader,' beamed Frost. 'I knew you were going to say that.'

He continued his rummage. 'More watches . . . keys . . . and, hello – what's this?' He carefully lifted out the mobile phone.

'It's a mobile phone,' said Kelly. 'I don't nick mobile phones.'

'Someone else got the franchise?' asked Frost. He held the phone aloft. 'Now I wonder whose phone this is?' He turned to Jordan, who had by now come in through the back door to join him. 'Isn't there some way a phone will tell you its own number so we can check the owner's name with the phone company, because Mr Kelly says it isn't his?'

'Yes,' nodded Jordan. 'I've got one exactly like that.' He carefully took the phone from Frost and turned it on. He frowned, switched it off and on again, then shook his head. 'Battery's dead.'

'Where's the charger?' Frost asked Kelly.

'You should have brought the flaming charger

along when you planted the phone,' he answered.

'I always forget little things like that,' grinned Frost. 'There's one back at the nick. We'll finishing searching your gaff, then we'll nip down to the station.'

The toilet flushed, the bathroom door opened and a sweaty, green-faced Bridget Malone staggered out. She was dark-haired and plump, in her mid-forties. She wiped her mouth with the back of her hand. 'I knew that lobster was off,' she snarled at Kelly. She focused blurry eyes on Frost and his team. 'What are the flaming police doing here?'

Frost held up the mobile phone. 'Ever seen this before, Bridget?' She stared, then shook her head, not looking at him. 'No.'

Guilty as arseholes, thought Frost. 'We're going to continue this little tête-à-tête down the station. Get your coats.'

'I'll go in a separate car to her,' said Kelly. 'She spews up every five minutes. My car's swimming in it.'

'Good point,' nodded Frost. 'Taffy – take her in your car.'

Frost stirred his mug of tea with his Bic pen, sucked the sugar from the cap and sighed. 'All this sodding hanging about.'

'Kelly won't talk to you until his brief arrives, Jack, you know that,' said Sergeant Wells.

'Give me back the good old days,' said Frost. 'If your suspect wouldn't talk you kneed him in the groin, wrote his statement yourself and forged his signature.' He sighed deeply. 'The golden days.' He looked up at the clock. Four thirty. 'How's Jordan getting on with that flaming phone?'

'Still looking for a battery-charger, Jack. Our one is the wrong sort.' He drained his mug and lowered his voice. 'Are you sure it's the girl's phone?'

'Of course I'm bleeding sure,' answered Frost. 'I checked it before I got the flaming warrant.'

Wells looked alarmed and moved hurriedly to close the open door. 'For Pete's sake, Jack, I don't want to know.'

Frost sank into a chair. 'I wish he'd hurry up with that charger. Even when Kelly's brief Slippery Sam arrives, without confirmation that it's Debbie's phone I can only question him on the drugs and the piddling jewellery and credit cards, nothing else – and that other kid, Jan O'Brien, might still be alive.'

He shook a cigarette from the packet and offered one to Wells, who shook his head. Frost lit up and moved over to the window, staring down to see if the solicitor's car had arrived. 'Bloody nine-to-five solicitors,' he muttered.

There was a tap at the door and Jordan looked in. 'I found a charger, Inspector, and it is Debbie Clark's phone.'

'I'd be flaming surprised if it wasn't,' said Frost, 'but well done, son.'

'And even better news, Inspector. The last call she received was from Kelly's phone!'

Frost punched the air with delight. 'Then

we've got the sod!' He peered out into the car park again. 'Where's that flaming brief?' He turned to Jordan. 'And how's Molly Malone?'

'Still throwing up,' said Jordan. 'I don't know where it's all coming from. She wanted us to send for a Harley Street specialist, but she's got the duty quack.'

'We've got to talk to her,' said Frost. 'She'll be the one who made the phone call to Sandy Lane about the video tape.'

Car doors slammed in the car park. Frost turned back to the window. 'Slippery Sam's here. Look at the bleeding posh car he's got.' He swilled down the dregs of his tea and cuffed his mouth dry. 'Right, let's get cracking . . .' He stopped dead and smacked a palm on his forehead. 'Shit! That last call on the flaming phone – that was me checking if it was Debbie's mobile!' He spun round to Jordan. 'Is there any way we can erase it?'

Jordan thought for a moment. 'We could probably wipe it off the phone's memory, but the phone company will still have a record.'

'Human dung!' cursed Frost. 'All right. If it comes to it, they will have to prove they didn't make the call and I'll do what every good police officer does – lie my bleeding head off!' He rubbed his face with his hands. He was always skating on thin flaming ice. One day it would crack and he'd fall in the freezing water.

PC Collier looked round the door. 'Sarge, Kelly's solicitor is here. He wants to see his client.'

'Coming,' said Wells.

Frost looked at his empty mug. They would have to wait until Kelly had briefed Slippery Sam on the lies he was going to tell before he could be questioned. 'Any more tea on the go?' he called.

Deadly silence.

'Then someone bloody well make some,' said Frost, giving Taffy an encouraging kick. 'Tea all round, Lloyd George.'

Taffy reluctantly pulled himself out of his chair, where he was half asleep. 'Tea, Guv? Right away,' he yawned.

Frost didn't have to wait long. Halfway through the next mug of tea Bill Wells came back.

'They're ready for you, Jack, and Kelly wants bail.'

'I want a sex-mad teenage virgin,' said Frost, 'and Kelly's got the same chance as me!'

With Morgan tagging along, he made his way to the Interview Room, where he nodded at the solicitor, a weaselly-faced man you definitely wouldn't buy a second-hand car from – he looked more of a villain than Kelly, who was sitting beside him. Frost waited for Morgan to set up the tape recorder, then opened his folder.

'As you know, Mr Kelly, on information received we obtained a warrant enabling us to search your premises, where we found you in possession of these items.' He reached down and pulled up a polythene sack filled with the packets of coke Kelly had been carrying in the house. He took out one of the packets and showed it to the solicitor. 'Forensic tests haven't yet been carried out, but we have every reason to believe they contain an illegal substance.'

'As I explained to you earlier, Inspector,' said Kelly, in his reasonable voice for the tape recorder, 'I found them in my airing cupboard. I had never seen them before. Someone must have planted them there.'

'You were found with these packets in your arms and were intending to flush them down the bog.'

'Hold on, Inspector,' interjected the solicitor. 'You have no idea what my client's intentions were.'

'It's all right, Mr Simpson,' said Kelly, still in his reasonable voice. 'The inspector is quite right. To my shame, I did intend to flush them down the loo. I wanted to get rid of them. I knew he would never have believed they were planted. Inspector Frost is not a very trusting man.'

'Planted?' scoffed Frost. 'Then who would have had access to your airing cupboard?'

Kelly smiled. 'Someone who wanted to get me into trouble, Inspector. Perhaps the very same person who gave you the information you used to obtain the search warrant.'

Frost reached down beneath the table and brought up the box containing the credit cards, jewellery and mobile phone. 'We found this hidden at the back of your airing cupboard too,' he told Kelly.

Kelly shrugged. 'Never seen it before in my

life. Whoever is planting these things is doing a good job.'

'Just a moment, Inspector,' interjected the solicitor. 'What is the significance of this? What have these items got to do with the drugs that were planted on my client?'

Frost took a swig of cold tea. 'Serendipity, Mr Simpson. We looked for drugs, the rest was a bonus.' He glanced at Kelly. 'Drugs might be the least of your client's problems, Mr Simpson.'

'Oh?' said the solicitor. 'Perhaps you could elucidate.' He leant back smugly, arms folded.

Frost pointed to the mobile. 'That phone, which we found hidden in your client's airing cupboard, was owned by Debbie Clark.'

Simpson gave a scoffing sniff. 'The dead teenager? Tut, tut, Inspector, you are scraping the bottom of the barrel this time. I am sure there are thousands of phones of that make and model.'

'But not with the same phone number,' said Frost, playing his trump card. He leant across to Kelly. 'We've checked the phone number. The phone we found in the airing cupboard is Debbie Clark's phone. We are now talking murder.'

Kelly jerked back as if he had been hit. 'I've never seen the bleeding phone before. It's been planted. It's been bloody well planted. Bloody hell. On my mother's life . . . Drugs, yes. Bleeding murder, no.'

'Then how did the phone come to be in your possession?' demanded Frost.

Before Kelly could answer, the Interview Room door crashed open and a red and sweaty-faced, angry-looking Detective Chief Inspector Skinner burst in, swaying slightly, quivering with rage. 'Frost! Out here. Now!'

It was Frost's turn to be angry. 'Didn't you see the red light? I'm interviewing a suspect.'

'I don't give a sod what you're doing. Out here – now!'

'Excuse me for a moment,' apologised Frost to the solicitor. 'I believe my superior wants to commend me for something.' He rose and walked out to confront Skinner in the passage. 'How bloody dare you interrupt me when I'm questioning a suspect?'

'Don't try your high and mighty larks on me, Frost,' retorted Skinner, breathing out clouds of whisky fumes. 'What are all these officers doing in the Incident Room – on overtime unauthorised by me?'

'We are following a line of investigation,' said Frost, trying to remain calm.

'You don't follow any lines of investigation without getting my approval first, especially for a tuppence-ha'penny-possession-of-illegal-substances and receiving-stolen-goods pull. Send all those men home, now.'

'I'm questioning a suspect in connection with the murder of Debbie Clark and Thomas Harris.'

Skinner stared at Frost with eyes he was finding difficult to focus. 'A suspect?' He grabbed Frost by the arm and pulled him into his office. 'Tell me about it.'

Frost told him, skipping the details about breaking into Kelly's house first.

Skinner leant back and considered this. 'You got a warrant on information received. What information?'

'An anonymous phone call, about the drugs,' said Frost. 'He's phoned me before and his gen is always bang on.'

Skinner folded his arms and grinned with smug satisfaction. 'You looked for drugs, you found the phone. Bleeding marvellous. You reckon they killed the kids and took the video?'

'They've got the girl's phone,' said Frost. 'That's a good enough start for me.'

'And for me,' nodded Skinner. 'OK, Frost. Piss off home now, I'm taking this case over. Don't try to muscle in on any of my cases again. You find a suspect, you find me. You don't try to steal the bloody glory.'

Frost stamped out to the lobby to commiserate with Sergeant Wells.

'At least you won't have to do all the questioning, Jack. He'd have taken the kudos for cracking the case anyway.'

'I laid my bleeding job on the line by breaking into Kelly's house,' wailed Frost. 'I do all the flaming dirty work—'

They both looked up as, with a blast of cold air, the doors opened and a young, flashily dressed girl in high heels tottered in. She had clearly been drinking and it was an effort for her to walk over to the desk. Over-made-up, her lipstick was smudged and her lavishly applied cheap perfume battled with the aroma of gin. 'Where is he?' she demanded of Wells. 'How much longer have I got to sit in that bloody car.'

'Where is who, madam?' asked Wells.

'John. That big copper – grey suit, red tie. He's supposed to have a room booked at the hotel for us. I'm bleeding shagged out waiting.'

Eyebrows raised, Wells and Frost looked at each other, silently mouthing the word '*Skinner!*'

'I'll go and get him for you,' volunteered Frost.

Skinner, who was just about to enter the Interview Room with a bundle of case files under his arm, scowled as Frost approached. 'I told you to piss off!'

'This is important,' said Frost. 'Your granddaughter is in the lobby. She's going off the boil waiting for you.'

Skinner glared. 'You're pushing your bleeding luck, Frost.' He dug in his pocket, fished out his wallet and extracted a twenty-pound note which he handed over. 'Stick her in a taxi. Tell her to wait for me in the hotel, and tell her I might be a bit late. And then leave me in peace.'

Frost stuffed the note in his pocket as Taffy Morgan emerged from the Interview Room, dismissed by Skinner. 'You got your car here, Taffy?' he called.

'Yes, Guv.'

'There's a load of quivering crumpet in the lobby. Take her to wherever she wants to go,' said Frost.

'Right, Guv.'

'And keep your trousers on.'

'Yes, Guv.'

* * *

Frost mooched back to his office, his spirits flagging. It was far too late to go to bed, and in any case his mind was still churning over the night's events and there was no way he would be able to go to sleep. He suddenly realised he was hungry. He'd send out to the all-night chippy for some nosh.

He gave Collier Skinner's twenty pounds. 'Who wants fish and chips?' he called. 'I'm buying.'

Everyone wanted fish and chips. As Collier was taking the orders the phone rang. 'It's for you, Inspector,' called Jordan.

Frost glanced up at the clock. Who the hell was calling him at this unearthly hour? 'It had better not be bleeding double glazing,' he growled, taking the phone.

It was Sandy Lane from the *Denton Echo*.

'What the hell do you want, Sandy?' asked Frost, putting his hand over the mouthpiece to tell Collier he wanted sausage in batter with his chips. 'Tell them that last bit of cod I had from them was off.' Everyone began changing their orders from cod and he had to shout to make himself heard on the phone. 'What do you want, Sandy? Couldn't you sleep?'

'I was in bed. The office phoned me. They've just had another phone call.'

Frost flapped an urgent hand for silence. 'Another phone call? When?'

'A couple of minutes ago. Same woman as before. She said, "Ask the fuzz about the whipping." '

Frost went cold. The lash marks on Debbie's back. They hadn't released that information to the press. 'Where did she phone from?'

'A call box – not the same one as before. I got the number, but the exchange wouldn't give me its location.'

'We'll get the location,' said Frost. All public call boxes were supposed to be under twenty-four-hour surveillance, but he'd pulled everyone off for the Kelly caper. His white-knuckled hand was squeezing the living daylights out of the handset. Whoever the tart was who had phoned, it certainly wasn't Bridget Malone.

'What's this about a whipping? Was she beaten up?'

'Later, Sandy, later. Just give me the flaming phone number.' He scribbled it down and banged the phone back on the handset. 'Forget fish and chips,' he yelled. 'That tart has phoned again about the video.'

'I thought we had her banged up,' said Lambert.

'Unless she's in two places at once, we're bloody wrong.' He gave Collier the phone number. 'Speak to the phone company and find out where this call came from.' As Collier picked up the phone he turned to the others. 'The rest of you, get in your cars and start driving around. There can't be many motors on the road at this hour. I want registration numbers of the lot, so shift . . . Now!'

They thudded out while Frost waited impatiently for Collier to finish the call.

'Shouldn't you let Skinner know about this, Jack?' suggested Wells.

'He said he wasn't to be disturbed and I always do what I'm told, especially when he asks so nicely.' He turned back to Collier, who still had the phone pressed to his ear. 'Come on, son . . .'

The other phone rang. He snatched it up. 'What the bloody hell is it now?' It was the Fortress Building Society – another five hundred pounds had just been withdrawn from the cashpoint.

'You've made my day,' he grunted, banging the phone down. Hell! Beazley would be on to him first thing in the flaming morning. It never rained but it peed down. Still, one lousy crisis at a time. He turned his attention back to Collier. 'Don't take all flipping day, son.'

Collier snatched up a pen and scribbled on a pad. 'Thank you.' He hung up. 'The call box under the railway arch by Levington Street – the one I should have been watching.'

'Don't rub broken glass in the flaming wound,' said Frost, grabbing his scarf. 'Come on, let's take a look.'

Levington Street, with its cobbled roadway, snaked up a hill, under a railway arch, then fizzled out. Redevelopment work which would have transformed it into a more modern slum area had been on hold for six years. There were no CCTV cameras anywhere near to film traffic. *That tart knew what she was doing when she picked this spot*, thought Frost.

The door to the darkened call box, with its smashed light bulb, was ajar. It stank of urine, with torn yellowing pages of the phone directory carpeting the floor and a batch of prostitutes' calling cards stuck to the wall. 'Mind where you put your feet,' grunted Frost. 'Hello.' He bent and picked up a small square of paper – a Post-it self-adhesive note. Holding it carefully by the edges, he shone his torch and read it. '655555.' He beamed triumphantly. 'That, my son, is the phone number of the *Denton Echo*, and this is what we call in the trade a clue!' He foraged through his pockets, found a used envelope and slipped it in. 'Just in case she's obliged us by leaving her dabs.' He plucked one of the calling cards from the wall. 'Flaming heck – is she still going? She went to school with my gran.'

With his handkerchief he carefully lifted the handset and studied it under the beam of his torch. 'Wiped clean. If I had a suspicious mind I'd reckon she didn't want us to find her fingerprints.' He replaced the phone, then thought for a while, staring at the coin box. 'You know, son, I reckon hardly anyone uses this call box. It's stuck out on the arsehole of Denton on a road leading to nowhere, and the way it smells you'd be better off making your phone calls down a sewer.'

'What are you getting at, Inspector?' Collier asked.

'I bet there's hardly any coins in that coin box and they'll all have fingerprints on them, and one will have the dabs of our lady caller.' He pulled his penknife from his pocket and began to saw away at the flex on the handset.

Collier looked on, horrified, turning his head from side to side in case anyone could see what Frost was up to.

Frost examined the flex. His knife had made hardly any impression. 'I don't know how these bleeding vandals do it,' he said. 'There's a pair of wire-cutters in the glove compartment of my car. Fetch them for me, son.'

The cutters sliced through the flex in one go. 'Give us the tools and we'll finish the job,' said Frost in his Churchill voice.

'Why did you do that?' asked Collier.

'Because I don't want anyone else using this phone until we've got all the coins out of the box for testing. When we get back to the station, phone British Telecom. I want one of their engineers to liaise with someone from SOCO at the crack of dawn. I want the coins removed and fingerprinted.'

'But she could have been wearing gloves,' said Collier.

'If she was wearing gloves, my son, she wouldn't have had to wipe the handset clean after using it. Oh, and you can tell BT that some vandalising bastard has hacked the handset off – give them Skinner's description if you like.'

Skinner charged out of the Interview Room and yelled down the corridor to Wells, 'That bleeding woman's thrown up all over me. Get her to Denton General. Look at my suit – it stinks of puke.' His jacket was splattered with vomit.

'Dear, dear,' tutted Wells, trying not to laugh.

'Get me a tea towel or something to wipe this off. Where's Frost?'

'Gone home, I think,' Wells told him.

'The bastard's never here when you want him. What about the rest of the team?'

'I believe Inspector Frost sent them home. He said you'd instructed him to do so.'

'He picks and chooses what flaming orders he wants to obey,' snorted Skinner. 'Sod it. I haven't got time to waste on a drug-possession and petty-thieving case. Bang Kelly up and I'll finish questioning him in the morning.'

'What about the dead girl's phone, sir?' asked Wells.

'That Malone woman probably nicked it. She threw up when I asked her. She claims she nicked the other stuff from lockers at the school. She also says there's about half a ton of bog rolls she knifed in their garage. If Frost had done a proper search he would have found them. I can't see anyone who nicks bog rolls being a killer, somehow. Bloody Frost. The sooner he's out of Denton the bloody better . . .'

The hands on the wall clock in the Incident Room crawled round to five fifty-eight. Frost yawned and rubbed his stubbled chin. His team had returned with the registration numbers of the few vehicles that had been spotted, but none had had woman drivers or passengers, so they didn't look at all promising. He yawned again. 'We'll check the CCTV footage later. Might find something we missed on there.' He stretched his aching back. 'The important question of the moment is this: do we go home and grab a couple of hours' kip before reporting to Skinner for a bollocking, or do we go down to the all-night café and have a fry-up?'

'I'm starving,' said Lambert.

'Then you speak for all of us,' said Frost, reaching for his scarf. 'Let's go.'

He turned his head as Morgan, looking well satisfied with himself, sauntered in. 'Sorry it took so long, Guv. Something came up.'

'Something went up, you mean,' said Frost. 'You were supposed to take that tom to the hotel and come straight back. Skinner will have your guts for garters if he finds out he's not a first-footer.'

'She didn't want to go to the hotel, Guv. She wanted to go home. She was shagged out.'

'And we all know by whom,' grinned Frost. 'Care for some brekker?'

He slept for a couple of hours at his desk and was woken by the clanging of the cleaners' buckets as they mopped up the corridor outside. He clicked on his desk lamp and looked at the wall clock. Eight forty-five. He'd had barely two hours' sleep and felt shagged out and dirty. He rubbed his eyes, reached for his cigarettes then pushed the packet away. He'd smoked himself sick last night and his mouth tasted like the contents of a week-old ashtray. The fried food from Nick's café was churning away in his stomach and making him feel queasy. Coffee, that's what he wanted. He detoured to the washroom on his way to the lobby, to splash cold water on his face. He looked at the weary, drawn, grey face staring back at him from the mirror. 'You poor old sod,' he muttered, dabbing himself dry.

The coffee helped a little. Johnny Johnson grinned as Frost came down the stairs.

'Had a rough night, Jack?'

'Bleeding rough,' nodded Frost. 'Has Skinner charged Kelly and the cockle-seller yet?'

'He's charged Kelly with the drugs, but the woman was taken violently ill and is in Denton General.'

'Ill?'

'Food poisoning, I think. She threw up all over Skinner's best suit.'

'I'm beginning to take to her,' said Frost. 'I think I'll nip over to Denton General and have a few words with her. What did she say about the phone?'

'He couldn't get much sense out of her.'

'And she's in Denton General? I'll just nip over and try and jog her memory.'

'Skinner won't like it,' said Johnson.

'Which adds to the pleasure,' smirked Frost.

The cleaners were mopping and polishing the seemingly endless corridor that crawled round the hospital to Nightingale Ward, where Bridget Malone was a patient. The staff nurse in charge had just come on duty and had to refer to the admission doctor's notes.

'Nothing too serious. Food poisoning. She can go home today.'

'I'll just pop over and cheer her up,' said Frost.

Bridget Malone's complexion was still tinged with green. A plate of cold, congealed porridge lurked sullenly on a tray beside her. She was sipping a bright-yellow mug of hospital tea with obvious distaste.

'We left a urine sample in a yellow mug on a tray near here,' said Frost, dragging a chair to the side of the bed. 'You haven't seen it by any chance?'

'Who the hell are you?' she asked, then she remembered. 'You're the copper who was at the house last night.'

'Once seen, never forgotten, love,' said Frost. 'I want to talk about that mobile phone.'

'What mobile phone?'

Frost sighed deeply. 'Don't sod me about, Bridget. You know damn well what phone. The mobile we found in your airing cupboard. The murdered girl's phone.'

The woman's jaw dropped. She stared wide-eyed at Frost. 'Dear Sweet Mother of God. Not little Debbie – not that poor girl?'

'Yes, that poor girl.'

'Dear Mother of God. I never knew . . .' She crossed herself. 'May I die in the bed I'm lying in, Inspector – I never knew. I'd never have taken it had I known.'

'Taken it? From where?'

She shook her head. 'I don't know.'

'You don't bleeding know? Don't sod me about!' roared Frost.

There was a clatter of footsteps as the staff nurse came over. 'Please keep your voice down. There are sick people here.'

'Sorry, love,' muttered Frost. He turned back to the woman. 'If you can't remember where you got it, I'm arresting you for murder and you'll be doing porridge as well as bleeding eating it.'

'Murder? I wouldn't have touched a hair on that poor innocent child's head. Those girls, they just left stuff lying around. They were just asking for it to be pinched.'

'You stole stuff from the kids' lockers?'

'All the lockers. I was teaching the school a lesson. I was going to put it all back.'

'I bet you bleeding were,' sniffed Frost. 'So when did this happen?'

'On my mother's life, Inspector, if I hadn't been taken sick, I'd have put it all back.'

'You're a lying cow, Bridget. When did you nick it?'

She screwed her face in thought. 'Let me see . . . Wednesday . . . Yes, it was Wednesday, the day before I was taken sick.'

'You're a bleeding liar, Bridget. Debbie was killed on Tuesday night and she had her phone with her. You and Kelly killed her, didn't you?'

Her eyes spat fire. 'Don't you dare accuse me of a thing like that, Inspector. You can go to hell. If you want to talk to me, get my solicitor. I'm not saying another word.'

Frost stood up and scraped his chair back against the wall. 'I'm going for now, Bridget. But remember what big Arnie said . . . "*I'll be back*."'

Back in the car, he radioed the station to send a WPC to stay with Malone until she was discharged and take her straight to the station. Then he turned the car off the main road and headed down the side streets to Debbie's house.

Mrs Clark was haggard with grief. Her hair was uncombed as before, her dress not buttoned properly. The house felt cold and empty – it felt like a place where someone had died. She took him into the living room. Cards of condolence were strewn on the carpet.

'It's about your daughter,' began Frost uneasily.

She stared at him as if deeply surprised. 'She's at school. My Debbie is at school . . .' Then her body shook and she collapsed into a chair. 'She's not at school . . . she's dead. My Debbie is dead.'

'I know, love, I know,' sympathised Frost. God, this was going to be bloody difficult. He sat himself down in a chair opposite her. 'A couple of questions and I'll be on my way . . . it won't take long.'

She stared at him intently, then leant forward, dropping her voice. 'Her father killed her. He lusted after her. He was jealous of that boy.'

'You might be right,' nodded Frost gravely, 'but we've got to get a few facts straight before we can make an arrest. It's about Debbie's mobile phone. You said she took it with her the night she went missing?'

She blinked at him. 'Her phone? I bought it for her twelfth birthday.'

'Yes, love. But the night she went missing, did she take the phone with her?'

'I made her take it. Every time she went out, I made her take it. I said terrible things might . . .' Her body shook, racked with sobs, '. . . terrible things might happen.'

'And she took it?'

'I always made her show it to me. She held it up. She said, "Look, Mum, I've got it."'

'You're sure about this, Mrs Clark? It's very important.'

'Of course I'm sure.'

18

'Skinner wants you,' said Wells, 'and he's spitting blood.'

'You did say "spitting"? I'm not going in if it's the other end,' said Frost. He groaned. 'Ah, well. Let's get it over and done with.'

He took a quick look in his own office on the way down. A heap of niggling chase-up memos from Mullett lay in his in-tray, together with a report from SOCO about the coins removed from the call box. Only ninety pence in assorted coins. One of the 10p pieces had a segment of a fingerprint which matched the fingerprint on the video wrapping paper. The same woman each time. Big deal! They now knew it was the same woman, but still didn't know who she was. But what else did he expect? He gave a deep sigh. Things were getting on top of him. The little unexpected lucky breaks that often came to his rescue seemed to be on unauthorised leave. He wished *he* was! Flaming fat-guts Skinner was no help. He'd dumped all the cases on him, ready to take the credit when they were solved and to bollock

Frost when things went wrong. And talking of bollocking, he'd better go in and see what Chubby Chops wanted this time.

The typewritten notice pinned on Skinner's office door read DCI SKINNER. ROOM 12, with an arrow pointing down the corridor. Frost poked his head inside. It was empty of furniture and a white-overalled workman was splashing paint on the walls. He looked up at Frost.

'You the gentleman from next door, squire?'

'First time I've been called a gentleman,' said Frost, 'but yes.'

'We'll be starting on your office next week. Understand you're leaving?'

'In my own bloody time,' snapped Frost, slamming the door. Bloody Skinner, ordering the coffin while the corpse was still phoning for an ambulance.

Room 12's door had a pinned notice: DCI SKINNER – KNOCK AND WAIT. Frost barged straight in.

Skinner sat behind a paper-laden desk in a tiny room jam-packed with furniture from his office. He glowered at Frost. Standing in front of him was WPC Kate Holby. She was biting her lip hard and looked on the verge of tears.

'I didn't hear you knock.'

'Ah – that's why I didn't hear you say "Come in",' said Frost.

Another scowl from Skinner. He turned to Kate. 'Now get out. You'll hear more about this.'

She brushed past Frost and left.

Skinner leant back in his chair. 'I'll give that

girl something to cry about. If she can't obey orders, she's out. I gave her a specific job to do and I find her out on surveillance at the Blue Parrot.'

'I ordered her to do that,' said Frost.

'I don't care a sod about you. She obeys my orders, not yours. She's on probation. I've got to do a report on her suitability. Well, I'm reporting that she's unsuitable and that will be that.'

'Even you wouldn't do that,' said Frost.

A nasty grin crawled over Skinner's face. 'Wouldn't I just?'

'You wouldn't,' said Frost as he sat down, 'any more than I would report you for having sex with an under-age prostitute and bringing her to the station. I wouldn't stoop so low – unless I had to, of course.'

The colour drained from Skinner's face. 'Under age?' he croaked.

Frost nodded. 'Fifteen this year.' He had no idea how old she was, but Morgan had taken her home last night so he knew where she lived, and he'd get her to lie if necessary.

Skinner was trying to pull himself together. He gathered up the papers on his desk and patted them into a neat stack. 'You're too bleeding clever for your own good,' he muttered.

'Thank you,' said Frost. 'Praise from you is praise indeed. What did you want to see me about?'

Skinner waved a hand at the papers on his desk. 'You know what these are? Overtime claims . . . *unauthorised* overtime claims. I'm the one who authorises overtime, Frost, not you.'

'Superintendent Mullett—' began Frost.

'And not Superintendent bleeding Mullett – you take your orders from me, not him. What did that Irish tart say about the phone?'

Frost told him.

Skinner snorted. 'She took it from the girl's locker? Just what I thought.'

'Mrs Clark said Debbie had it the night she was killed.'

'Then she's wrong. It can't have been in two bloody places at once, can it? The kid probably left it at school by mistake and lied to her mother. You're wasting everyone's time following that line of inquiry, so drop it. Bridget Malone is a petty, bog-paper-nicking thief, not a murderer, and Patsy Kelly's a drug-dealer – I'm letting the drug squad deal with him. I've phoned the school. They don't want to prosecute the woman, so that's that.'

His phone rang. 'Skinner.' He pulled the handset away from his ear as a stream of invective poured out. 'Mr Beazley, my name is Detective Chief Inspector Skinner. I think we have a mutual friend . . . yes, he's the one. Up to now this whole thing has been a complete mess. I'm going to kick arse to make sure it's dealt with as it should be. You have my word on that, Mr Beazley, you have my word.' He hung up and rubbed his ear. 'More bloody money was taken last night while you were gallivanting around picking up a bog-paper nicker. I want Beazley off my flaming back, so do a proper surveillance for a change tonight and catch the sod . . . *Comprende?*'

'*Arrivederci*,' said Frost.

Skinner stared at him, wondering as usual whether Frost was taking the mickey or was just plain stupid. A noise from his old office distracted him. 'How's that lazy sod next door getting on?'

'What, Superintendent Mullett?' asked Frost innocently.

'You know damn well who I mean. And he's doing your office next week, ready for your successor. Have you sold your house yet?'

'Not yet.'

'Then get a bloody move on. You start at Lexton the week after next.'

As Frost got up to go, Skinner suddenly remembered. 'Where's the change from my twenty quid?'

'I gave it to your granddaughter,' said Frost. 'The under-age one.'

Back in his office, he sat and smoked, staring at the nicotine-stained ceiling. The thought that he would have to give this up and move to some sterile cupboard in Lexton added to his depressed mood. He hated to admit it, but Skinner was right about Kelly and Malone. Villains, yes; drug-dealers and petty thieves, yes; but killers and torturers of kids, no. So, with them off the suspects list they now had to try and trace the woman who was making the phone calls to Sandy Lane about the video.

He made his way over to the Incident Room to see if they were having any luck with the registration numbers of the few cars that had been in the vicinity at around the time the woman made the call.

Kate Holby was sitting at the corner desk with stacks of box files around her, transferring the contents to the computer. It was a boring, seemingly never-ending job. She looked as depressed as he felt. He wandered over to her. She looked up and gave him a weak smile.

'I've just had a word with Skinner, love. He won't be doing an adverse report on you.'

Her face brightened. 'Oh, thank you. Thank you so much.'

'Don't thank me, love,' said Frost. 'I just pointed out one or two things to him and, living saint that he is, he realised he'd made a mistake.'

He moved across the room to Collier, who had the phone to his ear and was scribbling something down on a sheet of paper.

'What are you doing, son?' asked Frost when the call finished.

'Jordan and Simms are out checking on the cars that were in the vicinity last night when the phone call was made. All vehicles cleared so far.' He waved the A4 sheet at Frost. It was a list of registration numbers, ticked and marked when the owners had been traced and called on.

One registration number wasn't ticked. Frost jabbed it with his finger. 'What about this one?'

'That's a lorry, Inspector. You said check only cars.'

Frost stared at the number. A little bell started ringing deep in the dark depths of his memory.

Where had he seen that registration number before? It was on a list. It was definitely on a list of some sort. 'Check it out, son.'

He waited while Collier tapped away at the computer. A name flashed up on the monitor. 'Registered to Kenneth Taylor, Denton Farm Produce Ltd.'

Frost shook his head. It still didn't mean anything. 'By the way, we're back on surveillance duty at the Fortress cashpoints tonight. After midnight this time. Skinner has promised Beazley that he is going to crack this case personally, and we mustn't let our Chief Inspector down, must we?'

As Frost returned to his office, DC Morgan hastily stuffed the *Daily Mirror* in a drawer and pretended to be busily filling in forms.

'We're back on cashpoint surveillance again tonight, Taff, so it will give your dick a rest.'

Morgan grinned. 'I've got details of the cars picked up on CCTV around the time the money was taken from Fortress last night. No common factor.'

He passed the file across to Frost, who idly flipped through it while digging in his pocket for a cigarette. Then he froze. Staring up at him was the registration number of the Denton Farm Produce lorry. He turned another page. There it was again. He looked up. 'Taff, come here.'

Looking apprehensive and wondering what he had done wrong now, the Welshman joined him. 'Yes, Guv?'

Frost stabbed a finger. 'Why wasn't this one checked? The same vehicle on three of the four nights?'

'It's a lorry, Guv. You said don't check lorries.'

'You prat,' snarled Frost. 'Why do you only obey orders when it's the wrong flaming thing to do? The same flaming lorry turning up every night around the time the money was taken from the building society. Didn't you think that was more than a flaming coincidence?'

'Now you come to mention it,' began Morgan, but Frost was already on his way to the Incident Room.

'Collier, what was the address of that bloke from Denton Farm Produce?'

'Rose Cottage, Shadwell Road,' Collier told him.

Frost punched the palm of his hand. 'Shadwell Road? That's within spitting distance of where Billy King lives – the one whose cashpoint card was stolen. This could be the bloody lead we're looking for.' He snatched up the phone and called Control. 'Get on to Jordan and Simms. Tell them to drop everything and pick up a Kenneth Taylor, Rose Cottage, Shadwell Road for questioning in connection with the theft of a bank card. And tell him I want to thank him personally for hitting Morgan on the head the other night.'

The area car's headlights sliced a path through the darkness as it bumped and juddered up the unmade road that led to the farm building. It crawled up to a wooden gate which had fallen off its hinges, the headlights picking out the dim outline of an old farm labourer's cottage. No lights were showing. Jordan squinted through the windscreen. 'You sure this is the place? It looks derelict.'

'This is the place,' confirmed Simms. 'Look – there's the lorry by the side of the house.'

Jordan climbed out and adjusted his peaked cap as Simms slid from the driving seat. They scrunched up the weed-strewn gravel path. Suddenly there was the sound of shattering glass. They froze.

'What the hell . . .?' began Simms when a man's voice screamed out at them from one of the upstairs windows.

'That's far enough, coppers.'

Simms tried to make out the shape in the window. 'Now look, Mr Taylor,' called Simms in his 'let's be reasonable about this' voice. 'We just want to talk to you.' They were moving forward again when the man swung round and thrust something through the shattered window, something metallic which glinted in the headlights.

'Shit!' croaked Simms. 'It's a bleeding shotgun.'

Both policemen stopped dead.

'This is silly, Mr Taylor,' called Jordan. 'We only want to talk to you.'

'Another move and I'll shoot.' The voice was strained. The man seemed to be on the crumbling edge of a nervous breakdown.

Flaming hell, thought Simms. *What has Frost let us in for this time?*

The woman on the phone was near hysterical and Wells could hardly make out what she was saying. 'Now calm down, madam, please.'

'The baby,' she kept sobbing. 'He's got the baby.'

'Who has got the baby?'

'I keep telling you. My husband . . . I came home from work. I went to the childminder. She said my husband had taken him. He told her we were going away on holiday.'

'And what's wrong with that, madam?'

'We're separated. He doesn't have access. He gets violent rages. He's going to hurt the baby. I just know it.'

'Have you contacted your husband?'

'I keep telling you. You don't listen. I tried the last address he gave me. He's moved. I don't know where he is. He's got the baby and I don't know where he is.'

Wells picked up a pencil. 'Right, madam, let's have some details. First, your name and address . . .'

Jordan and Simms stood stock still. The barrel of the shotgun was moving slowly from one of them to the other.

Jordan tried again. 'You're prolonging the agony, Mr Taylor. If we can't sort this out calmly, we'll have to call in a whole gang of armed police and things would get really nasty. We don't want that.'

'I bloody want it,' screamed Taylor. 'Get your bloody armed police. Get the press. Get the telly. I'll tell them how those bastards ruined me . . . how they drove me to this.'

'Mr Taylor—' Jordan took a tentative step forward, jumping hurriedly back as the shotgun blasted out, shattering one of the area car's headlamps.

'I warned you,' screamed Taylor. 'I won't warn you again. Unless you want a faceful of pellets, clear off!'

'In the bloody car,' yelled Simms, grabbing Jordan's arm and dragging him back. Once at the wheel, even before the doors were shut, he hurriedly backed the car down the lane, out of shotgun range and snatched up the radio handset.

'Denton. We've got a problem. We're going to need back-up . . .'

'A bloody shoot-out,' moaned Frost, shuffling on his mac. 'Just what we flaming well need.'

Lambert looked round the door. 'Skinner isn't answering his radio or his phone.'

'Trust Fatty Arbuckle to piss off somewhere when things get nasty.' Frost turned to Morgan. 'He might be checking up on that tart. You did tell her to say she was fifteen?'

'Yes, Guv. She said she would. Are you going to call out Armed Response?'

Frost thought for a moment, then shook his head. 'Not yet. They'll take over and turn it into a flaming gun fight at the OK Corral. Let's try and keep things low key and talk Taylor out of it.'

Kate Holby came in and dumped some papers on Frost's desk. 'From DCI Skinner,' she said.

Frost smiled up at her. 'Grab your coat, love. We're going to a shoot-out.'

She looked doubtful. 'I've got to stay here. DCI Skinner said—'

'Sod Skinner. He's not here, so I'm in charge. Just get your coat.'

'Shall I come too, Guv?' asked Morgan.

'Yes,' nodded Frost. 'We might need an expendable human shield.'

Frost's ancient Ford made heavy going of the unmade road but it eventually staggered up to the area car. Frost switched off the headlights, then he and Taffy slid on to the rear seat of the area car. 'Where is he?' he asked.

Jordan pointed up to the shattered window. 'Up behind that left-hand top window – the one with the broken glass.'

Frost squinted. 'I can see sod all.' He wished he'd had the sense to bring the night glasses.

'He's up there all right,' Jordan assured him. 'Just try walking towards the house and see what happens!'

Frost passed his cigarettes round to delay the moment when he would have to come up with a plan of action. At the moment, his mind was a blank.

Morgan offered a suggestion. 'If you kept him talking, Guv, I might be able to sneak round the back of the house unnoticed and take him by surprise.'

'No,' said Frost. 'I only want you shot to pieces as a last resort.' He took one last drag at his cigarette and stubbed it out. 'Let's see if my silver-tongued eloquence will work.' He climbed out of the car and advanced cautiously up the path. 'Mr Taylor, my name is Frost. Detective Inspector Frost. I want to talk to you.'

No reply.

Frost took another couple of tentative steps forward. 'Can we talk?'

Movement at the window. A shot blasted out. Shotgun pellets bounded off the path just in front of Frost, who backed away hurriedly. 'I'll take that as a no,' he muttered.

'I said no further,' yelled Taylor.

'What's the point of all this?' shouted Frost. 'You've nowhere to go. Chuck out the gun and come out.'

'If you want me, you can bloody well come and get me.' The voice was quivering on the edge of total hysteria.

'I don't want to have to bring in armed police,' called Frost, his throat hurting from shouting against the wind. 'I don't want my men hurt and I don't want you hurt.'

'Then go away. Leave me alone.'

Frost shrugged and mooched back to the car for another cigarette.

'What now, Guv?' asked Morgan, who always imagined Frost had instant solutions to all problems.

'Gawd knows,' shrugged Frost. 'Sit it out, I suppose. He can't stay in there for ever.'

'He sounds suicidal,' said Kate Holby.

'If he tops himself, then hard luck. I'm not risking lives trying to stop him.' A tapping at the car window made him look up. He opened the door to Simms.

'Have you got your radio switched off, Inspector?'

Frost checked. 'Yes. Sorry.'

'Control's going mad trying to contact you.'

Frost switched on and picked up the handset. 'Frost. What's the panic?'

'Mullett wants you,' Lambert told him.

'And I thought it was urgent,' sighed Frost.

'Putting you through now,' said Lambert.

'Frost,' said Mullett, sounding annoyed as usual. 'We've been trying to contact you.'

'Sorry, Super. Radio went on the blink. We've just managed to fix it.'

'We've had Taylor's wife on the phone. She's frantic. She and Taylor are separated. He doesn't have access to their one-year-old son. Taylor picked the kiddy up from the childminder and didn't take him back home.'

Frost went cold. 'Shit. He must have the kid in there with him. I need back-up.' This completely changed the situation.

'DCI Skinner is coming over to take command.'

'Terrific,' muttered Frost. 'Our troubles are over!' He turned to the others. 'Taylor's got his one-year-old son in there with him.' He opened the car door. 'Let's have another bleeding fireside chat.'

He moved as far up the path as he dared and yelled, 'Mr Taylor!'

Movement at the window. 'What do you want?'

'Have you got your son with you?'

'He goes where I go.'

'He could get hurt. Let's get him out of there.'

'He stays with me.'

'What's the point of all this, Mr Taylor? You've got to come out some time. This is doing no one any good. What do you want?'

'I'll tell you what I want.' The man was screaming now. 'I want the world to know what that bastard supermarket has done to me . . .'

'And what has it done to you?'

'I had a market garden. I supplied all their vegetables – top-quality stuff, but they kept cutting the price they wanted to pay me. And then they wanted to cut it to below the cost of production. When I couldn't meet their price, they dropped me. I lost everything.'

'Tough,' said Frost. 'But how does this help?'

'I want the world to know what that bastard Beazley did to me. I want the press here . . . I want television . . . I want the bloody world to know what a shit he is.'

'All right, send your son out and I'll get the media here.'

'My son stays with me.'

'Is he all right, Mr Taylor? He's very quiet.'

A long pause.

'Mr Taylor,' repeated Frost. 'Is he all right?'

'He's sleeping . . . peacefully sleeping.'

'If I get the media here and you give them your story, will you end this? Will you come out quietly with the baby?'

Again a pause, then a none-too-convincing 'Yes.'

'Leave it to me.' Frost returned to the car and lit up. 'I don't like this,' he said. 'I don't like it one sodding bit. Still, we've got no choice. We'll have to go along with him. I get the feeling the bastard might make his point by doing himself in in front of the TV cameras and before the bleeding watershed.'

Headlights flared in the windscreen as DCI Skinner's car pulled up alongside. 'Our troubles are over,' muttered Frost. 'The United States Cavalry has arrived.'

Skinner yanked open the car door, then jerked a thumb for Morgan to get out so he could slide in beside Frost. He scowled as he noticed Kate Holby. 'What the hell are you doing here? Didn't I tell you—'

'We need her,' cut in Frost. 'Taylor's got a baby with him. We could well need a woman.'

'I told her to stay in the office. She's disobeyed orders once too often. By the way, I've checked with that tart . . . She's twenty-three.' He turned to face the WPC. 'You're out, sweetie.' Back to Frost. 'Fill me in.'

Frost brought him up to date.

Skinner frowned. 'And you haven't called in Armed Response?'

'I don't want to escalate things. I want to keep it as low key as possible.'

'Firing at police officers is hardly low bleeding key, is it?'

'He fired in their direction. He could have hit them if he'd wanted to.'

'OK, we'll keep them out of it for the time being. Those bastards like to steal all the flaming glory. And he's got the child in there with him?'

Frost shrugged his shoulders. 'He says he has, but we haven't heard a peep out of the kid. He says the baby is sleeping peacefully – that's got me worried.'

Skinner stared at him. 'What do you mean?'

'With all the shouting and noise, I'd expect the kid to be bawling its head off. He might have done him in.'

Skinner frowned. 'Done him in? You're a cheerful bleeding sod, aren't you? You've got no bloody proof of that.'

'Of course I've got no bloody proof. I hope I'm wrong, but Taylor's gone round the bend. He's not talking logically any more.'

The DCI chewed this over. 'Suppose we rushed him – drove the car at speed to the door, bashed our way in and charged up the stairs?'

'Even I'm not prat enough to try that,' said Frost. 'He's got suicidal tendencies. He'd have shot himself and the kid before you were halfway down the passage.'

'We can't just bloody well sit here,' said Skinner.

Then think of something, thought Frost. *I'm out of flaming ideas*. Aloud he said, 'He wants to pour his heart out to the media.'

Skinner shook his head. 'I don't want the media here at this stage. If anything goes wrong I don't want our mistakes broadcast all over the flaming country.' He tugged at his nose in thought. 'I'll talk to him. Do we know his phone number?'

'If he's got his mobile on him, we know that number. It's written on the side of the lorry.'

'Then try it.'

Frost dialled and handed his mobile over.

The call was was answered on the first ring. 'What do you want?'

'Mr Taylor?'

'Who the hell did you think it would be? Who are you?'

'Detective Chief Inspector Skinner.'

'I don't want to speak to you. Let me talk to the scruffy one.'

Skinner handed the phone to Frost. 'He wants to speak to you.'

'What is it, Mr Taylor?'

'The media. Where's the media?'

'On their way,' lied Frost. 'How's the baby?'

A pause, then, 'He's fine. He's at peace.'

A cold shiver crawled down Frost's spine. 'You're sure he's all right?'

'He's at peace.'

'Can we see him?'

'No. I want the media. I want Beazley. I want him here.' The line went dead.

Frost stared at his mobile, then turned it off. 'Did you hear that?' he asked Skinner.

Skinner nodded. 'Yeah. I don't want the

flaming media here yet. Hold on. Do nothing. I'm going to take a recce.' He opened the car door and stepped out into the darkness.

'A reccy?' said Frost to Morgan. 'Is that another name for a slash?'

'Reconnaissance, Guv,' explained Morgan.

'Oh!' said Frost, as if he didn't know. He lit up another cigarette he didn't want and watched the smoke writhe its way up to the roof. 'It might not be a bad idea to get his wife down here.'

More car headlights shone through the windscreen. A blue Porsche – Superintendent Mullett. 'Shit,' groaned Frost. 'Just when I thought things couldn't get any worse.'

Mullett tapped on his window and beckoned Frost over. 'Update,' he snapped as Frost slid in beside him.

'Up what?' asked Frost innocently.

'I want an update,' barked Mullett. 'What is the current position? Where is DCI Skinner?'

'Taylor's in that upstairs room. He's got a shotgun and is threatening to shoot anyone who comes too near. We think he's got his one-year-old son with him, but we can't be sure.'

'What does he want?'

'He wants the media and Beazley brought in so he can let the world know what a load of bastards Beazley and his supermarket are.'

'If that's what he wants, get the media here,' said Mullett.

'In case we make a complete balls-up, DCI Skinner doesn't want it splashed all over the TV screen,' said Frost.

Mullett nodded gravely. 'Yes, of course. Good point. But what do you intend to do, Frost? We can't just sit it out.'

'I'm waiting for Skinner. He's in charge.'

'Then where is he?' The possibility of a balls-up was making Mullett nervous. If things went disastrously wrong, he didn't want to be in the vicinity. He was already mentally composing his defence. *I knew nothing about it. I would never have sanctioned it if I had known*. 'Ah – here he is.'

Skinner emerged from the dark and slid into the back seat. He nodded to Mullett. 'Good to see you, sir. Do you want to take charge?'

'Good heavens no,' blurted Mullett, vigorously shaking his head. 'I'm sure things are in capable hands.'

The DCI grunted his acceptance of authority. 'The way I see it is this. The longer we leave things, the worse they could get. He's on the verge of cracking up completely. God knows what the hell he'll do when he does.'

'We should back off and let him calm down,' said Frost.

'That's just delaying what has to be done. We've got to bite the bullet. I managed to get round the back of the house without being seen. The back door doesn't seem to be locked. Since I'm an official police marksman, I drew a gun from the station before I came. I want you to keep him talking, Frost, while I sneak round the back with the gun. I reckon I can get in without him knowing, creep up the stairs and ram my gun in his guts before he has a chance to do anything.'

'But if he hears you . . .' protested Mullett.

'If he hears me and comes at me with the shotgun, I'll have no alternative but to shoot. I hope it won't come to that. The important thing is to save the child if he's still alive.'

Mullett blinked nervously. This could well go wrong and he didn't want to be around when it happened, but he could see no way of getting out of it. 'I don't like it,' he said. 'It's too risky.'

'The alternative could be him killing the kid, then topping himself. Do you want to risk that?'

Mullett winced. He hated being put on the spot. 'You're in charge of the operation,' he told Skinner. 'I must defer to your decision, but I'm calling Armed Response as a back-up just in case.'

Use your flaming authority, you spineless prat. Veto it, urged Frost mentally. This was going to end in disaster, he just knew it.

'Right, Frost,' ordered Skinner. 'Get him on the phone and keep him talking.'

'Hold on,' said Frost. 'Let's make one last attempt to get the kiddy out.' He climbed out of Mullett's Porsche and beckoned Kate Holby, then walked up the path with her so she was fully illuminated in the headlights. He called Taylor on the phone.

'What now?'

'I've got this young WPC here. She's trained to handle children. Why don't you let us have your son? He shouldn't be placed in danger like this.'

'No. He stays with me. She's not having him. Where's the press? Where's that sod Beazley?'

'On their way,' said Frost, aware that Skinner had slipped out of Mullett's car and was circling round to the rear of the house. He was sure Taylor wouldn't spot him behind the glare of the headlights. 'The local TV boys are sending a team and I've arranged for ITV news to send a full crew, but it may take a little time. I expect they'll want to send a cameraman into the house.'

'No!' cut in Taylor. 'No one comes inside the house.'

'Let them see your son. You'll get everyone on your side if they can see the kiddy.'

'No!' screamed Taylor. 'No one sees him. He stays with me.'

He's dead, thought Frost.

'And I want that bastard Beazley here. I want the world to see what a shit he is . . . what that bastard has done to me.'

'So you said. My colleague is on the phone now, trying to get him to come,' said Frost, glad to spin things out. 'We can't force him to come, but we're trying.'

'I want him here,' shrilled Taylor, his voice rising to a scream. 'Do you hear me? I want him here.'

'We're trying now,' said Frost, signalling to Mullett to make the call. The Superintendent was speaking quietly into the mouthpiece but didn't seem to be getting anywhere. 'He wants to speak to you,' he said, handing the phone over to Frost.

'What the hell are you playing at?' demanded Beazley. 'If you think I'm coming in front of the flaming TV cameras you've got another thing coming. I'm not the bloody villain here. I didn't try to kill bleeding babies. If he couldn't meet our prices there were plenty of people who could. You keep my bloody name out of this, do you hear, or I'll have your guts for flaming garters.'

'Thank you,' grunted Frost, handing the phone back to Mullett and returning to Taylor on the other phone. 'He's on his way.'

'Right . . . I . . . *What's that?*'

Shit, thought Frost. *He's heard Skinner*. 'Mr Taylor . . . Mr Taylor . . .' But Taylor had put the phone down. Frost could hear the thud of footsteps, and muffled voices.

The sound of a shot blasted through the phone and echoed over the open ground.

The colour seeped from Mullett's face. 'Did you hear that?' he croaked.

Frost nodded grimly. 'What's going on?' he yelled down the phone. 'Answer me, you sod, answer me . . .'

Slow footsteps. A rustling as the phone was picked up. Heavy breathing.

'Who's this?' demanded Frost.

It was Taylor. 'You tried to trick me,' he screeched.

'What the bloody hell has happened?' yelled Frost down the phone.

'You sent someone up with a gun. He was going to kill me.'

'What happened?' asked Frost again.

'I shot him. I've got his gun.'

'Is he dead?' Everyone around him held their breath, waiting for an answer.

'No, but he's bleeding badly. He could bleed to death.'

'We've got to get him out of there . . . get him to hospital.'

'No. If you want him, you do what I say. I want a car, with a full tank of petrol. I want that WPC to come with me. If anyone follows or tries to stop me, I'll shoot her. I've nothing to lose. So help me God, I'll shoot her.'

'And if we do what you say?'

'When I'm sure I'm not being followed, I'll let her go. I won't hurt her.'

'Hold on,' said Frost.

'I'm not bloody holding on. The way he's losing blood, I'd say he's got minutes. It's pumping out.'

'Hold on,' cried Frost. 'I'm calling an ambulance.' He put his hand on the mouthpiece and yelled at Morgan. 'Get an ambulance, Skinner's bleeding to death.'

'What's going on?' demanded Mullett.

'He says Skinner is still alive, but bleeding badly. He wants a car and Kate Holby as a hostage before he'll let anyone in to Skinner. He says if we try to follow, he'll kill her.'

'Right,' said Mullett firmly, 'then that's what we do.'

'No,' said Frost. 'No bloody way. I'm not giving him a hostage.'

'I'm willing,' said Kate. 'I'll do it.'

'Forget it,' said Frost. 'No bloody way.'

The phone rang. 'I'm not sodding about waiting,' yelled Taylor. 'Two minutes. If I don't get the car and the woman in two minutes, I'll finish the bastard off with his own gun. I mean it.' His voice rose to a shrill shriek. 'I'll finish him off.'

'Send in the girl,' ordered Mullett.

'No,' Frost replied. 'I'm not risking her life.'

'I'm ordering you,' said Mullett.

'And you'll take full responsibility if she gets killed?'

Mullett's mouth opened and closed. Damn Frost to hell for putting him on the spot like this. He jabbed a finger at the inspector. 'On your head be it,' he snapped.

Back to the phone. 'Mr Taylor—'

'Where's the car?' yelled the man, before Frost could say any more.

'You're not getting a car, you're not getting a hostage,' said Frost. 'Chuck the guns out of the window, then come out with your hands up. It's all over, Mr Taylor.'

Taylor's voice was now hysterical. 'Your last chance, or I shoot him.'

'Come out with your hands up,' repeated Frost. 'It's all over.'

The crack of a single revolver shot shattered the air.

Shocked silence, broken by Mullett turning to Frost, his face black as thunder. 'You hated Skinner. You wanted him dead. You killed him.'

Frost said nothing. Yes, he hated Skinner, hated his guts. If the man was dead, then he was sorry – or was he? Had he secretly been hoping this would happen?

More cars roared up the lane. The Armed Response team had arrived.

Frost quickly filled them in and watched as they ran, half crouching, to the house. He tried to raise Taylor on the phone, hoping to distract his attention as the team burst their way in.

'Mr Taylor, talk to me. What have you done?'

The armed police were at the front door, examining it to see if it would open with a kick. Heads shook and they silently made their way round the back to the door Skinner had used.

'Mr Taylor . . .' Frost was silently pleading for the man to answer, terrified he might be waiting, gun in hand, at the top of the stairs, ready to shoot as the men burst in.

Silence. Creaking sounds. A door charged open. Silence again. Then someone picked up the phone. One of the Armed Response team.

'Inspector Frost, we need an ambulance.'

'On its way,' said Frost.

'And you'd better get up here now.'

Skinner was sprawled on the floor by the door of the upstairs room. His clothes were sodden with blood. Frost bent to touch his neck.

'He's dead,' said one of the flak-jacketed Armed Response team. 'The other one is still alive, but he won't be for long unless that bloody ambulance hurries up.'

As if on cue, they heard the approaching urgent wail of the ambulance siren.

Frost had to step carefully over Skinner's body to get inside the room. Two of the team were waiting. Taylor was slumped on the floor, his back leaning against the wall. Frost winced. Half his jaw had been blasted away and blood bubbled from his throat. The wall behind his head was splattered with flesh, bone fragments and blood. On the floor, where it had dropped from his hand, was the police-issue revolver he had taken from Skinner, its muzzle wet and sticky red.

'Must have tried to top himself,' said the sergeant. 'Stuck the gun under his chin and pulled the trigger. Must have had it at an angle.'

'Silly sod couldn't even do that right,' said Frost sadly.

The ambulance pulled up below.

'Up here, quick,' yelled Frost.

The paramedics carefully and gently lifted Taylor on to a stretcher and covered him with a blanket. They had managed to stem some of the bleeding from the shattered jaw. Taylor's face was chalk white and his rasping breath was making blood flow again.

'Will he live?' asked Frost.

The paramedic looked down at the shattered wreck of a face. 'If his luck's in, he won't,' he said.

Frost watched them ease the stretcher down the stairs, then pulled his mobile from his pocket and switched it on. Seven unanswered calls, all from Mullett. It rang again.

'What the devil's going on up there, Frost?'

barked Mullett. 'Ah – I see they're bringing Skinner down.'

'No,' said Frost. 'That's Taylor. Skinner is dead.'

Stunned silence as Mullett took this in. 'What?'

'He's dead,' repeated Frost. 'It's now a murder scene. We need SOCO, Forensic, a doctor and a pathologist.' Then he suddenly remembered. He took the phone from his mouth and called to the sergeant. 'The kid. Any sign of the kid?'

'Next room,' said the sergeant, pointing.

Frost dropped the mobile in his pocket and followed the man to the adjoining bedroom.

The boy was fast asleep and completely unharmed.

'He slept through it all,' said the sergeant. 'I wish I could sleep like that.'

Frost sighed with relief, then remembered the phone in his pocket. He fished it out.

'Frost . . .' Mullett was shouting. 'Answer me.'

'Frost.'

'I hold you solely responsible for DCI Skinner's death, Frost . . .'

'I knew I could rely on your support,' said Frost, switching off the phone. He looked down at Skinner's body, now draped with a sheet from the bed, a sheet that was becoming more and more bloodstained.

'I hated your bleeding guts,' he told the corpse. 'I didn't want you dead . . . but I can't say I'm sorry.'

19

Frost woke with a start, screwing his eyes against the glare. The sun was hammering at the bedroom window and the room was as bright as day. Hell, he'd overslept with a vengeance. He fumbled for the alarm clock. Ten twenty-seven. A vague feeling of unease told him that something was wrong. His brain was out of focus.

Then it hit him.

Last night! That bloody disaster. Skinner, slumped on the floor, blood everywhere. Mullett bleating away, shovelling all the blame on to him. '*You are solely responsible for his death, Frost. As sure as if you pulled the trigger, you killed him . . . You could have saved him, but you let him die . . .*'

He lay back and stared at the ceiling, his head throbbing. As he tried to piece everything together, a jumble of flashbacks elbowed their way through his brain.

The visit to the hospital. Seeing Taylor unconscious, all drips, wires, blood-soaked bandages and tubes that gurgled from his throat, while the faltering monitors were bleeping away.

'He'll live,' the weary junior doctor had told him. 'We might be able to repair most of the jaw, but he's shot away the best part of his tongue, so there's nothing we can do there.'

'When will he be fit for trial?' asked Frost.

The doctor shrugged. 'God knows – if ever . . .'

He organised a team of uniforms to keep vigil, although it was a waste of time as Taylor wasn't going anywhere. But the man was a murderer and someone was bound to scream if he was left unguarded, even if he only had half a face.

Then back to the station, where the phones didn't stop ringing . . . the press, TV channels wanting facts and quotes, other forces offering condolences. Then the disgruntled Investigating Officer from County arrived, short-tempered at being dragged out of bed and trying to drum up some sense of urgency in the already knackered Frost, who he eyed with displeasure after accepting Mullett's version of events without question.

'An officer's life needlessly lost. There will be a thorough investigation. I want a full written report of what happened, and I want it now.' And this at four o'clock in the morning.

He'd staggered back to his office, opened the window to tip out the contents of an overflowing ashtray on to the roof of Mullett's car, then started on the report. He'd barely put his name, rank and number when the phone rang yet again. 'Yes?' he snarled.

It was Beazley. At that hour of the night, flaming Beazley. 'I've just heard on the radio that you've caught the bastard. What about my money?'

'We've recovered a substantial amount,' yawned

Frost. 'Too many other things to do than bother to count it.'

'It had better be all there. When do I get it back?'

'When we've checked that it's your money.'

'Of course it's my money. That prat Taylor didn't have two ha'pennies to rub together. Whose bleeding money do you think it is?'

'If the banknotes' numbers tally with those issued by the building society, you stand a good chance of getting your money back. Until then you'll just have to wait.' He slammed the phone down. It rang back almost immediately. He ignored it and pulled open the desk drawer for his whisky. He swigged it down from the bottle. It didn't make him feel any better.

He managed to catch young PC Collier, who was on his way to keep a watchful eye on Taylor at the hospital in case the man gathered up all the drips and wires and made a dash for it.

Collier drove him home.

He was still dead tired, fed up and miserable. Why had he had that flaming whisky? And he felt battered and bruised. Whether or not it was his fault that Skinner had died, guilt was chewing away at him. He still felt that part of him had wanted the sod to die and that he deliberately hadn't let the WPC go in to take his place as hostage.

Sod it. He didn't want to go to the station and face everyone, but with Skinner dead and no one to take over his cases, he'd have to bloody well go in.

After a quick wash and a half-hearted shave, he headed out of the front door. But his car wasn't waiting for him in the street outside. Had some bastard nicked it? Then he remembered leaving it at the station when Collier drove him home.

He called a minicab.

'Denton police station,' he grunted.

'What have the bastards nicked you for then?' asked the chatty driver. 'Speeding? The bastards copped me the other night. Driving in a bus lane . . . ten minutes to midnight, no bleeding buses until the morning and they nicked me. Passenger was in a hurry, so I took a chance and they nicked me. Police cars do it all the bleeding time. One law for them bastards, another for us.'

'There's no justice,' muttered Frost.

'See one of the sods got shot last night,' continued the cabby. 'Hope it was the bastard who nicked me.'

'Shouldn't these back seats be fitted with safety belts?' asked Frost, fishing out his warrant card.

'Honey, I'm home,' he called to Bill Wells, carefully stepping over the heaps of flowers and wreaths that covered the lobby floor. 'Mullett's mum and dad getting married?'

Bill Wells grinned. 'Morning, Jack. Seen the paper? Headline news.'

He held out a copy of the *Denton Echo* – the headline read: POLICE HERO KILLED SAVING CHILD.

'Nothing about Skinner, then,' sniffed Frost,

pushing it away. He'd seen it all happen. He didn't want to read about it.

Wells looked at his scratch pad. 'Everyone wants you, Jack. Mullett wants to see you the minute you arrive, Sandy Lane wants you to phone him and that nice Mr Beazley has phoned about eight times.'

Frost held up a hand to cut him short. 'They can all wait. I'm going to get myself some breakfast.'

The phone rang. Wells answered it and held it out. 'It's for you, Jack. Meyers from the Crown Prosecution Service.'

Frost took the phone. 'Yes?'

'Graham Fielding was granted bail.'

Frost's jaw dropped. 'What! . . . A bleeding murderer? He raped and killed a girl.'

'A long time ago, Inspector, and the defence are querying the DNA evidence. He's married, with a business to run. The bench didn't think he posed a risk. There was no one from the police to oppose bail . . . I thought Detective Chief Inspector Skinner—'

'Skinner's dead,' said Frost flatly.

'Oh . . .' said Meyers, not really taking this in. 'Sorry to hear that – then you, as second in charge . . .'

'I've been up most of the night. I've only just come in.'

'Well, it might have made a difference, but no use crying over spilt milk. He had to surrender his passport, his father-in-law met the £10,000 bail demanded and he's now a free man. The trial has been set for next March.'

'Thanks very much,' snapped Frost, banging down the receiver. 'They've only let Fielding out on bleeding bail,' he told Wells.

Before Wells could answer, a voice roared down the corridor. 'Inspector Frost . . . my office, now!'

'Flaming hell,' muttered Frost. 'Mullett! I thought he couldn't come out in the sunlight.' He called back sweetly, 'Coming, Super,' then turned to Wells. 'Probably wants me to put a stake through Skinner's heart in case he comes back from the dead.'

Mullett was wearing his best uniform, a black tie and a black armband. If the press or television wanted to interview him, he was ready. He frowned as Frost shambled in and flicked a finger at a chair. 'The Chief Constable is very upset,' he snapped.

'Few of us are laughing,' said Frost, flopping into the chair. 'What did you want to see me about?'

'What happened at court today?'

'Fielding got bail.'

'I know he got bail, Frost. I want to know why. Why weren't you there to oppose it?'

'Me? It was Skinner's case.'

'You knew he was dead. Who else could go in his place apart from you?'

'Things were a bit bloody abnormal last night,' retorted Frost. 'We did have other things to worry about.'

Mullett fluttered a dismissive hand. 'Excuses, excuses, always excuses. The case files are on DCI Skinner's desk. I want you to take them over for the time being until we get a replacement. This, as I am sure you will appreciate, makes no difference to your joining Lexton division, although that will depend on the result of the inquiry into Skinner's death. I can't back you up there, as you know, so your future in the force is in doubt. And in that respect, County want a full report from you on what happened last night. Detailed, Frost – not a couple of lines of your usual scribble.'

'Right,' said Frost, rising from the chair. 'Was that all?'

Mullett patted some papers into a neat pile on his desk. 'There is one other thing . . . the funeral. There will be a police presence, of course. You – er – have got another suit? That one is hardly appropriate.'

'I'll rake out my old Teddy Boy suit,' said Frost. 'It should still fit.'

Frost mooched into Skinner's office and shivered. The room felt cold. Why did a dead person's office have a different feel to a living person's office? He crossed to the filing cabinet where Skinner kept his fiddled car expenses and gave the top drawer a tentative tug, but it was locked. None of the keys on his ring worked, neither did his nail file or an opened-out paper clip. Skinner had had an expensive new lock fitted. Shit!

He sank into Skinner's chair and tried the deep filing drawer. It slid open to reveal a couple of bottles of Johnny Walker. Serendipity! Well, Skinner wouldn't want them any more. He took them out and scurried back to his own office, hid them in his desk drawer, then returned to Skinner's room.

A small stack of case files awaited his attention. He pulled them towards him. The one on the top was for the Fielding rape and murder case, which Skinner had had ready for his court appearance. Frost opened it and idly flicked through the contents, pausing as he reached all the old papers from that distant Christmas when the girl's body was discovered in that frozen churchyard. He shivered again, the cold of the room transporting him back to that frosty Christmas morning with hard-packed snow scrunching underfoot. And it put him in mind of his return home and his young wife, in that red dress . . . He shook his head to shake away the memories.

He closed the file and pushed it to one side. Then he paused. Something inside his head was telling him that he had spotted something in the file, something significant. There was something he had skimmed over, which had subconsciously registered in his brain. So what the hell was it?

He opened up the file again. Among the top papers were the computer printouts of Fielding's petty criminal record – all minor traffic offences. Nothing there – or was there? Speeding . . .

dangerous driving . . . Manchester. *Manchester!* He stared, snatched up the file and scurried into the Incident Room, waving the folder at Collier and Morgan, who were seated by the computer.

'Come and have a look at this.'

They crowded round him as he opened up the file. 'This is the list of Fielding's past offences, right?'

'Pretty trivial stuff though, Guv,' said Morgan. 'Motoring offences.'

Frost jabbed a finger. 'This one. Dangerous driving, Manchester, 22 September.' He looked at them expectantly. They looked back, puzzled.

'Are we missing something?' asked Collier.

'The date,' said Frost. 'The bloody date!'

They still stared back blankly.

'September 22nd. The day that girl went missing. The girl whose body we found on the railway embankment. Fielding was in Manchester the day the girl went missing.'

'Coincidence?' suggested Morgan.

'I don't believe in flaming coincidences, especially when they don't suit me,' said Frost. 'The girl was abducted on the 22nd September and we reckon she was abducted by someone from Denton. We have someone on a rape and murder charge who comes from Denton.'

'Possible,' conceded Collier begrudgingly.

'Try not to be too bleeding enthusiastic,' said Frost. 'There's other motor offences in other towns. I want you to check back with the forces concerned and see if any girls went missing or if there were rapes or attempted rapes on the day of the offences.'

'Right,' nodded Collier, taking the file and picking up the phone.

Wells came in. 'Mullett wants you again, Jack.'

'What, again? He's man-mad,' said Frost.

The Superintendent was standing in Frost's office, the bottles of whisky from Skinner's filing cabinet on the desk before him. Mullett was glowering and pointing an accusing finger at them.

'When I went into DCI Skinner's office this morning there were two bottles of whisky in his drawer. When I checked just now, they had gone. I come into your office and there they are. This is outrageous, Frost. Stealing from the dead – absolutely outrageous.'

'I thoroughly agree with you, Super,' said Frost. 'Sneaking into someone's office and going down their private drawers. I expected better of you.'

'Me?' croaked Mullett, pointing a finger at himself in shocked outrage. '*Me?* You take whisky from a deceased colleague . . . a colleague in whose death you are deeply involved. This is despicable, Frost. It is nothing short of theft.'

Bloody right, thought Frost, his mind racing, trying to think of a way to get out of this one. Then he had an idea. He pulled open a desk drawer and took out the note Sandy Lane had sent with the whisky he had given him. 'If you had looked more carefully in DCI Skinner's drawer, Super, you would have found this note from Sandy Lane of the *Denton Echo.*' He handed Mullett the scribbled note, which read: '*You kept asking for whisky in return for inside information, so here it is.*'

'Skinner seems to have been taking bribes from the press. I'm sure even you wouldn't have wanted that to come out, Super.'

Mullett frowned at the 'even you'.

'In respect to the Detective Chief Inspector's memory,' said Frost, wiping away a non-existent tear, 'I thought it best to remove the evidence. I'm sorry you found out, Super, but the last thing I expected was that you would sneak into my office and rummage in my drawers, trying to prove I was a thief. I'm afraid I thought better of you.'

Mullett's mouth opened and closed like a gulping goldfish. 'My dear Frost . . . what can I say?'

'You've hurt my feelings, but your apology is enough,' said Frost. 'In your own way, you probably meant well.'

Mullett squeezed out a smile of gratitude. 'What do you intend doing with the whisky?'

'I shall take it to a charity shop,' said Frost, putting the bottles back in the drawer. 'I think Skinner would have wanted that.'

'Charity shop?' Mullett frowned. He didn't know charity shops took whisky, but being wrong-footed by the inspector had completely thrown him. He nodded. 'A good idea, Frost . . .

yes, an excellent idea.' He made a hurried exit.

Frost looked up hopefully as Collier came in. The PC shook his head. 'Nothing on record for any of those dates, Inspector.'

'Damn. I suppose it was too much to hope he would oblige us by getting tickets every time he did a bird in.' He drummed his fingers on his desk. 'It's him. He's our rapist and killer. I just know it. His DNA matches that old murder and rape case, he was in Manchester when the other girl went missing and turned up dead, and his car was picked up on CCTV when that girl was raped in the car park. It's just too much of a flaming coincidence.'

'His DNA didn't match the sperm sample from the girl in the car park,' reminded Collier.

'Don't put bloody difficulties in my path, son. The bastard did it.'

'But we've got no proof.'

'Proof? I don't need proof. I just know.' He leant back in his chair and sighed. 'OK, son. Thanks for trying.'

He opened up the next box file, which contained details of the Debbie Clark/Thomas Harris killings, as well as copies of the video tape, and the mobile phone. Skinner had dismissed Patsy Kelly and Bridget Malone as possible suspects. Skinner was probably right, but they were all that Frost had. And the mobile phone . . . was her mother wrong? Did Debbie leave it behind in her locker for Malone to steal? He held the phone aloft in its sealed plastic bag. 'If only you could speak, you sod.'

The last file was on the missing teenager Jan O'Brien. They'd searched everywhere they could and found sod all. They'd reported her as a missing person. Nothing. She could have run away from home as she had done so many times before, but she'd always come back before. She had no money and, like Debbie Clark, they had found her mobile phone. Skinner had scrawled 'Don't waste too much time on this one' across the main report sheet. Frost wasn't so sure. The woman who had phoned Sandy Lane about the video of Debbie Clark had mentioned a video of the other girl. Was she talking about Jan O'Brien? If so, were they still holding her, or was she dead? Shit! Bridget and the mobile were the only leads they had got. They were not going to get anywhere until they could clear up the mystery of the phone. If Mrs Clark was right and Debbie took it with her that night, then the only way Bridget could have got it was from the girl. If the mother was wrong, then Bridget could have pinched it from Debbie's locker. But back to Jan O'Brien. There was nothing they could do until they either heard from the girl or found the poor kid's body. He shuddered. They had enough young girls' dead bodies. He didn't want any more. What next? The flaming detailed report County wanted. Shit. He was in no mood for that.

Bill Wells poked his head round the door. He had an envelope in his hand. 'Like to contribute to Skinner's wreath, Jack?'

'No,' snapped Frost. 'I hated the bastard.'

Wells grinned. 'We all did, Jack, but we're still chipping in.'

'Because you haven't got the courage of your flaming convictions. Now pee off. I've got a detailed report to write for County about the shooting. How do you spell "Good riddance"? And I want to stress that Mullett, the senior officer, was there throughout – how do you spell "slimy bastard"?'

'Be careful how you write it, Jack,' warned Wells. 'They'll be looking for a scapegoat.'

'If I caused his death, I'd be proud to take the credit,' said Frost. 'The silly sod killed himself. Creeping into a house he'd never been in before, knowing that the bloke inside was round the bend and armed – he was a prat.'

'He didn't deserve to die in that way, Jack.'

'No – he deserved to be eaten to death by rats. This was too good for him.' He looked at the blank report sheet with distaste. 'Sod it. County will have to flaming well wait.' He tossed it into his in-tray and pulled the files towards him. 'As a reward for killing Skinner, Mullett is moving forward my transfer. The new Inspector – a friend of Skinner's, so he'll be a charmer – arrives at the end of next week.'

He drummed his fingers on the files. 'I want to get these outstanding cases cleared before I go, but there's little chance of that.' He tucked the files under his arm. 'I shall miss this bloody place.'

'We'll miss you, Jack,' said Wells.

'Bleeding car expenses,' snorted Frost. 'It

wasn't as if I needed the money. It was my way of jabbing two fingers up at the system. And now the bastards are jabbing two fingers up at me.'

'You got anything black for the funeral?' called Wells after him as he left the office.

'Yes – black fingernails and a black look for Hornrim Harry.'

Frost surveyed his team in the Incident Room. Most of them looked as tired as he felt. 'Right, let's stop sodding about. I'm definitely being booted out in a couple of weeks and I want to tie up at least one of our outstanding cases before that happy day.'

He passed his cigarettes around and perched himself on the corner of a desk. 'Debbie Clark and Thomas Harris. We've missed something. I don't know what it is, but we've bloody missed something. So let's go over it, step by step. If anyone has any bright ideas that I can pinch as my own, don't be coy – shout them out.' He flipped open the file. 'Right. Girl beaten, raped and strangled on video. Woman phones wanting us to tell the press about the video. The theory so far, a snuff movie. They haven't got an up-to-date photo of Debbie so they don't get any money unless we confirm it is her. The boy went with her, was caught and killed to keep his mouth shut. The girl took a bikini and we reckon was expecting a photo session – she always wanted to be a model. Whoever killed her must have known this. There's at least two people involved – a man and a woman. The girl calls out a name – Millie, Molly or something similar. The mother is positive the girl took her mobile with her. Bridget Malone reckons she pinched the mobile from the kid's locker the day after the girl disappeared – kids should lock their lockers, but too often they don't bother, so she just helped herself.'

'Guv—' Taffy Morgan was waving a hand.

Frost looked up wearily. 'You should have done one before you came in.'

'Not a wee, Guv. If you remember, I searched Debbie's locker the morning after she went missing.'

'And the phone wasn't there?'

'That's right, Guv . . . just an envelope with a fiver inside, for a school outing.'

Frost frowned. 'Hold on, Taff. A fiver? How come Bridget didn't pinch that? She took the mobile. She would have taken the readies too, surely.'

'That's the point I'm trying to make, Guv. Debbie's locker was locked. I had to get the key from the headmistress to open it.'

Frost leant back in amazement. 'Locked! You never mentioned this in your report.'

Morgan looked shamefaced. 'I didn't think it was important, Guv.'

'Every bleeding thing is important in a murder case, you prat. But locked? That tart Malone said she only went to the ones she could open and she wouldn't have bloody well locked it up again.'

'Exactly, Guv. What I'm saying is, if it was

locked and there was no phone when I unlocked it, then Bridget Malone never got the phone from there.'

'Then she's lying,' said Frost. 'The cow's lying. Bring her in.'

'This is harassment,' she screamed. 'Sheer harassment.'

'Shut up, Bridget,' sighed Frost. 'You're giving me a headache.' He slid Debbie's mobile in its polythene bag across the table. 'I want the truth about this phone.'

She glared at him. 'So I nicked a flaming phone. What am I going to get – life?'

'You don't know how right you are,' said Frost. 'Only the charge won't be nicking, it will be conspiracy to murder.'

'Murder? You must be hard up for suspects. I told you, I pinched it from her locker.'

'There was a fiver in an envelope. Why didn't you take that as well?'

'So I'm guilty of not taking a fiver now? This is all rubbish.'

'No. Your story is rubbish, Bridget. There is no way you could have got into her locker. Debbie's locker was locked. The only way you could have got hold of that phone was by taking it from Debbie the night she was murdered.'

'Then it must have been in someone else's locker. I don't bother with locked ones, and I certainly wouldn't have missed a fiver. Can I go now?' She stood up.

Frost flapped a hand. 'Sit down, Bridget.' He

squeezed his chin in thought. Somebody else's locker. Bloody hell. He should have thought of that. Bridget was a tea-leaf, but in no way a killer. He raised his head and looked thoughtfully at the woman. 'Prove your story to me, Bridget. Think hard. Which locker did you get the phone from?'

She shook her head. 'As sure as there's a God in heaven, I don't know. I just went round quickly in case anyone caught me. I tried locker doors. If they opened I saw what was worth pinching and I took it. It came from one of the lockers, that's all I can tell you.'

Frost nodded wearily in despair. 'All right, Bridget. I believe you. But if you can remember . . .'

She shrugged. 'If I remember, I'll tell you, but I don't think I will. There were lots of lockers and it was all done in a rush.'

'I'm clutching at flaming straws!' moaned Frost. 'Her and Kelly are not the type to do this sort of thing. I know that, so why did I suddenly decide they were guilty?' He rammed a cigarette in his mouth. 'Snuff movies. Bloody snuff movies, and the kick of seeing yourself doing these things to a kid.'

'It's lucky that bloke spotted the bodies,' said Morgan. 'They were so well concealed, they could have remained there like the other one.'

Frost stopped dead in his tracks, the match for his cigarette still in his hand. 'I'm a prat, Taffy, a flaming prat. That's what's been nagging away at me all the time and I've not been listening. Get your car. We're going round to where the bodies were.'

They were in the field with its burnt stubble where the corn had been harvested. Frost had made Morgan bump his car into the heart of the field. 'Stop here, Taff. This is about it.'

Morgan stopped the car and switched off the engine. 'Why here, Guv?'

'Because, my little Welsh wonder, this is where the tractor driver was when he spotted the bodies.' Taffy followed as Frost headed out into the field.

Frost pointed. 'They were behind that bush up there.' The blue marquee had been removed.

'I know, Guv,' said Morgan. 'I was here, remember?'

'Don't get sarky with me, you Welsh git. Debbie was wedged behind that bush, Taff. Now there's no way you could have seen her body from here.'

'The driver wasn't on the ground, Guv. He was higher up, in the cab of his tractor.'

'Right. Get on the roof of your car . . . come on.'

Morgan looked doubtful, then clambered on to the bonnet. His foot slipped and his shoes scraped across the paintwork. 'I've scratched the car, Guv,' he said plaintively.

'I thought you might,' said Frost. 'That's why I said we should come in your car.' He rubbed his thumb along the scratch mark. 'Nothing much to worry about – a complete respray ought to hide most of it. Now come on, hurry up.'

The DC heaved himself up on to the car roof, then stood gingerly, bracing himself against the wind. 'Even up here I can't see anything behind those bushes, Guv.'

Frost rubbed his hands with glee. 'We've got the sod, Taff, we've got him. He couldn't see Debbie's body, but he knew it was there, because he planted it there.'

'He could have stood up in his cab, Guv,' offered Morgan. 'He might have been able to see it then.'

'Why the bleeding hell should he stand up in his cab? He was cutting bleeding corn, not looking for bodies hidden behind a bush. Right, let's get back to Denton nick.'

'Thomas Henry Allen,' reported Collier, reading from the computer monitor. 'Couple of speeding offences, nothing else. We've got him down at an address in Bristol.'

'Bristol?' queried Frost.

'Yes, Inspector. He's living in temporary rented accommodation in Denton, which is why he never showed up before. He's working part-time for the farmer, who lets him live in a tied farm cottage.'

Frost nodded. 'Right. What else?'

'You're going to love this, Inspector. He used to work for that modelling agency.'

Frost punched the air in delight. 'We've got him. We've got the sod.'

'A possible suspect, but not enough evidence yet, Jack,' said Hanlon.

'Proof,' snorted Frost. 'All you bleeding well think of is proof. In—'

'In the good old days . . .' cued Hanlon with a grin.

'Exactly. We didn't need proof in the good old days. If we didn't have proof we faked it.' He leant back in his chair and stared at the ceiling. 'Right. I don't give a monkey's what it costs, I want 24/7 surveillance on the sod. There's a woman involved. They must meet up some time. And I want it doing properly. We mustn't let him know he's under suspicion, so leave your bloody helmets at home and let the only thing dangling be your dicks, not your handcuffs – don't have your police radio blazing away.' He nodded to Hanlon. 'Sort out a rota, Arthur.'

'Mullett will have to authorise it,' said Hanlon.

Frost snorted. 'Consider it authorised, Arthur. The four-eyed git is going to have to do what he's told this time.'

'You haven't got enough to go on,' protested Mullett. 'He might have stood up in the cab.'

'To scratch his arse? He was driving the flaming thing. It was moving. You don't stand up in a moving tractor on the off chance that you might see a body.'

'Couldn't it wait until Skinner's replacement arrives?' *Someone else to take responsibility for the outlay*, Mullett thought, *in case it blows up in our faces like so many of Frost's enterprises.*

'He's a temporary worker. He lives in Bristol. He could move back there any time now the harvesting is finished.'

Mullett sighed. 'All right, I agree, but on a strictly limited basis. Two days, no more.'

'Of course,' said Frost, making for the door. He had no intention of packing in the surveillance early.

He was back in his office, waiting for something to happen. A break of some kind . . . a break of any flaming kind. His phone rang. It was Harding from Forensic. 'That rape case, Inspector. We've got a DNA match on the sperm sample.'

'Please tell me it's Superintendent Mullett,' said Frost, reaching for a pen. The break he wanted at last.

'An eighteen-year-old boy. He was arrested nicking a battery-charger from Homebase. His DNA matches.'

'Let's have the details,' said Frost, his enthusiasm taking a nosedive. Somehow he didn't think an eighteen-year-old was the serial rapist they were after.

'Peter Frinton, 22 Victoria Terrace, Denton. He's currently out on police bail.'

'Thanks,' grunted Frost, hanging up. He stared at the name he had scribbled on one of Mullett's memos, then shook his head. It didn't ring a bell.

Peter Frinton, a sullen-looking, greasy-haired

youth, glowered at Frost, who was sitting opposite him in the Interview Room.

'Why have you dragged me in again? I've been bailed out. I told that other cop, I walked out of the store without thinking. I intended to pay, but forgot.'

'You forgot to bring any money with you, either,' Frost reminded him, flipping through the arrest report. 'You didn't have a brass farthing on you when you were arrested . . . and I see from your form sheet this isn't the first time.'

The youth glowered at Frost and said nothing.

'Actually, son,' continued Frost, 'this is about something a tad more serious than nicking a battery-charger. We're talking rape.'

Frinton leant back in his chair and stared at Frost, wide-eyed. 'Rape? I should be so lucky. You're bloody joking. Who am I supposed to have raped?'

'A fifteen-year-old girl – Sally Marsden.'

Frinton gave a derisive laugh. 'Sally Marsden? You don't have to rape Sally Marsden, you have to bloody well fight her off.'

Frost frowned. 'You know her?'

'Of course I know her . . . she's one of my girlfriends.'

'Where were you last Thursday night, around ten, eleven o'clock?'

'A Thursday? I would be indoors. I always stay indoors Thursdays.'

'Can anyone verify that?'

'Yes, flaming Sally Marsden – ask her. She was

with me. Came about seven, left at a quarter to ten.'

'She told us she was with her girlfriend.'

'She always pretends that's where she's going, and the girlfriend always backs her up if mumsy asks. Her mother thinks she's too young to go with boys . . . she'd go berserk if she found out her darling daughter hasn't been a virgin for at least a year.'

'She was with you that night – and you had sex?'

'That's right.'

'Unprotected sex?'

'She's on the pill.'

Frost chewed away at a hangnail. That bleeding girl. Steering them in the wrong bloody direction. He stood up. 'We're going to put you in a cell for a little while, son, and if your story checks out, you can go.'

He knew it was going to check out. The little butter-wouldn't-melt-in-her-mouth mummy's girl had lied her head off and steered them away from Fielding, because the DNA in the sperm sample didn't match his. 'The bleeding trail's gone cold now,' moaned Frost. 'If we could have caught him with his dick still steaming, we might have got something – more DNA perhaps from his clothes, but he's been on remand, mixing with all types of villains, his brief would tear our evidence to shreds.'

The girl was tearful. 'I'm sorry,' she kept saying. 'I'm so sorry.' She wiped her eyes and looked pleadingly at Frost. 'Please don't let me mum know. She'll murder me.'

'If it goes to court, of course she'll flaming well know,' said Frost. 'If I was you, I'd tell her.' He shook his head as Kate Holby took the girl back home.

He spotted Bill Wells in the far corner of the canteen and carried his tray over. 'Hope you're getting your five a day, Bill.'

Wells grinned. 'So Fielding could be back in the frame for the first car-park rape?'

'Yes. DNA evidence no longer clears him. He was in the vicinity. He had the opportunity, but that's all we've got on him.' He bit into a Jaffa Cake. 'But it's him, Bill. He's the bloody rapist and I know it, I just know it. And I'm bloody sure he topped the girl from Manchester too.'

'We ought to get him for the old crime, Jack,' said Wells. 'But there's no way the court would convict him when the only evidence we've got is that he was in Manchester when that girl went missing and his car was seen near where Sally Marsden was raped. The fact that she lied won't help us. You're going to need a hell of a lot more than that.'

'The bastard's out on bail,' said Frost. 'I want 24/7 surveillance.'

'Flipping heck, Jack. Mullett will never agree to that – you're already watching the tractor driver.'

'Right, then I won't ask Mullett. I'll do it on

my own authority ... By the time the overtime returns come in I'll be in Lexton anyway and he won't be able to touch me.'

'But Jack ...'

'Just do it, Bill. Just flaming well do it.'

20

The estate agent, his pen hovering over his clipboard, sucked air through his teeth and shook his head despairingly. 'It's rather cramped, Mr Frost, and it badly needs a woman's touch.'

'So does my dick,' said Frost, 'but it doesn't get one very often.' He wished the supercilious sod would hurry up. He was itching to get back to the station. Surely someone would have spotted Allen or his car by now.

The estate agent squeezed a sour smile. 'I suppose we could say it would suit a DIY enthusiast. There's rather a lot that wants doing to it.'

'Say what you flaming well like,' said Frost. 'Just sell it.' He looked around, seeing the house for the first time through a prospective buyer's eyes. Yes, it did veer on the tatty side. He had let it get run down. Memory clicked back to that day, so many years ago, when his young wife first saw the house. She had fallen in love with it the minute they stepped inside. She didn't think it was cramped. 'Just right for the two of us,' she had said, and they had raced back to the estate agent with the deposit in case some other well-heeled buyer got there first. They'd had some bloody happy times here. And then it had all gone wrong . . . He shook the thoughts from his head. No point getting maudlin and sentimental. Thanks to Skinner and Mullett, he had to sell the flaming place. 'So how much?'

The man consulted his clipboard and again shook his head. 'If it was in better condition . . .' He spread his hands and shrugged. 'But there, it isn't. We can only go on what we have got.' He tapped his teeth with his pen and did a few mental calculations. 'I suggest we offer it at eighty-nine thousand but be prepared to come down to eighty-five, or thereabouts. As I said, if it was in better condition . . .'

'And if it was flaming Buckingham Palace, but it isn't,' snapped Frost. Eighty-five thousand would just about buy a one-bedroom flat in a not-too-salubrious part of Lexton. But he had no flaming choice. 'All right. Put it on the market at that.'

'I see,' said Mullett. 'Yes, I see. Thank you for telling me.' He put the phone down. 'That was my contact in County,' he told Frost. 'A bit of good news for us. They've just had the post-mortem results on DCI Skinner. It seems he died instantly from the gunshot wound.'

'So he was already dead when Taylor was asking for a hostage?' said Frost.

'Er – yes, it would appear so,' conceded Mullett begrudgingly.

'Which means that if I had sent in Kate Holby as you wanted, we'd have risked her life and got sod all in return?'

'Ah – yes,' mumbled Mullett, wishing Frost wouldn't keep rubbing his nose in it. 'But we weren't to know that at the time, of course. With hindsight—'

'You don't get the benefit of hindsight in this job,' snapped Frost. 'You have to use your common sense.'

'Yes, quite,' nodded Mullett. 'My thoughts exactly.' He quickly changed the subject. 'Any news on the tractor driver?'

'Nothing yet. So if that's all . . .' Frost was out of his chair and away before Mullett could reply. Back in his office, he snatched up the phone.

'No, Inspector,' said Lambert patiently. 'Still no news. When there is, I promise you'll be the first to know.'

'Flaming heck, Jack. Are you still here?'

Sergeant Wells's voice woke him with a start. He blinked and scrubbed his face. He'd fallen asleep at his desk. 'Damn. I must have dropped off.' He yawned and stretched. 'What time is it?'

'Half past one in the morning.'

'Has Allen been sighted yet?'

'We'd have told you if he had. Look, Jack, go home and get some proper kip. If he's spotted we can phone you.'

Frost yawned again and shook his head. He didn't feel tired any more and he certainly didn't feel like going back to that empty house. 'Do you know how much that smarmy estate agent reckons my house is worth? Eighty-five flaming K. He says it's a tip.'

'Estate agents always over-price houses they want to sell,' grinned Wells.

'What sort of a place am I going to get in Lexton for that sort of money?'

'An even shittier tip than yours, Jack,' said Wells, ducking as the inspector hurled a file at him.

Frost reached for his cigarettes and rammed one in his mouth. A tip. It hadn't been a tip when he was first married. His wife had kept it beautifully. He dribbled smoke through his nose. Why was he constantly harping back to those days? It must be that ancient Christmas Day murder and the girl Fielding killed. 'I'll hang on here for a while. Any chance of some tea?'

'We're not a flaming all-night café, Jack.'

'And I wouldn't say no to some toast.'

'Bloody hell. What about a four-course dinner? You'd better leave a big tip.'

'Leave my big tip out of this,' said Frost.

He wandered into the Incident Room, where DS Hanlon and Taffy Morgan were on standby. His mobile rang.

'Inspector. PC Williams – Traffic. I'm by the Dedham roundabout on the Denton Road. That car you asked us to look out for – it's just gone past.'

'You mean Allen's car?'

'Yes. It drove past here about two minutes ago.'

'Didn't you go after him?'

'Inspector, I'm at the scene of a traffic accident . . . a car and a motorbike. Two teenagers killed and the car driver badly injured. I've got enough on my flaming plate.'

'Sorry, sorry. Which direction was he heading?'

'Away from Denton – going north. Man driving. Woman next to him.'

'A woman?' Frost was now excited. 'Did you get a good look at her?'

'Yes. They had to slow down. It's single-lane traffic here at the moment.'

'What did she look like?'

'Dark hair, buck teeth – in her forties, I'd say.'

Frost was squeezing the phone so hard his hand hurt.

'Bloody hell,' he said. 'Bloody, bloody, hell! Thanks, Williams. I owe you one.' He hung up, then looked round the room, rubbing his hands together with glee. 'You,' he announced, 'are looking at the biggest prat in Denton.'

They stared open-mouthed at him.

'Well look bleeding surprised. Don't look as if you knew that all the time.'

They grinned.

'Why are you a prat, Guv?' Morgan asked.

'Millie . . . Molly . . . Maisie . . . Misty . . . It was none of those bleeding names. That wasn't what the poor kid was saying. And it was under my flaming nose all the bleeding time and I never flaming twigged. The bitch who was videoing her was her form teacher, that toothy cow Janet Leigh. Miss Leigh. Miss bleeding Leigh!'

Hanlon's eyes widened. 'Miss Leigh? Debbie was saying Miss Leigh?'

Frost nodded. 'Someone the poor kid trusted . . . her form teacher – Miss bleeding Leigh. When Bridget went on her nicking spree, she went down the staff lockers as well and I bloody missed it. That's where she found the phone – in Janet Leigh's locker.'

DS Hanlon stood up. 'Shall I run her through the computer, see if she's got form?'

Frost shook his head. 'She won't have form. Everyone dealing with kids has to be thoroughly vetted. If she had form she'd never be allowed to teach.' He clicked his fingers. 'The fingerprints on the wrapping paper that came with the video tape. I bet a pound to a pinch of poo they are hers.' He drummed his fingers on the desk. 'Taffy – get on to Control. I want a message putting out. Allen's car has been spotted on the Denton Road. I want all patrols to be on the look-out. If they see the car, they should stop it and arrest the occupants on suspicion of murder.' He turned to PC Collier. 'Get the Electoral Roll up on the computer. I want that tart's address.' He beckoned DS Hanlon over. 'Arthur. Bit late for a social call, but we're going to do her place over. She could have Jan O'Brien locked away there.'

'We'll need a search warrant,' said Hanlon.

Frost looked at the sergeant sternly and waggled a finger. 'Wash your mouth out with soap, Arthur. I don't want to hear that sort of filthy talk from you again.'

* * *

Morgan and Collier were sent to cover the back way while Frost, DC Hanlon at his side, hammered the door knocker. The sound echoed inside the house. Frost frowned. 'I don't think there's anyone in, Arthur.' He knocked again.

Frost bent and examined the lock. 'Do you know, Arthur, I think this is the sort of lock you can open with a credit card.'

Hanlon looked alarmed. 'Now watch it, Jack. You've already pushed your luck with the Kelly house.'

Frost found his wallet and extracted his Mastercard. 'I've got my Crime Prevention Officer's hat on. I just want to check to see if I can open it with a credit card, then I'll advise the good lady bitch to get a more secure lock.' He slid the card in the side of the door and wiggled it. 'Come on, you stubborn bastard,' he hissed. A satisfying click. 'There. What did I say? If I was up to no good, I could walk straight into this place and search it from top to bloody bottom.' He pushed the front door. It creaked open. 'Look at this. An open invitation for no-good coppers to exceed their authority.'

Hanlon, looking very worried now, stepped back. 'Shut it, Jack, for Pete's sake.'

Frost ignored him. He pushed the door open wider and called, 'Anyone at home?'

Dead silence.

'Noise from upstairs,' hissed Frost. 'Must be a burglar. We'd better check, Arthur.' He dragged

Hanlon inside and shut the front door behind them.

'I don't like this, Jack,' moaned Hanlon.

'If we get caught, I'll take all the flak,' said Frost. 'I'm a better liar than you. But we won't get caught.' He tugged his mobile from his mac pocket. 'Taffy, we're in the house. Get round the front, keep out of sight and warn me if they come back.' He turned to Hanlon. 'You search downstairs, Arthur. I'll do the upstairs. Don't switch on lights, use your torch. Let's see if we can find that kid.'

They searched. No trace. Frost peeped out of the back window. 'There's a shed in the garden, Arthur. See if she's in there.'

Frost was beginning to feel despondent. He had been banking on finding Jan O'Brien in Janet Leigh's house. Hanlon came back, shaking his head.

'She's not there, Jack. There's no sign she's ever been here. Let's get the hell out of here.'

'Don't let's waste a flaming golden opportunity, Arthur. Do a more thorough search. See if we can find the video camera and the tapes or anything to tie her to the murders.'

They went round each room methodically, looking everywhere where tapes could be hidden. There was a sideboard in the dining room which looked promising.

'Quick, Arthur. You look in the cupboards, I'll go through the drawers.' They found nothing.

The pantry. Nothing.

The airing cupboard. Nothing.

The bath was free-standing without panels, so no hiding place there.

Frost flashed his torch to the landing ceiling. No trapdoor to a loft.

'The bedroom, Arthur. Our last hope – don't trip over the po.'

Frost went through the dressing-table drawers while Hanlon poked about in the wardrobe.

Nothing.

'Shit!' cursed Frost.

He nearly missed the A4 manila envelope in the drawer of the bedside cabinet. He wasn't interested in it – he was looking for videotapes – but something made him look inside.

He whistled softly.

'Bloody hell, Arthur. We've got them.'

It wasn't the tape. It was two colour photographs of Debbie Clark, bound, gagged and naked.

He pushed the photos back in their envelope and sighed with relief. 'We've got the bastards, Arthur.'

'But without a search warrant, Jack.'

Frost carefully put the envelope back in the drawer where he'd found it. 'Then we'll get one. Morgan can stay outside and arrest them if they come back. We're going back to the nick to make out a search warrant, then I'm dragging old Miller out of her pit and getting her to sign it.'

They were halfway back to the station when a wailing siren made them pull over to one side to allow a fire engine to go roaring past.

'Off to get some chips,' grunted Frost, but then he saw a red glow cutting through the night sky way over to the north of Denton. He nudged Hanlon and pointed. 'Look over there, Arthur – a fire, and a bloody big one.'

His radio crackled. 'Control to Inspector Frost.'

He clicked on the mike. 'Frost.'

'999 call, Inspector. House fire.'

'We can see it from here. Where is it?'

'Dunn Street, Inspector. Number 23.'

Frost frowned, and then he jerked back in his seat. 'Twenty-three Dunn Street. Kelly's house!'

'Yes, Inspector. The fire brigade have recovered two bodies. They suspect arson.'

'We're on our way,' said Frost, screeching the car into a U-turn.

There were fire engines and police cars with flashing blue lights, which gave a macabre tinge to the cluster of dressing-gowned figures woken by the noise who had come out to gawp. Most of the lights in the street were on and a uniformed officer was trying to keep the onlookers back.

A traffic policeman flagged Frost's car down. 'Sorry, sir, you can't—' he began, before recognising the inspector and waving him through to park behind an ambulance, its rear doors wide open.

The chief fire officer spotted Frost and hurried over. 'Definitely arson, Inspector. Petrol doused everywhere.' He looked across to his men. One team was rolling up their hoses, the other was spraying water as small pockets of flame re-ignited. 'We've got the fire under control, but there's not much left of the house.'

'You found bodies?' Frost asked.

The fireman nodded. 'A man and a woman . . . burnt to buggery. The ambulance crew are taking them to the morgue now.'

Two ambulance men were humping a body bag on to a stretcher. 'Hold it a minute,' called Frost, hurrying over. They put down the stretcher and waited.

Frost knelt and unzipped the black body bag, turning his head at the smell of burnt flesh that seeped out. The face was twisted, distorted, blackened, the hair burnt off, but there was no doubt about the identification. It was Bridget Malone. He pulled the zip down further. The body was clad in the charred remains of a dress. Frost stared down, shook his head, then straightened up. 'Let's have a look at the other one.'

One side of Patsy Kelly's face had missed the flames, but the other was burnt away, showing blackened jaw and cheekbone. He was dressed in a charred jacket and trousers. 'Has a police surgeon seen the bodies?'

'Yes, Inspector,' said the ambulance man. 'He didn't stop long. Said to tell you that they're dead and could have been burnt in the fire and if you wanted to know more . . .'

'. . . ask that bastard Drysdale,' said Frost, finishing the sentence for him.

'You're a mind-reader, Inspector,' grinned the ambulance man. Frost stepped back and told them to carry on, then returned to the chief fire officer.

'What time did the fire start?'

'About an hour ago. We got a phone call from a neighbour about fifteen minutes later. It was well alight by the time we arrived and we were here within minutes.'

Frost checked his watch. 'So it would have started around two o'clock. They're fully dressed – bloody late to be fully dressed and not in bed. And if they were fully dressed, how come they didn't raise the alarm themselves and get out of the place?' A slamming of doors made him turn his head to watch the ambulance back out and drive off to Denton General.

His mobile chirped. Taffy Morgan.

'Allen and the woman have just returned, Inspector. We've arrested them, like you said. They're yelling blue murder. They want to pick up some things from the house.'

'Don't let them in the house,' warned Frost. 'Cuff them, bung them in your car and wait for me. Don't take them to the station yet.'

They were halfway there when Morgan phoned again. 'The woman's demanding to use the bathroom in the house, Inspector. Says she's busting for a pee.'

'She can pee all over your car seat if she likes,' replied Frost, 'but don't let her into the house.' He knew what she was after. The cow wanted to destroy those photos and flush them down the loo. *Well, hard luck, darling, it's not going to happen.*

* * *

'What is this all about, Inspector?' asked Allen. 'I bring my ladyfriend back to her house and that Welshman arrests us and handcuffs us and tries to make out we killed those kids.'

'And I really must go to the toilet, Inspector,' said Janet Leigh. 'It is urgent and this is intolerable.'

Frost gave a deceptively sweet smile. 'We're going to nip you down to the station in a minute, love, where you can pee to your heart's content. In the meantime we'll be getting search warrants for both your houses, and if we don't find photographs and videos tying you both to the murder of Debbie Clark, I'll apologise before you've had a chance to pull the chain.' He stopped abruptly and sniffed, then pressed his nose to Allen's jacket. 'Fee, fi, fo, flaming fum!' He beckoned Hanlon over. 'Take a sniff at the gent's jacket, Arthur, and see if you can smell what I can smell.'

Hanlon took a tentative sniff. He frowned. 'Petrol?'

Frost turned back to Allen. 'We've just come from a house fire with two dead bodies. The place stunk of petrol.'

Allen gave a scoffing laugh. 'You're surely not suggesting we had anything to do with it?'

'Then tell me why your clothes reek of petrol.'

'I filled the car up when we were out. I spilt some on my coat.'

'I knew there must be a reasonable explanation,' beamed Frost. 'Show me the petrol receipt, so I can apologise for my evil thoughts.'

'I don't keep receipts. I threw it away.'

'Ah well, it will be on your credit-card statement.'

'I paid cash.'

'Never mind. All of these garages have got CCTV cameras in case punters drive off without paying, or buy petrol to burn houses down. What was the name of the garage?'

'I forget.'

'Don't worry about it, son,' said Frost. 'We've got teams of cops who can go round every petrol station and check through their CCTV footage, and as soon as they find one of you dousing your coat in petrol, I'll be grovelling my apologies.' He snapped his fingers. 'I almost forgot.' He called to Morgan, 'Take the gentleman's car keys and have a look in the boot. Don't touch anything, just tell me what's in there.'

Allen and Janet Leigh stared at each other grimly, but said nothing. Morgan unlocked the boot. 'Two empty petrol cans, Guv, and they stink of petrol.'

'Petrol cans usually do,' said Frost, beaming at the pair. 'You're making it too easy for us. Lock up the boot, Taff, and get Forensic to examine the car in situ and see if they can tie it in with the fire at Kelly's place.' He turned back to Allen. 'Where's the girl?'

'What girl?'

'You know bloody well what girl. Jan O'Brien.'

'I don't know what you're talking about,' said Allen.

Frost turned to the woman. 'Please, Miss

Leigh,' he said. 'You're already in this up to your neck. Where is Jan O'Brien?'

'I'm sorry, Inspector. Like my friend, I don't know what you're talking about.'

Frost wound his scarf round his neck and opened the car door. 'To save us smashing your front doors in when we get the search warrants, you might like to give us your keys.' He held out his hand.

They gave him their keys.

Frost breezed into the lobby at four a.m., no longer tired. Morgan followed him in, clutching the envelope containing the photos Frost had found in Janet Leigh's house, together with a polythene sack containing clothing for forensic examination.

'We've got the bastards,' Frost told Bill Wells. 'Photos and a camcorder from the tart's house, and Bristol police have found more photos and tapes at Allen's pad. There's still no clue as to where they've hidden the girl, but I'll beat it out of them.'

From the cells at the end of the corridor a drunk was roaring a filthy song. Wells frowned. 'Listen to the ignorant bastard. He doesn't even know the right words.' He yelled down the corridor, 'If you don't shut that bleeding row, I'll pee over your breakfast.'

The singing stopped immediately.

'Appeal to their better natures,' nodded Frost. 'It always works. Let's have Allen in the Interview Room.'

* * *

Frost watched his cigarette smoke wriggle its way to the ceiling, past the red lights which indicated that the cassette recorder and the video camera were functioning. He felt good. He had enough evidence, without any admission of guilt, to send Allen and Leigh down for life. He tapped one of the camcorder cassettes. 'We found these video tapes hidden under a pile of clothing in the wardrobe in your girlfriend's bedroom. We played them through. They show a naked Debbie Clark being raped and strangled.'

Allen wouldn't look at them. He spoke to the floor. 'No idea how they got there.'

Frost took the camcorder from the box. 'Is this your camcorder?'

Allen gave it a brief glance, shrugged, then resumed his study of the Interview Room floor.

'Just in case you need a memory jog,' said Frost, 'we've checked out the warranty and it's in your name.'

'Yes,' muttered Allen, 'it's my camcorder.'

'There's a slight fault on one of the runners – it scratches the tape . . . did you know?'

'No.'

'There's scratches on those tapes, which our Forensic boys say proves they were taken with that camcorder.'

'No comment,' muttered Allen.

Frost sighed. 'Not the old "no comment" lark? I find that dead boring, even though it always convinces the jury of a person's guilt. When me and my mates are in the station late at night and can't decide who to beat up, we always pick the "no comment" ones.' He pushed the camcorder to one side. 'Right. We've got you nailed for that, let's turn to the other girl.'

'What other girl?' Allen asked.

'It's late and I'm tired,' said Frost. 'Don't sod me about. You know bloody well what other girl. Jan O'Brien.'

Allen's eyes widened and he gave a scoffing laugh. 'You must be hard up for suspects – I know nothing about any other girl.' His brow creased in thought, then his expression changed. 'Look . . .' He paused. 'Turn off the tapes.'

'No flaming fear,' said Frost.

'I've got something to say off the record that will be of interest to you. You'll get the conviction you want for Jan O'Brien, even though I'm not involved.'

Frost signalled to Morgan. 'Turn them off.'

Morgan pressed the Stop button and the little red recording light blinked and went out.

'And the video,' said Allen.

Morgan switched that off.

'This had better be good,' said Frost.

Allen leant back in his chair. 'Right, as you're going to find out, I'm on those tapes without the mask, so it's sodded up my chance of claiming I know nothing about it. What do you reckon I'll get?'

'Well, it won't be community service or a flaming fine,' said Frost. 'Life, without a doubt.'

'And Janet?'

'That bitch,' snorted Frost, 'was worse than

you. Debbie trusted her. Life as well, probably in solitary confinement otherwise the other inmates would tear her to pieces.'

Allen shuddered. 'I want to do a deal.'

'We don't do deals,' said Frost, 'and in your case we don't flaming have to. We've enough on the pair of you to get convictions, even from a jury of do-gooders.'

'Listen to what I'm offering first. I'll put my hand up to the two kids. That will avoid a long-drawn-out trial with people screaming abuse at us. I'll give you the name of the bloke who was going to distribute the tapes to his customers. I'll even put my hand up to Jan O'Brien, although I know nothing about her.'

'What do you mean, you know nothing about her? When Janet Leigh phoned the *Denton Echo*—'

'Never mind what she said. It wasn't true. Bridget Malone was blackmailing us. She threatened to tell the police where she found the kid's phone if we didn't come up with ten thousand quid. Neither of us had that sort of money. The bloke who was going to buy the tape wanted solid proof it was Debbie Clark before parting with the cash. We wanted the fuzz to admit it was Debbie, but you wouldn't, so we tried pretending we had Jan O'Brien as well, but that didn't work either.'

'Which is why you killed Bridget and Kelly?'

'Yes.'

'Flaming heck,' snorted Frost. 'Pierrepoint would turn in his grave if he knew what we were giving life sentences out for. Then what about Emily Roberts – the body we found on the railway embankment? You'll be telling me you didn't kill her either?' This was a long shot. Frost's money was still on Graham Fielding.

Allen shook his head. 'Nothing to do with us, but I'll put my hand up for her as well if you go easy on Janet. Get her on a lesser charge – posting the tape, making the phone calls. Don't involve her with the killing.'

'Very bleeding chivalrous,' said Frost. 'That kid pleaded – *Please, Miss Leigh* – and she just carried on filming as you choked the life out of the poor child. She's going down with you, buster.'

Wells slammed the cell door shut on Allen and chalked up the time on the board by the door. 'Well, Jack?'

'He and the tart are denying it on record and admitting it off record, but the evidence is watertight. They'll go down. But they both claim they know nothing about Jan O'Brien.'

'What about the other girl – the body on the embankment?'

Frost shook his head. 'They both deny having anything to do with her and I believe them. Fielding killed that girl, I just know it.'

'The old feeling in your urine, Jack?' grinned Wells.

'It's never let me down yet,' replied Frost, '– except sometimes.'

'Lots of flaming times,' said Wells.

Frost waved this to one side and told Wells about the off-the-record conversation. 'He admitted killing the kids and he'd have put his hand up for Emily Roberts if he'd killed her as well. He had nothing to lose.' He yawned. After the high of the arrests, he now felt drained. He had pinned everything on Allen and Leigh having abducted Jan O'Brien, but now he would have to start from scratch.

His phone rang. He signalled to Wells to answer it. He was too tired.

'It's Mullett for you,' said Wells, handing the phone over.

'Mullett?' gasped Frost, shooting a glance at the wall clock. 'Four o'clock in the bleeding morning. What woke him up?' He took the phone.

'I've had the *Denton Echo* on the phone. Have you made an arrest in the Debbie Clark case?'

'Yes, Super,' said Frost. 'I've just come from questioning them. I'm charging them for the two murders and taking them to court tomorrow.'

'What sort of case have you got?'

'Watertight, Super. Fingerprints, DNA, photographs, videos, the lot.'

'Good. What about their statements?'

' "No comment" to the lot, but the forensics are more than strong enough.'

'Excellent. Leave all the details on my desk. I'm calling a press conference tomorrow. We might as well trumpet our success. Oh – no need for you to attend, Frost. You've had a busy night.'

'You're too kind, Super,' said Frost with all the insincerity he could muster.

'And – er – this was DCI Skinner's case, wasn't it?'

'It was,' agreed Frost.

'He had obviously done most of the hard work. It would be a tribute to his memory, don't you think, if we attributed the successful outcome to him?'

'Yes, he did do all the hard work,' agreed Frost. 'He actually handed me the file and told me to get on with it, but if you want him to have the credit . . .'

'Excellent. I understand there's still the other girl's death and that missing teenager outstanding?'

'Yes. We're nowhere with them yet.'

'Well, your successor will probably spot something you've missed.'

'Not without the benefit of Skinner's unselfish help,' grunted Frost, banging the phone down.

'The *Denton Echo* woke him up,' he told Bill Wells. 'How the hell did they know we'd made the arrests?'

'They listen in on police radio frequencies, Jack, you know that.'

Frost nodded. 'Anyway, the case has been posthumously solved by DCI Skinner and Hornrim Harry is holding a press conference tomorrow to which Cinderella is not invited.'

'My heart bleeds for you, Jack,' sniffed Wells, looking up as PC Collier came in.

'The woman wants to see you right away,

Inspector. She wants to make another statement.'

'Another statement? She said sod all in her first one,' said Frost, heaving himself out of his chair. 'Ah, well, let's see what Fanny wants. It's not as if I wanted to go to bed early.'

WPC Kate Holby brought Janet Leigh into the Interview Room. Frost stubbed out his cigarette and pointed to the chair. 'Take a seat. I understand you want to make a statement?'

She nodded and dabbed a handkerchief at dry eyes. 'I'm going to tell you everything. He made me do it. I didn't want to. He forced me. I was terrified of him. He made me watch. I had nothing to do with it.'

Frost nodded for Kate to start the cassette recorder. 'Right. Tell us about how you are the innocent victim. Make my heart bleed for you.'

As Kate Holby led Janet Leigh back to her cell, Wells came into the Interview Room and sat in her vacated chair. Frost rolled a cigarette across the table for him.

'Well?' the sergeant asked.

'She's coughed the lot,' said Frost. 'She had nothing at all to do with it. It was all him. She took no part in the killings, she was just an innocent bystander. He dragged her along for the ride and he's a lousy bastard making her watch the disgusting things he did to poor Debbie Clark. Allen was prepared to take all the rap as long as she was left out of it, and the lousy cow can't wait to drop him in it.'

'Do you believe her?' asked Wells.

Frost shook his head. 'Do me a favour. She enjoyed it. She bloody well loved every minute of it. I wouldn't be surprised if she took the lead in all this. It was she who told Debbie her friend was a photographer and might be able to get her a modelling contract . . .'

'I suppose there's always a chance, if Allen still wants to take all the blame, she'll get away with it.'

Again Frost shook his head. 'I'll make certain the jury see the tape with Debbie pleading for Miss Leigh to make Allen stop it, while the cow just pointed the video camera. They'll find her as guilty as hell.' He yawned. 'I'm too shagged out to drive home. Have you got an empty cell I can kip in? Preferably one not stinking of stale pee?'

21

It seemed as if he had just shut his eyes when some silly sod was calling his name.

'Jack. Wake up!'

He opened his eyes and blinked at the light. Bill Wells was bending over him, shaking him.

He yawned and checked his wristwatch, stared at it in disbelief and checked again. 'Five to six? Flaming heck, Bill, I've only been asleep five minutes. What do you want?'

Wells waved a mobile phone. 'Taffy Morgan's on the blower, Jack.'

'Then tell the Welsh prat to phone at a more convenient time – and switch off that bleeding light.' He turned over, but Wells shook him again.

'Taffy's doing the surveillance at Fielding's house, Jack. Fielding's on the move.'

Frost sat up. 'At five to six in the morning? He's doing a bunk. The sod's doing a bunk.' He snatched the phone from the sergeant. 'What's happening, Taff?'

'It's Fielding, Guv. He's just left in his white van. I'm on his tail.'

'Don't lose him, for Pete's sake.'

'You can rely on me, Guv.'

'I can rely on you to sod things up. Don't let him see you.'

'Don't worry, I'm well behind him.'

'Where are you?'

'I'm on Felwick Road. He's heading north out of Denton. Shit! . . .'

'What the hell is it?' yelled Frost.

'He's spotted me, Guv. He looked back. He recognised me.'

'You prat. I told you not to get too close.'

'Bloody hell, Guv, he's roaring off like the clappers.'

'Then get after him like the clappers, you silly sod. Put the bleeding phone down. Drive with both hands.'

For a while Frost listened to the drone of engine noises down the mobile, then there was a scrabbling noise as Morgan picked up the phone again. 'I've lost him, Guv.'

'What do you mean, you've bloody lost him? You were supposed to be on his tail.'

'Not my fault, Guv. He swerved ahead in front of two articulated lorries and jumped the lights at the crossroads. I didn't see which way he turned. I must have gone the wrong way.'

'You prat,' said Frost. 'If he's trying to get away the bastard's got something to hide. Where the hell are you now?'

'Three miles west of the Denton bypass.'

Frost slammed the phone down and dashed into his office to study the wall map, closely followed by Sergeant Wells. He banged his palm on the bypass area and yelled to Wells, 'Bill, I want every car, motorbike bobby, even foot patrols, to stop what they're doing and get there to look for the sod. Now . . . do it bloody now!'

'County won't let you have the helicopter, Jack, not without Superintendent Mullett's authority.'

'Mullett's not bloody here . . . I could phone them in my Mullett voice.'

'You bloody dare, Jack!' gasped Wells.

'All right, forget it. By the time they get the damn thing off the ground he'll be miles away anyway.'

He snatched up the phone on the first ring. 'Yes?'

'Jordan here, Inspector. I'm after him. He's on the Lexton Road, heading north. He's going to crash that bloody van the speed he's going.'

Frost spun in his chair and again checked the wall map.

'I'll try and set up a roadblock.'

He dialled Lambert in Control, jabbing the wall map and giving instructions.

'I hope all this is worthwhile, Jack. Every available bit of manpower is out there – we're even ignoring 999 calls. Suppose we can only nick him for speeding?'

'If that's all there is, I'll frame the bastard,' said Frost.

Five minutes later, an excited Jordan called

again. 'We've got him, Inspector. He nearly smashed through the roadblock, but braked just in time.'

'Drag him out of the van, cuff him and charge him with anything you like. We're on our way.'

As he snatched his scarf off the hook, WPC Holby came in with a mug of tea.

'Dump it, love,' said Frost, grabbing her by the arm. 'You're coming with me ... you can drive.'

Traffic roared past the white van. Fielding, handcuffed in the back of the police car, was fuming. 'Would someone have the courtesy to tell me what the hell this is all about? Do you need an army of cops just for a speeding offence? Give me a ticket and let me go. Why am I handcuffed?'

'To stop you picking your nose,' said Frost, sliding into the car seat alongside him. 'What was all the rush?'

'I was in a hurry. I had a delivery deadline to meet.'

'A delivery? So what's the name of the firm in such desperate need of your services you have to be out at this time of the morning?'

For a while Fielding was silent. He chewed away at his lower lip. 'You know ... with all this harassment, I've completely forgotten.'

'So what have you got in the back of the van that they need so urgently?'

'Packages. I don't know what's in them.'

Frost held out his hand. 'Give me the key and I'll tell you.'

'I haven't got the key. I want a lawyer.'

'I haven't got time to sod about,' snapped Frost. 'Give me the key or I'll smash your bloody face in.'

Fielding leant back in his seat and stared back defiantly. 'Just try it!'

Frost opened the door and called Jordan over. 'Search the bastard. Get the van keys.'

Jordan patted pockets and dragged out a bunch of keys. Frost gave them to Kate Holby. 'Little job for you, love. Find the right key and see what he's got in the van that he doesn't want us to see.'

Suddenly Fielding jerked forward, spinning Jordan to one side, and tried to make a run for it. Kate shot out her foot and, as he fell face-down to the ground, kept her foot crushing down on Fielding's neck until Frost dragged him back into the car. Blood was streaming from the man's nose. The handcuffs meant he couldn't do anything about it.

'When we get the keys back,' beamed Frost, 'I'll drop them down the back of your neck – they're marvellous for a nose bleed.'

There was the sound of the key being turned and a click as the rear doors unlocked, then clanged open.

'Oh my God!' cried Kate. 'Oh my God! It's the girl. It's that missing teenager.'

Frost was out of the car in a flash. Kate Holby was bending over a girl stretched out on the floor of the van, naked, bound hand and foot, and gagged. She looked up, white-faced, at Frost. 'I think she's dead, Inspector.'

Frost pushed her out of the way and felt for a pulse in the girl's icy neck. Was there something or was it bloody wish-fulfilment?

'Get an ambulance,' he yelled. 'Right now ... Paramedics and a bloody ambulance.'

'He's had that poor kid tied up in the van ever since we arrested him,' Frost told Mullett. 'No food, no drink, freezing cold, terrified ... He'd have strangled the poor cow and dumped her body miles away if we hadn't kept him under surveillance.'

Mullett frowned. 'Surveillance? What surveillance? I didn't authorise any surveillance.'

Frost pretended not to hear. 'If it wasn't for your thoughtfulness in stretching the budget to the limit and letting us carry on with the operation, we'd have had another dead teenager on our hands.'

Mullett considered this very briefly and instantly accepted it. 'Yes ... I'm so glad I did the right thing.' He rubbed his hands together in satisfaction. 'Another excellent result for the Denton team, which means, of course, your successor will be starting out with a clean sheet, although you must still have a few loose ends you want to clear up.'

'Yes, you know me,' sniffed Frost. 'Always like to leave things neat and tidy.'

'How's the questioning of the two murder suspects going?'

'The man's decided to "no comment" everything unless we let the woman off the hook. The woman is blaming everything on the man – saying he made her do it. They killed Kelly and Malone because Malone was going to blackmail them and tell us she found Debbie's phone in Leigh's locker. They arranged to call with the blackmail money, but once inside, smashed Kelly's and Malone's heads in and set the place alight . . . thought we'd never guess it was arson.'

'And we will get a conviction?' asked Mullett, slightly worried.

'He can "no comment" as much as he likes – the forensic evidence is solid and the woman's given us a statement.'

'And Fielding?'

'The CPS want to do him on the old murder first, then the rape and kidnap of Jan O'Brien. There's no doubt in my mind that he killed Emily Roberts and dumped her on the railway embankment, but it's all circumstantial – no forensics, and the CPS aren't keen on pushing it.'

'Excellent. I've arranged another press conference with Jan O'Brien's parents – they are over the moon at getting their daughter back. The hospital say she will be able to go home in a couple of days. No need for you to attend, of course – I expect you're very busy arranging for the move to Lexton.'

'Yes, I'm counting the minutes,' said Frost.

'Yes . . . well, we will obviously want you to come back from Lexton for the trial . . . we will need your evidence. Oh – er – one other thing.' Mullett began doodling little circles on his scratch pad and avoided looking at Frost. 'I haven't told Lexton about your misdemeanour with the car expenses. I hope there will be no repetition in your new post.'

'Not if there's any chance of my being caught,' said Frost.

Mullett's smile flickered on and off like a failing light bulb. He never knew how to take Frost's flippant remarks. 'Quite.'

Frost yawned. Tiredness was beginning to creep up on him and he was finding it a job to keep his eyes open. He was even too tired to try and read the memos in Mullett's in-tray.

'Oh, one other thing. The autopsy on Kelly and Malone is at ten o'clock. You'll be there, of course.'

Shit! thought Frost. Aloud he said, 'Of course.'

He was late. It was ten fifteen. He had gone up to the canteen for breakfast and must have fallen asleep over the plate of uneaten food. He had been shaken awake by Sergeant Wells. 'I thought you were going to the autopsy?'

'Knickers!' cursed Frost, snatching a cold slice of toast and ramming it in his mouth as he raced downstairs.

He parked his car in its usual place. Like a milkman's horse, it seemed to know the way unaided. He glanced quickly round the car park. No sign of Drysdale's black Rolls Royce, so perhaps the great man himself was late for a change. He could only hope.

Shrugging on a green gown, he hurried into

the autopsy room to be greeted by the cloying smell of burnt flesh. A police photographer was moving forward to take a shot of a body on the autopsy table. Sod it, the post-mortem was under way. Then, as the photographer moved back, he saw the wobbling buttocks of a plump figure. His heart leapt. It wasn't Drysdale. It was Carol Ridley.

He hurried over. 'Sorry I'm late.'

She flashed a smile. 'At least you've turned up for a change.'

'Sorry about that. I was called out on a case. I couldn't get to a phone.'

She nodded as she took up a scalpel and scraped a red line across the blackened flesh of Bridget Malone's stomach. 'For new readers,' she said, 'the woman and the man died of asphyxiation from smoke inhalation, but before death they were hit heavily on the head with our old indispensable friend the blunt instrument. This fractured their skulls and would have rendered them unconscious before the fire started.'

'Just what I thought,' said Frost.

She flashed him another smile. 'You are a clever dick.'

'Kindly leave my dick out of this,' said Frost.

She chuckled and began prodding about inside the stomach. 'Want to know what her last meal was?'

'It's not on my list of priorities,' replied Frost, turning his head away.

'I understand you're moving to Lexton. I don't know the place. What is it like?'

'I'd rather take a look at her stomach contents than go there,' Frost told her. 'You doing anything tonight?'

'Eight o'clock,' she said, 'and don't bloody well let me down this time.'

Frost gave her a happy thumbs up.

She leant forward and lowered her voice. 'And bring your dick with you, you might need it.'

The autopsy over, he removed the green gown and dropped it in the bin, then went over to the desk to sign himself out.

'If you're going back to the station, Inspector,' said the mortuary attendant, 'perhaps you could give this to Superintendent Mullett.' He took a bulging A4 manila envelope from his desk drawer. 'He's been asking for it. It's the items that were in Detective Chief Inspector Skinner's pockets when they brought him in.'

'Right,' said Frost, tucking it under his arm.

He chucked the envelope on the passenger seat of the car and switched on the ignition. Then he stopped. He picked up the envelope and rattled it. Metallic chinking. He ripped it open and tipped the contents on the seat. Some folded papers, receipts, a wallet with Skinner's warrant card and . . . a bunch of keys. He snatched them up, not daring to hope. They were Skinner's office keys – including the key to the filing cabinet in his office. The filing cabinet which contained all the dodgy car-expense claims, plus the form Skinner had made him sign requesting a transfer. All the evidence against him.

He leant back in his seat, lit up a cigarette and smiled happily to himself.

Frost dropped the complete file into the central-heating furnace and watched it wither, curl and crumble to grey powder. Then he went upstairs to tell Mullett he had changed his mind about leaving Denton.

THE END

A TOUCH OF FROST
by R.D. Wingfield

A DI Jack Frost Investigation

DI Jack Frost, officially on duty, is nevertheless determined to sneak off to a colleague's leaving party. But first the corpse of a well-known local junkie is found blocking the drain of a Denton public lavatory – and then, when Frost attempts to join the revels later on, the nubile daughter of a wealthy businessman is reported missing.

Sleepy Denton has never known anything like the crime wave which now threatens to submerge it. A robbery occurs at the town's notorious strip joint, the Coconut Grove, the pampered son of a local MP is suspected of a hit-and-run offence and, to top it all, a multiple rapist is on the loose. Frost is reeling under the strain, his paperwork is still in arrears and now, more than ever, his self-righteous colleagues would love to see him sacked. But the manic Frost manages to assure his superior that all is under control. Now he has only to convince himself . . .

'WHAT IMPRESSES MOST IS THE EXTRAORDINARILY VIVID INTERPLAY BETWEEN THE POLICE CHARACTERS. FROST HIMSELF IS SPLENDIDLY DRAWN'
The Times

'A FUNNY, FRANTIC, UTTERLY REFRESHING BREW'
Sunday Telegraph

9780552145558

FROST AT CHRISTMAS
by R.D. Wingfield

A DI Jack Frost Investigation

Ten days to Christmas and Tracey Uphill, aged eight, hasn't come home from Sunday school. Her mother, a pretty young prostitute, is desperate. Enter DI Jack Frost, sloppy, scruffy and insubordinate. To help him investigate the case of the missing child, Frost has been assigned a new sidekick, the Chief Constable's nephew. Fresh to provincial Denton in an oversmart suit, DC Clive Barnard is an easy target for Frost's withering satire.

Assisted and annoyed by Barnard, Frost, complete with a store of tasteless anecdotes to fit every occasion, proceeds with the investigation in typically unorthodox style. After he's consulted a local witch, Dead Man's Hollow yields up a skeleton. Frost finds himself drawn into an unsolved crime from the past and risks not only his career, but also his life . . .

'A CRISP, CONFIDENT, RIPELY-CHARACTERIZED NOVEL; EXCITING, INGENIOUS, ROUNDLY SATISFYING. MORE PLEASE'
Literary Review

9780552139816

NIGHT FROST
by R.D. Wingfield

A DI Jack Frost Investigation

A serial killer is terrorizing the senior citizens of Denton, and the local police are succumbing to a flu epidemic. Tired and demoralized, the force has to contend with a seemingly perfect young couple suffering arson attacks and death threats, a suspicious suicide, burglaries, pornographic videos, poison-pen letters . . .

In uncertain charge of the investigations is DI Jack Frost, crumpled, slapdash and foul-mouthed as ever. He tries to cope despite inadequate back-up, but there is never enough time; the unsolved crimes pile up and the vicious killings go on. So Frost has to cut corners and take risks, knowing that his Divisional Commander will throw him to the wolves if anything goes wrong. And for Frost, things always go wrong . . .

'MEATY POLICE PROCEDURAL; BAWDY, FUNNY . . .ENOUGH MATERIAL HERE FOR CULT HERO STATUS'
Literary Review

9780552145589

HARD FROST
by R.D. Wingfield

A DI Jack Frost Investigation

A young boy is found dead in a rubbish sack, suffocated and with one finger cut off. Another boy of the same age, Bobby Kirby, is missing. A psychopath is stabbing babies as they lie sleeping in their cots. A fifteen-year-old has been abducted, then found naked by the roadside. The corpse of a petty criminal is discovered, with the tops of three fingers chopped off. The small children of a carpet-fitter are murdered; his wife's body is found on the railway line. A supermarket MD is sent a ransom demand for the missing boy Bobby, accompanied by one of the child's fingers.

DI Jack Frost, scruffy and insubordinate, foul-mouthed and fearless, staggers from crisis to crisis, his bumbling *modus operandi* disguising his extraordinary powers of detection.

'INSPECTOR JACK FROST (IS) DEPLORABLE YET FUNNY, A COMIC MONSTER ON THE SIDE OF THE ANGELS'
Guardian

9780552144094

WINTER FROST
by R.D. Wingfield

A DI Jack Frost Investigation

Denton is having more than its fair share of crime. A serial killer is murdering local prostitutes; a man demolishing his garden shed uncovers a long-buried skeleton; there is an armed robbery at a local minimart and a ram raid at a jewellers.

But DI Jack Frost's main concern is for the safety of a missing eight-year-old. Nine weeks ago, Vicky Stuart didn't return home from school. Then another girl is reported missing. Her body is found . . . raped and strangled.

Frost's prime suspect hangs himself in his cell, leaving a note blaming Frost for driving him to suicide. Subsequent evidence points to the man's innocence.

Coarse, insubordinate and fearless, DI Jack Frost is in serious trouble.

'FROST IS A SPLENDID CREATION, A CROSS BETWEEN RUMPOLE AND COLOMBO'
The Times

9780552147781